Praise for the novels of Karen Harbaugh

The Vampire Viscount

"Blends the sparkling elegance of Regency England with a spellbinding touch of fantasy into a dazzling love story . . . sheer reading delight!"

—*Romantic Times*

"A distinctive supernatural Regency romance that readers of both genres will enjoy . . . effectively turns the mixing of the two genres into a very satisfying reading experience." —*Affaire de Coeur*

"A wonderful twist of a Regency, with wit and delicate eroticism, a wicked villainess and a splendidly happy ending. For anyone who loves Regencies, vampires, or simply appreciates a terrific book."

—Anne Stuart, author of *Lady Fortune* and *Nightfall*

"A well-written, unusual vampire story that is a nicely done example of genre-blending." —*Library Journal*

The Devil's Bargain

"A highly original, absolutely fascinating love story."

—*Romantic Times*

continued . . .

Night Fires

"Paints a poignant portrait of all forms of faith lost and reclaimed, and of redemption, against a richly detailed canvas of the chaos of the turn-of-the-nineteenth-century France. —*Booklist*

Dark Enchantment

"The emotional power of her writing, [the] originality of her story, [and] unique plot lines grip the reader. With characters that leap from the pages, the eternal battle between good and evil takes on a new slant." —*Romantic Times*

The Reluctant Cavalier

"A must-read for Regency fans." —*Literary Times*

Cupid's Kiss

"Poignant, wonderfully romantic, and laced with more than a little myth and magic." —*Library Journal*

Cupid's Mistake

"Peppered with witty dialog and humorous repartee." —*Library Journal*

The Vampire Viscount

and

The Devil's Bargain

Karen Harbaugh

A SIGNET BOOK

SIGNET
Published by New American Library, a division of
Penguin Group (USA) Inc., 375 Hudson Street,
New York, New York 10014, U.S.A.
Penguin Books Ltd, 80 Strand,
London WC2R 0RL, England
Penguin Books Australia Ltd, 250 Camberwell Road,
Camberwell, Victoria 3124, Australia
Penguin Books Canada Ltd, 10 Alcorn Avenue,
Toronto, Ontario, Canada M4V 3B2
Penguin Books (NZ), cnr Airborne and Rosedale Roads,
Albany, Auckland 1310, New Zealand

Penguin Books Ltd, Registered Offices:
80 Strand, London WC2R 0RL, England

Published by Signet, an imprint of New American Library, a division of Penguin Group (USA) Inc. *The Vampire Viscount* and *The Devil's Bargain* were previously published in separate Signet editions.

First Printing, September 2004
10 9 8 7 6 5 4 3 2 1

Printed in the United States of America

The Vampire Viscount

I would like to dedicate this book to my good friend, Deborah Wittman, for introducing me to vampires when I thought I wouldn't like them; to Leonore Schuetz for letting me borrow her lovely name; to my local critique group and the GEnie ROMex critique group for their encouragement and nit-picks; and to my agent, Ruth Cohen, who found a home for this odd little book.

Most of all, I would like to dedicate this book to the memory of my father, John Eriksen, who taught me how to read, who introduced me to myths and legends, who gave me a love of books and history, and who knew his daughter would be an author someday.

And thanks to all the readers who still remember and cherish *The Vampire Viscount* after all these years, and have written to me to tell me so.

Author's Note

I hope vampire fans will forgive me for departing from the fairly recent tradition in vampire lore of having the vampires incapable of seeing themselves in mirrors. This idea came mostly from Bram Stoker (who wrote *Dracula* at a much later time than the Regency era), and I thought it better thematically to do something different with mirrors in my story. I am supported in this by Lord Byron, who did not even mention mirrors with regard to his vampires, and Byron's contemporary and personal physician, Dr. John Polidori, whose vampire, Lord Ruthven, was too impeccably dressed not to have looked in a mirror from time to time. However, vampires have been known not to like looking in them, whatever they may or may not see. That piece of folklore, at least, I have included.

There are many conflicting traditions and "rules" in vampire history, and an author must choose with care which ones she will use. I hope I have sufficiently done so.

Chapter 1

The Viscount St. Vire closed his book with a snap and shoved it away from him. He was tired of being reclusive. He would go out tonight instead of staying in his study, reading ancient texts. He eyed his solicitor's report upon his desk and shrugged. At least his research in that direction was finished, and he need select only one—fortunate—candidate. But not tonight.

Rubbing his eyes, he sighed. He would definitely go out. Perhaps mingling with others once again would dispel the memories of the dreams. They were getting worse. The last time he woke, the images continued to move before his eyes even though he knew he was no longer sleeping.

He went to his chamber, donned an impeccably designed waistcoat, tied his neckcloth with precision, and selected a finely tailored coat. He pondered over a selection of walking sticks, then rejected them all. The last time he'd gone to a gaming hell, he had lost one.

He stepped out of his house and walked through the barely moonlit night to a house that he remembered from many years ago; happily, the gaming hell was still there. He knocked at the door, and a burly guard opened it slightly.

"I need the secret word from yer, sir," he growled.

St. Vire only smiled at him and shrugged. The guard hesitated for a long moment, then opened the door wide. He shook his head as if to clear it, then resumed his post as St. Vire walked past him.

The air was heavy with the smell of sour wine, smoking candles, and the heat of crowded humanity. Even he could smell it. The decor had changed since last he had entered this room, for the better, thankfully. Heavy gold curtains draped the windows, and the rugs were relatively new and soft. Clearly, the owner of this gaming hell did very well for himself—or herself. A gaudily dressed woman turned in his direction. She smiled and glided toward him.

"I see we have a new guest, hmm?"

"Nicholas, Viscount St. Vire. I heard there was some interesting play here and thought I'd see what it was about," St. Vire replied. He grinned at the woman, and a dazed look came into her eyes. "I take it you are the proprietress of this establishment?"

"Why yes, my lord. . . ." She moved closer to him and ran her fingers across his chest. "And what is your preference?"

Clearly, she was hoping his preference would not be at the gaming table, and he considered it. No. He had to take care upon whom he slaked his lust, and it would be awkward if it were the gaming hell's proprietress. A tide of ennui washed over him, and he glanced at the gaming tables. He needed something to stimulate his mind tonight.

"Faro or whist," he said. "Or vingt-et-un." He let his gaze wander with relish over the woman's voluptuous figure, however, so that she would know he appreciated her efforts. She gave a little pout, but led him to a table where three men sat, proposing a game of vingt-et-un.

"May I introduce you to the Viscount St. Vire, gentlemen?" the proprietress said.

He bowed, regarded each of the men in a friendly manner, and nodded as each introduced himself: Lord Eldon, Lord Bremer, and Mr. Edward Farleigh. Of the three, Mr. Farleigh seemed out of place; he was a burly older man, whose eyes would have seemed intelligent had they not been so bloodshot. His clothes were stained, and shiny spots appeared at the elbows from wear. Lord Bremer was a well-dressed man with a bored expression; Lord Eldon, also impeccably dressed, could not be over thirty years of age and had a look of good humor about his eyes and mouth.

St. Vire noticed, when he glanced at Mr. Farleigh, how that

man's expression shifted from a vague discontent to speculative greed as he gazed over his wineglass at the newcomer. St. Vire smiled a little to himself as Lord Eldon dealt the cards. It seemed Mr. Farleigh deemed the new player a pigeon to be plucked.

The viscount played, won, lost, and won again. He knew how the game was played, more than mere stakes and the turn of a card. One lured one's opponent with an innocent manner and baited the trap with a lamb's guise. He knew he looked very young, and he almost smiled as Mr. Farleigh's greed caused him to stake more against him than was wise. Lord Eldon put down a modest wager, and Lord Bremer grimaced and made out some vowels.

Half an hour passed in silent contemplation of the cards. The play came around to St. Vire, and he laid down his cards, looking up at his opponents. Wry humor twisted Lord Eldon's lips as he spread his cards on the table. "Your luck is in, St. Vire! Damned glad I didn't get taken in by your innocent looks and stake more than I should have." The viscount grinned at him.

Lord Bremer grimaced and slapped down his cards. "If you'll give me your direction, I'll settle this tomorrow, St. Vire."

"Of course; I shall be here tomorrow night if it's more convenient for you than calling upon me," St. Vire replied.

"Good of you." Lord Bremer's voice was grudging; he regarded St. Vire with an ironic eye, which the viscount returned with one of bland innocence. A laugh broke from Bremer, and he shook his head ruefully.

St. Vire looked at Mr. Farleigh expectantly. A slight sheen of sweat gleamed upon the older man's brow, and his expression was one of anger. He had wagered a substantial amount. He looked up and caught St. Vire's gaze, and his smile seemed forced. "You're a good player, my lord." He placed his cards upon the table.

Farleigh had lost, but his smile remained. "Another game, my lord?" He looked at the other gentlemen as well.

Lord Eldon yawned and shook his head. "I'm out!" He

looked slightly embarrassed. "Promised m'sister I'd attend my niece's wedding in the morning, and it's getting on a bit."

Lord Bremer barked out a laugh. "It is not even nine o'clock! Your sister still pulling you about by your leading strings, boy?"

Lord Eldon raised his brows. "*I'm* not the one living under the cat's foot, my lord."

A guilty expression passed over Lord Bremer's face. "I'll have you know my Hester is a damned fine woman, Eldon." He looked even more uneasy. "I suppose I should look in at her musicale." Lord Eldon only grinned.

Farleigh looked at St. Vire. "Well, my lord?"

The viscount looked at the large number of vowels before him, more than half of which were Farleigh's. He raised his eyes from the pile of paper and caught a brief look of frustration in the older man's eyes. St. Vire put on an uncertain expression. "I . . . don't know, Mr. Farleigh. It seems my luck has been in tonight, but I have no idea how long it will last. It rarely does with me, you see."

Farleigh visibly relaxed, and this time his smile seemed more genuine. "Perhaps a different game will make it last longer," he said.

At a brief touch on his sleeve, St. Vire looked up to see concern in Lord Eldon's face. The young man bent toward him. "Don't bother, St. Vire," he said in a whisper. "It will not be a challenge at all with Farleigh. Worst luck I've ever seen in a man, give you my word!"

"All the more reason to play, don't you think?" St. Vire replied softly. He glanced at Farleigh, but the man was occupied with pouring himself another drink.

Eldon shook his head. "I hear the man's a drunkard and a brute; my brother lives next to him—told me so. Takes his losses out on his wife and daughter. You can hear him rage right across the square. I only wager with him when I've got money to lose."

St. Vire suppressed a smile at Eldon's inadvertent admission to charity. "Perhaps I have some money to lose as well," he said, and a relieved look crossed Lord Eldon's face. The young man straightened himself, smiled, and took his leave.

Lord Bremer gazed after Lord Eldon with some indecision. He grimaced. "Devil take it! I suppose I really should look in at Hester's musicale. She would have my head on a platter if I did not." He, too, rose, bowed, and left.

Farleigh's gaze settled on St. Vire. "Well, my lord? Are you going to leave as well?"

The viscount hesitated, looking at the older man. Farleigh was one of the men his solicitors had mentioned in their report, and Farleigh had a daughter. The words he had read in his study earlier rose before his mind's eye, and a sudden electric exhilaration rushed through him. He had decided to take no action tonight, but perhaps this was a sign that he should. He smiled. "Faro, Mr. Farleigh?"

Relief crossed Farleigh's face. "Of course." He turned around in his chair, searching the room for the proprietress. "Rosie! Bring me brandy!" he roared.

"That's Mrs. Grant to you, Mr. Farleigh!" the woman retorted. "And I'll not be bringing you another bottle until you've paid for the last!" She held out her hand and glared at him.

Farleigh thrust his hand in his pocket and shoved some coins at her. "There, devil take it!"

With a complacent smirk at St. Vire, Mrs. Grant signaled a servant to bring the brandy. When it arrived, Farleigh poured himself a glass and gestured with it toward St. Vire, who only smiled politely and shook his head.

This time St. Vire did not need to pretend unskilled innocence for Mr. Farleigh to wager more and more money. The brandy did that for him. The man's luck was phenomenally bad, and his skill only mediocre. Even when the viscount deliberately discarded some excellent cards, Farleigh still lost.

St. Vire won once more, and boredom crept in. Really, it was finished. He'd won enough in vowels from Farleigh to bargain for the soul of a saint, and this man was no saint. And this in the space of less than one hour. He stood up and smiled.

"Well, it was a pleasure playing against you, Mr. Farleigh. Shall I expect to meet you tomorrow?"

Mr. Farleigh raised a gaze full of confused rage to St. Vire's face. "I am not done yet! Another game!"

"Hush! You disturb the other players," the viscount said softly. The man looked furtively around at the other gamesters, some of whom did indeed stare with distaste toward them.

He grasped St. Vire's sleeve. "Another game," he said hoarsely.

"Please, Farleigh. You are wrinkling my coat."

"Damn you, St. Vire! I want another game!" Farleigh stood up abruptly, and the other guests glared at him.

"No."

Farleigh's fist shot out, but St. Vire caught his wrist almost effortlessly and held it away from his face. The man breathed heavily and struggled. St. Vire did not let go, but smiled, watching the fear grow in Farleigh's eyes.

Mrs. Grant ran to them, alarm clear on her face. The viscount gave her an apologetic glance.

"I am terribly sorry, Mrs. Grant, but it seems Farleigh and I are at some disagreement." He pushed the man backward into a chair. Farleigh rubbed his wrist, staring at St. Vire, who returned the look contemplatively. "Perhaps we should go somewhere more private to discuss this."

"To be sure, my lord, I've got a private parlor if that's what you'll be wanting," Mrs. Grant said, eyeing him uneasily. As she looked at him, her face softened. She leaned toward him and lowered her voice. "He's a bad man, that Farleigh is. I'll send Grundle to you if you need 'im. He used to fight with Gentleman Jackson himself before he ruined his knee."

Farleigh's face flushed red. "Why, you blowsy—"

St. Vire cut him off with a sharp glance, and Farleigh looked down at his feet. The viscount turned to Mrs. Grant and brought her hand to his lips, smiling at her. "You are most kind, Mrs. Grant, but I will not need your servant. Merely a room in which Farleigh and I can be private."

A blush appeared upon her cheeks, and she simpered. "Well, and so you shall have it!" She turned, then looked back at him and beckoned.

St. Vire repressed a smile, then stared hard at Farleigh. "You will come with me if you please."

The man rose and dragged his feet as he followed.

Mrs. Grant opened the door to the parlor and was disposed to linger, but St. Vire put some coins in her hand and gently pushed her away. "Later," he whispered in her ear, which put a gratified look upon her face. He smiled. He had promised her absolutely nothing; it was amusing what meaning people could put into a single word and tone. He closed the door behind her.

St. Vire turned to Farleigh, staring at him meditatively for a while before gesturing to a chair. "Sit, please."

Farleigh complied, eyeing him warily. "I'll pay you, my lord, if that's what you're wanting to talk to me about."

St. Vire's lip curled slightly. "Pay? I doubt it. I have it on good word that you are very much in debt. I wonder that you are not in prison for it already." He sat and leaned his chin upon his hand, gazing at Farleigh's rumpled, worn clothes, his ill-tied and stained neckcloth. The man's eyes were filled with both resentment and fear. A vulgar man, thought St. Vire. Remarkable how an old family such as the Farleighs had come down in the world. He winced inwardly. Did he really want to ally himself with this man? The devil only knew what his daughter would be like. He shrugged to himself. Well, he would find out first.

"What do you want?" Farleigh said. He wet his lips and looked about the parlor as if trying to find an avenue of escape.

"I want to be sure you will pay me what you owe in some way. Either in money or goods. And be honest with me, for I have no hesitation exerting the right amount of . . . pressure to gain my ends."

"I can pay . . . perhaps a sennight from now." The man's eyes shifted and looked away.

"I am not stupid, Farleigh. The moment a few coins drop in your hands you spend it on drink—or game it away."

He looked about to argue, but did not. His eyes held a bleak, desperate look. "I . . . I do not have anything, my lord."

"Nothing?"

"I . . ." He stopped, then a hopeful expression came over his face. "Wait! I have a daughter. . . ."

St. Vire rose and turned away until he controlled the expression of disgust and triumph he was sure was on his face. God, the man needed no prompting at all to offer his daughter for sale. He wondered if perhaps he had made a mistake. One had certain standards, after all, and if the Farleighs had fallen so low as to breed a man like this, it could very well be that he would have to bear more than good taste could stand. He mentally reviewed the rest of the families on his solicitor's list. Really, the Farleighs would cause the least amount of trouble. The rest, however poor they'd become, still had respectable reputations. Farleigh's daughter could probably expect no help from her father if she did not like his agreement with St. Vire. And she would be only a means to an end, after all.

"A daughter." He turned back and looked hard at Farleigh. "Is she a virgin?"

Farleigh smiled sourly. "She's an ape leader, a skinny thing—naught to tempt a man, there—and waspish, too. No reason to suppose she's not a virgin. There's better game in town than a shrew, I'm sure."

"I am looking for a wife, Farleigh. You do not make her seem a very attractive prize."

"A wife!" Farleigh's brows rose in surprise, then greed shone in his eyes. He looked at St. Vire and shifted uncomfortably on his seat. "Well, she ain't a prize. But you wanted the word with no bark on it, so there it is," he said resentfully.

St. Vire considered it. If she was as her father said, she'd be glad to marry at all. He sighed impatiently at himself. He need not be so particular. It would only be for a year, after all, and then he could be rid of her. He'd see her first before he'd make an offer, however. He pulled a calling card from his pocket and flicked it at Farleigh, who managed to catch it.

"Bring her to me tonight, at this address. I want to see what I am buying."

Farleigh's eyes filled with relief. "Straightaway, my lord."

St. Vire rose from his chair. He leaned toward the sitting man and stared at him intently. "And if I find you are lying to me, I shall make sure you suffer for it." He smiled cheerfully at him. "I can, you know."

A shudder went through Farleigh's bulky frame. "Yes, no, of course, my lord."

"Go, now."

Farleigh stood hastily and almost ran from the room.

St. Vire frowned. The whole thing was in very bad taste, but there was no help for it. It was necessary for the spell to work. He sighed. What a pity it was that magic had no sense of good *ton*.

Chapter 2

Tick. Tick. Tick. Tick.

Once more Leonore Farleigh's eyes rose from the book on her lap to the parlor clock. Except for this action, she showed nothing of what she was feeling, for she kept her face emotionless, her posture straight, and her hands steady upon the pages. She gazed dispassionately at her mother, who was embroidering a purse by the light of a branch of candles, and said nothing. It was not necessary. The clock made enough conversation for both of them. She turned her eyes to her book.

A loud voice sounded in the hallway outside the parlor. Mrs. Farleigh gasped. Leonore looked up slowly, her gaze cool as she stared at the parlor door. Carefully, she smoothed the pages down, then closed the book. She clasped it, white knuckled, on her lap. Mrs. Farleigh dropped her needlework and twisted the rings on her fingers.

"Leonore! Martha!" came the voice again, and a large, heavy thump made the door tremble. Leonore caught her mother's frightened glance and looked once more at the clock. It was a little past nine o'clock; early for her father to return from the gaming hells he frequented.

"I think you should open the door for him, Leonore."

Leonore cast an angry glance at her mother. "No. I want to know how inebriated Father is by how long it takes him to open the door."

"Leonore, please—"

But the door opened, and Leonore smiled to herself cynically. Her father must have won something at the gaming table to be less intoxicated than usual. Indeed, his red face was full of smiles as he gazed upon both his wife and daughter.

"Congratulate me, Martha!" He wove his way forward and draped himself upon the sofa on which his wife sat. He gave his wife a smacking kiss on the cheek, and she visibly tried not to wince. "I have got our Leonore here a fine husband."

A cold chill seized Leonore's heart, and she could feel herself grow pale. She could smell the brandy on her father from where she sat. *He is inebriated,* she told herself. *He does not know what he is saying.*

"Did you hear me, Leonore?" Mr. Farleigh turned his wavering gaze toward his daughter. "A husband!"

"Yes, Father."

"Well, are you not going to thank me?"

Leonore caught another frightened, warning glance from her mother, but it was for nothing.

"I am convinced you must be mistaken, Father."

He rose up like an angry bear and cuffed her ear. "I am not mistaken. It is Lord St. Vire, I tell you!"

Leonore put her hand to her stinging ear and stared at him, expressionless. "I am afraid I have not heard of him." Her voice trembled only a little, and she was glad of her control. Perhaps if they were lucky her father would tire soon and leave. A great weariness came over her as she looked at him. She yearned to leave home, and marriage might be an avenue of escape. Being a governess gave her some relief, but it did nothing for her mother or her sister. On the other hand, marriage could be worse; there was no guarantee of relief from her father's rages—or indeed those of a husband—and still it did nothing for her family.

Her father seized her shoulders, pulled her from her chair, and shook her. "Stupid girl! He has an estate near Avebury. It was rich in my father's time, and I am certain it is still so. You will marry him, for I have promised you to him."

"Edward, no!" cried Mrs. Farleigh. "I have heard nothing good about the St. Vires, for all they are reclusive."

He turned reddened eyes to her and raised his fist. "Silence, woman! I know what is best for my family!" His wife shrank away from him. He turned to his daughter again.

"How much money did you lose this time?" Leonore bit her tongue, but it was too late to take back the words she had blurted. Her father shook her again, then pushed her away. Slowly, she sat down on the chair again.

"It matters not—he has agreed to marry you, and he will pay all our debts as well. Do you see?"

"Yes, Father." There was both relief and greed in her father's eyes, and Leonore knew it was not some drunken dream of his, but the truth.

Her stomach turned, and she pressed her lips together to keep down the rising nausea. She had been sold to this St. Vire, no doubt an old, lecherous man, one who had probably worn out his prior wife, trying to get sons on her. Why else would he want to wed a young woman like herself, whom he had never seen?

"Good girl," Mr. Farleigh said, and he released her. "We will go to him now."

"Edward, it is very late! Why, it is not decent to have a girl go to a man's house at this time of night! Indeed, not at any time at all!" his wife cried.

This time it was his wife whom he seized by the arm and shook until she sobbed. "Decent! Not decent! She is my daughter, and she is going with me, woman!"

"Father, stop!"

He turned, staggering.

"I will go with you. I cannot promise I will marry him, but I will at least see him for myself." *Perhaps if he thinks I am willing, Father will not cause trouble. Then I will take my savings from my wages and take Mother and Susan with me to Aunt May's house to visit—to gain a little quiet for once. No one can object to that, not even Father.* She wished she had taken a governess's post away from London, so that she need not feel obliged to come home on her days off. She sighed mentally. She had, after all, chosen to stay close to home; it was useless to regret it now.

"You will keep your mouth shut and say nothing, do you hear?"

"Yes, Father."

Mr. Farleigh was all smiles again. "Good."

Leonore had not even time to nod at her mother reassuringly before her father seized her arm and pulled her out the parlor door.

The hackney took Leonore and her father to a fashionable part of town—Pall Mall, she believed, looking at the new gas lamps. The lamps lighting the street were brighter than the moon and shone upon the gleaming brass fixtures on the door of the house. About that, at least, thought Leonore, her father had not lied. St. Vire must indeed be wealthy to live on this street. She wet her dry lips as her father nearly dragged her up the steps to the door, his fingers digging into her arm. She closed her eyes briefly, more from shame than from the pain. No matter how many times she had been humiliated by her father and his actions, each new humiliation was as nauseating as the last.

The door opened slowly at Mr. Farleigh's pounding, and the butler acknowledged them with a slight bow. He led them through the silent house, and Leonore could not help staring all around her, for the walls were covered with brocade, the draperies heavy and rich. Fine paintings lined the hallway, suggesting finer ones within the rooms. The clean smell of beeswax and polish came to her, and as she went up the stairs, she felt the smooth and sturdy banister beneath her hand. Lord St. Vire must be very wealthy indeed.

Lightly knocking at the door in front of them, the butler announced their presence.

"Come in." The door muffled the voice, and Leonore could not tell from it if the owner was young or old. Shame and anger overcame her in that instant, heating her face, and she felt she could not look at her host without showing it. She stared down at her hands clasped tightly in front of her instead and stepped into the room.

"Welcome, Mr. Farleigh, Miss Farleigh. Please sit down."

The voice in front of her was soft and deep and did not quaver with age. Perhaps he was middle-aged, instead of old, thought Leonore . . . not that it made her situation any better. She pressed her lips together firmly, choosing a chair well away from her father. It was best to face things as they were instead of guessing and pretending, she knew, however much less it hurt to pretend and imagine. But still she did not want to look at him; just for a moment she wanted to pretend she was not here. Leonore swallowed and castigated herself. She would control her emotions once again, and show a face as serene as she could make it.

"Miss Farleigh," the voice said, soothingly. "Do look up. I would very much like to see your face." Somehow she could not take offense at his words, for his voice pulled at her, the sound of it curling up around her ears so that she felt impelled to do just as he asked. For one moment she fought it, then took a deep breath and looked up.

He was beautiful.

Her breath left her in a rush. He was tall, much taller than herself, and she was considered well over average height. He could not be much older than her own five-and-twenty years, Leonore thought. His hair was dark and glinted red in the candlelight—it would show dark auburn or chestnut in the sun, she was sure. Two dark, arched eyebrows were set in a face perfectly oval and smooth of lines. Beneath those brows were eyes, large and of an impossible green—grass green, almost—fringed with thick lashes. His lips, smiling gently, were austerely formed and yet oddly sensual. She would have thought him too beautiful to be a man, except that the lines of his face escaped the feminine with a firm, cleft chin, a strong jaw, and a classically straight nose.

But he was pale, pale as a marble saint in a medieval church, and there were shadows beneath his eyes. The cause of that must be dissipation, Leonore thought, or illness. Her mother had said that there had been little good said of the St. Vires; perhaps that was why he wished to marry her, sight unseen. Perhaps his reputation put him beyond the pale for marriage with any well-born young lady, although his wealth and looks must have attracted many. Here was a puzzle, she thought.

St. Vire gazed at her up and down, his eyes lingering upon her figure, but with the coolness of an experienced horse trader. A blush warmed her cheeks, though Leonore kept her face impassive. How dare he! she fumed inwardly, then thought, how dare my father! For she was being sold as surely as a well-bred horse would be at Tattersall's. She began to resent him, almost as much as she did her father.

Something of her thoughts must have reflected in her face, for St. Vire smiled at her gently, saying, "I understand how awkward this must seem, Miss Farleigh. But you see, I need a wife quickly and could not wait to do it in the usual manner." He glanced at Leonore's father and returned his gaze to her. "I believe you came here willingly?"

"I came to see what you were like. So yes, I suppose you might say I came willingly. I made no promises to my father, and neither do I make any to you."

Her father rose from his chair in a stumbling rush. "I told you to keep your mouth shut, you little—!"

"Silence!" The room filled with an almost palpable threat as St. Vire leaned across his large desk toward Mr. Farleigh. The older man shrank down upon his chair again.

"Thank you," St. Vire said. His tone was cordial, and Leonore realized with surprise that his voice had never risen above a conversational level. He returned his gaze to her.

"Now then. Your father told you I wished to marry you?" He smiled at her, almost sympathetically, she thought.

"Yes. But unlike you, I did not want to make a decision that would affect the rest of my life without seeing what I would be living with."

St. Vire's smile turned into a wide grin. "Fair enough." He stood up and spread his arms wide. "You may look all you wish."

Leonore felt a blush rising in her cheeks again, but she looked him over as purposefully and as assessingly as he had her.

"Are you satisfied?"

She gave him a level look. "Not yet."

A low grumble came from her father. St. Vire gave him a sharp look, and Mr. Farleigh subsided. The younger man seemed to come to a decision and pulled the bell rope. "I think, perhaps, it is best if Miss Farleigh and I talk alone."

"Leave her alone with *you*!" Mr. Farleigh exclaimed. "You said you'd marry her right and tight, and I'll not have you tell me this night she's damaged goods!"

Silence reigned for one tick of the clock on the mantelpiece.

"I think it is best if Miss Farleigh and I talk alone," St. Vire repeated. The door opened, and the butler looked respectfully at his master. St. Vire nodded his head toward Mr. Farleigh. "Our guest wishes to wait in the parlor. Do provide him with some refreshment if you please, Samuels."

"Very good, sir."

Leonore's face grew more heated with mixed shame and wonder as she watched her father follow the butler out the door. If she did not know her father better, she would have said he had been cowed into submitting to St. Vire's wishes. She had never seen her father submit to anyone. How had St. Vire done it? She dared glance at him and found him looking at her again, seated and resting his chin on his hands.

"Interruptions are distressing, are they not?" he said.

A reluctant smile lifted the corners of Leonore's lips.

"Ah, that is better. You have a most charming smile."

"Are you relieved?"

St. Vire raised his eyebrows in question.

"That I am not an antidote," she explained.

This time he laughed—a pleasant, husky sound. "Truthfully, I did not think about it, although I must say to be wed to a lovely woman cannot be unpleasant."

Leonore's smile faded, and she looked away, remembering the times that sort of comment did her harm.

"You do not like to be complimented upon your looks?"

She raised her eyes and found him looking at her intently. "Attractiveness is not a useful attribute in a governess."

"Ah. Your father neglected to mention this."

"My family is poor," she said bluntly. "As the eldest, I

thought it better I earn my way in the world than be a burden upon my family's slight resources."

"And a respectable way to escape, I imagine." He pushed himself from the desk and leaned back in his chair, his expression contemplative.

Leonore looked at him in wary surprise. The man was perceptive; she needed to keep herself from displaying much of her feelings, lest it make her vulnerable in some way.

"Your father told me you are five-and-twenty. How is it that you are not married?"

"Quite easily: I am poor, have no dowry, and no entrée to the higher circles of society, despite my lineage. I am very much a creature betwixt and between."

"And yet you are clearly a lady of good breeding and intelligence."

She smiled wryly. "The first is of little worth when compared with the lack of other attributes, and the second is a liability, I assure you."

"But not, I assure *you*, to me."

Leonore blinked. To him? Of course. He wished to marry her. It was odd how she had been lured into talking with him as if she were actually considering it, responding almost automatically to his soft, sympathetic voice. Her intention had been to say little or nothing. Quickly, she went back through their conversation in her mind and realized she had revealed a great deal about herself, but he had said little of himself. How had he done it? She seldom spoke of her feelings, her thoughts to anyone. It had been his voice, perhaps, for it was deep and musical, lulling her into a comfort she seldom felt around people, dissipating the resentment she'd felt earlier.

"Why?" she asked."Why do you want to marry me?"

There was silence as he watched his finger trace an aimless design upon the surface of the desk. Then he looked up at her.

"I need a wife. Soon. For . . . the usual reasons."

She watched him, his pale perfect face and the faint shadows under his eyes. A tired expression crossed his features, then a certain sad frustration replaced it. Clearly, he was not telling her everything. But she could guess, and pity for him rose within her. He was not well, it seemed. Perhaps that was why he wished to wed so quickly, to beget an heir before his illness overcame him. She shook her head, however. Regardless, he had no right to require that she marry him in return for her father's gaming debts.

"No. I am sorry, but no. I do not know you, and though I understand your troubles must be grievous, I am not the one. I am sure you will find another young woman more than happy to become your wife."

The frustration in his eyes grew, and he said, "May I ask why?"

"Simply this: I will not be sold."

He hesitated, then said bluntly: "My dear lady, do not all marriage arrangements concern a certain trade of favors? However much a pair may proclaim affection for each other, one gives and the other takes, and vice versa. A woman may bear her husband children in exchange for a comfortable living. In return, the husband protects her from all harm. Sometimes property is involved. I am offering that same comfort to you and will extend the same to your family. I only ask that you be my wife and live with me for a year. In that respect, it is no different from what any other man might ask in a proposal of marriage."

Leonore shook her head again. "I have no guarantee that you will deliver what you promise."

"Come here, please, Miss Farleigh."

She would have preferred staying in her chair, but she rose, nevertheless, and came to him. Lord St. Vire rose as well; he was tall, indeed. The top of her head came to his chin, and she had to tip back her head to look at him. Leonore felt suddenly small in front of him, and she did not like the sensation. She looked away from him.

A light caress circled her sore ear and then her chin, gently lifting her face so that she looked at him again. A fleeting expression of anger crossed his face, and Leonore took a quick step back.

"Your father hit you." It was not a question.

Shame suppressed all her words and she turned away from him.

"I promise, he will never do so again. And I swear I will never lift my hand to you, for as long as we are married."

Leonore looked at St. Vire, into his impossibly green eyes and thought she saw honesty there. Should she trust it? She thought of not having to constantly school her features so that an unguarded expression would not spark her father's wrath. Glancing about the room, she noted the beautiful tapestries that hung on the walls and rubbed her feet upon the soft richness of the carpet. Here she would have some comfort and would be surrounded by beauty instead of ugliness. Perhaps, also, she could ask that Susan stay with her, for she knew her shy and sensitive sister had almost become a recluse in her own room in an attempt to escape their father's drunken rages. St. Vire offered generous settlements; certainly a steady flow of money would keep her father's rages under control most of the time, and thereby offer some peace to her mother and sister. Could going to St. Vire be any worse than returning home? No, it could not. A tendril of hope pushed through her resistance, and she let out a breath she did not realize she'd been holding.

"Do you promise, then? Truly?" Leonore gazed at him intently.

"Yes, I do. I swear it." He looked straight and solemnly at her, then hesitated, glancing away briefly. "I hope to be a good husband to you. However, in all honesty, I must warn you that my habits are not those of other men."

Her brows rose in question, but her body tensed. The prospect of marrying St. Vire was so terribly tempting in many ways, and though she believed she could bear anything that resembled her father's intoxicated outbursts, she was not sure if she could bear anything worse.

"I cannot squire you in any daytime activities, although I can accompany you to all the society functions at night. I have a . . . condition that prohibits me from going out in the sunlight. I am very sensitive to it and will become quite ill."

Leonore wet her lips nervously. "Is . . . is it catching?"

Wry humor suddenly sprang into St. Vire's eyes. "No, I assure you, you will not catch it from me."

She smiled at him then and felt an odd regret. She had wondered what his hair would look like in the sun, and now she would never know. Regret turned to pity, and she extended her hand comfortingly to him.

"Very well, then. I shall marry you." The words came from her abruptly, rattling the brief silence between them. She surprised herself. She had not thought about it at all, but had spoken on impulse. It was a thing she rarely did; she was far more used to measuring her words carefully with people she did not know. Governesses did not keep their posts, else. But then, what did she have to lose? She would be away from her father and his drunkenness and be able to offer at least some support for her mother and sister. Marriage to St. Vire could be considered a form of employment, to be sure.

There was silence again, while St. Vire watched her. "Do you say that willingly? Your father has not forced you to agree? And I have not put undue pressure upon you, I hope?"

Leonore made sure to think carefully now. She thought of the advantages and looked at St. Vire's pale, earnest face. Perhaps he was, indeed, quite ill, and the one year he had spoken of was the amount of time he had left to him. Her pity for him grew stronger, overcoming the resentment she had felt earlier. Regardless of the way he took advantage of her father's debt to him, he still offered her more choices than she had ever had before. Though she was not so naive as to think he would tell her all, she felt that what he did tell her would be the truth. It was a thing she could sense about people, a skill she had built from sheer observation and from necessity. An urge to become free pressed from inside her, and the direction it pointed was away from her father's house and from his influence. She would have a measure of freedom here, with Nicholas St. Vire, more so than she would at home, or as a governess. She closed her eyes briefly, then said: "Yes. I say it willingly. I agree to marry you."

This time it was St. Vire who sighed, and his shoulders visibly relaxed. "Thank you," he said. "You have helped me immensely." He took her hand in his, lifting it to his lips. "I shall do my best to make sure you will live in comfort."

"And I shall do all I can to be a good wife," Leonore replied, letting out a breath as he released her hand. His touch was cool and soft, yet there seemed to be a controlled strength in his grasp. She almost shook her head, puzzled. Was he ill, or not? She gazed at his pale skin and decided on the side of illness.

He smiled brilliantly at her, almost dazzling her. "I am sure you will," he said.

Chapter 3

She was lovely.

St. Vire had not expected it, for surely someone like Farleigh could not have sired anything except brutishness and vulgarity in his offspring. But Miss Leonore Farleigh was tall and slender, unlike her burly father. Indeed, he would have almost thought her one of the *sidhe*, rather than human, with her gray eyes set in an elfin face and her delicate hands.

He contemplated the idea, as he put on his waistcoat. Perhaps it was her eyes that made him think strongly of the fairy folk, for though her expression had been neutral almost throughout their interview, her eyes had a wary, wild look in them. She belonged, not amongst the cobblestones and bricks of London, but in the wildwood, dancing beneath the moon.

St. Vire shook his head and smiled at his fancy. He was too old to be enthralled by a pretty face. Yet, he had always loved and admired women, the way they looked, the way they talked and laughed and moved. It had been, in the end, his downfall. All that was past, however, and the remedy for his . . . condition was in the present, and he hoped in his future with Miss Farleigh.

Taking a neckcloth from his valet, he wrapped it around his collar, keeping his eyes firmly on his hands reflected in the mirror. Glancing to the side, he noticed his young valet watching his actions carefully and almost smiled again. Edmonds was well on his way to becoming an excellent valet, for he was diligent, memorizing all he could about the tying of neckcloths, the polishing of boots, and the general care of clothes. He would definitely deserve a praise-filled reference when the time came to discharge him. It was too bad, but he could not afford to keep his personal servants for too long a time.

The *ton*, thankfully, was less observant. He never went to social functions, preferring his own company, but now he was to be married, and it was necessary that he enter society once again. He should recompense Miss Farleigh in some way for becoming his wife, after all. Thinking of his betrothed brought her image to mind again, her soft white-blond hair and slender form—especially that slender, womanly form. He chuckled at himself. He was truly incorrigible.

St. Vire turned away from the mirror with a last tug on his neckcloth. Lady Jersey, he had heard, would be at Lady Bremer's card party tonight, to which he had been invited. He had won a bit of money from Lord Bremer. He smiled cynically. Lord Bremer had been all too eager to issue him an invitation in return for debt, as the man was known to live in fear of Lady Bremer's stringent eye and sharp tongue. Once there, St. Vire would cultivate Lady Jersey's acquaintance. He had known her father long ago, and was sure he could claim the acquaintance once again—obliquely, of course.

He dismissed Edmonds, then changed his mind and stopped the young man with a raised finger. "Oh, by the way, I understand you did not request a clothing allowance when you were retained."

"No, my lord," replied the valet. "The wages were generous enough, I thought."

St. Vire smiled. "You are an honest man, Edmonds. But I give all my servants a clothing allowance. I will write my solicitor later, but meanwhile, do take that yellow waistcoat from the wardrobe—I have taken a sudden dislike to it."

"Not . . . not for me?" stammered the man.

"Yes, for you." His smile grew wider. "The color offends me."

Edmonds grinned in return. "Thank you, my lord! I'll take care not to wear it in your presence."

"Good. Is the carriage ready?"

"Yes, of course, my lord."

"Excellent." He turned and left the room.

St. Vire descended the stairs to the waiting carriage. Gaining entrance once again into the heart of the *ton* should be easy. He had the initial entrée through Lady Bremer's card party, and he could employ the special talents he had gained so long ago if he had to. He would only need to be persuasive. There should be no trouble obtaining vouchers for Almack's from Lady Jersey, after all.

The lights from the Bremers' town house shone almost as bright as day. But as the lights had nothing to do with the day, and everything to do with staving off the night, St. Vire did not mind it. A brief hush came over the room when he made his entrance, startling him, but he supposed it was because he was a stranger, and odd-looking. Lord Bremer greeted him as if he were an old friend and introduced him to his wife, a stern, aristocratic matron. St. Vire smiled his best smile for her, and she turned pink, fluttering her fan like a young girl. She, in turn, brought him to Lady Jersey.

Sally Jersey. She had aged well. St. Vire could see the little girl he had once known in this mature and pretty lady. He bowed most gravely to her.

"Do I know you?" she said after Lady Bremer introduced them. Lady Jersey had a puzzled, interested look on her face as if she were trying to recall him. "You seem familiar to me."

He smiled. "Yes, of course. I knew you when you were a little girl. I see you have not changed at all."

Lady Jersey looked as if she did not know whether to be affronted or amused. "Nonsense! You cannot be more than five and twenty, if that!"

St. Vire put on a concerned expression. "Have I offended you? You did say I seemed familiar, and it seemed to please you. So, I decided to be even more familiar, to see if it would please you further." He let his gaze linger avidly over each of her features as he bowed over her hand.

She burst out laughing, lightly tapping his hand with her fan. "I see you are a rogue! Now I am certain I have seen you before! Tell me!"

He smiled. "I think you may have seen my . . . father. He

was acquainted with yours. Perhaps you might have seen him once or twice. I am said to resemble him greatly."

Lady Jersey's face cleared. "Of course! I do remember your father! A most charming man, even to the child that I was. I never did hear of him since, though. Is he well?"

St. Vire shook his head. "I am afraid he passed away years ago, when I was young. I hardly knew him."

"Ah! I am sorry. But you!" She gazed at him assessingly, and a determined light grew in her eye. "Why is it I have not seen you in London?"

He took her hand, put it on his arm, and led her to the supper table. Another, older man—apparently Lady Jersey's supper companion—gave him an angry glance and started forward, but St. Vire only smiled sweetly at him. The man stopped, and though he continued to glare, he did nothing. Lady Jersey did not seem to notice, for all her attention was on St. Vire.

"Alas," he said. "I did not know such beautiful ladies abounded in London, else I would have hurried here, hot-footed." He was pouring the butter boat over her, and he was certain she knew it. He gave her a mischievous look, and she tapped his arm smartly with her fan again.

"Double rogue! I do not know why I am even speaking with you, for you seem incapable of answering me straightly. Indeed, where is Colonel Stoneworth? *He* was to be my supper companion!"

"Was he? He is a poor soldier, then! One glance from my fiery, jealous eye, and he was thoroughly routed, I assure you." He brought her, unresisting, to a table.

Lady Jersey burst into laughter again and tried to stifle it beneath her hand. "Oh, dear! You really must come out more often, St. Vire!"

"I would, Lady Jersey, but I have been so secluded on my estates, that I know no one, other than poor Lord Bremer and his most charming wife."

She gazed at him, her lips pursed in consideration. "I *could* give you a voucher for Almack's, but I suspect *that* is why you cultivated my acquaintance."

"No!" He put a hand over his heart. "You wound me, saying such a thing! Have I asked for one, after all?"

Lady Jersey pressed her hand against her lips again to stifle her laughter and failed. "How vexatious you are! I am *certain* now you only wish entrée to Almack's." She gnawed her lower lip and considered him. He put a ludicrously expectant, hopeful look on his face, and she laughed again. "I vow, you look like a naughty boy with that expression! Oh, very well! But you must promise to be amusing, and *no* naughtiness."

St. Vire gave an exaggerated sigh of relief and gazed soulfully into her eyes. "I can but try, my lady."

The patroness of Almack's tried to look stern but failed. "You are *incorrigible*!"

"Yes, my lady," St. Vire said obediently and grinned.

It would be two months until they married. Leonore fingered the delicate lace of the dress she had laid upon her bed. She did not know whether the time before her wedding was too long or too short. She dreaded the marriage, as anyone would dread the unknown, but she dreaded more staying much longer with her family, wondering when the next violent outburst would happen. At least her father was all smiles now and his temper well in check; St. Vire had advanced him some money from the settlements.

Leonore stroked the fine silk gown she had bought. The cloth was pink and shimmered in the late afternoon sunlight, one of the few bright spots in her drab and faded bedroom. She was not to be shabbily attired, it seemed. St. Vire had sent her a note, recommending a particular dressmaker, Madame Etoile in New Bond Street. When she had gone there with her mother, the dressmaker had looked upon her drab clothes with some disdain. But then her mother had timidly announced their names, and the woman had become eager to do business with them. Apparently, St. Vire had sent a note to Madame, saying all purchases Leonore and her mother made would be charged to his account.

There were more dresses coming in the next week, but Leonore wanted the pink silk one soon, even though she knew she would have no occasion to wear it. The dress was lovely, lovelier than anything else she had ever owned, and she was content to look at it, letting its smooth folds slide through her hands. She felt daring at the indulgence and would put the dress away again, only to pull it out not a few hours later.

A knock on the door startled her from her thoughts.

"Who is it?"

"It is I, Leo," came her sister's voice.

"You know you can come in, Susie. You need not wait." Leonore rose from the bed and opened the door, smiling affectionately at her sister. The girl was seven years younger than Leonore, her parents' last attempt at siring a boy after years of stillbirths. Perhaps it was fortunate that her father generally ignored Susan's existence after his initial disappointed rage.

Susan smiled eagerly at Leonore. "I came to see your new dress. Mama said you had brought one home, and I did so want to see it." She hesitated. "It is permitted, isn't it? For me to see it, I mean."

Leonore laughed. "Of course, silly! I was just looking at it myself." She picked up the dress from her bed and held it up against her. "See?"

"Ohhh. . . ." Susan's eyes were round with awe. "May . . . may I touch it?"

"Here." Leonore held out the dress to her. "Indeed, you may even try it on."

The girl stared at Leonore, then broke out in laughter. "Oh, you are such a tease, Leo! You know it would never fit me! You are so tall and pretty, and I am just a little squab of a thing."

Leonore looked at her sister's golden blond hair and large, beautiful blue eyes. True, Susan was six inches shorter than herself, and very slight of frame, but she was very pretty.

"Nonsense, Susie! You are just turned seventeen, and I did not reach my height until I was nineteen. You shall undoubtedly be as tall as I, and beautiful, besides."

Susan shook her head, blushing, and Leonore smiled. She turned to a chair at the side of her bed and picked up a package from it. "And this, my dear sister, is for you." She held it toward Susan.

The girl did not touch it, but looked uncertainly at Leonore. "Is it allowed? For me to have it, that is?"

"Yes. Yes, it is." Leonore leaned toward her. "*I* bought it, do you see? St. Vire wishes me to buy whatever dresses I like, and for you, too." Her sister still hesitated. "Open it, Susie!"

Susan looked once more at Leonore, then took the package. She unwrapped it and let out a long, awe-filled sigh. "Ohhh. Is this really for me?" Pulling out the blue round-gown, she gazed at it with wide eyes.

"Have I not said it?" Leonore said. "Do try it on! I want to see if it fits you properly."

Hastily, the girl pulled off her clothes and put on the blue gown while Leonore lit a branch of candles, the better to see in the growing dimness. She tied the ribbon at the back of the dress, then pushed her sister in front of a mirror. "Now look!" she said.

Susan stared at herself in the mirror. "This is mine," she whispered. "This is truly mine." Tears welled up in her eyes, and she turned to Leonore. "Oh, Leo, thank you! I don't know . . . I've never had Ohh!" The girl cast herself into her sister's arms and hugged her fiercely. "You are the *best* of sisters! You should be *sainted*!"

Leonore burst out laughing. "Hardly that, silly! Now, don't cry, please! You will stain your very pretty dress, and I shall then regret giving it to you."

Wiping away her tears with her fingers, Susan smiled mistily at her sister. "Well, *I* think you should be sainted. I am sure you cannot love St. Vire in such a short time, so I know you are sacrificing yourself for our family."

Leonore glanced away. "Oh, it is hardly a sacrifice! St. Vire is a gentleman and seems kind besides. And I shall be living in luxury, to be sure! Why, if you could only see his house! It is full of the richest draperies, and the furniture is of the finest. Not only that, but—"

"But you don't *love* him."

"What has that to say to anything?" She glanced impatiently at Susan. "People marry for many other reasons than love."

"You will be unhappy; I know you, Leo. We have talked of this, I remember, long ago."

"Oh, well, long ago!" Leonore replied. "It has been a long time since we have read fairy tales together and, after all, that is all they were—fairly tales. You cannot base your life on made-up stories."

"But you told me there was a seed of truth in all those stories!" Leonore could hear a note of bewilderment in Susan's voice.

"Well, there might be, but *only* a seed. And, as I said, that was long ago. I am older now and must face facts: We cannot all have the luxury of marrying where there is love." She gazed at Susan and saw the lost look in the girl's eyes. "Oh, Susie! It will be different for you! Why, you will receive a dowry and will be able to choose whom you will wed! And you are so pretty, I am sure you will have many suitors from which to choose."

"It isn't right, Leo, it isn't right!" cried the girl passionately. "I cannot be happy that you are marrying an old, ugly man! Not for *my* sake!"

"Oh, my dear Susie!" Leonore took her sister in her arms, hugging her tightly, glad Susan couldn't see the tears in her own eyes. "You are mistaken! Did no one tell you? St. Vire is young and handsome. Exceedingly handsome! Why, I am sure everyone will think me an absolute hag when I stand next to him."

"Oh!" Susan moved away from her, blushing. "I have been very stupid, I think."

Leonore sighed. "No, my dear, you have only been good-hearted and loyal, and the best of sisters." Susan was so reclusive that apparently not even their mother had bothered to give her any of the particulars of Leonore's betrothal. Their father barely spoke to Susan at all. She felt a pang of guilt. Neither had she, for she had avoided thinking of her impending wedding, and so was not wont to talk of it.

"I am certain he will come to love you, Leo. He must know

how beautiful you are and will come to see how good you are, too, and then will love you forever, I am sure of it!"

Leonore smiled slightly. "Perhaps." Just a little longer, she would allow Susan her dreams. Certainly, the girl would have a better chance at it than herself and would marry a man who would adore her as her little sister deserved. Such a thing was not for Leonore, herself. Was she not making an arranged marriage? And she did not, truly, know St. Vire. In real life, beasts often lurked under the face of a prince, rather than the other way around. No spell would change that, and neither was she a princess to kiss away an enchantment.

"And, if he is indeed as kind as he has been so far," Susan continued, "and since he is so handsome, *you* will come to love him, too."

"Perhaps," replied Leonore, forcing herself to smile wider still.

A knock on the door startled the young ladies, and they both looked at the door, then glanced at each other. "Come in," Leonore said. A maid entered.

"Excuse me, miss, but there's Lord St. Vire wishing to speak with you."

Leonore rose, her hands clasped tightly together. It was past the hour for callers, just beyond twilight. What could St. Vire want of her? "Yes, Annie, of course. Do let him know I shall be down directly in the drawing room." The maid bobbed a curtsy and left.

"Do . . . you wish for me to be with you, Leo?" Susan asked anxiously. "Mama is not well today; she has the headache."

Through the years Mama's headaches had increased in frequency and duration. Leonore bit her lip and wished she did not feel so nervous; there was something about St. Vire that intimidated her, and this angered her. She had had enough of intimidation throughout her life and had sworn she'd never be under it again. No doubt it was his undeniable handsomeness, or his exquisite elegance; she felt a drab mouse beside him, and he disconcerted her with his words and his manner, and the lingering way he looked at her.

She tried to smile at her sister reassuringly. "Only if you

wish to see what St. Vire looks like. I am betrothed to him, after all."

Susan bit her lip, considering the idea. She glanced at Leonore, then nodded. "I think I shall, just for a little, for perhaps he would like to be private with you, and I would not like to intrude."

Leonore almost sighed with relief. It was proper for her to be alone with her betrothed, but she did not feel comfortable about it yet. She smiled. "And I am sure you would very much like to see if he is as young and handsome as I have said he is," she said, teasing.

A blush suffused Susan's cheeks, but a dimple appeared as well. "Well, I only wished to see who our benefactor is . . . and all the better if he is young and handsome."

"Minx!"

Susan only grinned.

It had been two weeks since Leonore had seen St. Vire for the first time, and that late at night. She sometimes thought perhaps she had exaggerated his handsomeness and his youth, that wishful thinking had tainted her memory of him. But she only had to look at her sister's awe-filled gaze upon their entrance into the drawing room to confirm her own perception.

For St. Vire was more handsome than she had remembered, perhaps because she was not so tired now as she had been two weeks ago. He was impeccably attired, apparently for some evening event, instead of in the more casual fashion she had seen him that night. His well-fitted jacket showed off his broad shoulders, and a silver-chased waistcoat peeked beneath it. A single ruby pin glowed in the midst of the immaculate folds of his neckcloth. In all, he looked magnificent, even more so in contrast to the faded wallpaper and the worn furniture around him.

He greeted her and bowed over her hand with exquisite grace, and then over Susan's, which made the girl giggle.

"Miss Susan Farleigh, I presume?" he said smiling.

The girl nodded shyly. "I am pleased to meet you, my lord." She looked at Leonore and then back to St. Vire. "Shall I leave, now, sir?"

"Susan!" Leonore exclaimed at her sister's abruptness. She was hoping Susan might stay a little longer, at least until Leonore felt more comfortable in St. Vire's presence.

St. Vire chuckled. "Only if you wish to leave, Miss Susan."

Susan cast a mischievous glance at her sister. "Oh, I think I shall. I have some mending to do."

"Susan—!" Leonore hissed as the girl passed her on the way out the door. But Susan ignored her and shut the door firmly.

Her face was hot, and Leonore was sure she was blushing furiously. She could not look at St. Vire, could not say one word because of her embarrassment and her frustration at being put at such a disadvantage. Silence was a wall between them, and she tried to breach it with a small laugh.

"You must excuse her, my lord. She is young and full of romantic notions."

"And you, of course, are an ancient, too full of years to have such ideas."

This time she could not help smiling, and this gave her courage to glance briefly at him. He was also smiling at her, and his gaze was kindly. "Of course not," she said.

"Ah! I have hope that you, too, have romantic notions."

Blushing, she shook her head. "You mistake me. I meant I am not an ancient. But I have enough years to know our match is not at all romantic."

"One never knows how anything will turn out. You should have enough years in you to know that." He took a step closer to her. She looked up at him then. Their eyes met and held. "You are lovely, Miss Farleigh—Leonore. I could easily have romantic notions about you." He took another step closer.

She was but a handbreadth away from him. His eyes shifted from her own and focused on her lips.

"Nonsense," Leonore said, surprised her voice came out in a whisper. "Nonsense," she said more clearly. "We have met only once, and that two weeks ago." She hated herself for her weakness, for showing even slightly that he discomposed her.

He grinned. "I see you have been counting the weeks, Leonore."

She took a step backward and breathed deeply. "Not I! I have been too busy for that. And . . . I have not given you permission to use my Christian name."

"How remiss of you. I, however, will do my part: My name is Nicholas. You may use it whenever you wish." He took another step toward her, but when she stepped back, she found herself against a wall. She dropped her gaze from his.

His hand came up to rest on the wall next to her head. The other touched the same ear he had touched when they first met. A finger traced a tingling line from ear to jaw, making her face flame hot again.

"In fact, I would very much like to hear you say it. You have a lovely voice, you know. I have always like my name, and I think I shall like it even better if you were to say it."

"Nicholas."

"Ah. I was right. I do like it better when you say it."

An unwilling chuckle bubbled up from within her and made her look at him again. It was a mistake. St. Vire had bent his head toward her so that his face was very near hers. A considering look crossed his countenance.

Her breath came and went quickly, making a sound like a little moan. A spurt of anger at herself for her loss of control came after it.

He moved away from her. "You are frightened of me."

"No, I—"

"You need not be, you know. I have said I will never raise my hand to harm you. I keep my word."

"It . . . it is just that I do not know you, my lord." Leonore glanced at him and saw he was not angry. Her heart slowed its hammering beat, and she let out a slow breath.

He smiled and took her hand, kissing it. "Then my errand to you is most opportune. In the interests of getting to know one another better, perhaps I can persuade you to come to the opera with me?"

"The opera?" She felt a little dazed at this change of subject. "When?"

"Tonight. Now. And, if you feel uncomfortable about being

alone with me, you may ask your mother and sister to come with us."

"Tonight?" Her mind was in a flurry of confusion. "The dresses I have ordered have not come yet—or wait! There is one I brought home, and Susan can wear her new one. But my mother—oh, she is ill with the headache. I do not know—"

"Then you and your sister can come with me," he said patiently.

Susan would be ecstatic at a chance to go to the opera. Leonore gazed up at St. Vire and smiled gratefully at him. "You are very kind, my lo—Nicholas. I shall tell my sister, and be ready quickly."

" 'My Nicholas.' I like the sound of that." He took her hand again and kissed it. His lips were soft against her skin.

Again the thoughts scattered in her mind. "I didn't mean . . . That is to say . . ." She looked at him, saw laughter in his eyes, and pulled her hand away, saying, "You are teasing me!"

"I?" His expression was wounded. "You accuse me unjustly, my dear."

This time she could not help laughing. "You *are* teasing, and for that I shall take my time dressing and make you late for the first act." She went toward the door.

"Oh, horror!" he cried and put his hand theatrically to his forehead.

Leonore did not reply, but laughed again before she shut the parlor door behind her.

St. Vire stared contemplatively at the closed door for a moment. He sighed. His betrothed was a truly delectable woman, but she was as elusive and as easily startled as a wild deer. The wooing of her would take some time, and he had only two months before the wedding. And it was necessary that she give herself willingly on their wedding night.

He grinned suddenly and widely. At the very least, he would enjoy the pursuit.

Chapter 4

Leonore captured one's gaze, thought St. Vire, and made it linger. He was conscious of the speculative looks at their box in the theatre, and knew she and her sister were attracting much attention. There was something gratifying about it, after his lengthy seclusion from society.

He watched Leonore, who leaned forward in her chair, her whole focus on the stage. It was more amusing watching her than the opera itself. Her face, ordinarily quite controlled, now clearly showed the emotions the opera evoked in her. Gone were the guarded look and the wary watchfulness, and he thought her more lovely for it.

As for himself, he had seen Mozart's *Don Giovanni* many times before. Since Lord Byron had published his poem *Don Juan*, all things even remotely related to the story were revived for public consumption. Perhaps he was becoming jaded from overexposure to the character, but St. Vire thought Don Giovanni—Don Juan, for that matter—singularly stupid. No man who truly appreciated women would treat them as that character did.

His lip curled as he watched Don Giovanni struggle upon the stage to escape from the seduced Donna Anna and end up killing her father in the process. What a fool the man was, with no finesse whatsoever. A woman was to be wooed gently, seduced into understanding that nothing mattered but the moment; and a wise man chose experienced women who expected nothing else. Don Giovanni had no discrimination whatsoever. St. Vire shrugged. He recalled the music was sublime, and if he did not reflect on the story, he could concentrate on the sounds coming from the stage and perhaps recapture the experience he'd once had.

St. Vire let his gaze wander appreciatively over his betrothed, considering her. He *had* wooed her gently this evening, giving Leonore most of his attention when he was not playing host to both her and her sister. And yet, though this usually would have thawed the iciest of dowagers, it only brought the wary look into her eyes again. Should he not press his attentions upon her as much? But then, he had only two months until their wedding day. It was not much time, to be sure.

The second act ended, and he watched Leonore sigh and lean back in her chair. She turned to look at him, her expression still unguarded.

"Are you enjoying the opera, Leonore? Miss Susan?"

"Oh, Lord St. Vire!" Susan exclaimed, her eyes glowing with wonder. "It is the most wonderful treat! And such a story! I cannot wait to see what happens next."

A light laugh came from Leonore, and she leaned toward St. Vire. "I agree and would add to that the wonder of such beautiful music." She put out her hand in an impulsive gesture and touched his sleeve. "Thank you. It was very kind of you to bring us here."

An odd warmth rose within St. Vire, surprising him. "Nonsense," he said. "I wished for company. Who else more appropriate than my betrothed?" He almost wished he had not spoken, for his voice sounded cool and abrupt. He had been surprised out of his customary urbanity, and he frowned briefly.

Leonore gazed at him, her wary expression returned, and then it disappeared again with a wide smile. "You need not have asked Susan to accompany us, however. I still think it very kind of you to do so."

St. Vire gazed at her, arrested. Here, now, was Leonore's expression open again, and for what? Not flattery, but a simple act of what she termed kindness. He had thought he'd seduce her with his words and his manners, as he had done with other women. But one simple invitation for herself and her sister had sufficed to have her look upon him more favorably.

He smiled and raised her hand to his lips. "No, again it was merely self-interest. I merely wished the whole *ton* to be envious of me that I have two lovely ladies in my box."

Leonore withdrew her hand from his, but this time her gaze was uncertain rather than wary. A blush rose in her cheeks, and she shook her head. "You are too kind."

St. Vire leaned back in his chair. "I am not, really. In truth, I am a selfish fellow, concerned only with my own wishes. However, if you are determined to think me otherwise, please do so. Indeed, I will give you another reason to heap praise upon my head: I have ordered refreshments be brought here, so you needn't venture forth and be mobbed by the enormous number of gentlemen who have been training their quizzing glasses for the last half hour upon you both."

"*Have* they?" Susan inquired, her eyes round. She leaned forward and looked out of their box, then shrank back. "Oh, no!"

Leonore put her hand on Susan's arm. "It is only that we are strangers, I am sure. Once we are better known, they will not stare so." Her sister relaxed and continued looking about the opera hall with more interest. Leonore seemed to hesitate, then leaned toward St. Vire and lowered her voice. "My lord, my sister is normally reclusive and only agreed to come because music is so dear to her heart." She pressed her lips together and looked at him uncertainly. "I do not want her to . . . she needs to . . ."

St. Vire took her hand and squeezed it gently. "She is not used to society, eh? And the attentions of strangers tend to frighten her a little and make her more reclusive?"

She sighed and smiled at him gratefully. "Yes, that is it. Susan is not at all used to having attention paid to her, and she would not know how to respond to it."

"Very well then. I will be careful in what I say, so we may ease her into society with as little trouble as possible." He noticed Leonore had not pulled her hand from his grasp and, indeed, pressed his hand in return. "Am I wrong in thinking this might be true of you, also?" he asked.

A flustered expression briefly flickered over her face, and she withdrew her hand. The refreshments came, and as she sipped a bit of wine, she seemed to gain some measure of composure. She looked at him, a bit of defiance in her gaze. "Oh, I shall manage quite well, I am sure."

He merely nodded and suppressed a smile. He really could not resist teasing her. "I am certain of it. But there are so many rules and restrictions, it would be easy even for me to falter."

"Oh, really?" Leonore's eyebrows rose. "I would not have thought it." Her voice was ironic.

"Truly. I received one set-down after another from Lady Jersey the other night, and there was nothing for it but I must persist in blundering toward my goal."

"And that was . . . ?"

He opened his eyes wide in innocence. "Why, procuring vouchers for Almack's of course."

There was silence.

"Almack's?" Leonore croaked.

"Yes. Do you not wish to go?"

"For me? I . . . I will go to Almack's?" She stared at him, hope and disbelief crossing her features. She shook her head and smiled ruefully. "No, of course not. You are teasing me. If you are such a blunderer, and if Lady Jersey gave you set-downs, then you cannot have received any vouchers."

St. Vire shook his head as well. "Alas, it's true. She called me a rogue and double rogue and slapped my hand with her fan time after time."

"No doubt you deserved it . . . and I suspect, my lord, that you are a hopeless flirt."

"Never hopeless, Leonore," he said. He took her hand and smiled into her eyes.

It was an intimate smile, and Leonore could feel her face grow warm. But she could not look away, for his gaze held hers as firmly as his grasp on her hand. The lights dimmed, St. Vire turned to glance at the stage, and Leonore was able to look away. She tried to move her hand from his, but he held it firm.

"Don't pull away, Leonore," he whispered as the music started. "No one will see. I would like to hold your hand. It . . . pleases me to do so."

She gazed at him again, at his face that showed nothing but kind friendliness. Surely it was not such a terrible thing to allow him to hold her hand for a while. He was her betrothed, after all, and he had been kind to her and Susan. What he asked for was little compared to what he had given. She relaxed, nodding slightly.

"Thank you," he said and gently pressed her hand.

Leonore gave him a hesitant smile, then leaned back in her chair, letting the opera's music flow over her. But this time, she could not immerse herself in the story of Don Giovanni. She was too conscious of St. Vire's hand upon hers. He pulled her hand toward him, lacing his long fingers through hers, and settling it upon his knee. She could feel the firm muscles of his leg upon the back of her hand, glad the theatre was dim enough to hide her blushes.

She did not know how such a simple, innocent thing could seem so intimate to her. He released his fingers slightly from hers, and though she could not see it in the shadows of the theatre box, she could feel his thumb rubbing gently the palm of her hand. It was at once distracting, soothing, and oddly comforting.

His thumb stopped for a moment, and then she felt her glove slipping off. His hand came down upon hers again, flesh upon flesh, for he was gloveless also. His skin was dry and cool, growing warm as his thumb again caressed the hollow of her hand; but this time a fine tingling shimmered across her palm, radiating through her fingers and up her arm.

She trained her gazed upon the stage, but it was as if she saw nothing. All her attention was upon his bare hand entwined with hers, alternately still and caressing, the sensation of knitted silk breeches over muscle pressing upon the back of her hand.

"Don't," she said at last and was annoyed at the breathlessness in her voice.

St. Vire turned to look at her, his brows raised in question.

"What you are doing," she explained, beginning to feel foolish. He took his hand from hers and she felt strangely bereft.

"You do not like me to hold your hand?"

Leonore glanced at Susan, but the girl was oblivious, totally absorbed by the music and the singers on the stage.

"Your sister has noticed nothing," he said, smiling.

"It is just . . . you were not just *holding* my hand," she said, feeling even more foolish for protesting what now seemed a trivial thing.

His smile turned apologetic. "I am sorry. You seemed to find it soothing, perhaps comforting in a way. It was at least to me."

A strange sensation, a soft tenderness, unfurled within Leonore, and she drew in her breath, half afraid of the feeling. It *had* been comforting, and therefore seductive, for there had been little tenderness in her life, except for Susan's sisterly affection. He had said it was comforting to him, too. Suddenly, she remembered why he wanted to marry her, and sadness came over her. He probably had not long to live and took comfort in what signs of affection he could find. She smiled at him and took his hand again. "You need not be sorry. It was foolishness on my part. I am not used to signs of . . . affection."

St. Vire cocked his head a little to the side in a considering manner. "Could you become used to it, in time?"

Leonore could feel her face grow warm, but nodded. "I think I could learn. It is not . . . unpleasant."

He smiled widely at her. "I am glad," he said, and brought her hand to his lips.

It was almost dawn by the time St. Vire readied himself for sleep. It had been a good evening. Apparently Leonore had decided to allow him a first step toward intimacy, and it seemed likely he could, indeed, persuade her to come willingly to him on their marriage night. He thought of it, the coming marriage, with a mix of anticipation and dread. He would know then, that night, if he could be cured eventually of his condition. And even if he found he could, there was still no telling whether it would all end in regaining full use of his senses or if he would die at the end of a year. How ironic it would be if all his efforts resulted in achieving all he held dear in life, only to be snatched away.

St. Vire took off his robe and caught sight of the cheval mirror, hidden under the curtain he had specially made for it. Turning, he stretched out his hand toward it, hesitated, then jerked the curtain aside.

Pale, pale as death. The familiar urge to smash the mirror rose in him, but he thrust the feeling down. He forced himself to look upon his reflection: feet, legs, sex, stomach, arms, and chest—all normally formed, all that was necessary to a living, breathing man. Yet the sight of his body mocked him, for other than the fact that he breathed and was standing, there was no other sign of life upon him, no fleshly color to his skin.

And then his face. St. Vire made himself stare into his reflected eyes, and his hand rose up involuntarily, as if to strike the reflection. He lowered his clenched hand and made it relax. It was an alien face, the only alive thing in it his eyes—an old man's eyes set in a face obscenely young.

Why did no one see it? Was it that everyone else was stupid, blind, or was it himself? *He* could see his pale, translucent skin, his teeth just as white, the canines sharp and longer than in humankind. Sometimes he thought he had gone mad, for no one had ever commented on his looks, and indeed some seemed to gaze upon him with favor.

Yet every time he hunted, and every time he came upon his prey, he would be shocked into sanity again, for certainly he'd glimpsed the horror in the eyes of his victims—the horror that should be there in anyone else who looked upon him. But it was not.

Perhaps he was mad. St. Vire shuddered and thrust the thought away. God, no. Not yet, not before he could feel, hear, smell, and taste of life again. Even an hour of it would be enough for him, after sixty years of being one step removed from life. Sixty years of touching but scarcely feeling, of eating but not tasting. Music, with its sublime sweetness and agony, could not pierce through the confusion of noise his ears heard; the glory he had heard so long ago was only a memory. Not even sexual desire could stand against the wash of thirst that overcame him, the thirst for blood.

"A vampire," he whispered. "I am a vanrpire."

There, he had said it. Anger and despair muddied his emotions, but he pushed the feelings aside. There was no use bemoaning his fate. He smiled slightly. Besides, it was of more practical use to enjoy what he had at the moment. There were certain advantages to being a vampire: preternatural strength and swiftness, the ability to cast a glamour over those he wished to influence. Indeed, he had enjoyed these talents when he had first discovered them, and a heady sense of power had filled him when he had first exercised these gifts.

But it had soon palled, and it was not enough for him. He never was one to exult in an advantage unless it was intellectual. Now, even that advantage he was beginning to question. Never had he thought that the enjoyment of one's physical senses fed the intellect, but now he was certain it did. He wondered how far into madness one could slip without the daily sensory sustenance the mind needed. If the woman who had made him a vampire had known or had cared to know, certainly she had had no wish to tell him. He grimaced, not wanting to know the answer. She had disappeared long ago, and he would not find out from her.

St. Vire sighed and pulled the cloth over the mirror again. He did not know why he bothered to ponder these things, why it made him want to smash the mirror and anything else inanimate—

Ah, but who was he trying to fool? Of course he knew why. He was not at all sure he would ever be fully alive again, regardless of his plans, not sure that he could escape the madness he was sure would overcome him at some time. One tended to wonder and fear, hate and deny when one's plans had small hope of success. But there was hope, at least.

St. Vire went to the window and noted the first faint lightening of the sky. The dawn was but a few minutes away. He had stayed up too late; he could feel the sharp tingling on his skin that promised pain if he did not protect himself from the sunlight. Almost, almost, he was tempted to keep the curtains open just a little longer. The pain would be real, and there was no blandness about it. He did this from time to time, just to prove to himself he was truly alive.

The tingling sharpened even more, and he pulled the heavy curtains across the window, making sure there was no place for light to come through. He did the same for the equally heavy curtains around his bed once he climbed into it. He lay down upon the cool sheets, pulled the covers over him, and sighed once more. Perhaps he would not dream this time, he thought, as he closed his eyes. He never knew what to make of his dreams, for sometimes they were full of portent, and sometimes only shifting images.

A brief picture of Leonore flitted through his mind as he drowsed. He wondered if she would hate him when she found out. But the thought faded into sleep.

Chapter 5

It must be, reflected Leonore cynically, the glamour of near-nobility that made her acquaintance so desirable now. She sat in the drawing room of her father's house, hoping she could maintain her smile for one more guest, glad her father had left for his club, and wishing her mother had not retired with yet another headache.

Once her betrothal had been announced in the *Gazette*, she achieved instant popularity. Five invitations to balls and routs had come to her within the week, and the callers she had received today had given her more. She was no fool, however; it was St. Vire they were curious about, and then secondarily herself as someone who had snared a most intriguing and eccentric, if not mysterious, man.

She smiled politely at Lady Brunsmire, a widow still young enough to look pretty in the frivolous dress she wore. The lady looked around the Farleighs' shabby drawing room with curiosity. No doubt she is wondering what it was that attracted St. Vire to someone like me, Leonore thought.

"Lord St. Vire is such an intriguing man, I vow, and so handsome!" Lady Brunsmire was saying. She looked toward the door expectantly and then glanced at the mirror near it, tucking a lock of her red hair back beneath her headband. The lady brought her gaze back to Leonore. "I have tried to invite him to my alfresco luncheon, but he says he cannot come." Clearly, the woman was hoping St. Vire would appear, and that Leonore would persuade him to go to the luncheon.

"I am sorry, my lady. But Lord St. Vire does not go out during the day. Not even with me."

The lady's eyebrows rose. "Surely he . . . You are his betrothed! Certainly you could persuade him."

"No, I doubt Lord St. Vire will change his ways. It quite amuses him to live as he does."

"Perhaps you have not been . . . persuasive enough. Few men are proof against a lady's charm." Lady Brunsmire looked at her pityingly as if to say that Leonore had no charm at all.

Leonore smiled slightly. "Oh, but you must admit he is quite out of the ordinary, certainly an original. And an original, especially such a charming one as St. Vire, should be allowed his little fancies, should he not? Why should he attend the usual common activities that everyone else does?"

Lady Brunsmire shot her a sharp glance, but Leonore kept her face politely bland. The lady's glance took in the worn furniture and rugs in the room, and she smiled, apparently deciding that Leonore was too gauche to have meant anything by her words.

"So true, Miss Farleigh. St. Vire is a clever man, is he not? He kept me so very amused a few evenings ago." A complacent smile came over the woman's face.

A sharp pang shot through Leonore's heart. Was infidelity the thing she must bear when she married him, just as her mother bore Father's rages? At least it would not be drunkenness . . . but somehow this did not comfort her. She made herself smile.

"Yes, he is a terrible flirt, is he not?" Leonore laughed lightly. "You must beware he does not break your heart, my lady! No one can take his compliments literally. You must know what a rogue he can be. Why, I have had all of four ladies admit to me this afternoon that he has quite stolen their hearts!"

The look of chagrin that flitted over Lady Brunsmire's face almost made Leonore laugh aloud. But enough was enough. This would be the last caller, she promised herself. She smiled politely and attempted to bring the call to a close, but Lady Brunsmire leaned forward in a confidential manner toward Leonore.

"But tell me, Miss Farleigh, how did you meet—"

Fortunately, Simpson, the butler, entered the parlor once again, interrupting Lady Brunsmire's question. Leonore sighed, resigned to more company.

" 'Tis Lady Jersey to see you, Miss Leonore," Simpson announced, clearly impressed, and opened the door wide.

Leonore rose hurriedly, as did Lady Brunsmire. She had not expected Lady Jersey to call upon her! St. Vire had surely been teasing that night at the opera. He could not have persuaded a patroness of Almack's to condescend to visit a relatively unknown young woman. It wasn't done!

But Lady Jersey it was. She smiled kindly at Leonore as she entered the drawing room, then turned to Lady Brunsmire. "I am so sorry to have broken into your farewells!" she said brightly. "Please do not let my presence keep you from any appointments you might have, Lady Brunsmire." She smiled and inclined her head regally.

Chagrin was writ clear now on Lady Brunsmire's face. "Of course, Lady Jersey! I was just taking my leave." She threw a slightly angry look at Leonore. "I hope to see you at some time in the near future, Miss Farleigh."

Leonore nodded politely. The door shut behind the widow, and she turned to find that Lady Jersey was looking at her with approval.

"Nasty woman!" she said. "I cannot abide her. You dealt well with her, and with good address, too."

Lady Jersey must have been eavesdropping at the door. Leonore suppressed a smile at the thought. It was not something she would have thought someone of supposed strict propriety would do.

"I think Lady Brunsmire was merely curious about Lord St. Vire."

Lady Jersey laughed and waved her hand dismissively. She took a seat near the fireplace. "Oh, you must be prepared for the curious, Miss Farleigh. Your betrothed is a singularly handsome man and eminently eligible, and he affects an intriguing mysteriousness as well. But it is just as well he does; if he wishes to be known, he must have a few affectations."

"Very true, my lady. St. Vire does like to amuse and be amused." Leonore silently congratulated him on making his need to avoid the sunlight into an asset. How clever he was! She wondered how long it would be before it was revealed as a symptom of his illness, rather than a fashionable whim. But clearly the mysteriousness with which St. Vire had surrounded himself made Lady Jersey curious enough to call upon Leonore. She relaxed at the thought.

"*You* do not have affectations, do you?" Lady Jersey asked.

"No, I hope I do not." Leonore smiled wryly. "I do not aspire to compete with St. Vire. I merely follow in his wake."

"The silent and devoted bride, Miss Farleigh?" Lady Jersey cast her an assessing glance.

"Oh, most certainly, my lady," replied Leonore, and her smile turned mischievous.

Lady Jersey laughed again and rose from her chair. "Oh, now I see why it was St. Vire settled upon you for his betrothed! I should have known he would not choose an insipid miss." Her own smile turned wry. "Well, I have promised St. Vire I would call upon you, however irregular it is, and so I have."

A shock went through Leonore, though she inclined her head gravely as she rose also. "And I am very honored that you have condescended to do so."

The older lady turned to the door, then hesitated. "Why *is* it that St. Vire refuses to attend functions during the day?" she asked.

"I am afraid I cannot say, Lady Jersey."

The lady's gaze turned sharp. "Then you know."

Though Leonore gave her an apologetic look, she said nothing.

An expression of discontent crossed Lady Jersey's face, then she chuckled. "Oh, that odious man! I vow he has half the *ton* wondering about him. Very well then! I know he wished me to send you vouchers for Almack's, but I could not do so until I called upon you—those are the rules, after all! Well, I have seen you, and just as he wished, I have approved. There now! You can expect the vouchers within the week."

Leonore felt a little dizzy. "I? Vouchers?"

This time Lady Jersey's smile was kind. "Yes, Miss Farleigh. You did not expect them, did you?"

"No . . . of course not."

"Good." The patroness's smile grew wider. "I never send vouchers to people who expect them." She nodded and extended her hand to Leonore in farewell. "And do make sure St. Vire attends with you. I have given him vouchers as well, but he has not come. It is to keep us all in suspense, I am sure!" With a last smile, she left the room.

Leonore sat down abruptly, then absently rang for Simpson to refuse any further callers. She thought St. Vire had been teasing when he had mentioned getting vouchers for Almack's. However, he had not only procured some for himself, but had persuaded Lady Jersey to call upon her so that she could have them as well.

She had not expected this when she had agreed to marry him. He had said he would help her family, but she did not think it would extend to launching her into society. Once she received the vouchers, she, herself, could approach one of the patronesses to call upon her again and perhaps offer some for Susan. Then she could see to Susan's welfare and see her well established in a good marriage.

She did not know quite what to think of St. Vire. Certainly he was extraordinarily handsome, and he had promised that he would treat her well. And so he had. More than that, he had gone to great lengths to please her, going so far as to insinuate himself into Lady Jersey's good graces to procure vouchers. He had an occasionally frivolous manner, had a clever tongue, and was even a little vain at times. Clearly he took great care over his clothes, for he dressed with impeccable taste. And . . . he liked her. Or so he seemed to imply by his wish to hold her hand and in the way he complimented her.

Leonore pushed the thought aside. No doubt he treated all ladies the same. Did he not manage to make Lady Jersey do as he wished? She smiled wryly. She was sure he had used the same wiles upon Lady Jersey as he had upon herself. He was a wicked flirt, to be sure!

And yet, there was something else. . . . Perhaps it was his illness that caused him to seem a little sad, made him seem as if he were a little on the edge of . . . Of what? Leonore was not sure.

Most certainly, sadness. She had seen it herself, flickering across his countenance from time to time when he did not know she was watching him. An answering sadness crept into her heart at the thought, and then a growing warmth. He had been kind to her, and even to Susan, which she felt sure he did either from the kindness of his heart or to gain her approval. What had she offered him in return? Surely, at the very least, she should give him her trust. He had asked nothing of her so far, except to hold her hand that once in the theatre.

She blushed, remembering it. That was all he had done, but it had been as intimate as a kiss. She had not known what to think of it at first, but she understood that certain intimacies were allowed between betrothed couples, and even more between married ones. Her mind went back further, to when Susan had left them alone in the parlor, how he had stepped close to her and had leaned forward as if he had been thinking about kissing her.

Leonore wet her dry lips at the thought. She had not liked the kisses that some former employers or employers' sons had tried to press upon her when they had caught her alone. She had rightfully repulsed them. But this, now, was different. It was not a forbidden thing to kiss one's betrothed.

She shook her head at her thoughts. What nonsense! Did she truly know that St. Vire had wanted to kiss her that evening before the opera? No, she did not. Most certainly, she did not know if he had wanted to do so lately. He had been the soul of courtesy and propriety each time he called upon her after the opera.

A glance at the clock made her rise hurriedly from her chair. It was late in the afternoon, and if she was to ready herself for Lady Bennington's ball, she had to start now.

St. Vire glanced up at the clock from the ancient *grimoire* he was reading. It wanted but an hour and a half until the start of Lady Bennington's ball, and he was not at all sure if he wanted to go. He had replied to the invitation tentatively, saying he might have to attend to some business at that time. He gazed again at the book of spells he had been studying for the last hour. His sleep had been full of shifting images, and he did not know if any of them held a clue to his fate, but the *grimoire* had instructed that he take note of his dreams. He was almost certain he was very close to finding the additional information he needed. Impatience flickered through his mind at the thought of delaying the gathering of knowledge by yet another day, just so he could make an appearance at a ball.

Yet, Leonore would be there. He felt an unfamiliar eagerness at the thought, and his smile became crooked. She had become the icon of his restoration to humanity. In reality, it was his research and knowledge of the magical arts that would restore the full use of his physical senses to him and stem the onslaught of madness. But somehow he had come to look upon Leonore as the embodiment of all his hopes.

Well, it was true after all that he could not do it without her willing participation. With luck, he'd be able to effect the transformation without her knowledge of his true nature, and so elicit her willingness all the more easily.

But of course, it would not happen if he stayed away from her. With Leonore, it seemed that gentle attention from him softened her to him more and more. If he stopped now, it was wholly possible he might lose ground with her. He would, therefore, go to Lady Bennington's ball. Marking his place in his *grimoire*, he closed it.

St. Vire sighed and after a long look around the room, grimaced. He would have to tidy the place soon himself, as he never let servants into his study. Some tiny shards of glass still sprinked the floor from the time he had smashed the single mirror that had hung above the mantelpiece many years ago. It did not bother him, as he knew where they were and avoided them, but from time to time it irritated his sense of order. He'd tried sweeping them up before, but he always seemed to find some slivers of glass scattered across the rug.

He shrugged. He would deal with cleaning later. A sense of

anticipation grew in him as he thought of the ball. He had not told Leonore he would attend, so perhaps she would be surprised. It occurred to him that he had not danced with her yet, as this was the first ball Leonore had attended since their betrothal. Leaving his study, he smiled slightly. He imagined her in his arms in a waltz—his hand on her waist, his legs brushing hers. It would be amusing to see how she reacted to such a public embrace. He chuckled to himself. It would be even more amusing to see how she reacted to a private one.

It was Leonore's fifth social function, but she was not accustomed to the brilliant lights, the laughter, and the gaiety she found amongst the *ton*. Most of all, she was not used to the attention. She had not thought about it when she first agreed to marry St. Vire, that she would have to make a change in attitude, different from the governess's diffident manner she had acquired. Regardless, she must now do her duty and present the best face she had to the world; she could not shame her betrothed after all he'd done for her so far, and that before they even wed.

As she and her mother descended from their coach and ascended the steps to Lady Bennington's house, Leonore smiled reassuringly at her mother. Mrs. Farleigh had been invited as well, as chaperon to her daughter. The change in status was difficult for her mother, who was more used to seclusion than Leonore. As a result, Leonore had to deal with the brunt of the attention. Her father had declined to attend any of these social functions, and she was thankful for it. He disliked balls and routs, and preferred to keep to his gaming hells and his taverns. She was ashamed of her relief when he told her this. What was worse was that she knew she'd be more ashamed if he decided to accompany her and her mother.

Leonore shook off these thoughts. Castigating herself over it was useless. She was used to her father's habits and had steeled herself against the humiliation he heaped upon her. He had once been the cause of her dismissal from a governess's post, banging at her employer's door and in his drunkenness demanding to see his daughter. But her life was changing now, and she would not have to bear the humiliation of being dismissed again.

The chandeliers within Lady Bennington's house sparkled as if hung with diamonds instead of glass. The jewels on the guests were as bright, and the laughter brighter. Leonore could feel people's attention upon her as she entered and saw a few guests whisper to each other. She raised her chin in defiance and smiled at Lady Bennington, who welcomed her and her mother warmly.

"Mrs. Farleigh, Miss Farleigh, I am so pleased to see you here," Lady Bennington said. "Please do partake of the refreshments, and there is a retiring room should either of you feel fatigued after dancing."

Mrs. Farleigh murmured a few polite though awkward words, but Leonore noticed her mother looked less anxious at the mention of a retiring room. Her mother would probably not stay in the ballroom for very long, and so she'd best resign herself to either finding a friendly guest to whom she could talk, or wearing her slippers thin from dancing all night.

Lady Bennington leaned toward Leonore a little. "I was wondering . . . will Lord St. Vire be attending? I sent him an invitation, but he had only replied that he might."

"I am sorry, my lady, but St. Vire has not informed me whether he would or not." Leonore could see a flicker of disappointment in Lady Bennington's eyes, but that lady was too polite to let it show on her face. She smiled instead and introduced Leonore to a blond young man who seemed eager to dance with her. She noticed that her mother retreated immediately to another room, and Leonore resigned herself to dancing most of the evening.

Leonore enjoyed the first dance and went from one partner to another for the next three dances. A part of her, nevertheless, kept wondering if St. Vire would appear after all.

An hour passed, and she mentally shrugged. No doubt he had decided not to come. Disappointment rose within her at the thought, surprising her. After all, she had not come to the ball expecting to see him. Yet, she wished he had come. She wanted to thank him for persuading Lady Jersey to call upon her and offer vouchers for tickets to Almack's assembly rooms. As she sat, resting between dance partners, she fingered the light blue silk crepe of her dress and smiled to herself. She may not have expected to see St. Vire, but she had hoped to. Her gown was of the latest fashion, and she had dressed with care, just in case St. Vire might attend the ball. Well, it was not a wasted effort, for one should always look one's best, after all. She fanned herself lazily, for the ballroom was quite warm.

"May I have this dance?"

Leonore looked up, startled, and her heart began to beat wildly. "Lord St. Vire! I . . . I had not thought you would attend."

She had not heard him approach—of course she hadn't. The noise in the ballroom would have drowned out anyone's footsteps. He looked impeccably elegant. He was dressed all in black; the only color upon him was his green eyes, his chestnut-red hair, and the ruby he seemed to be so fond of, set within the folds of his neckcloth. In all, he was a singular figure, and it was no wonder that people turned to stare at him as he passed.

He gazed at her, smiling, and brought her hand to his lips. "My dear, do try to call me Nicholas. I hear 'Lord St. Vire' from everyone, and I *am* fond of variety." He pulled at her hand gently, and she stood. "And of course I had to attend. I realized I did not know whether you danced well or not. I thought perhaps I should find out."

Leonore's breath became short. He was looking at her, and his smile was intimate . . . or so it seemed to her. "Of course, my lord," she said and went with him to the dance floor. She chided herself. She was sure he looked so at all women—it was nothing, really, just his usual manner.

A shock went through her when she felt his hand upon her back. It was a waltz! Heavens, but she should not be dancing the waltz, not now, before one of Almack's patronesses gave approval for her to do so. She stared, alarmed, at St. Vire. "My lord—"

"Hush, Leonore, and simply enjoy the dance." His smile

turned mischievous as they moved to the music. "Mrs. Drummond-Burrell is here, and I asked if I might dance the waltz with you; she allowed that it was proper for me to do so. I am your betrothed, after all."

Of course he would ask; he was a gentleman after all. She relaxed, and an answering smile turned up the corners of her mouth. "Do you *always* get your way, my lord?"

"Except when I ask my affianced wife to call me by my Christian name."

Wife. Her smile left her; she gazed into his eyes, his handsome face, then looked away. She knew she was not yet ready to wed this man, for the idea of herself being anyone's wife still seemed a foreign one. The idea of being a governess forever still had some hold on her.

"If you wish to call off the betrothal, you know you may do so," St. Vire said before she could speak. She thought a tight, bereft look crossed his face before it became pleasantly cordial again.

"I— No," she said firmly. Perhaps he truly did wish to marry her, perhaps for herself, for here he was clearly giving her a choice in the matter. A warmth rose within her at the thought and caused her to smile at him. "No. I do wish to wed you . . . Nicholas. You have been so very kind to me and my family. How could I not wish to wed a man like you?"

An expression of ironic amusement came upon his face. She felt his hands tighten upon her back and hand. "You need not feel obligated to me, Leonore. I am not as good as you think."

"Well, then, if you will not be complimented, then I shall be obliging enough not to do so," she replied. "Besides, I know you are not a saint."

"No?" He put on an expression of extreme chagrin.

She chuckled. "I think you are a terrible flirt and a little vain, also."

"Am I? How so?"

"Why, I know you flirt because half the ladies in London profess to be in love with you."

"And how do you know this?"

"Half the ladies in London have come calling at my house, inquiring after you, and all of them have said it."

He grinned widely, then his eyes half closed, assessing her. His hand shifted to her waist, caressing it lightly. "And to which half do you belong, Leonore?"

She felt a shiver pass over her as his hand moved up from her waist and his thumb made little circles upon her ribs. She gazed at him, and her breath came a little short, for his eyes held a caressing warmth. She firmly gathered her scattered thoughts together and raised her eyebrows. "Oh, I will not tell you that."

"And why not?"

"I have already shown that you are a flirt, and telling you would only inflate your vanity."

St. Vire laughed. "Well, that cannot be, for I am sure you would prick it with your words and it would burst."

"Alas, I fear my words would have little effect on you, as you fence so well with your own," she replied.

He gave her a wide smile and drew her a little closer to him. "You underestimate your effect on me, my dear."

The dance ended, and Leonore fanned herself, glad that she had the excuse of a vigorous dance to explain her heated face. They had ended their dance near some windows that opened to the terrace. Fanning helped her gain some measure of composure, though she thought her face must still be quite pink.

"A trifle warm, are you?" St. Vire asked solicitously.

She shot him a suspicious glance, but his expression was smoothly polite. "Yes; the dance was a particularly spirited one."

"Perhaps a short walk outside on the terrace would refresh you."

The ballroom was indeed oppressively hot, and the thought of a cool breeze was very tempting. She gave a little nod, and St. Vire left her briefly to fetch her shawl, which she had left draped over a chair.

The air was cool outside, and Leonore shivered slightly at the first brush of a breeze. She felt a light caress upon her arms; it was St. Vire drawing her shawl about her shoulders.

He smiled down at her, then took her hand and placed it upon his arm. The noise and music of the ballroom faded behind them as they walked a little upon the terrace. They said nothing for a while, but there was no awkwardness between them. It was as if St. Vire was content to be silent, demanding nothing of her. They came to the low stone wall that separated the terrace from the gardens below, and he drew her to it.

She gazed at him, seeing how the moonlight outlined each of his features precisely so that his pale profile seemed etched upon the darkness of the sky. The night suited him, she thought, for night was full of contrasts, when all things seen were either black or white. He, also, was full of contrasts; at once kind and vain, generous while he protested he was wholly selfish.

He leaned against the stone wall, looking over it to the gardens. He breathed in deeply, and an odd expression, a mix of longing and frustration, crossed his features. He breathed out again in a quick rush of air.

"Is there something the matter, Nicholas?" She moved toward him and touched his sleeve.

He turned and smiled at her. "No. I was merely thinking it has been a long time since I have been in a garden."

A sudden sadness and strange warmth curled around Leonore's heart. Of course it would be unlikely he'd venture into a garden. It was a thing best seen during the day, and Nicholas could only come out at night. He could not see the open faces of flowers or breathe in the full perfume that scented the air only during the day. Their colors would be varied shades of gray under the moon, and never the rich panoply of hues that would show so clearly under the sun. A wild impulse moved her to tug at his arm.

"Come," she said and pulled him away from the terrace wall.

St. Vire's smile turned quizzical, but he followed nevertheless. He watched her step quick and light upon the terrace steps to the garden. Moonbeams touched her form, and her dress shimmered as she walked, clinging and releasing, hinting at feminine curves beneath. Only the faint strains of music reached his ears now instead of the murmur of voices and instruments combined. His feet soon touched earth instead of stone, and his legs brushed low shrubbery.

His eyebrows rose. He had not expected this, that Leonore would bring him here to the garden. He had thought her somewhat staid, for she had been all that was proper with him, never giving into any impulse. But now they were in the middle of the garden, the moon illuminated the clearing, and roses surrounded them. Their scent was not strong, or rather, he could barely smell them. But then an abrupt, sharp fragrance filled his nostrils, for Leonore had plucked a rose and brushed his cheek with it.

"I will give you this," she said, and she gazed intently into his eyes. "You have given me and my sister much, and I do not know how to return it. But when we are wed, I will give you roses, fill the house with them, and you will see their color even in the night."

Nicholas's breath left him suddenly as he looked into her eyes. They were no longer wary, but looked upon him with trust and even warmth. The light from the waxing moon shone upon her elfin face and silvered her blond hair, and the silk of her dress as she breathed shimmered upon her breasts like water. He had dreamed this today, of Leonore and the moonlight, fairylike and unreal. Even the scent of roses had come sharply to him, as it had in his dreams, as they never had since his change into a vampire. He took her hand, and then reached up and gently touched her cheek with his finger.

"Dance with me," he said.

She said nothing, but put her hand in his. The faint, lilting sounds of a waltz reached them from the ballroom. Slowly they moved and began to dance.

This time there was no proper distance between them, for he could feel the brush of her legs against his own through her skirts. He drew her close to him, sliding his hand from her waist to her hip, and she did not pull away. Instead, she looked at him, saying nothing, as if her whole concentration was upon him, trying to penetrate to his soul. Her head tipped back to look at him, exposing the long column of her throat.

The bloodlust caught him, almost making him gasp.

No. Not now, and not Leonore. His life would sink further into unreality if he gave into it now. He shuddered, and the thirst receded.

"What is wrong, Nicholas?" Leonore asked. The distant music from the ballroom faded, and their steps slowed, then stopped.

"A chill." He gazed at her, at her eyes and lips sculpted by the light of the moon and the shadows of the dark. Her body was still pressed against him, her legs almost entwined with his through her gown's thin silk cloth. A different sort of lust overtook him. He bent his head, and his lips seized hers in a fierce kiss.

At first Leonore froze. Then his kiss softened, and she moved into his embrace. It was proper, he was her betrothed, she told herself, and then all rationality fled. No one had ever held her so close, and the closeness was suddenly a thing to be cherished. For all that it was foreign, it was also rare, and a hunger rose in her for it.

He must have sipped Lady Bennington's champagne before their dance, for his lips tasted of wine. Beneath the scent of bay rum was a wilder tang, like a forest in autumn, and it mixed with the scent of the roses and the night. She moved her hands to his shoulders, and her hand came up behind his neck to touch the thick curls at the nape. His hair was soft and flowed between her fingers like silk.

"Nicholas . . ." she murmured against his lips, wanting to hear the sound of the name she'd said over and over again in her mind, but hadn't willingly allowed herself to say aloud.

In answer, his lips came down upon hers again in a deeper kiss. His hands caressed her hips, pressing her hard against him. Heat flared there, and Leonore trembled and sighed a low moan. His mouth moved across her cheek to where her hair curled around her ear.

"God, Leonore, how I want you. . . ." His whisper ended in a husky laugh, and his kisses trickled just below her ear down to her shoulder. He hesitated at her neck, and his tongue flickered out briefly to touch her there, before his lips descended further.

Her skin tasted sweet and salt to his tongue, and the agony of denying himself more than this taste transmuted into hot desire. He wanted to pull Leonore down to the grass and take her there, but he could not if he were to save himself from madness, and he groaned in frustration. It was madness itself, his desire for her: an amalgam of bloodlust and the abrupt hyperacuity the thirst always brought to him. Now he could feel her breasts and thighs against him, as if her silk dress and his own clothes were nothing but mist. The heady scent of roses and lavender water made him dizzy; the music of her sighs seized his heart and made him want to weep. It was ten times the agony, for he knew once the thirst faded, he'd sink into the mind-killing dullness of the senses again.

One more taste of her, he thought, once more before I stop. He pushed aside the gathers of fine silk crepe that covered her breasts and kissed the revealed skin. Her breath came fast, and her hands clutched his shoulders tightly.

"Nicholas . . . I don't . . . I want . . ." Her voice came out in a breathless sob.

He turned his face so that his cheek rested on her breast and, taking a deep breath, briefly closed his eyes. He pushed himself away from her, and though he tried to keep his hands steady, they trembled as he gently pulled up her bodice again. He did not want to look at her face, for he felt perhaps she would see his shame at his lack of control. The shame surprised him, for he had not felt it with other women—women whom he had seduced in the past. It was, no doubt, because he had not had to control himself with them, and anything that he took from them was amply paid for in coin or sensual pleasure.

"Nicholas . . ." He felt her warm fingers touch his cheek, the sensation already dulled, for the bloodlust had faded. It was as if a transparent cloth had formed itself about his body and muffled all his senses. He looked down into her eyes at last. A light dwelt within, and her mouth smiled, still soft with passion.

"Kiss me again," she said.

A husky laugh erupted from him, and he gently did so. She responded eagerly, and Nicholas pushed her from him after a moment. "No, Leonore. You don't know—" He stopped, then sighed. "You are altogether too tempting. And I am sure we are causing something of a scandal, for though I am certain we have not been seen, we have been gone long enough from the ballroom for people to notice."

"Oh, heavens." Leonore's hands went to her face, covering her mouth, and she stared at him, obviously embarrassed. She had apparently not thought of the possible consequences of being alone with him outside. "I didn't mean—"

He grinned. "I know. Let us hope our betrothal makes our absence more acceptable than it normally would."

A distressed expression crossed her face. "They will know that we— How can they not guess when they see my blushes? For I do not think I will be able to look at anyone without doing so."

Nicholas bent and picked up her shawl, which had fallen to the ground, and shook it out. Gently he placed it around her shoulders. "Never mind. We need not enter the ballroom again. It is late, and I can simply make an excuse for you to Lady Bennington, find your mother, and have you return home."

She looked gratefully at him. "Yes, thank you." He put her hand upon his arm and they walked around the house to the entrance.

He signaled a footman to fetch the coach and felt Leonore press his arm. "Please . . ." She glanced away, wet her lips, and then looked up at him again. "I hope you didn't think I was—I am usually very much in control of myself and do not do improper things. . . ."

Nicholas chuckled and caressed her cheek with a finger. "My dear, sometimes it is a pleasant thing to lose control." He raised her hand to his lips, helped her into the coach that had just arrived, then went into the house to find her mother.

Chapter 6

Some thought it was scandalous, but most smiled indulgently. Clearly, it was a love match between Lord St. Vire and Miss Leonore Farleigh. For though no one had ever *seen* them in any sort of compromising situation, many noted they disappeared together at times, and when they were seen together, each glance they exchanged was as intimate as a private embrace.

It was worse than that, thought Leonore, if anyone really knew. Even thinking of it brought a heat to her cheeks. She brought her fan up to cool her face and tried to train her mind upon the musicians who were tuning up for the next piece—and failed miserably. She hoped none of Lady Rothwick's guests would glance her way and see how discomposed she was.

She felt almost helpless against the onslaught of St. Vire's—Nicholas's—attentions. She could not even continue to keep a formal and mental distance from him by calling him St. Vire, for he was Nicholas to her now. It was unnerving how her gaze would inadvertently follow him about a room, how her hands seemed unable to keep from touching his hand, his sleeve, or his arm. Or how, when she would glance at him, she'd find him watching her, whether it was from across the room or beside her.

And Nicholas was expert at finding secluded places for their kisses—and not so secluded. That was the danger of it, what made it at once frightening and infinitely exciting. She never knew when he would draw her aside and kiss her, how long it would last, or if anyone would discover them. Every sense was achingly on edge because of that uncertainty, and when he touched her, even so much as a hand on her elbow, she felt her body begin to tingle in readiness for a possible caress.

Yet, he confused her, for he'd call her "sweet" and all manner of endearments, but surely he could not be in love with her in less than two months. And his attentions had a flavor of wooing. But for what reason? They were already betrothed, after all.

Did she take joy in it? A small part of Leonore's heart was not certain. When he looked at other women, he might be admiring, and a mischievous light might enter his eyes. But never did he look on other women as he did her, as if she were wholly desirable. He never said he loved her, and she told herself again it was not something she expected.

There was nothing to dislike in Nicholas, and much to admire. She should be content with that, she knew. More than his looks and charm, were his cleverness, intelligence, and undeniable kindness and generosity toward her. He refused any thanks for his little gifts to her, or the large account he had with Madame Etoile's dressmaking establishment, laughingly saying that he was vain enough to want his wife-to-be to be dressed as well as he. But there was no need for him to extend his kindness to Susan. Leonore's heart warmed to him for this. At first she'd been suspicious, for Susan was a pretty girl, and Leonore trusted no one. But it was clear even to her that his attention was wholly upon herself, and his kindness to Susan disinterested. For it was Leonore whom he watched, and he seemed to glance only reluctantly at others when she was near him.

And heaven only knew she was highly attracted to him . . . almost obsessed. That was the word with no bark on it. She knew if she so much as shook her head at his advances, he'd stop. She had managed to do it once, and he had ceased his kisses immediately. But just as immediately she felt bereft and shamelessly sought them again.

Even now, as she sat at Lady Rothwick's musicale, she felt intensely aware of Nicholas's thigh pressed against hers as he sat on the chair next to her. She wet her dry lips and tried to focus on the music. She was partially successful: Lady Rothwick had engaged superb musicians, and they played the Mozart divertimento excellently. She could not help herself; she wanted to see what he thought of the music. Turning to look up at him, she saw he was already looking at her. You wanted to ask him about the music, she told herself. But then his gaze lingered on her lips, and a slow smile grew on his own, as if he were thinking of kissing her.

"The music," she blurted.

Nicholas's eyebrows rose. "Yes?"

"Do . . . do you like it?"

He turned his eyes to the musicians, and Leonore felt she was able to breathe again.

"They are very competent." His voice sounded indifferent, however, and she remembered he had been equally blasé about the opera they had attended. She frowned, thinking.

"You are not very musically inclined, are you?"

"No," he replied.

"Why do you bother to come to the musicale, then?"

"To see you, of course."

"Nonsense," Leonore said testily, though she blushed. "You have seen me five times this week, and you need not come to a musicale for that. Why *do* you come?"

Nicholas gazed at her, and she thought she saw indecision in his eyes. Then he said, "I used to appreciate music very well. I cannot seem to do so now. Sometimes I come, hoping I can remember what it was like." He still smiled as he had a moment ago, and she could almost think he was joking, but something in his eyes told her he spoke the truth.

"I see," she said.

"You believe me?" His voice held a note of surprise.

"Yes."

"Why?" The word seemed to come involuntarily from him.

She said, looking up at him, "Because I've come to trust you."

Oddly, she knew it was true. She did not know quite how it had happened, or why she should, but she did trust Nicholas. Though he had teased her and was sometimes oblique in manner, he had—so far as she could see—never lied to her. When he stated a thing, he made sure it was so, time and time again. More than anything, he was the only man who did as he promised. Perhaps it was not saying much, for the men she had encountered at her students' houses—fathers, brothers, guests—promised only things they could not give, each hoping to make her his mistress. She'd refused them all, for she was no fool and no harlot.

His face showed incredulity mixed with gratitude, and strangely, regret. "You should not trust me, you know," he said.

"No, I should not, for in general I do not trust anyone except perhaps Susan. But I do, nevertheless."

Nicholas stared at her, then looked away. "I thank you," he said, and his voice sounded strained, even to himself. "But again, you should not. You know little of me, after all." A curious feeling, warm and aching, twisted through his chest. He had intended to seduce her, slowly and carefully, and he had expected she'd succumb to it—as she had, so far. But trust? He had not expected it, had not thought of it, really. In truth, he did not want it. It was better she be a conduit for his goal, only a part—needed part, to be sure—of his cure.

Yet, he felt compelled to warn her . . . of what? He was being foolish. She would never know, for if she did she would never come to him willingly. Of course, that was it—if he told her a little bit of the truth, even warn her, and she still wanted to marry him, then it only proved how willing she was.

The musicians ended their piece, and the guests rose to exchange greetings and walk about a little. After nodding and smiling to a few new acquaintances, Leonore gave him a wry smile. "It is true. You do not reveal much of yourself—in words. But the very fact that you would warn me against you, shows me you are not as untrustworthy as you would make yourself out to be." They also rose, and Nicholas took her hand and placed it on his arm.

He gazed at her coolly. "Beware, Leonore. Ours will be a marriage of convenience. I hope you are not falling in love with me." *I cannot afford to return it. If the magic does not work, your short life will have no place in mine.* He thrust away the confused emotions that accompanied the thought. Better to train his attention on the moment.

"How very vain you are, to be sure!" Leonore replied lightly. "Have I said it?"

He grinned, relieved at her tone. "No, you have not, and you have caught me out again." He brought her hand to his lips. Though she smiled, he could see the guardedness in her eyes again. He felt satisfaction at it but also regret, then almost grimaced at himself for being so contradictory. "You are very good for the state of my soul; I am sure when we are wed, you will improve me to sainthood."

"No fear of that, my lord." She looked about her, clearly startled, and Nicholas smiled to himself. He had taken her out of the conservatory, where the musicale was held, and down a long hall. She had apparently not noticed it. A fleeting uncertainty slowed his steps. Did she not notice because he had unconsciously put a glamour on her? Sometimes people did as he wished even when he did not purposely put a glamour upon them. What did it matter, after all? he thought impatiently.

He pushed open a door, and it opened to a small room, dark and apparently unused, for the moonlight streaming through the windows illuminated the Holland covers over the furniture. He reflected with a smile that it was certainly convenient he had been in most of the noble houses in London so many decades ago and knew the arrangement of the rooms well. He shut the door behind them.

The dim light showed her eyes, wide and vulnerable. He did not kiss her immediately, but cupped her chin in his hand, stroking her jaw with his thumb.

"You are quite right, my dear," he said lightly. "I am irredeemable, a very bad man. I am surprised you have not guessed it yet, for I have led you to the edge of scandal more than a few times. Do you really think you should marry me?"

He throat moved in a swallow. "I . . . have known of worse men."

"Have you? But you do not know me well—yet." He slid his fingers down onto her neck, feeling the pulse of blood at the base of it. He could put a glamour on her now, and she would never know if he drank of her. His hand tightened slightly as the bloodlust surged within him.

He looked down at her; Leonore did not move, but simply stared at him. She trusted him, or so she said. He had told her when they first met he would never hurt her, and she appeared to believe it, for he never had—yet. Would he go against his word? He searched her face. Never had he put a glamour on her, but he could see her breath came quickly as she stared at him, definitely in his thrall. Or was it her damned trust again?

"I . . . know you well enough—more than many betrothed couples might in an arranged marriage," she said. He saw her swallow again and felt the pulse quicken at her throat. "We have never gone over the edge of scandal, I think."

Moving his hand lower still, he pushed the small puffed sleeve from one shoulder and her bodice from one breast. He watched her, the way her teeth bit her lower lip, the way her eyes closed at his touch. Ah, but she was delectable! Desire for her rose in him, and he smiled. He was becoming quite good at controlling his bloodthirst now, so that it burned low and fused instead with his lust for her lips and breasts and thighs.

"And what if we did now?" He ran his fingers up to her collarbone and then back down beneath her breast.

She shivered, opened her eyes, and stared at him. "Then we should have to marry immediately, of course. It wants but two weeks to our wedding, after all. Whom else would you be able to get to wed you at this late date?"

Nicholas laughed softly at her practical answer and seized her lips with his own. " 'Would she could make of me a saint/Or I of her a sinner,' " he quoted in a whisper against her mouth.

"The poet . . . Congreve," she replied, her voice trembling now, obviously trying to retain some control over herself.

He laughed again, amused that she let it slip that she knew this poem. "*Such* a good governess you are!" He kissed her again below her ear, then down her neck to the pulse beating wildly there. Carefully he let his teeth run against her skin. He was on the edge of letting his thirst overcome him again, but

he could not resist the tantalizing possibility, even though he knew he would keep himself from piercing her flesh. "You cannot make me a saint, Leonore. Shall I make you a sinner?"

"We are sinning *now*."

"Oh, no, only somewhat close to it. Trust me to know more of sin than you, sweet one." He moved her backward until they came to a chaise longue and pushed her gently down upon it.

"What . . . what are you going to do?"

"Make us come closer to sinning than we have done before," Nicholas replied and kissed her full and deeply on her mouth.

Leonore moaned, a despairing sound. He parted from her, ready to stop, but a wild look came into her eyes. She seized his face with her hands and brought him down again, kissing him just as deeply as he had her.

This time his husky laugh held a note of triumph. Her lips moved upon his as he had taught her; her tongue slipped within and touched his own as he had done to her before. Her fingers slid behind his head and pulled a little at his hair. The former governess was a good student, and he chuckled again at the thought. He dipped his hand between her breasts and freed the covered one from her bodice. One last time he kissed her deeply before descending to the skin of her neck, her shoulder, and then the tips of her breasts.

Leonore felt hot and cold and hot again, and a fine tingling brushed across her skin. Sinning. He had called it that, or said what they were doing was close to it. He had said he was a bad man, and though she did not think this was entirely true, every touch upon her body told her he was a rake and a seducer. But if he were bad, then so was she, for she did not want his seduction to stop. Despair mixed with her desire; she was certainly her father's daughter, for she drank of Nicholas's lips as uncontrollably as a drunkard took wine. Where was her control? She had little; Nicholas had it all.

His kisses were both sweet and fierce, his embraces tender, and because she received so little of either in her life, she had no head for them. Nicholas's caresses were a fine liqueur upon her body, pouring over her breasts and belly and thighs. The scent of him, full of wildness and spice, made her feel dizzy. She opened her eyes wide when she felt his hand on her bare hip and realized with a shock he had pushed up the hem of her gown. Her eyes met his own, watching her; his smile was gentle, and his eyes full of warm desire.

"Let me touch you here . . . and here. . . ." His fingers played over her, and he kissed her throat and chin, then took her lips once again. We are betrothed, Leonore told herself. It is only two weeks until we are wed. It does not matter. But it did, for even she knew what they did was not right, most certainly not before they were married, however much it might be mitigated by their betrothal.

For a moment she let him touch her as he willed, biting her lip as a shimmering heat rose from her secret places to course through the rest of her body. I must stop this, she told herself.

"Stop," she said aloud, but her voice came out as a whisper. But his caresses ceased, though he was still pressed against her, and he took one last long kiss.

"I would not have taken you, Leonore, before our wedding night." He moved from her, as if reluctant to do so.

Slowly she pushed herself upright upon the chaise longue and breathed deeply. Her legs felt odd and shaky, so she did not rise immediately. She glanced at him in the dimness, glad he could not see the color rising in her face. "I thought you *had* taken me," she blurted.

A husky chuckle came from him. "Oh, no. That truly would have been sinning."

Leonore swallowed. "There is more?" she asked. She should not be talking of this with him at all, but she blurted the words before she could stop herself.

Nicholas pulled her up from the chaise longue and drew her to him gently. "Yes, sweet one. Much more. Shall I tell you what will happen on our wedding night?"

She did not answer him, for he kissed her deeply before she could reply.

"I shall continue to do all I have done to your delectable body so far, until you cry out with the delight of it." He bent to kiss her neck, her ear, and then her lips again.

Drawing up all her resolve, she pushed against him and stared at his face. His gaze was still hot upon her, and she knew he would kiss her again if she let him. "I do not think I want to do that. It does not sound proper." She felt foolish saying it, for she really did not know what was proper within the confines of marriage, but saying it brought a measure of control over herself. Putting on an air of briskness, she pulled up her bodice and adjusted it as well as she could.

He laughed softly. "Oh, but you will. And it is not proper at all. I told you I was a bad man, did I not?"

Chapter 7

He was becoming obsessed with Leonore.

St. Vire did not know if this was a good thing. He had enough control over himself so that he did not take her blood, but each time he tamped down the urge, the sensitivity that came with it changed the bloodlust into a lust for the touch of her skin, the sound of her sighs, and the scent of her perfume.

It was something he could not separate from his vampirism, and so seemed tainted somehow. Tainted. He smiled wryly to himself. Was she making him yearn for sainthood, turning him from being a contented sinner? He remembered their encounter at the Rothwicks' musicale, how she had allowed him to touch her intimately and how she had pulled him down for a kiss. His smile turned into a wide grin. Oh, he doubted he'd become a saint.

Looking in the mirror in his chambers, St. Vire adjusted his neckcloth with care, frowning a little until he achieved the precise folds he wished. He glanced up at his face and dared smile into the mirror, showing his sharp teeth. His reflection did not seem so repulsive to him now; he had refrained from drinking blood two months before the consummation of his wedding, as the spell required. Now it was his wedding day—or rather, wedding evening—and at least he could slake one kind of thirst. It had been, he admitted, somewhat frustrating seducing Leonore into willingness. His smile turned rueful. No, loin-twisting agony came closer to it. He could not even take any recourse with whores, either, for the spell did not allow it.

He took the hat his valet held out to him, set it at a rakish angle, then descended the stairs from his room. Sometimes he wondered if all this saintly abstinence was worth the cure.

Perhaps it was easier in ancient times to find a willing virgin who would give herself for a year. These days it was impossible without searching for one in a well-born family, woo the girl, and then marry her. The thought of being wed had almost made him give it up, for he'd always seen marriage as a nuisance. He remembered, however, the madness he'd seen long ago in another vampire's eyes before St. Vire was forced to kill him. He shuddered at the memory, and he decided it was worth it.

On the other hand, there was the church. St. Vire wondered how long he was going to be able to bear being inside one while he said his marriage vows. His mouth went dry at the thought. The spell in the *grimoire* had said if he had done everything correctly, he would survive it. But he'd seen what had happened when he had locked that other vampire into the church: It was how he had killed him. Thankfully, the church in which he was going to be wed was a different one, so he would not have to be reminded much of the unnerving incident while he said his vows.

As he climbed into the coach that would take him to the church, St. Vire became aware of the tension in his body and made himself relax. Perhaps he could pretend his apprehension was merely wedding nerves. He rolled his eyes at the thought. He was the furthest thing from a trembling virgin he could think of. God, but he was becoming ridiculous over it all.

The coach stopped in front of the church at last, and he hesitated before descending. He could sense the odor of sanctity emanating from the church even from the carriage, a sweet and bitter scent. Go to it, man! he said to himself. I might die, said another part of his mind. But I am undead; what, after all, is the difference? he told himself wryly. It was that or madness—and he would never choose madness.

He climbed up the steps to the church's open doors. The wedding company was small, for only Leonore's family would attend, and his few new friends. It was an odd thing to think of having friends; all the ones from his youth were dead. Thankfully, it was not the fashion now to have large weddings, and Leonore had not wanted a large one, either. St. Vire looked at the altar, at the lines of the beams and arches leading the eye upward to the cross near the roof. He took in a deep breath and stepped within.

The sharp tingling that coursed through his body started as soon as he put his foot upon the marble floor of the church. He made himself ignore it and stared at the altar instead. The vicar there eyed him sourly, for an evening wedding was quite irregular. However, once he knew that Leonore's family approved, and once the very large contribution from St. Vire's bank was in his hands, the vicar had agreed to do it.

His bride. St. Vire turned his gaze to the doorway at the sound of carriages. The tingling now became a slight sizzling pain, and in order to block it out he concentrated on the figures coming toward him. He wished he could better appreciate Leonore's loveliness as she came up the aisle on her father's arm. He could not feel the pleasure he normally would looking at her, for the pain increased with each minute he stood before the altar. Her sister, Susan, sat next to her mother in one of the pews, but he barely noticed. He spared one glance for her father, glad for her sake that he was sober for once.

At last Leonore was beside him, and St. Vire turned to the vicar. "Hurry," he whispered to the man and put a glamour upon him so that he would obey. Even so, the ceremony lasted longer than he ever thought it could, for the pain that seemed to burn his flesh seeped within until his lungs felt as if they were on fire. He wanted to cry out, but he did not have the breath to do so. His vision blurred, and he blinked to clear it.

"I do," he heard himself say, but he was not sure to what he agreed, for his mind now burned as well. *God help me,* he thought, *I must stay upon my feet.* But the red-streaked darkness descended upon him, and his knees hit the marble floor. . . .

A faint voice: "He needs air and quiet, I am sure. None of you need stay, for I will attend him. I am sure he will recover soon." A door shut—too loudly.

Cool air. Silk upon his cheek. Something wet upon his

brow. The scent of lavender came to him. It reminded him of someone . . . Leonore. He opened his eyes, and it was indeed she. She drew in her breath, and the tight, tense look in her eyes faded.

"Oh heavens, Nicholas! I thought . . . I thought . . ." A confused expression of anger and fear crossed her face, and she seized his face in her hands and kissed him fiercely. "Do not ever, ever do that again!"

"I assure you, I did not do it on purpose," he whispered when she released him, and closed his eyes. His lungs still burned a little, and coughing, he groped for the handkerchief he usually had in his coat pocket. His coat had disappeared, and he was in his shirtsleeves.

"Here." He felt a handkerchief thrust into his hand.

He coughed fully into it, and the sharp tang of blood came to his tongue, but he felt too tired to do anything about it. A sharp gasp burst in the air above him. He opened his eyes again and shifted his head; smooth silk rubbed against his hair. It seemed his head was resting upon Leonore's lap. How pleasant.

A small, distressed moan came from Leonore. "You *are* ill, then! I had wondered . . . I shall call for a doctor immediately." She eased herself from under his head, but he grasped her arm.

"No. I am merely thirsty . . . water, please. . . ."

"Nicholas, you stained the handkerchief with blood when you coughed into it," Leonore said, her voice impatient, but reached to a table beside her and poured him a glass from a ewer nearby. He drank it, washing the blood from his mouth.

"I shall be well presently." He pushed himself upright to prove it. He was in an unfamiliar room, plain and utilitarian. "Where is this place?"

"They—the vicar and the curate—brought you to the vicar's sitting room. You collapsed at the very end of our wedding ceremony."

"How embarrassing," he said lightly. "We are, however, married?"

A light blush suffused Leonore's cheeks, and she smiled. "Yes."

"Good. I think we should proceed to the wedding supper—unless I have been unconscious for too long?"

"No, it has been only a quarter of an hour—but you must let me find a doctor!"

"Nonsense, my dear; you see I am quite recovered." He stood up and was relieved to find he did not feel at all as weak as he had when he awakened. He looked about the room. "My coat?"

She gave it to him reluctantly. "Nicholas . . . you have consumption, do you not?" Her voice was tense.

He gazed at her face; it was as strained as her voice. He smiled crookedly. "No, not consumption. It is not something a doctor can cure, believe me." He put on his coat and spied a mirror. His neckcloth was creased inappropriately, and he ran a thumb under a fold.

He found his arm seized, and Leonore pulled him around to face her, her expression one of angry fear. "You vain, stupid man! You collapse at the altar, you cough blood, and now you say you are well and must adjust your neckcloth!"

"I can hardly greet the wedding guests with a badly tied one, my dear."

"The *devil* take your neckcloth!" Her face flamed at her own words and at Nicholas's raised eyebrows. "How long—How ill are you? How long will you live?" He heard aching desperation in her voice, and her words stumbled from her lips.

Surprise and troubled tenderness curled around Nicholas's heart. He touched her cheek softly. "You care how long I might live?"

She turned her face and pressed her cheek against his hand, closing her eyes briefly. "Yes. Yes, of course."

"You are very sweet, Leonore." He pulled her to him and kissed her softly.

Her lips moved hungrily against his, then parted from him by only a hairsbreadth. "Tell me, Nicholas. How long?" she asked.

"Mmm . . ." Nicholas could feel his strength returning steadily, and with it, desire. He kissed her again, deeply.

Leonore pushed him away, gasping a little. "Tell me."

He gazed at the clear desperation and longing in her eyes, and a curious ache grew within him. "I do not know. A year . . . or I could live forever. . . ."

"A year!" The word came out from her in a sob, and she bit her lip.

"Don't—" He took her in his arms again. "Don't cry." He stroked her hair and pressed a kiss upon it.

"I am not crying," she said, her voice muffled against his chest.

"Good." He chuckled. "I mean what I say. I could live forever." He thought about stopping the course of the spell and remaining a vampire, living forever. Leonore could even be by his side, also a vampire and his eternal consort. Just a very little he was tempted. . . . The image of Leonore rose before his eyes, her face moon-pale and twisted with the bloodthirst, going slowly insane. God, no. He shuddered.

"Nonsense! No one lives forever." Leonore the governess was back again. She moved away from him, her lips pressed together in a disapproving line. He reached out and ran his thumb over her lips.

"Smile for me, Leonore. Perhaps I will not live forever, but I could live for a very, very long time—as long as any man might. I shall know by the end of the year."

She grasped his hand and held it hard. "How will you know?"

He felt his smile turn crooked. "I shall be alive," he said simply.

"That is not enough! A doctor—"

"Can do nothing." He made his voice stern. "Enough! We have wedding guests to attend to." He glanced at the clock on the mantelpiece. "Another quarter hour has passed while we argued. I have given our guests enough to think about for now. If we delay more, I am sure they will wonder if they should turn the wedding supper into a funeral feast."

A bitter smile came to Leonore's lips. "A little early for that, I think."

"*Much* too early." He kissed her once more. "Come, come, Leonore! It is not as bad as you think." He caressed her cheek with his finger. "Besides, I am sure it is no less than I deserve. After a year, you may well wish to be rid of me. I am, no doubt, not at all easy to live with, with all my bad habits," he said lightly.

This time she gave a reluctant laugh. "No doubt!" was her dry reply before she took his hand and led him out of the vicar's sitting room.

How could anyone laugh and drink when the groom at a wedding party was to die in a year? Leonore made herself smile and nod cordially to another guest, then sipped her wine. It was acrid on her tongue, though she knew the wine was of the best vintage, for Nicholas prided himself on his cellar. She set down the glass with a snap on the table next to her. But of course, no one knew how ill Nicholas was, and she would not tell anyone.

Everyone had retired to the large drawing room in Nicholas's house after the wedding supper. It was a merry group, composed mostly of his friends, and of course Leonore's family. Even Susan came out of her shell a little, smiling shyly at Nicholas's jokes and the admiration she received from the gentlemen.

Nicholas was clearly enjoying the company. Leonore smiled wryly. He liked to be in a crowd, preferably in the center of it. It would destroy all his pleasure if she were to let anyone know he was so ill. He made a joke of it; even now he grinned as someone twitted him about the incident at the ceremony.

"I never thought you would come to the altar as nervous and fainting as a schoolroom chit, St. Vire," said Lord Eldon, whom Leonore remembered was one of Nicholas's friends.

"Not I!" Nicholas replied. "It was the prospect of ending my bachelorhood and deserting all my dear . . . companions." He eyed the ladies with exaggerated lasciviousness. They all blushed or hid their giggles behind their hands. As one they seemed to look at him with longing and regret, which made Leonore laugh in spite of herself. Incorrigible! She supposed he would never stop being a flirt.

He sighed theatrically. "I suppose my poor wife will now have to bear the brunt of my attentions." Suddenly he seized her around the waist and pulled her to him.

"Nicholas! Really!" she hissed, her face flaming hot. Nicholas wiggled his eyebrows at the guests like a villian in a bad farce, and their chuckles turned to laughter. "For heaven's sake! Do let me go!" she protested, half laughing and pushing her hands against his chest.

"A kiss first," he said.

"I— No, stop, oh surely you— Nicholas—"

"A kiss, a kiss!" cried the guests, laughing.

She looked helplessly at them, and then at Nicholas. "Oh, very well then!" She primly pursed her lips.

He grinned at her. "None of that, my lady," he said, and his lips came down over hers, kissing her until she gave in and kissed him in return.

Cheers came from the gentlemen, and Leonore could hear envious sighs from the ladies as well. She broke away at last, covering her heated cheeks with her hands, unable to look at anything but her feet. She felt a hand caress her chin, and she gazed up into Nicholas's amused eyes.

"Come, my dear. Surely it was not so bad."

She eyed him sternly. "You, my lord, are a shameless rogue."

"Yes, I know. I depend on you to reform me."

"I think it may be far beyond my powers to do so," she retorted.

"You can but try," he said and put on an innocent, hopeful look. The guests broke out in laughter again, and Leonore gave a reluctant smile. She wanted to laugh along with the others, but a heaviness in her chest weighed her down every time she looked at Nicholas. He smiled at her, then his attention was taken by another guest. She felt suddenly cold and alone, despite the smile she kept on her face.

Leonore did not want him to die. The heaviness became an ache, and she drew in a slow breath. When he died, she would be alone, more so than she had ever been in her life. In the short space of time she'd come to know him, her days had been filled; filled with his laughter, his touch, his kisses. When he held her, she felt comforted of much of the pain of her life, the loneliness.

She understood, suddenly, that she had been lonely all her life. There was Susan, but Leonore was the older sister and Susan's support, the strong one. She rarely revealed her thoughts and feelings to anyone, including her sister. No one really knew her, knew what was inside of her. She'd taken pride in her invulnerability; it was a thing that protected her heart, like a hothouse sheltering a rare rose. And yet, Nicholas had encouraged her to talk and listened to her, had opened a door and let in the wind. Sometimes the wind was warm, and sometimes it was chillingly cold; Leonore did not know if her heart would survive being exposed to such extremes. She had protected it so very carefully.

But now her gaze followed Nicholas around the room; she noted how he chuckled at a guest's gibe, how he looked mischievously into a lady's eyes as he kissed her hand. Should she close the door and protect herself once again?

He may die in a year. Leonore closed her eyes briefly, then made herself smile and nod at a gentleman who congratulated her on her marriage. What would she have after Nicholas was gone?—a title, and if he continued to be generous, funds enough so that she might live in luxury. A shudder went through her, a cold current of grief. These things seemed meaningless somehow. Nicholas looked up from his conversation with Lord Eldon and smiled at her from across the room. Leonore smiled in return, then bit her lip, for bleak desolation threatened to overwhelm her. She would give up the title and all the riches in the world if it would keep him alive.

She loved him. The thought startled her. Impossible! she said to herself. Her father had sold her to Nicholas; it was a marriage of convenience. But that argument and the resentment that had always accompanied it were long expired. A rising panic made Leonore's hands clench in her lap. What would she do? What *could* she do? She felt exposed and vulnerable and weak.

It came to her then, that her weakness was none of Nicholas's doing. It was she, herself, who had caused it. Protecting her heart from all the pain in the world had weakened it, for she had risked nothing, had not become strong from the exercise of risk. She'd never let herself receive any tender gesture, denied she had need of it. She had even refused to acknowledge the hopeful and proper approach of a gentleman at a student's house, and she had known at the time he would have meant honorably by her. But she could have been wrong, was her thought at the time, and it was not proper that a governess marry any man of the house in which she taught.

There had been nothing proper about Nicholas's advances toward her, however, though they had occurred within the bounds of their betrothal. He had wanted *her*, and he had made it clear that it was herself alone he wanted. He had spoken no word of love, and she'd not expected it. But he had treated her with—yes—respect. Her wishes had some value to him. Even his improper caresses had ceased when she had said no. And when she had inadvertently shown distress at his illness, he had taken her in his arms to comfort her. She was sure, in his own way, in some slight way, that he cared for her.

And all this would be taken away from her in a year. The pain of it almost made her groan aloud, but she swallowed it down. No, no, surely it was not "would" but only "could."

The sound of music startled Leonore from her thoughts. She looked for the source of it and found to her surprise that Susan had come to the pianoforte and was playing a dance tune. Some guests were already standing up for a set. She felt a touch on her shoulder and looked up to see Nicholas at her side.

"Dance with me," he said, an echo of his words that time they danced in the moonlit garden at the Benningtons' house. Wordlessly, she took his hand and stood up.

She had no occasion to dwell on her feelings, for the country dance was a sprightly one, and it took all her breath and attention to keep up. Even when she was not looking at him, she could feel Nicholas's eyes upon her, and even when the figures of the dance caused them to part. He looked at her as if studying her, as if he was trying to make a decision. Of course she could not ask him, for the dance kept them apart too much of the time. Later, she thought. Later I will ask.

The dancing continued, and even Susan blushingly agreed to dance while her mother or another lady played the piano. A quadrille came to an end, and a few yawns were suppressed here and there amongst the company, and Leonore looked at the ormolu clock upon the mantelpiece. It was not very late according to the hours society generally kept—only eleven o'clock. She looked at a few of the people who had yawned and caught laughing looks from them. Heat rose in her cheeks, for she suspected they had some notions about leaving the newlywed couple alone.

The room became thin of company then, for the guests began to leave. Leonore's family was the last to depart, and she dutifully allowed her mother to kiss her cheek and shook her father's hand. Then she smiled and held out her hands to Susan, who rushed into her arms and gave her a fierce hug.

"Oh, Leonore, I am so glad for you! Lord St. Vire has been so kind to us all! I am convinced you cannot be anything but happy you have married him."

"Of course I am happy," she replied and swallowed a small lump in her throat. "How can I not be?" Nicholas moved closer to her side and placed his hand on her shoulder. She looked up at him and gave him a slight, uncertain smile. Turning back to Susan, she said, "I would like you to visit me often—promise me, now!"

Susan looked uncertainly at Nicholas. "I . . . if it is permitted. . . ."

"Of course, Miss Susan, you are always welcome here," Nicholas said. "You may visit your sister whenever you wish."

Susan blushed shyly. "You are too good, my lord."

Nicholas grinned at her. "You must call me Nicholas, as you are my sister now, are you not?" He bent and kissed Susan briefly on her cheek. The girl's face blushed fiery red, and she put her hands to her cheeks.

"Yes, sir . . . that is, Nicholas." Susan looked shyly down at her feet.

Leonore gave her a hug and whispered loudly in her ear—loudly enough for Nicholas to hear. "You must not heed him, Susan, for he is a terrible flirt and delights in discomposing everyone about him."

Susan looked up and grinned. "That *is* true, isn't it? He did kiss you in front of everyone, didn't he?"

This time it was Leonore's turn to blush, and Nicholas laughed. "Touché! Leonore, your sister catches you out!"

Leonore turned an ironic eye to him. "I think it was you she caught out, not I!"

"Susan!" Mr. Farleigh called from the doorway. Susan looked hurriedly back at her father.

"I must go! But I will see you soon!" She gave Leonore one last hug and left.

The door shut behind her, and Leonore breathed out a long breath. It echoed in the now empty room . . . empty except for herself and Nicholas. His hand was still upon her shoulder, and now his thumb was caressing the skin of her neck. She gave him a tentative look.

"Are you glad, Leonore?" he asked, gazing at her intently.

"Glad of what?"

"That you married me." His thumb continued tracing a line up and down her shoulder and throat. She swallowed and looked away from him.

"Of course I am," she said. "You have been all that is kind to me." There was silence, and she glanced up at him. He was watching her, his eyes speculative.

"Shall we retire, then?"

She nodded and turned toward the door. Then she stopped and looked at him. "But you sleep only during the day."

"True."

"Oh!"

"Yes, 'oh!' " His smile turned into a grin, and he kissed her. She could not help kissing him in return for a moment, then gently pushed him away from her. She felt suddenly afraid, for what her mother had told her—in a vague, furtive manner—seemed a terribly intimate thing, and her emotions were almost too raw this evening to consider it. She gazed at his face, serious now, and touched the pale skin of his cheek, then let her fingers brush his lips. He has perhaps a year to live, she thought. He took her hand and kissed it.

"You are frightened, yes?" he asked.

"Yes," she said.

"I will be gentle with you, Leonore, I promise it."

She looked at him, surprised, then realized that he meant he would be so to her in the marriage bed. Her mother had told her it would hurt and that she should think of the clothes she would buy when next she went to the dressmaker's shop. But she did not want to think of clothes, for she knew the pain she'd feel when he was gone would be woven in with regret if she did not let herself know him fully. Then she could always remember and never wonder "if" later. She did not want to regret anything.

Abruptly, Leonore tugged his hand, and pulled him toward the door. His brows rose, but he said nothing, and only followed her.

They went up the stairs, and Leonore finally stopped in front of a chamber door, which earlier a maid had told her was her own room. She turned to Nicholas then and put her hands behind his neck to pull him down in a kiss, fierce and passionate. He was still for an instant, then brought her close to him. After a moment, she pushed him from her and stared into his eyes.

"Come to me. Soon." Her face flamed red in the candlelight at her brazenness. She turned, went into her room, and quickly shut the door.

Chapter 8

St. Vire stared at the closed door, then let out a quiet, triumphant laugh. She was willing—more than willing. Leonore wanted him. Everything was in place now; he needed only to take action.

He went next door to his room, where the conscientious but yawning Edmonds waited to help him remove his clothes. Perhaps his valet thought he had to help his master to bed this night. St. Vire gave him a quick smile and waved him away after removing his jacket. "You need not change your routine, Edmonds. I will not need you this evening."

"Very well, your lordship." Edmonds gave him a grateful look, bowed, and left.

Taking off his waistcoat, St. Vire glanced at the clock on the wall. It was almost eleven o'clock, midsummer night. He smiled in satisfaction. Each part of his plan had fallen into place, all on the schedule the spell indicated. He frowned. That was the thing . . . the spell indicated, but rarely stated. Then, too, the spell book was old and the words faded. He had abstained from both blood and whores prior to his wedding, enticed a virgin to the point of desiring his embrace, and married her in a church on midsummer night. Now he would bed her. The sign that he had succeeded so far was that he had survived in the church. The next step, however, told of releasing the maiden's blood . . . and this could either mean taking her virginity or her lifeblood, or even both.

To his surprise, his hand clenched into a fist. His whole body had tensed. He made himself relax and smiled wryly. He was acting as if he were the virgin, not Leonore.

But what if it was indeed her lifeblood that he needed to take? One would think, after all the austerities the spell had demanded, that it meant the lesser of the two, the taking of her maidenhead. What would happen, then, if it were not? What if he must draw her blood from her veins? Oh, God. If he did not do the right one, he would have no other chance to avoid the madness that was sure to come. He had already stepped upon the path by marrying Leonore. There was no going back.

And would she come to hate him if he drank her blood?

Why should he care if she did? She was just the means to cease the march toward insanity, after all. He could drink of her blood every week, and she would have no power to refuse, for Leonore was his wife. An image of her came to his mind's eye, her face filled with revulsion, flinching from his touch where she had sought it before. His breath left him suddenly. No, no, she had to be willing—that was what the spell required. It would ruin everything if she were not, and he much preferred her willing. Yes, that was it. It was better that way; it would be awkward otherwise, and he always did prefer finesse in all things.

His fingers became suddenly clumsy, and his neckcloth tangled in his hands; he tore it off and threw it on the floor. He was tired of this dance, this mincing around and about the spell. It made him feel things he did not want to feel, made him think he wanted Leonore's regard, made him obsessed with her. Why look at him! He'd been wondering *if* and *when* and *how* about the marriage bed as if he'd never eased his lust upon a woman before. He sneered. How stupid he'd become, all because of a spell . . . and a woman. He was more than eighty years old now. Perhaps he was coming into senility. What was more repulsive was that he, as old as he was, lusted after a woman sixty years younger than himself.

A laugh broke from him, at once exhilarated and angry. But he was not old, was he, after all? His mirror could show him that. He turned, thrust aside the curtain he had put over it, and stared at himself—stared at the face smooth of any sign of aging. Not even laugh lines showed around his eyes, though he laughed much. God, he was still young. He'd seen his friends die of old age—no, only noted they had died when he read their obituaries, for he could not let them see him after the years had scored their faces with lines but had left his alone. No one was still alive who knew him when he first was turned into a vampire. No one knew what he was, who the real Nicholas St. Vire was.

He knew, of course. He could see it in the old eyes that stared back at him, the colorless skin, the canine teeth long and sharp. And why could not anyone else see it? What did he, in truth, look like to others? He let out an impatient breath. He should be dead, for what was the use of living when all who once knew you were dead?

Stupid, stupid! This was old ground—he had walked this path before in his thoughts. A fire heated his mind, and he paced the floor, glancing at the mirror from time to time. He shouldn't have a mirror in his room, not at all. What he saw was all a lie, anyway. His whole damned, immortal life was a lie. Why should his mirror tell him anything different? He stopped before the mirror and laughed again, angrily. What was truth, after all, and what was reality? His fist shot out, and the sound of shattering glass and the crash of the mirror upon the floor pierced the night's silence.

He stared at the pieces of glass scattered upon the rug, his breath still coming quick and harsh. The fiery mist receded from his mind, leaving him feeling dull and slow. The scent of his own blood came to his nose. It sharpened his senses, and pain spread across the knuckles of his hand. He sighed and shook his head. He had broken another mirror. Really, he should not have put one in his room to begin with. And yet, how was he to tie his neckcloth properly without one?

"Nicholas! Nicholas, what has happened?"

Leonore . . . her voice sounded frantic with worry. St. Vire stared bleakly at the connecting door he usually kept locked, at the mirror, and then at his hand. His hand was oozing blood . . . he should do something about it. He shook his head, trying to clear his mind of the fog that had settled in it.

"Nicholas! Open this door!"

She cared for him. He could tell by the anxiety in her voice, and she had said she cared if he lived or died.

"Nicholas!" The doorknob rattled, and he could hear Leonore pounding her hand on the door.

He blinked and shook his head again. He had broken the mirror. He let out a shuddering breath. What a fool he was. The madness had not seized him for a while, and he thought perhaps he had controlled it totally. Of course, he had not. He supposed he should be glad he had not gone on to destroying other furniture, as he had done before. Or destroying people, for that matter, as he'd seen that other vampire do long ago. He took another deep breath, and it seemed to clear his mind.

"Please, Nicholas, open the door, or I shall call for Edmonds!"

Abruptly, he strode to the door and opened it. There Leonore stood, her hair disheveled and her eyes wild. "Yes?" he said calmly.

Fear and anger burned in her eyes, and she thumped his chest with her fist. "Is this all you can say? I thought you were ill again, and you would not answer! For all I know you could have died, and then what would I have done?"

He smiled slightly. "Why, then you would have been a rich woman and could choose another husband at your leisure."

She pushed at him, and he caught her hands. "I do not *want* to be rich!" Her breath caught in a sob. "I want *you*, Nicholas, only you, and— Oh, heavens, your hand is bleeding!" He saw her bite her lip to control its trembling.

"Never mind . . . it is nothing." He drew her close and kissed her, but she pushed him away again.

"Nonsense! You must tell me what happened."

"I . . . tripped and grasped the mirror—it fell and broke upon my hand."

Shooting him a skeptical look, she pulled him to her turned-down bed and made him sit.

"I was not ill again, Leonore."

"Hmm," she said. He watched her while she wet a handkerchief from the washstand. She wore a thin white wrap drawn over her breasts and tied with a single ribbon. The cloth shifted, outlining her limbs as she moved, and he could see her form, lithe and graceful, as she passed in front of the candles and the fireplace. His breath quickened. He wanted to touch her then, untie the ribbon and push away the bodice of her gown. He put out his hand toward her, but stopped himself, for it was yet another obsession, a little madness like the one he'd experienced just minutes ago, and he was not sure he was fully in control of himself yet.

She brought a brace of candles and set it upon the table next to the bed. A smooth spiral of her hair dropped forward from her shoulder as she leaned over his hand, and his other hand closed tight against the feeling that he must follow the line of the curl to where it lay upon her breast. She pulled with care a fragment of glass from between his knuckles and wiped away the blood. She began to wrap the handkerchief around his hand, but he stopped her.

"You need not bind it. It is but a small cut, after all."

She looked at his hand and raised her brows; it had indeed stopped oozing blood. She brought his hand to her lips and pressed a kiss upon it, then gave him a wavering smile. "There, then. Perhaps that will help if you do not want me to bind it."

"Yes, I am sure it will." He returned her smile and drew her to him, down to the bedsheets.

Now, now he pulled the ribbon and the robe fell open, now he slipped the gown from her shoulders, now he kissed her lips softly, tasting them. A salty tang was upon her lips, the faint residue of his own blood from when she kissed his hand, and he drew in his breath at the desire that rose in him, hot and feral.

"The candles—" She struggled up and reached toward them.

He grasped her hand and brought it down again. "No. I want to see you. All of you." His gaze went over what he had exposed so far: her shoulders and her breasts, round and full. He sighed deeply at the sight of it. He had been very good, bearing his abstinence with great fortitude, he believed. Damned saintly, in fact. He pulled the robe from her. Slowly he unbuttoned her gown from bodice to hem, kissing the skin he exposed as each button came undone. A glance at her when he released the last fastening made him smile. Her face was blushing, and her eyes were squeezed shut.

"Look at me, Leonore."

She opened her eyes and stared at him.

"You need not be afraid. You are familiar already with some of what I will do with you," he said and slid his hand up to her breast. She let out a long sigh, and he felt her body relax a little.

"I suppose I should think of the clothes I shall buy."

St. Vire let out a soft chuckle. "Is that what your mother told you?"

She smiled a little at him. "Yes."

He shifted atop her and kissed her. "Sweet one, very soon you will not be able to think of clothes at all," he murmured against her lips.

It was true. Leonore could not think of anything except his hands caressing her as they had before in the moonlit garden, in the Holland-covered room at the Rothwicks' house, in the many secluded places he had found to draw her close to him. She did not *want* to think of anything but how his lips tasted of wine and how his hands stroked her. She had thought too much already of his illness, the possibility that he would be gone from her someday. A fierce grief and tenderness overcame her, and she pressed her face into his shoulder to hide her emotions. The feelings almost banished the tingling that coursed over her body, but they merged with the sensation into a bitter longing, an aching passion to give him whatever he wished, whatever she could give him.

She put her arms around his neck and kissed him as he had taught her all those times, wanting to please him, but Nicholas's caresses caused her to moan and close her eyes, kissing him as she pleased—wildly, and with all the love she had and all the heat that rose in her body. Briefly, he parted from her, and then she felt him unclothed against her. She dared run her hand upon his bare flesh, her eyes still closed, feeling now the coolness of his skin warmed under her touch. His breath came short and she was glad, for perhaps he also felt as she did.

"I can make you . . . feel, as well," she whispered.

His lips slanted across her cheek and down her neck where his tongue touched her throat. "Yes. God, yes."

His touch brought a trembling upon her body that caused her to press herself to him, and his words brought an exhilaration that burned in her soul. She could give him back touch for touch, kiss for kiss, give him the heat and the joy she herself felt.

I love you. I love you, she said to him in her mind and her heart, said it with the passion she put into her kiss. She could not say it aloud, not now. Those words would die if she spoke them, for they were brief things that would hang between them only a moment. Better than she impress her love through her body's movements upon his body and her lips upon his lips, for these things were real and not mere breaths upon the air. Then, she was sure, he would remember it until the end. *I love you, Nicholas,* she murmured in her heart, and the pain of silence made her moan and kiss him fiercely. She slid her hands along his body. He gasped and kissed her cheek, then moved his lips and teeth against her neck.

He was on the edge of the bloodthirst, of the urge to drink of her from where his tongue lay against the pulse on her neck. He did not, relying on the practiced control he had exercised each time he had kissed and touched her before. Relief washed over him. He was not in the madness now, for the thirst's acute sensitivity brought him alive once again. The smooth contours of her shoulders and breasts were like silk to his fingers; her lips were sweet and hot against his own. Her hair flowed over his hands like a pale gold river, and her eyes were the color of slate. He breathed in her woman's scent and the silvery scent of lavender.

The onslaught of sensation at first overwhelmed him, but he controlled it, just pressing his mouth to her neck, and drawing back to put his tongue against the faint blue line that pulsed just under her skin. He pushed down the desire for blood, and it resurfaced as desire for her, as it had before. This desire was a common thing, he told himself. It was allowed, they could do this, and he would make another step away from the madness. He wanted to sink another part of himself into her and take her warmth into himself. But he could not hurry her, for he needed her to be willing.

Yet, he did not need to slow his pace at all. Leonore pressed herself against him without hesitation or shame and kissed him with passion. He parted from her to gaze into her eyes and threaded his fingers through her hair. She said nothing, but stared back at him, a soft smile upon her lips, her eyes tender and warm. Her hand came up, and she traced his brow and his cheek with her fingers until they rested upon his lips. A tightness in his chest made him draw in his breath.

"Do you . . . care for me?" he could not help asking. He felt as if the words had been pulled from him, as if she had put a glamour upon him and willed him to say it. *Say no,* he pleaded inside of himself, then, *say yes.*

Leonore's smile grew wider, and she put her hand behind his neck and drew him down to her. She kissed him full on the mouth, and he felt afire as her lips moved upon him, as her body moved beneath him.

"Yes," she said, parting from him for a moment. "Yes, and yes, and yes." Nicholas felt her hands slide down his back, and he pressed himself between her thighs in response. Her eyes widened, and she released her breath in a rush.

His laugh had a hint of triumph in it. It was as before, during all the times when they had been private together. He could make her respond as he wished, make her want him. Moving his lips across her cheek to her ear, he whispered, "Do you remember, at the musicale, what I told you?" He moved a little aside and brushed his fingers along her hip. Leonore shivered, but did not reply. "I said that I shall do all I have done to you so far, until you cry out with the delight of it. Do you remember?" Her head nodded slowly next to his, and a sighing moan came from her when he moved his hand between her legs.

"I lied," he said, sliding his lips from her neck to between her breasts and then to her belly. "I will do . . . so . . . much . . . more."

She closed her eyes and clutched at his shoulders, and her breath came short. The sound of it made him feel wild. Nicholas kissed and stroked her until he could not stand it, could not stand her sinuous movements beneath him without release. He thought he'd be in control, but that was a lie, also, for he was not. A madness descended upon him, a fine madness of the flesh instead of the mind, and he wanted to feel all of her, inside and out.

"Nicholas—" Leonore sobbed, and he could hear the dawn of heaven in her voice. *She wants me*, he thought, *she cares for me*. The knowledge was the thrust of a knife into him; he groaned as if on the edge of death, closing his eyes as he pushed inside of her. Her cry of mingled pain and ecstasy, the pulse within her, made him breathe in sharply.

The scent of blood—the maiden's blood. It seized him and shook him and rattled him until his soul was no longer his. She cried out in pure pleasure again, and it was music and torture for him. He thrust into her until his mind and body burst into a flash of light and darkness, then sighed and sank his teeth into the fine skin of her neck.

No. No. No. The pain was fierce as he drank of her, the pain of a man dying of thirst in a desert and given his first mouthful of water. A flood of power came into him, and his senses surged into a keen, tingling receptivity.

No. The word echoed in his mind more strongly, forced a semblance of rationality into him. His mouth was against Leonore's neck, the metallic taste of blood upon his tongue. She was tense beneath him, he could feel it. *No*. A leaden feeling pressed into his chest, pushing an abrupt groan from him. Quickly he cast a glamour upon her. "Forget," he whispered in her ear. "Forget the pain, and the . . . bite."

She put her arms around him then, and Nicholas drew her to him so that they lay on their sides. He closed his eyes and stroked her hair, then moved his fingers to the small wound upon her neck. He remembered a spell for speedy healing he had learned decades ago. Only a bruise would show in the morning.

He felt her fingers upon his cheek, and he opened his eyes. Leonore was gazing at him, a sleepy smile on her face.

"Thank you," she said.

"You are welcome. At any time, in fact." Nicholas made himself grin in return and kissed her forehead, then rested his chin on her hair. His smile faded. The heaviness was still within him, an unfamiliar emotion. He did not know what made him want to name it instead of pushing it away. Perhaps it was the oddly comforting sensation of Leonore pressed against him and the even sound of her sleeping breath that lulled him into it.

He had never been an introspective man. His mind had always delved into things outside himself, esoteric though these things might be. It had led him into rituals and practices both light and dark, but never had he been touched by them. He had even been amused by the fervor of others and was usually the onlooker, sometimes a detached participant. The most satanic of meetings and the most sublime of angel invocations had not moved him, for they were of only intellectual interest to him, and made him want to seek further and strip away yet another veil between himself and the essence of all magics.

But now the heaviness within him felt close to regret—he who regretted little or nothing in his life. More than regret, in fact, for as Leonore moved to curl herself into him in her sleep, the heaviness became an ache only somewhat assuaged when he held her close to him. He breathed in the scent of lavender that emanated from her, and the faint scent of roses came to him as well. He glanced up and saw a vase of roses near the bed. He had not noticed them when he had entered Leonore's room, for all his attention had been on her alone.

He remembered he had asked his servants to put flowers in her room, for she seemed to like them that time they had danced in Lord and Lady Bennington's garden. He had done it on impulse; all his actions regarding Leonore these days seemed to be sudden and without thought, he reflected wryly. He examined the impulse the way he examined ancient texts for hidden meanings—turning it over and over in his mind, seeking patterns. The patterns were there: He desired Leonore, whether she was near or not; he enjoyed her presence; she seemed . . . *real* to him, more so than other people seemed. What man would not feel so? She was a lovely woman, after all. And yet, he felt dissatisfaction with his conclusion.

What else was there? He acknowledged that he felt regret. He wished he had not taken the blood from Leonore, but he had no choice about it if he were to keep the madness away. Then, too, the thirst had caught him suddenly; it was at present his nature to take blood after all. It was no use regretting it. Would it have been different had it been another woman? He let out a quick breath. He wished it had not been Leonore—anyone else, but not Leonore. He had not thought she'd come to care for him, wished she hadn't, but would not have her change now that she did.

Fully asleep now, Leonore moved a little apart and onto her back, and Nicholas gazed at her profile. She had a sweet countenance, kind and a little sad when she slept. It was different from the careful neutrality of expression she usually wore. A small quiver went through her. She woke and turned toward him again, her smile sleepy and warm.

Nicholas could not help himself. He moved over her again, kissing her softly, and then with more heat. The heaviness within him made his chest feel tight; he felt as if he were breaking. It was no use searching his thoughts for the reasons behind the things he wished to do for Leonore, for the answer was not in his mind.

He feared it was in his heart.

Chapter 9

Warmth stroked Leonore's face, and she fancied it was Nicholas's fingers upon her until she opened her eyes and admitted to herself it was only the morning sun. She ran her hand across the sheets next to her, then rolled into the slight depression there, as if she could take that last evidence of his presence into herself somehow.

It was all foolishness, of course. He would not be in the bed beside her, for he could not have the sun upon him. Still, she burrowed into the sheets that had been under him and breathed the faint scent of bay rum from the pillow. The warm summer sun was persistent, however, and conspired with her growling stomach to move her from the bed.

"Oh, very well, then!" she said in a cross voice. She pulled on her robe, pushed aside the bed curtains, and went to the washstand. To her surprise, the water in the pitcher was lukewarm, probably from standing in the sun. She glanced at the clock on the mantelpiece. Good heavens! It was already past noon. She had never slept so late in her life. An image came to her of Nicholas smiling down at her in bed. Well, she supposed she had a good reason for her late awakening. He had been intimate with her three times last night. Her face grew hot. She'd been wanton, totally uncontrolled. His touch had done that to her.

No, she had to take the blame as well. She had not cared to exert any control upon her behavior, had touched and kissed and opened herself to him. Leonore pressed a wet cloth against her face, hoping to cool her blushes. It did, a little, but did nothing to cool the heat that stirred in the pit of her stomach at the thought of Nicholas. She bit her lip at the sensation, trying to quash it, but the memory of his touch and his kisses were too sharp and clear for her to banish.

For goodness sake, she could not forever be thinking of him; other things needed to be done. She must dress, put away all thoughts of him, and try to occupy herself until she saw him again. Leonore pulled the bell rope to summon a maid. First, she would speak with the servants and learn their names and their function. Then she would look about the house and see if she might do something to while away her time. Perhaps she might be useful, and when next she saw Nicholas, he would be pleased with her, pleased enough to take her in his arms and—

She groaned, despising herself for thinking such slavish thoughts. Never would she be like her mother, cringing or cautiously happy at whatever glance Father cared to throw her way. Leonore had never shrunk from her father, no matter that he raised his hand to her. She had taken pride in that.

But she could not stop thinking of Nicholas and wished he were here now so that she might curl herself into him and hold him close. It was what she craved most of all: the way he held her, stroked her hair, and soothed her after the almost unbearable shock of heat and light that came upon her at the end of their joining. The loneliness she'd always had within her would disappear then, and the sensation was like the warmth of the sun after a long, hard winter.

Her mother had not told her of this, that she would feel such things for Nicholas. She thought over the rage and the fear that was ever-present between her parents, and thought perhaps her mother could not tell what she did not know. Her observations of her parents' marriage did her, Leonore, little good, however. They gave her no clue to what she must do about it, if what she felt for Nicholas—both in her body and her heart—were what she should feel, and if it were proper.

A knock at the door startled her.

"It's me, Betty, my lady."

"Come in."

A pink-cheeked, round-faced girl peeped timidly in. "I was

hopin' you was awake, my lady," said the maid. "I'd like to do my best fer you, ma'am, this bein' the first time I've been a lady's maid, and all." The girl blushed.

Leonore smiled at her. "Do come in, I'll not bite." Betty smiled widely and entered the room. "I will need some breakfast—something hearty, for I am quite hungry—and I wish to dress."

"Yes, my lady." Betty gave a curtsy and hurried to the bell rope. She rang it vigorously. When another maid appeared, Betty said in a whisper quite loud enough for Leonore to hear, "Sal, you go tell Cook to fix up some victuals for m'lady, and be sharp about it! Good stuff, rib-stickers, like. And no skimping, mind, or I'll skin yer silly arse for yer." Sal nodded quickly and ran off, while Betty beamed proudly at her new mistress.

Leonore winced. The girl would definitely need some training in deportment. She hoped the rest of the servants were more refined. She smiled at the maid and said, "Let's see if my clothes have arrived in good order, shall we?" Betty nodded eagerly and opened the wardrobe door.

The dresses looked nothing like what Leonore had bought in the past few weeks. They were beautiful creations done in the latest style or in innovative designs, bold pieces of cloth she'd never dreamed she'd ever wear, or even dare to.

"Oh, heavens!" she said. "These cannot be mine. I am sure I did not order them."

A worried frown crossed Betty's face. " 'Tis what his lordship ordered, my lady. Who else would it be for?"

A courtesan, a woman of pleasure, thought Leonore as she gazed at one dress she had pulled out of the wardrobe. It was a diaphanous thing of stars and moonlight and the bodice but a whisper of silk and gauze. And yet no one could say it was gaudy or vulgar, for the shifting colors of deep blue, white, and pale pink were subtle and elegant. A vision of herself in the dress came to her, of Nicholas seeing her in it and smiling his seductive smile, of him taking her in his arms, kissing her. . . .

She could feel her face heat with blushes and hastily shoved the dress back into the wardrobe. "Well," she said and took a deep breath. "Well. That is obviously not a morning dress, or, or even an afternoon dress, so of course I cannot wear it now."

"Yes, my lady," Betty said, her face a picture of concentration. Leonore could not help smiling. Her maid was obviously trying her best to learn. Leonore hoped the rest of her gowns were not so daring, or the maid would have a difficult time selecting appropriate clothes should she ever go on to another mistress.

She went through one dress after another and finally picked a relatively plain, high-necked gown. Even so, it fit with precision around her body, making the best of any asset she had. She looked in the mirror and did not feel like herself at all; she was used to thinking of herself as practical and sensible, and this dress was impractical and frivolous to boot. It made the gowns she had selected in the weeks before seem drab in comparison. She was used to wearing cottons and sturdy woolen cloth. This dress slid over her limbs like warm water, a sensuous thing that made her think of Nicholas's hands upon her body. Leonore let out a swift, impatient breath. *Stop it,* she told herself. *Stop. You are obsessed with him, and this cannot be right, even though he is your husband.*

"My lady?"

Startled out of her thoughts, Leonore turned to look at her maid.

"My lady, is anything wrong?" Betty's face was anxious.

"No . . . no, you have done quite well." Leonore smiled at her. "We need only to put up my hair—simply, please—and I shall go down to my breakfast."

"Yes, my lady."

Betty did a credible job with Leonore's hair, and she smiled at her maid in approval. The girl blushed and grinned, then left, leaving the door of her chamber ajar. Leonore shook her head and closed the door.

She hesitated, thinking that she should go down to breakfast, but as she passed the connecting door to Nicholas's room, she could not help gazing at it curiously. She wondered if he rested well, or if he had any recurrence of his illness. Perhaps

. . . perhaps she should look in on him. She turned the doorknob and pushed open the door.

The room was dark as night, for the curtains were drawn tightly against the windows, allowing no light to pass through. Of course, Leonore remembered, the sunlight made Nicholas ill. She retreated to her room, found a tinderbox, and lit a lamp. Making sure to close the door behind her, she approached the bed.

Only her footsteps made any noise in the room, and that was only a soft padding sound upon the rug. She stopped and heard nothing, not even the sound of breathing. Her heart beat quickly, anxiously, for the silence almost made her think there was no one else in the room—or perhaps that Nicholas's illness had overtaken him. She touched the bed curtains surrounding the bed and castigated herself for her worries. The cloth was thick and heavy; any soft sound would find it impenetrable.

Slowly, Leonore drew aside the curtains and sighed. Nicholas was indeed within, and she felt foolish for thinking he had not been there at all. She lifted her lamp, and its light shone softly down upon him. His face was turned toward her, his eyes closed. He did not move at all, and a sudden fear seized her. Quickly, she put her hand out to him, hesitated, then laid it over his heart.

His skin was cool and this alarmed her, but then she felt a slight, steady pulse, the small rise and fall of his chest, barely perceptible. She felt almost dizzy with relief. Perhaps it was his illness that made him so, or perhaps he took some medicine that made him sleep this way. Feeling a little bold, she kept her hand upon his chest, for he did not wake or even stir, and seemed very heavily asleep.

She had not thought to touch him last night as he had touched her. She marveled at the way he felt, his skin softer than she thought it would be, the light curling hair upon his chest like feathers upon her fingers. His skin had warmed under her touch, and slowly she moved her hand up to his neck and cheek, then smoothed the tousled hair from his forehead.

He moved and Leonore jumped back, almost upsetting the

lamp in her hand. But still he did not wake, merely lifting his chin as if trying to feel her hand again. How silly she was! He had been so still, his movement had startled her.

Lingering was useless, she told herself. Nicholas certainly needed his rest, and she would not disturb him. She closed the curtains about the bed. It was time, anyway, for her to have her breakfast. Staring at her husband while he slept accomplished nothing, after all.

She looked at the clock hanging on the wall. It would be almost eight hours until twilight when her husband would awaken. Husband. She'd always thought—when she thought of the vague possibility—that if she should ever marry, she'd marry a staid, placid man. Once in a while, she let herself fancy such a thing and imagined a pretty cottage in the country, a simple life with an undemanding man, perhaps a scholar of some sort who would be busy with his own interests. She'd go about her own business, and they'd live together in peace and quiet.

Impossible to have had that, she knew. She knew she had to marry to advantage, so that her sister would have a better life than she did. She gave a soft, incredulous laugh. What she had now was the furthest thing from any idyllic dream or practical imaginings. Yes, she had married to advantage; yes, Nicholas demanded little from her. But placidity? Nicholas, staid? Heavens, no. Leonore shook her head and went down to the breakfast parlor.

A footman came in with her breakfast. The food was well prepared, and she ate hungrily of the coddled egg, ham, and toast. Finally, she sat back and sipped her tea, feeling refreshed. Perhaps after she met all the servants, she would explore this house a little, perhaps claim a sitting room for herself. Nicholas had said she could arrange things as she liked in the house. It would at least, she thought, give her something to do.

When she arose from the table, she rang for the butler, Samuels, and requested he bring the servants before her. She knew Nicholas thought well of Samuels and Edmonds, the valet, but beyond that she was not sure he was aware of the rest of the staff.

Cook was a clean and competent-looking woman, but the maids looked young and inexperienced, and Leonore was certain she smelled liquor on the housekeeper's breath. That would not do, she thought, but she would not say anything unless she saw signs of neglect in the house. So she merely smiled at the housekeeper and requested the keys to the house.

The house was probably one of the largest on Pall Mall, for it had many rooms and three floors, not counting the attic rooms. The housekeeping was uneven—some rooms were well kept and others quite dusty. Leonore breathed a relieved sigh. She would have some occupation during the day and not just spend her days in idle pleasure. The thought that she would have nothing to do had made her feel oddly anxious, though she had thought otherwise before she was married. She could distract herself from thoughts of Nicholas by taking Susan out and about town and keeping house as well . . . until she saw her husband again in the evening.

She was almost done with her tour of the house and had selected a particularly pretty room—unused, she saw, and full of light once the curtains were drawn—for her own sitting room. She had memorized which key went to which room, but one key remained that did not seem to go to any room at all. She had not gone into the attics, however; perhaps the key fit something there. Leonore shrugged and almost put the keys away, but the thought of the long time until twilight and Nicholas's presence made her pull them out again. She found and lit a lantern, for she was sure the place would be ill-lit, and turned in the direction of the attic.

Grimacing, Leonore brushed at the dust and cobwebs that clung to her skirts as she ascended the stairs to the attic. The middle of the steps themselves were relatively clear of dust, which told her the attic was occasionally used. If so, the maids had little excuse for leaving the railing and the banister so dusty and dirty. She frowned and resolved to speak with the housekeeper about it.

The door to the attic opened to a short hall, and on either

side was a door. One had no lock at all and opened easily. She peered in, holding her lantern high, and sneezed, for the room was quite dusty. Pieces of old furniture and trunks were stacked within. She went in and looked about her and discovered some old aprons, fabric, and other clothing within the trunks. She wished she had discovered the aprons earlier, for her dress was becoming quite dirty. Nevertheless, she pulled one apron from the trunk and put it on. Better late than never, thought Leonore. She noted a few promising pieces of furniture, which she might have brought down to grace her sitting room.

She came into the hall again and tried the other door. It was locked. Well, now, she thought, this must be the door that goes with the last key. She took the key from her pocket and turned it in the keyhole. She heard a click, and the door opened.

The room was larger than she supposed it would be and surprisingly well apportioned. A large, thick rug lay on the floor, and thick curtains hung over the windows so that one would almost think it was night, for no light showed through. She was glad she had thought to bring her lantern, for it kept her from walking into furniture. She went to the windows and thrust aside the curtains.

The action made her sneeze again, for the curtains were obviously dusty; dust motes swirled in the beams of sunlight that weakly streamed through the dirty windows. And yet, the room had obviously been used, and that, recently. A rag lay on a table next to a used candle, and a line marked the rag's progress across the table, as if someone had made a halfhearted attempt at dusting. The room contained a large armchair and a daybed next to a small fireplace. Dust lined only the top of the armchair and not the arms or the seat. Someone had sat there not long ago.

Obviously, this was no servant's room. Nicholas . . . this must be his room, she thought, and her puzzlement grew. Why did he choose an attic room when there were better rooms below?

A tall bookshelf lined one wall, and these had little dust on them, as if the books had been taken out and read recently.

Some of the books were very old, held together in their bindings with pieces of string. She ran her fingers over the book spines; she could not read the titles, for they seemed to be in Latin or some other language she did not know, and in badly faded lettering, at that. It seemed as if Nicholas was a scholar, perhaps a collector of antique books. She wondered why he had never mentioned it before; she, herself, enjoyed books immensely and would have been interested in anything he cared to mention about his collection.

One book seemed newer than the others, and she pulled it out, opening it at random. "Ministrations and Communion with Angels," it read at the top of one chapter. Leonore raised her brows. Did Nicholas collect religious works, then? An image of him rose in her mind, of all the times he'd been scandalously alone with her before they were married. A burst of laughter escaped her. Good heavens, but she never would have thought him religious! She covered her mouth, trying to stiffle her giggles, but it only caused tears of laughter to come to her eyes.

Finally, she sighed and dabbed her eyes with her apron. Heavens, but she was becoming irreverent. Certainly, Nicholas could be devout if he wished . . . although she felt the chances of that were small. That he was not a churchgoer was probably what he meant when he had told her he was a bad man. Well, she thought, perhaps it was only old and rare books in general that he collected. She pulled out another volume—*An Historical, Physiological and Theological Treatise of Spirits* by John Beaumont. Another religious book, it seemed. She shook her head and took down a very old book, then opened it carefully.

"*Discoverie of Witchcraft,*" Leonore read. An uneasy feeling rose within her. This was certainly not a religious work. She shrugged her shoulders and pressed her lips together firmly, dispelling her uneasiness. Nicholas obviously collected unusual books, that was all. Besides, witchcraft is not real, and neither is magic, she told herself and smiled. What nonsense! Perhaps she would tease him about it when next she saw him, for he deserved a little teasing; he all too often won their verbal fencing, and she never would have thought he'd take an interest in such superstitious nonsense as witchcraft. She turned to leave the room, determined to ask Nicholas about the books and to do something about tidying the room.

"Ahh!" A sharp pain in her foot surprised her, and Leonore hobbled to a chair. She brought her foot up and examined it. A thin sliver of glass pierced through her slipper, and gingerly she removed it. The cut was somewhat deep, but not bad; she needed only to put a salve on it and bind it, and she was sure it would be well. She looked about her for a cloth to stanch the blood, but all she could see was the dusty rag, which she would rather not use. Grimacing, she pressed a clean corner of the rag to the cut. It stanched the bleeding a little, but not much. Well, she'd best get downstairs as quickly as possible so that she could find something better with which to bind it.

Leaving the rag upon the table, Leonore left the room and locked it. Surely, Nicholas could not object to having the room cleaned a little. She would have to see to it that any slivers of glass on the rug or floor be swept up so that no others would cut their feet on it. She shook her head. Nicholas should have had it done long ago. Perhaps he did not mind the dust much, although she would not have thought it of him. He was always so impeccably dressed and tidy, it did not seem quite like him to let this room be such a mess.

St. Vire did not dream this time. Or at least, he did not remember his dreams when he woke, but retained only a sensation of warmth and comfort that seemed to center in his chest. Perhaps this was a sign that the spell was beginning to work; he did not know, for the ancient *grimoire* said little of changes he might encounter as he went through the course of the spell. He only knew that he was glad he did not wake to watching images dancing before his open eyes, wondering whether these were real or not, or if he was still asleep or not.

He hesitated before he drew aside the bed curtains. Would it be daylight, then? Would the success of his actions last night make it so that he would be able to see the sun a little during the course of the spell? Briefly, he clenched his hand, then thrust open the draperies around his bed. He went to the heavy curtains at the windows and pushed them aside.

A frustrated sigh escaped him. It was night and quite dark. He would not see the sun yet, it seemed. A faint hope persisted, however; his room faced away from the setting sun, and it could very well be that if he went to a room with a western exposure, he would see it. His attic room faced the west—perhaps he could go there.

Quickly he pulled on a dressing gown, ascended the steps to the attic, then unlocked the door. A faint scent came to him as he entered the room and his senses sharpened, but he ignored it. He went to the windows and thrust aside the curtains.

Dark. The windows were dirty, however, and perhaps . . . perhaps . . . Nicholas hesitated again, then with an exasperated breath, he pushed the windows open and searched above the buildings in front of him to the horizon.

He did not feel the usual tingling across his skin when in the presence of the slightest bit of sunlight, because he could see no light. It seemed he had missed the setting of the sun. His shoulders slumped. He put his hand upon the window latch to close it again, then his eyes caught a faint color at the horizon. He was imagining it, surely, for he had seen no color in the sky but the blackness of the night and the whiteness of the moon and stars. Could he even remember what a sunset looked like? He stared hard at the horizon again. It was there, the last bit of light and color reflected upon the clouds from the sun setting below them, a thing he had not been able to see for sixty years without at least the beginning of pain.

St. Vire turned away from it, his hands clutching the window ledge. Perhaps he was imagining it. Had he not experienced some of the madness just the night before? He did not want to assume that what he saw was real. How could he tell, then?

Leonore. Leonore could tell him. He strode swiftly to the door, then let out a breathless laugh and stopped before he came to the door. Of course it was too late to do that, for no hint of light colored the sky now, and he would not importune her to stay up until dawn. Or, perhaps he could ask her. . . . He was not sure she would indulge him in this, waking just before dawn to watch the sunrise. He thought of the night before, of the way she had reacted to his caresses, and smiled. Perhaps he could wake her in a way that would make her more inclined to accede to his request.

His smile faded. He had taken blood from her and put a glamour upon her so that she would not remember it. He shivered. Going to the fireplace, he placed some wood in it. His hands shook a little as he used the tinderbox and failed to make a spark. He let out an impatient sigh, and gesturing with his hand, he murmured a few words. A little salamander of flame lit within his palm, and he emptied it into the kindling. He shifted the wood with the poker until the fire burned steadily. He twisted his lips ruefully. He did not know why he persisted in lighting fires the old way when he could do it with a few words.

Perhaps it was because it tied him to humanity still. All the vampires he had met feared fire and could not have it around them. Perhaps the warding spell he had put upon himself before he became a vampire had given a little twist to his condition and left him this last human attribute.

Finally, a vigorous fire burned in the hearth. The work of building a fire brought him some composure, and he smiled again. He'd been too eager to see the transformative spell succeed, and he knew it would take a year from midsummer before he was totally changed. Apparently the transformation would be gradual. He sat in a nearby chair. Really, he had no reason to regret that he had put the glamour upon Leonore. It was for her own protection, after all.

Staring into the flames that licked at the wood, he grimaced. No, it was not for Leonore's protection, it was for his own. He had not known whether he had to take her blood or merely her maidenhood and so had done both to ensure he would not descend into madness. It was beginning to work, too. Did he not see a bit of the sunset this evening? And, he realized, he had felt the night's cold, enough to start a fire in the fireplace, a thing he had not needed to do for a long while.

He'd done what he had to, that was all. He had needed her

willing in bed, and what woman would want to lay willingly with one such as himself—one who might drink of her blood from time to time? None, he was sure, unless he offered money.

You are a coward, Nicholas, admit it. He pressed his hands upon his closed eyes, rubbing them wearily, and sighed. He did not want her to know what he was. The thought of her cringing from him brought the tightness of the night before to his chest. It felt as if something were expanding from the inside, and it hurt him. He did not like it, for it was foreign to him, and he preferred the familiar when it came to the emotions. Such things were uncomfortable when he encountered them in himself or in others, for that matter.

And such musings were useless. There was nothing he could do about it, after all. Much more to the point was getting proof of his perceptions from Leonore. Perhaps if he pleased her in some way, she would do this for him. What would she like? A trinket of some sort? She had not spoken of any interest in jewelry to him; indeed, she did not wear much jewelry at all, even though he had given her some very fine necklaces as a wedding present. St. Vire frowned. She had asked nothing of him, really; nothing for herself, only for her family or for her sister. He put his hand on the small table beside him, tapping his fingers upon it impatiently. Was there nothing she wished for? His fingers touched the rag he had left on the table some days ago, and the scent he had encountered when entering the room came to him again.

Blood. Blood was near, recently shed. Someone had come into this room within the last day and had cut himself, perhaps on the shards of glass that were still scattered on the floor. He clenched his teeth in anger. No one should be here but himself, for he had told his servants that he did not want anyone to disturb anything in the attic. Whatever servant had disobeyed him would be out on the streets this night.

The books he had were valuable, and he'd had a devil of a time finding them; he trusted no one with them. And the implements he'd collected when he'd experimented with the more elaborate spells—many of them were of strange and foreign construction. While he cultivated his eccentric reputation, he could not let anyone come close to realizing his vampiric nature. It was hard enough to attend to daily business matters during the night without that.

He drew in his breath and found that the scent came from the rag. Smoothing it out, he found a large, dark spot upon it. Apparently whoever had come into this room had stanched the wound with the rag. Well, the culprit would be easy to find, then. Anyone who showed a cut would be suspect. St. Vire rose from his chair. He would find out as soon as he dressed.

Chapter 10

It was past twilight. Leonore cast another glance at the parlor clock as she turned the page of her book. Nicholas must appear soon. She brought her attention back to her book, then realized she did not remember what she had read for the last half hour. Sighing impatiently, she closed it with a snap. This was useless! Surely Nicholas would not think her forward if she went up to his chambers to see if he was up and about yet. Perhaps he had forgotten that they were to go to the theatre tonight, or overslept. She rose from her chair.

You are being quite silly, Leonore told herself as she ascended the stairs to his room. Nicholas would come to see her in good time, and he had promised they would go to the theatre. Had he not kept all his promises to her so far? There was no reason why he shouldn't keep this one. Her footsteps slowed, then halted. She smoothed her hand over the deep blue silk of her evening gown; she had dressed in one of the gowns Nicholas had bought for her. It was beautiful, but she felt awkward wearing it, for it was not in a style she had thought would suit her. She shook her head. Perhaps Nicholas thought fine clothes would make her look pretty; but peacock feathers on a sparrow did not make the sparrow a peacock.

But he had bought it to please her, as he did with other things he had given her and her family, and she didn't want to slight his generosity. He had asked nothing of her except that she marry him, and she supposed by implication, that she bear him an heir. The least she could do was show her appreciation for his gifts. She stepped quickly up the remaining stairs to his room and knocked at the door.

"Enter!"

Leonore opened the door and peered in. The room had no mirror in it now; she could see the imprint of the mirror's base upon the thick rug. Only the fire in the hearth and one brace of candles lit the room. Nicholas was looking into a small hand mirror that Edmonds was holding up for him. Leonore said nothing while he carefully tied his cravat and pressed his chin gently down upon its folds. She smiled to herself. How vain he was! But it was his only fault, and one which she found quite amusing. She wondered, too, if it was just one more piece of playacting that he performed, for she often had the distinct feeling he thought his own vanity amusing as well.

Finally, with a last glance at the mirror, Nicholas dismissed Edmonds and turned to her, smiling as the door shut behind the valet. His gaze went slowly from her face to her dress, as if he measured the gown upon her body with his eyes.

Leonore's face grew warm, and she turned away, blurting the first thing that came to her: "My, Nicholas, but you keep your room quite dim, even though it is night. I know candlelight doesn't hurt you, so there is no reason for so little of it." It was a stupid thing to say, she thought, but she felt she couldn't look at him without remembering last night and what they had done in her bed.

It was useless trying to avoid the thought, for Nicholas's arm went around her waist, and he cupped her chin with his hand so that she could not help looking at him. He was still smiling at her, but there was an assessing look in his eyes.

"And a good evening to you, too, Leonore," he replied.

A chuckle bubbled out of her, and she felt more at ease. "*Good evening,*" she said. "There, have I retrieved myself?" His measuring expression disappeared and he grinned.

"No. Lack of courtesy is anathema to me, and I exact a stiff penalty for it." He pulled her closer to him, and a fine anticipatory tingling came over her skin.

"Oh? And what is this penalty?" she managed to say.

"A kiss," he replied and moved his lips upon hers. "Or perhaps two . . . or three. . . ." He kissed her eyes, then her mouth again. "No, four is better." His lips moved down to her neck.

"Five is *much* better, actually. Or, no, six," he whispered at the edge of her décolletage. She gave a gasping laugh.

"Heavens, Nicholas, do stop!" He moved a little away from her; she was blushing furiously, she was certain, and her breath came quickly now. "I . . . I thought we were to go to the symphony tonight, you had said. . . ."

He grinned at her. "I suppose I did say that. But I can be persuaded otherwise if you wish for some other . . . activity."

"Yes, no, that is— Oh, for goodness sake, Nicholas, how you tease!" She felt her face grow hotter and put her hand to her cheek. She had forgotten another fault of his: He somehow always managed to get the last word. She pressed her lips together, trying to gather her thoughts together for a stinging reply.

"I? Tease?" He put a wounded expression on his face. "I live only to serve you, my dear," he said and bowed low.

"Nonsense!" Leonore said and tried to look stern. "How odious you are, to be sure! For that, we shall go to the theatre, where you will have to behave yourself."

"I suppose I will . . . ," he said, but the look he gave her was totally unrepentant.

"Besides, you are dressed for the theatre, so you cannot tell me you had forgotten it."

He looked down at his clothes in mock dismay. "Alas! Betrayed by my own vanity."

Leonore burst into laughter, for his grin made him look like a naughty boy.

A knock at the door interrupted her. "The servants are assembled, my lord," came Edmond's voice.

Nicholas's expression cooled to ice as he glanced at the door. "Very good. I shall be down directly," he said. An odd, uncertain feeling came over Leonore at that look. She had mostly seen him in a pleasant mood, but now her watchfulness came to the fore again.

"I hope you are not gathering them so as to introduce me. I have met them already; I needed occupation this afternoon and thought I might meet them myself." She watched him. He still smiled, but his body seemed tense.

He turned to her, and his smile grew a little warmer. "You did well. I am seeing them about a matter of discipline. One of the servants has gone into a private room of mine, a thing I have forbidden." He turned toward the door.

A chill went through Leonore. "I . . . Is it one of the attic rooms?"

His foot seemed to catch upon the rug, and he steadied himself with his hand upon the closed door. "Yes," he said, though he did not turn around.

"I . . . I am sorry if you don't like it, Nicholas, but I took the housekeeper's keys and toured the house. I thought I might find something useful in the attic, and I found some furniture I could use for the sitting room." She was babbling, and she hated how her voice sounded nervous even to herself, but the words kept tumbling from her lips. "There was a key—you didn't say you had a room up there—I thought perhaps I would find more furniture. I never knew you had . . . had . . ." Her words trailed off, for he had turned and stared at her, his eyes remote.

"Had what?" His voice was sharp and wary.

"So many books!" Leonore blurted. "You never told me you were a scholar."

He let out a sigh and smiled, though his eyes were still cool. "Yes, I am, and have been for a long time."

"And a collector, too. Although I never would have thought you would have collected religious works."

Nicholas laughed, and his eyes lost their remoteness. "No, I suppose not, considering. . . ." His gaze lingered at her lips, and she was sure he was not thinking of religion.

Leonore blushed again. Her shoulders relaxed; she had not been aware that she had tensed them. She returned his smile, but the disturbance within her did not leave. She had felt, for a moment, threatened. Perhaps she was so used to her father's rages that her fear had come over her, but Nicholas had promised he'd never raise his hand to her. He had kept all his promises to her, and more, since the time they were betrothed.

"Yes, especially *considering*," she replied and felt her composure returning. She held out her hand to Nicholas. "No more nonsense, now! Shall we go to the theatre before the concert ends?"

Nicholas brought her hand to his lips. "As you wish, my dear," he said, and this time his smile was warm.

And yet, thought Leonore as they left the room and descended the stairs to the carriage, she felt uneasy. It was not his nearness that gave her discomfort—that had disappeared after she had admitted her love for him last night at the wedding party. It was something else quite familiar that she had experienced before she had come to know him.

Nicholas smiled at her as he helped her into the carriage, and she returned it. While they rode to the theatre, she was glad the carriage's interior was dim. For though he took her into his arms again and kissed her until they arrived at their destination, she was conscious that a wall had arisen tonight. She knew Nicholas never told her everything of himself; she had believed it didn't matter. But there was something of import he did not want anyone to know, more than his illness, she was sure.

For when she had told him she had entered the attic library, there had been an emotion she hadn't thought to see in his eyes: fear. She'd seen it before, but had ascribed it to his fear of his illness. This time it had nothing to do with the illness, she was sure, but something about the attic room. Why else would his eyes reveal his feelings thus when she talked about it?

Though his kisses were intoxicating, a small part of her mind was still clear, holding the puzzle secure to examine later. When they parted at last, Leonore looked into her husband's eyes as if it were possible to see into him. But though they were penetrating and smilingly seductive, she found only desire there.

The carriage stopped in front of the theatre, and the groom opened the door to let them out. An ache grew in her chest, and Leonore sighed as she descended the carriage steps. Once more she felt her defenses rise. It hurt to put them up, for she had become accustomed to openness with him. Now, it seemed, there was to be none of that, or perhaps there never had been. No doubt she had been indulging in a fantasy the whole time.

As the concert began, she looked at Nicholas once more. A frown crossed his brow, then it cleared as he caught her gaze, and turned into concern instead.

"Is anything the matter, Leonore?" he asked.

She was silent for a moment, then shook her head. "No, Nicholas. Let's listen to the music. It is a very fine rendition of Mozart's last symphony."

Nicholas nodded and turned his attention to the orchestra. Leonore looked at him one last time, then transferred her gaze to the pit as well. No, something was, indeed, the matter, but she would discover what it was in time. She had taken down the walls around her heart, and though her defenses had risen once again, she knew they were useless, for she knew they made her weak. She would find out what made that flicker of fear appear in her husband's eyes. At least she could do that for him and help him with whatever he feared, and never again would he look at her so remotely as he had this evening. She would make sure of it.

Nicholas hadn't precisely forbidden her to enter the attic library, and Leonore believed the best approach was to go boldly into it and proceed to tidy it. Though she wanted to find what it was that disturbed her husband so, she also found a simple comfort in the activity.

She was dusting a table when Nicholas entered. When he caught sight of her, he stopped in the threshold. He said nothing, but merely stared. She could not discern anything from his expression; he seemed indecisive, for he hesitated before he stepped farther into the room.

She said lightly, "Since you won't allow the servants in to clean this room, I thought I should do so. I cannot see how you can go about your studies in such a dusty, dirty place. You are such a tidy person yourself, I was astonished to see this room in such a state."

A reluctant smile touched his lips, and a twinkle entered his eyes. He went to the fireplace and held up his hands toward the fire. He glanced about the room. "It does look better than it did before," he said.

"Thank you. I have not got to the books, however. Many of them are sadly dirty and in disrepair."

"You needn't attend to them, I assure you."

She looked at him carefully, for his voice seemed to have cooled. He still smiled at her, but though his face was half in shadow, she saw his hand tense briefly. The books, then. The books held a clue to his fear. If so, there would be little good in denying she had looked at them; he was too perceptive to be fooled. She made herself smile and laugh lightly.

"Are you afraid that I shall damage them further? I assure you, I am good at restoring books. The ones in my father's library would have been in worse condition than yours if I hadn't taken the time to mend and clean them. I have examined a few of your books and can repair them with little trouble."

Nicholas walked over to her and put his hand under her chin so that she looked him in the eyes. "Is that all you are interested in, Leonore?" he said softly. "Being the consummate housekeeper? Or is it that there is something you wish to know about me that you think to find in here?"

So, he was going to be direct about it. Very well, then. Leonore made herself stare into his eyes. "Yes. I do wish to find out more about you. You may call me nosy if you like, but I . . . I care for you, Nicholas, and there is something you fear. I wish you would tell me."

He released her chin. "I? Fear?" He chuckled. "I think not." He kissed her gently, then more with more passion. "There is little you could do that would make me afraid, Leonore."

For a moment she moved into his kiss, then pushed against him. "No, Nicholas. You won't seduce me away from finding out. You may not wish to tell me everything, but someday I will know what it is that frightens you."

He moved away from her impatiently. "There is nothing, I assure you. I wish you would stop prying, my dear, for you would find little of use to you. And if you did, what would you do with it?"

Leonore gazed at him as he looked into his reflection in one of the windows to adjust a fold in his neckcloth. His voice was nonchalant—almost. She had spoken only about some unspecified fear that he might have, not one that she could cause. *He* had voiced the possibility, not herself. She played a part, then, in the thing he feared. A familiar feeling—cold loneliness—filled the pit of her stomach. But she would never hurt him! And why did he marry her if he thought so? She went to him and laid her hand upon his arm, making him look at her.

"Nicholas, I would never do anything to hurt you. How could I? You've been kind and generous to me and my family. It would be unjust and cruel if I were to return all your goodness with anything painful to you. Haven't I said I care for you?" She touched his cheek with her fingers and at his uncertain look felt tears come to her eyes. She drew him down to her, kissing him so that he would not see them.

Nicholas's sigh sounded like a groan, and he pulled her to him hard, kissing her breathless. "Ah, God, Leonore, you don't know . . . you don't know . . . ," he murmured as he kissed her eyes and lips and throat. His hand came to her breast, and he pushed away her bodice, tearing the delicate fabric. She didn't care, for his touch was fire and life to her. He drew her down to the daybed, pressing himself against her. She felt his hands pull up her skirts, then felt him hard against the apex of her thighs, and she closed her eyes, shivering with the pleasure of it.

"You hurt me now, the way you make me feel," he said. His words made her put her hands against his chest and open her eyes again. He pressed himself against her, moving sensuously, and his eyes were closed tight, as if he were indeed in pain.

"I don't want to hurt you," she whispered, then gasped at the pleasurable ache he produced in her.

He looked at her, his eyes confused and lost. "When I hurt, I know I am alive," Nicholas said. "It is worth more to me than anything." He pushed himself into her, and she could not puzzle over his words, for she was lost in pleasure. He trembled as he thrust into her until she cried out twice, three times with the heat and ecstasy that burst within her. At last he groaned himself and thrust hard into her, breathing in sobbing gasps. "God, oh, God, Leonore. how you make me feel," he murmured against her ear. "Sometimes I cannot bear it."

Leonore sighed and relaxed. but said nothing. A still distrustful part of her mind wondered if he had seduced her once again for the purpose of distracting her. His arms came around her then and held her tightly; perhaps he had not meant to seduce her this time. She took some solace in the thought. In this, at least, he wanted her and seemed to take comfort in it as well.

But a still, lonely voice inside her heart mourned for him and for herself, for now she knew there was something in her that caused him fear, and she did not know what it was.

Chapter 11

St. Vire sat up with a gasp. His hands shook, and he pressed them to his eyes to suppress the images that had come to him—more vividly this time, as if to make up for their long absence. It had been months since he had dreamed anything; he had not dreamed since he was wed, and that was four months ago. This dream had a clarity that transported him sixty years to the night when he had been made a vampire.

In it, St. Vire had smiled at the whore who accosted him. The orgy—for that was what it was—was a farce, nothing more than men and Covent Garden ware dressed up as monks and nuns, profane and stupid with drink. Discarded bagwigs and buckram coats littered the floor of the abbey, and the scent of spilled wine made him grimace.

He absently stroked the woman's exposed breast as she cooed in his ear, and looked across the crowd at Sir Francis Dashwood, whose dissipated countenance was now fired with lust. Dashwood had said he'd knowledge of certain forbidden magical arts, and so lured Nicholas to this idiot's gathering.

The Hellfire Club. He should have known any group with true knowledge would not have let itself be advertised with such a flagrantly provocative title. A group with any knowledge of the magical arts would not have advertised itself at all. They had also called themselves the Amorous Knights of Wycombe, and he should have suspected the meetings were nothing but a debauch.

However, he was not averse to harmless diversion. He looked down at the woman pressed against him and this time noted with surprise that she was beautiful. She had black hair, unpowdered, contrasting with flawless white, translucent skin. Her eyes were black as well—large and heavy-lidded with impending seduction, and her lips were full and red as ripe plums. He smiled at her with growing interest and she returned it, her teeth white and delicately small.

A loud thumping at the center of the room took his attention. Sir Francis had seized a curiously shaped staff and brought it down forcefully once more on the ground.

"We have taken profound delight in our unholy gathering," Sir Francis intoned and paused. The noise quieted to just under a dull roar. "In thanks, let us send an invocation to our dear Lord of Darkness."

St. Vire felt bored and looked about him for an exit, but the woman pressed herself to him insistently.

"Stay," she said. "There is more to come . . . more delightful things, I assure you."

Her voice had an interesting lilt—foreign, though she spoke English clearly enough. He shrugged. She was beautiful, and she felt sinuously sleek against him. Why not?

She pulled him behind a pillar and dragged at his clothes, taking off his cravat and lace, kissing him hard upon the mouth. He heard Sir Francis's voice chanting some rhyme and calling upon infernal spirits. The hairs on the back of his neck rose at the sound. He ignored the sensation, for the woman pushed him down with surprising strength to the floor. She gazed into his eyes and smiled slowly, seductively.

"You want me. . . ." she murmured, her voice barely above a whisper. Yet, he heard her over the noise in the room, and he wanted her then, indeed—badly, savagely. He took her quickly, behind the pillar upon the floor. She moaned with pleasure, pressing her lips to his throat, and reaching her crisis faster than he'd thought she would despite the lack of caresses on his part. She laughed huskily. "You are mine, now," she said. "Always."

And she sank her teeth into his neck. The pain of her bite and the pleasure of his climax combined to make him cry out and clutch her arms in a bruising grip. Red darkness flooded his mind, and he felt as if he were dying, dying. . . .

Nicholas groaned and shook his head to dispel the images that rose up again before his eyes. It was only a memory now, but the memory of his foolishness made him wince. He had learned to be more cautious since that time, learned more than he ever had thought anyone could of magic, but it was too late. He'd been tricked and made into a vampire by that woman who took the opportunity when it presented itself.

Moving from the bed, St. Vire shrugged his robe over his shoulders, then pulled the bell rope for his valet. He had not thought of her for a long time. He did not know her name—not her real name, for she had changed it often, and lied easily. She had told him to call her Mercia, and after he'd got over his initial rage at her trickery, he'd been intrigued by all that she could tell him of his new powers. They'd traveled to Paris, where they had quarreled, and she'd left him for easier company. He had caught glimpses of her in his yearly travels to the rest of Europe, but they had avoided one another.

A knock on the door interrupted his thoughts. It was Edmonds, carrying freshly ironed neckcloths. St. Vire selected his clothes for the evening, a little less particularly, for the memory of his dream distracted him. He wondered what it meant, for surely a dream so vivid and occurring after months of no dreaming at all had some meaning. He hoped to God it did not mean he would see her again. Surely not now. Mercia had always said that next to Rome, she detested London.

St. Vire sighed and made one last adjustment to his neckcloth. The last time he had seen her, he had not been so caught up in discovering the extent of his powers or in his studies that he did not see the unrest that was the beginning of the French Revolution. He had left amidst Mercia's scornful laughter and retreated to his estates in Avebury to study and find the spell that would reverse his condition. He had heard or seen nothing of Mercia since that time, and in fact had rather hoped she had been done in by the French mobs for her association with the aristocracy.

He grimaced, thinking of her indiscretions, then shrugged. He would ponder the dream later, after he had his supper with

Leonore. He would much rather think of his wife, after all, than some vulgar woman he detested.

"Leonore, will you watch the dawn with me?" St. Vire asked abruptly. The sound of his voice echoed in the dining room, rattling the silence that had descended between him and Leonore often these days. He did not mean to ask her right then, for it was in the middle of supper, and he had thought he'd ask when he was giving her something, perhaps a necklace or a ring. He had put it off for four months—never finding exactly the right time, or at least the right time in which he felt comfortable. And how was he to ask it, after all? "Leonore, will you stay up so that I can confirm that I am not going mad?" Or, "Leonore, I need to see if I am going to stay a vampire for eternity?"

But she had smiled at him just then, her eyes warm and tender over the wineglass as she sipped. She looked beautiful, and he had been caught up in gazing at her, forgetting that he wanted to time his request at the right moment. He had simply opened his mouth and blurted out the words, graceless as a nervous schoolboy. He made himself look steadily at her and was, for once, glad he could not blush.

"The dawn?" Leonore's eyes widened, and her hand nervously twisted her pearl pendant. "I thought . . . I thought you could not have sunlight upon you."

Nicholas looked away from the clear concern and pity in her eyes and pressed his lips together in frustration. He did not want her pity, only her cooperation. He let out a breath, releasing an emotion that came too close to disappointment, and made himself smile at her. "I thought I might try to see if I could bear it this time." He could see her indecision, how her teeth worried her lower lip. "Please," he said.

She gazed at him and nodded slowly. "You must tell me if it hurts you, and I will close the bedroom curtains quickly."

He shook his head. "No, that room faces west, and I cannot see the dawn clearly from there. I would like to see it in the attic library if you would not mind."

"Of course," she replied and with a quick, uncertain smile lowered her gaze and returned to her supper again.

"Thank you," he said.

There it was again, her reticence. He had thought he'd eliminated it before they had wed, but it cropped up again and again since a few days after their wedding night. He was not sure what had made it appear. Did he not please her with his gifts, and did he not pleasure her in bed? He did not like her to act in this manner, alternately elusive and pitying. When she lay with him, she was not this way, but wholly herself—fierce and ardent, giving and receiving in equal measure. He had seen how tender and caring she was to those she held dear. Now, he only glimpsed that passion when they joined together, as well as that unrestrained naturalness of her laughter and tenderness when she protectively shepherded her sister Susan about to balls and assemblies.

Dissatisfaction made him tap his fingers impatiently upon the table. Leonore had carefully partitioned herself depending on whom she was with, and he knew he received a scrupulously dished out part of her attentions. He shook his head at himself. How greedy he was, to be sure! He did not need her regard, tenderness, or her passion to effect the completion of the spell, but he wanted it anyway. Well, he had been right when he had told her she'd prick any bubble of vanity he had left. She had told him he was vain, and now she showed him—not in so many words, it was true—that he was greedy. He wondered what other deadly sins in him she'd reveal and hold before his eyes, however unintentionally.

He grinned to himself as he let his gaze linger over the soft expanse of breast revealed by her low-cut evening gown. Certainly lust was another one of them, but it was not one he regretted. They were married, after all, and surely it was not a *deadly* sin to lust after one's own wife.

His grin turned wry. More foolishness! Here he was, concerning himself with the idea of sin when he never considered it much before—certainly not during his life as a vampire. It was a novelty to think on these things, however. He shrugged and sipped his wine.

Meanwhile there was Leonore . . . sweet and lovely and wholly desirable. He had thought her pretty when he first saw her, and now she was more beautiful to him with each night that passed. Indeed, as the weeks went by, it seemed his senses became slowly more acute, even when the bloodlust was not upon him. Surely, he had set his foot on the right path where the spell was concerned.

But with Leonore? He watched as she picked the sharp bones from the salmon on her plate. That was what she was when she was with him—careful, as if there were some hidden threat she might happen upon.

He looked down at his own plate then and pushed the vegetables about with his fork. There *was* a threat to her, and he did not want to think about it. Little chance she'd turn into a vampire, not without the proper rituals and circumstances. But once in a while, not more than once a month, when he lost himself in combined passion and bloodlust, he'd drink her blood at last. She could become weak from the lack of blood, and he knew it, and so he kept himself from slaking all of his thirst so that she would not become ill.

And truth be told, it disgusted him now. He had accepted the taking of blood as a necessary condition of his survival. Now it seemed it was not so. He'd always enjoyed being in control of any situation. Now that he was regaining his senses again, now that he felt the thirst with far less frequency than he had before, each time he drank from Leonore's veins, he . . . he . . .

He hated himself. He pushed his plate away and swallowed down bile. He took and took from her, and she asked nothing from him. *That* was why he had hesitated asking Leonore to watch the dawn with him for so long. *That* was why he offered her time and time again trinkets for which she thanked him, but in which she clearly had little interest. A short, mirthless laugh escaped him, and when he looked up, he encountered Leonore's questioning look.

"A joke, my dear," he said in explanation, and even he

could hear a tinge of bitterness in his voice. "A private joke that means little to anyone but myself."

Leonore nodded and looked away from him, down at her plate again..She seemed to shrink into herself.

"Stop it, Leonore."

She glanced at him again, her brows rising in question.

Nicholas let out an exasperated breath. He was making matters worse. How was he to bring her out again? He wanted her natural with him, not only in bed, but when they were in the same room, in the theatre, in the dining room, anywhere.

"What have I done to make you withdraw from me?" he asked.

"Nothing. And . . . I was not aware I was withdrawing from you. I am sorry."

"You have nothing to be sorry for, my dear." This was getting nowhere, Nicholas thought. He looked at her again and saw the loneliness in her eyes as she gazed back at him. Relief washed over him. That was it, certainly. She had little company during the day, especially since he was not available. She needed companionship. "Are you lonely, Leonore?" he asked.

A relieved expression crossed her face. "Yes . . . yes, that is it. I miss my sister, and I worry about her. I see her at assemblies and such, but there is no one to talk with when you are not here."

"Well, then, you must invite Susan to stay with you here—unless you feel she will not like it. You may even bring her out for the Little Season if you wish."

His reward was her wide, grateful smile and sparkling eyes, and he found himself smiling in return. "Oh, Nicholas— If it would not be an imposition, I would like it of all things!"

"Not at all," he said. "It displeases me to see you moped, that is all." He frowned. "Do you not have friends, then? I thought perhaps you might make some and accompany them to luncheons and such."

"Not really . . . I do not always know what to say to people."

"Oh? I had heard from Lady Jersey that you put Lady Brunsmire firmly to rout when she called upon you."

Leonore blushed lightly, but put up her chin. "I fear I manage to find my tongue when I lose my temper, and Lady Brunsmire made me do so."

"Did she? I shall be sure to give her the cut direct when next I see her, then."

"Oh, you need not do so," Leonore said hastily. "Lady Jersey gave her a set-down as well, so Lady Brunsmire has become quit amiable."

He felt a little disappointed and smiled ruefully at himself. Did he want to play the knight errant, now, as well?

"I am rather bookish, too," Leonore continued, and her smile grew crooked. "It is not popular thing to be, and it's difficult to strike up a conversation about the things that interest me."

"No, I suppose it is not popular, which is why I keep my bookish habits a secret, you see." It occurred to him that he had never asked her what she liked to read and knew only a little of her interests. He looked down at his plate again, and his smile turned ironic. He was wholly self-centered and selfish, too, in addition to being vain and greedy. Again, she did not say it and showed no hint of even thinking it. That she thought him generous and kind was clear. He knew he was not. The contrast between what she thought and what he knew threw his faults in his face as no accusation could have. Well, he knew he had no virtues; perhaps at least he could assume a few of them.

"Is that why you keep your library in the attic, then?" Leonore said, her gaze clearly curious.

The truth trembled on the tip of his tongue. He wanted to tell her everything, for he was tired of the secrecy, and a part of him wanted her to know everything. It would be a relief, even if it meant she would run from him in horror. But he would go mad if she left him, and he could not risk that.

"No," he blurted and felt a flash of irritation. How impulsive and graceless he was becoming! He'd tell part of the truth, then. Perhaps she would accept that. He poured himself a glass of wine and drained it. Glancing at the footman who came forward to take the empty bottle, Nicholas rose from his chair. "Perhaps we should remove ourselves to somewhere more comfortable than the dining room?"

Leonore nodded, clearly curious now, and stood up. "My sitting room, perhaps?" she said. He nodded and requested the footman to bring some refreshment to them there.

He went to her and put her hand on his arm as they left the dining room. She glanced at him, her eyes puzzled as they walked down the hall.

He had not been to her sitting room before, though she must have claimed it for her own for quite a few months already. An embroidery table was set next to a cozy-looking chair in front of the hearth. A cheerful fire played amongst the logs in the fireplace, and a folded, prettily embroidered fire screen leaned against one wall. It was a comfortable place, he noted with some surprise. He had not thought much about it, but it reflected what he glimpsed of Leonore when she let down her guard. He thought of his library in the attic. It was not comfortable at all, and he wished for the first time that it was. She gestured invitingly to a nearby plump chair that also faced the hearth.

"This is a restful place," he said as he sat. "Very pleasant."

"Thank you. I have always wanted a room for myself where I could have some quiet and do what I wished." She smiled gratefully at him. "You were generous to let me have one."

A pleasing warmth flowed over him. Here, then, was something he *had* given her, something she valued. He was glad of that. He waved his hand dismissively. "No, not generous at all. I have my own room, after all. Why should you not?"

Leonore frowned. "I do not know why yours should be in the attic, however. Would you not like a room like this one?"

He looked about him, at the fire and the ornaments upon the mantelpiece. The rug was soft beneath his feet, and the wing chair in which he sat held him snugly. It would be pleasant to have a room like this. But he shook his head.

"Not with the books I have," he said. "I do not collect just any ancient volume, however. They are books on arcane lore, on witchcraft, and magic."

Leonore leaned back in her chair and smiled. "Is that all

there is to it?" she said. "I cannot see that as a reason why you should keep them hidden away in the attic. Magic is not real, after all."

He felt his responding grin turn crooked. "Are you so sure?"

"*I* am not so superstitious. If magic were real, then why have I never seen it? Or anyone else, for that matter?"

"Have you never read fairy tales, Leonore, or ancient legends?"

"Oh, for heaven's sake, Nicholas! They are *only* fairy tales. I know the difference between fantasy and reality." She opened the table at her side, took out some embroidery, and began setting precise, even stitches. She gave him a derisive glance before attending to her needle again. "We live in the nineteenth century and are not uneducated serfs in fear of some sorcerer's curse or witch's evil eye. Magic? I think not." She said it firmly, as if she had once believed in it as a child, but would not believe any longer.

Should he show her otherwise? He grinned, thinking of how shocked out of her good sense she would be. Well, perhaps not now. She would no doubt prick her finger on the needle and ruin the embroidery she was stitching so diligently. "Many people are not as sensible as you are, Leonore," he said. "Our servants, for example. What will they think if they should come upon my books? They are not as educated as you or I."

"We will tell them not to be so foolish," Leonore said firmly.

"Really? And what are they to think of that, with my habit of waking only during the night?"

She bit her lower lip and lifted her eyes from her stitching. "Of course . . . you are right," she said. "Thoughtless of me. We never had many servants, so I am not used to having them about." She looked away from him, as if embarrassed by the admission.

Nicholas nodded, not commenting on her words, for he did not want to embarrass her further. A small porcelain figurine on the table beside him caught his eye. It was in the shape of a fairy, delicately made and painted, and its wings were those of a butterfly. He picked it up and turned it over, then looked at Leonore with a grin.

"So, you do not care for fairy tales, eh?"

She blushed lightly. "It was a gift from Susan, long ago. She fancied I would like it."

"Now, I wonder why?"

"If you must know, it is because I used to read her stories and legends at bedtime, when she was a little girl."

"And you thought fantasy was appropriate material for a young girl, oh Leonore-the-governess? On the other hand, I do seem to remember your fondness for the love poems of Congreve." Nicholas shook his head dolefully. "My, my. I am amazed your employers allowed you to teach such . . . provocative material."

"For goodness sake! Of course I did not teach these things to my pupils! How you tease!"

"Your sister, then?"

"I did *not* read any Congreve to Susan!"

He breathed a sigh of mock relief. "How thankful I am that you are not a corrupter of children," he said, then eyed her sternly. "But definitely fairy tales?"

Leonore primmed her lips, but a laugh broke from her nevertheless. "Have I not said it?"

St. Vire gently rolled the figurine about in the palm of his hand. "May I hope, then, that you once believed in them when you were a child? That sometimes you wished they were true?"

"I have grown up since then and know these things are fantasy only." Her hand came up to twist her necklace again.

"Really?" He put down the figurine on the table and reached over to caress her cheek. "Sometimes it is not a bad thing to dream and wish for things that seem impossible." He snapped his fingers, and a cool puff of air next to her cheek made her start.

"This is for you," he said. She stared at the red rosebud in his hand, and then at him.

"A trick," she said.

He grinned at her. "If you wish." He rose and went to her

embroidery table, selected a pin, and fastened the flower to the bodice of her dress. She gazed at him uncertainly, and he gave her a brief kiss before sitting down again.

"What do you like to read, then, Leonore?"

She looked a little relieved at this change of subject and said, "Oh, some philosophical works—"

"Like Congreve."

She burst out laughing. "Oh, for heaven's sake! That is not a philosophical work, as you well know!"

"What do you read for pleasure, then?"

Leonore's lips turned up in a smile. "Congreve, as you have so insistently pointed out. Keats, Byron, and Sir Walter Scott's works, as well as Jane Austen's."

He reached beside his chair and pulled up a book. "And Walpole's *The Castle of Otranto*, I see. Gothics, Leonore?"

"Where did you . . . I didn't . . . I thought I had returned that to the library—"

"So you admit you have a fondness for gothics, then, eh?"

"Well, yes."

"So do I. Shall I read for a while?"

She stared at him a moment, then nodded. He opened the book and began to read.

Leonore plied her needle while she listened. Her stitching slowed, for Nicholas read with such expression that she could almost imagine she was seeing the story as if she were in a theatre, watching a play. Occasionally he sipped the brandy that had been brought to the sitting room, but the pause in his reading did not disturb the pictures that were in her mind. Finally, he ceased reading, and she found she had stopped her needlework and was staring into the fire. She looked up at him, still in a haze from the sound of his voice and the lulling warmth of the fire in front of her.

Nicholas had the book open in his lap, his hand about to close it. "You seem tired . . . would you prefer to retire to your bed rather than go to Lady Russell's ball?" he asked.

"No . . . oh, I am a little tired, perhaps, but I am sure it is because of all the housework I have been doing. I would like to go out tonight, for I have been indoors all day and wish to do something different, but I don't wish to stay past eleven."

Was there disappointment in his eyes? But she thought she would please him by agreeing to go to the ball, for she knew how he liked to be in company. She almost retracted her words, but thought perhaps he felt disappointed because they would not be staying long at the ball, rather than that they were going at all. Well, they would go, and if he wished to stay past eleven, so be it.

She dressed in good time, but still in the most modest of gowns she had in her wardrobe. After all these months she would have thought she'd become used to the way her husband looked at her, but she was not. It made her think about him too much, a thing she had not resolved yet. She hadn't given in to the impulse to stay at home tonight, however, despite the thought that if she had retired to bed as he had suggested, it probably would have been with him in it. Perhaps she was regaining a measure of control over herself, after all.

But when she saw Nicholas downstairs ready to leave for Lady Russell's ball, his appearance a study in black, white, and red, she did not see how anyone could resist thinking of him. His coat was night black, and beneath it his waistcoat was black also, chased with silver designs. Pale knit breeches hugged his thighs so that she hastily looked away from them, blushing. Within the folds of his linen cravat winked his favorite ruby, the single touch of color in the chaste white cloth. The starkness of his dress made his face seem almost translucent, unearthly, as if he were some elemental spirit instead of a man, and the dark red of his hair and his vivid green eyes emphasized it all the more. He is all fire and air, thought Leonore, and then dismissed the thought firmly. She smiled ruefully to herself. Their talk of fairy tales and legends had made her think it.

Nicholas's smile turned into a grin as he watched her, and he spread out his arms. "I hope you approve?"

Leonore smiled primly at him. "*I* will not cater to your vanity," she said.

He shook his head morosely. "How grudging you are with

your praise! I am sunk in despondency, certain you think me a hideous beast."

"Oh, not hideous!"

"A beast, then?" He leered comically at her bosom.

"Silly man!" Leonore said, blushing. "If you must know, I think you quite beautiful, and a terrible beast for putting me to the blush. There, now! I have fed your vanity and there will be no bearing you for the next week I am sure."

"Beautiful?"

Leonore glanced at him and saw that his expression was just as astonished as his voice. "Why, yes. You have a mirror. Certainly you can see that for yourself."

"Well." He cleared his throat. "Well, I . . . I don't know what to say." There was a tremor of laughter in his voice. "It is not how I would describe myself, certainly."

"What you must say, is 'thank you kindly, ma'am,' and then take my hand and proceed to the carriage so that we may go to Lady Russell's ball." Leonore smiled triumphantly at him and could not help feeling a little gleeful that she had caught him short of words at last.

He laughed and took her hand, placing it on his arm. "Thank you kindly, ma'am," he said.

They reached the Russells' house in good time. Leonore danced a waltz with Nicholas, enjoying his gracefulness and the ease with which he led her around the ballroom. The dance ended, and she found herself next to Lord Bremer. He had been at her wedding, and she quite liked him and his wife, so she smiled at him.

He returned her smile, then looked at Nicholas. "Well, St. Vire, I hope you will not keep your wife all to yourself while at this ball." He looked at Leonore and bowed. "May I request a dance, my lady?"

Nicholas grinned at him. "I shall be watching with a jealous eye, Bremer, so do watch your step." He nodded at his friend and smiled at Leonore as Lord Bremer took her hand.

They danced a vigorous country dance, which left Leonore too breathless to make much conversation. She could not help glancing at Nicholas, who was also in the set, partnering a red-haired lady who was looking at him avidly. He caught her eye, and after sending Leonore a mischievous glance, gazed soulfully down at his partner, which nearly sent the lady swooning, if her dazed look and stumbling feet were any indication of her state of mind. Leonore bit her lip, trying to keep herself from laughing. If he did not know how handsome he was, certainly he knew how he affected the ladies and could use it to purpose.

"Beast!" she hissed at him as she passed him during the dance.

She caught Nicholas's innocent expression from across the circle of dancers as Lord Bremer led her around a turn and had to bite her lip again to keep from bursting into laughter. She became warm from the effort, then was glad when the dance came to an end and she was able to fan herself.

Lord Bremer smiled at her and bowed over her hand. "A pleasure to dance with you, Lady St. Vire. Perhaps I can be so bold as to ask for another— Good Lord!" he exclaimed and groped for his quizzing glass. He put it to his eye and looked past her shoulder.

It must have been something quite astonishing for the impeccably polite Lord Bremer to break off and stare in such a manner. Leonore turned and looked past the crowd to the door of the ballroom.

Half the guests must have held their breath for a moment, for she could hear a definite lull in the noise in the room—the male half of the guests, reflected Leonore wryly. For the vision who had stepped into the room was the most extraordinarily beautiful lady she had ever seen. Her hair was black and thick, curling around her pale face in a dark halo. Her eyes were large, her lips sensuously red. As she moved, her fashionably low-cut gown shimmered green and blue over her limbs, like the waters of a lake in summer. Her escort, a handsome, well-dressed young man, looked at no one but her, even when Lady Russell came to greet them. Leonore could not blame him. How could any man resist anyone like this lady?

"I wonder who she is," Leonore said, turning to Lord Bremer. But he had already left her and was wending his way through the crowd to the lady. Leonore grimaced. She had not thought Lord Bremer a ladies' man. Judging by the way Lady Bremer was looking at him, Leonore was sure his lady would have a thing or two to say to him once they went home.

Leonore sighed and made her way to a chair at the side of the ballroom. She wondered where Nicholas was. When the country dance had ended, he had been directly across from her and Lord Bremer in the set. The next dance was a waltz, and though Nicholas had not requested it of her, he usually did not dance it with anyone else.

Looking about her, she spied him at last, only three feet away from her. She managed to catch his eye and smiled at him, but Nicholas only looked at her gravely for a moment. Then he, like Lord Bremer, looked across the room at the newcomer.

Suddenly, Leonore found that she could not look at her husband. She had seen him look at other women, beautiful women, and it had not bothered her, since Nicholas did not seem to take them very seriously. Now it was different. The woman across the room was also beautiful, and Leonore assumed any man would want to look at her. And yet she felt as if a hot, sharp knife had been thrust into her chest.

She wanted to run, pretend that she was not here, for the sight of her husband staring at this woman tore at her, and Leonore was horrified to find that she was jealous. An acquaintance paused for a moment beside her and said something cordial she did not hear, though she murmured—she knew not what—in response. Stop it, Leonore, stop it! she thought fiercely to herself. Nicholas has looked at other women before, talked with them, danced with them, and you never cared one whit. This is no different.

But she was not convinced. The expression on Nicholas's face disturbed her, for there was recognition in his gaze. He knew this woman, and his stare said that he took her presence very seriously indeed.

Chapter 12

The nape of his neck tingled, as if the hairs upon it had risen in response to some threat. Nicholas looked up from the tittering redheaded lady at his side and searched the ballroom. There was nothing. He frowned.

"Oh, Lord St. Vire, I cannot think it is all that bad!" complained his partner. He looked at her blankly. Ah, yes. Mrs. Bradley.

"Not at all," he replied, not caring what it was he had missed in their conversation. "But I think perhaps some lemonade would refresh you. Allow me to procure you some." He moved away from her, ignoring her puzzled expression, and signaled a servant to bring a glass to his former dance partner.

Leonore was a few feet away from him, chatting with Lord Bremer, and he moved toward her. The tingling began again, and he hunched his shoulders to rid himself of it. He saw Lord Bremer start, his jaw dropping, and St. Vire followed his gaze. He froze.

Mercia had not changed at all. Of course she had not, despite the decades that had gone by. Her hair was still black, and Nicholas knew it was not from the dye pot. Her skin was as pale as his own, and her carmined lips as sensuous as he'd remembered them. She was still extraordinarily beautiful.

And no doubt just as dangerous.

He looked at Leonore for a moment, and then at the ballroom door. He was not sure if they could leave without drawing attention to themselves, for the door was across the room and the well-mannered Lady Russell would stop them with her long, polite good-byes. Damn! How could he be so stupid? The dream that had woken him this night had been a warning—he knew that now. He should have gathered up his belongings at once and taken himself and Leonore to his estates at Avebury, but all his thoughts had been on Leonore and the pleasure of her company.

Then Mercia looked away from her escort and saw him, and it was too late. She turned again to the young man at her side and laughed. St. Vire was conscious of her attention now, even though she did not look at him. He gave another glance at Leonore. The next dance was to be a waltz, and he preferred to dance it only with her, for she danced gracefully, and he liked the opportunity the dance gave him to touch her.

But to dance with Leonore would be a risk—perhaps even a risk to her life. He did not know why Mercia was in London, and he could not presume his presence would not attract her in some manner. She was unpredictable; she had told him she hated this town, but it had not prevented her from coming here. Until he knew Mercia's purpose, he should stay away from Leonore until they could escape the house. He saw Lord Eldon speak to Leonore. Perhaps he could depend on his friend's good nature to escort Leonore home while he, Nicholas, left the ball alone. Yet, he'd be a fool to think Mercia would never know that he had wed. He had no choice. Ignoring the hurt look in Leonore's eyes, he made his way toward Mercia.

The desire he had felt for her was decades gone, but he smiled charmingly at her. He let his eyes linger upon her half-exposed breasts, obscenely white and firm like those of a nubile maiden, before he lifted his gaze to her face.

"Why, I do believe it is Nicholas St. Vire!" Mercia exclaimed in her lilting voice and put her hand on her chest in apparent surprise. The gentlemen around her eyed him with envy.

"How fortunate I am that you remember me, Miss Mercia. . . ."

"Lazlo. I am Lady Lazlo now, can you believe it? But alas, my poor Constantin was not long for this world, and I am all alone in it now." Her lip trembled dolefully. A murmur of sympathy arose from those within hearing, and the young man at her side patted her hand.

Nicholas looked at her fine, diaphanous gown, at the jewels at her neck and wrists. A rising nausea made him press his lips together. Perhaps she had married; it mattered little. She was conducting herself as she always had. He did not doubt that she had lured some rich man to her bed, put a glamour upon him so that he lavished upon her all his worldly goods, and then killed him. It was her way, and always had been.

He bowed, lifting her hand to his lips. "My poor Mercia. I hope he did not leave you in dire straits."

She sighed and lifted a finger to her eye, as if to remove a tear. "Ah, my dear Constantin was always so generous! But I must have company, you know I must! I cannot bear to be lonely."

St. Vire's gaze passed innocuously over the group of gentlemen around her, then returned to her. "I cannot suppose you will be for long . . . as lovely as you are, my lady."

A slow, satisfied smile formed on her lips, and she hid it with her fan. "Charming as always, eh, Nicholas?"

"For you, always, Mercia." He still held her hand, and he put it on his arm, leading her away from the crowd she had gathered around her. "I see the musicians are starting up for the next dance. Dare I ask that you be my partner?"

A belated protest rose from the men behind him, and he grinned at them over his shoulder. Lady Lazlo tapped his arm with her fan.

"I should refuse . . . ," she murmured, then cast a seductive look at him. "But I will not, this once."

They stepped up to the line of dancers. Nicholas did not see Leonore amongst the guests sitting by the ballroom walls; he assumed she had also decided to dance. He hoped she would not approach them, that she would stay away after the dance, but it was a small hope, he knew.

Mercia was light in his arms, feather-light, as if she had little substance to her. He gazed into her eyes, wondering if the madness he had seen so long ago was still there. He did not see it now, but it meant nothing.

"I thought you did not like London, Mercia," he said, smiling at her.

"Oh, one changes, over the years," she said carelessly. "Perhaps I thought to renew some friendships . . . or make new ones. I grew bored with continental society."

They grew suspicious, is what you mean. Still preying on the aristocracy, and indiscreet as ever. He grinned and pulled her a fraction of an inch closer. "I am sure you will not be bored here," he said. He glanced at her escort, who was leaning against the wall, staring at them jealously. "Who is the young fire-eater who came with you?"

"Oh, that is Sir Adrian Hambly. Such a lovely boy, don't you think? And so . . . passionate." Mercia's eyelids drifted half-closed, as if remembering how passionate the young man was. "I do love passionate men." She gazed with wide eyes at Nicholas.

He almost grimaced, remembering how passionate he, himself, had been when she had first caught him in her web so long ago. The winter solstice was approaching, and he wondered whether she intended to turn Sir Adrian into a vampire at that time.

"But you know, my dear Nicholas, I came to London to see how you were faring." She smiled gaily up at him. "Yes, it's true! You didn't think I would visit after our unfortunate disagreement so long ago, but I am not one to hold grudges, you see."

"You don't know how delighted I am," he replied, even as his heart sank, leaden, to his shoes. It only needed this, he groaned inwardly. He'd have little chance of shaking her off now. The dance parted them for a moment, enough time for him to form a pleased smile upon his lips. "I am flattered, Mercia, but I cannot see the attraction, truly."

"So modest!" she murmured and cast down her eyes. "But you see, I still need a consort."

"There is young Sir Adrian, very willing, I am sure, to be at your side forever. As you said, he is so very passionate and, even better, is no doubt quite malleable."

She raised her head, and a flame of anger sparked in her eyes. "But there is no guarantee he would last as long as you, dear Nicholas. He might be like poor, dead Henri. I think you owe me a little consideration, truly I do."

Henri, who had gone mad, and whom he had killed. St. Vire placed a smug and gratified smile on his face. "You flatter my stamina, my dear."

The anger grew hot in her eyes, and he was sure she would have slapped him if he had not held her hand tightly.

"Ah, ah!" he chided. "What a scandal we should cause if you should strike me now. It would never do, for it would put off your admirers, and you would not want that."

The tension left her, and she gave him a resentful glance. "I can find more, I am sure."

"But in such refined company? I think not." The music ended with a flourish, and St. Vire released her hand and bowed. "A most . . . revealing . . . dance, Lady Lazlo. I thank you." He breathed a sigh of relief. *Now, now I will leave, and see what I can do about traveling to Avebury.*

It was a foolish hope. Before St. Vire could turn away, he felt a hand upon his sleeve—Leonore's hand. She smiled up at him uncertainly. He could not escape; St. Vire had no choice but to introduce them, especially with Lord Eldon at her side.

"My dear Leonore, and Lord Eldon, may I introduce you to Lady Lazlo? I met her long ago, when the Russian tsar came to visit England. Lady Lazlo, this is Lady St. Vire, my wife, and my friend, Lord Eldon." He made his voice cordial, and he continued to smile. He knew he must measure his words and tread a fine line between de-emphasizing Leonore's importance to him and letting Mercia know he would protect his wife.

The lady's eyes scanned Leonore's face and form, and she smiled lazily. "So Nicholas decided to wed! What a pretty little bride you have chosen, my dear. And quite young, too. I never would have thought it."

"There was something very appealing about the idea of

marital bliss, Mercia. A very convenient arrangement, as I am sure you know. I thought I should try it," replied Nicholas. He stepped close to Leonore and put his hand upon her shoulder. Leonore gave him a puzzled smile.

Lady Lazlo's gaze sharpened at the movement, then she turned and smiled at Lord Eldon. "And you, Lord Eldon? Have you thought of emulating your friend?"

Lord Eldon grinned. "Not I. I've not been so lucky as Nicholas here." He looked at her as if he hoped his luck would turn, and Lady Lazlo's smile widened. Taking her hand, he bowed over it. "Dare I hope that I am the next gentleman to ask for a dance?"

"You need not hope at all," Lady Lazlo said. "I would be very pleased to dance with you." She glanced at Nicholas and nodded. "Another time, my dear."

Nicholas's hand tightened on Leonore's shoulder, then he bowed. "Perhaps," he replied. He watched Lady Lazlo leave, her hand on his friend's arm, then let out a sigh and turned to Leonore.

"I hope you do not mind, but I believe we should leave. I think you said that you wished to return at eleven o'clock?"

"Yes, but if you wish to stay—"

"No," he said and smiled at her. "No, you must not sacrifice your own wishes for me, Leonore. You must allow me some respite from my selfishness. Otherwise I shall become a dead bore, and that would be a terrible blow to my self-consequence."

She smiled slightly. "Very well, then. I do wish to go home."

"Thank you. You have saved my vanity from a severe downfall."

Leonore chuckled—a reluctant one, it seemed to him. Nicholas was conscious of discontent, even disappointment. He had wanted her to laugh and realized he liked to make her do so. He took her hand; her body felt tense beside him, her hand tight upon his arm. Though she smiled and thanked Lady Russell very graciously, her eyes held no smile at all.

Leonore spoke little during the ride back to their home, replying cordially to any of his questions, but contributing almost nothing of her own. At last he gave it up, and they continued in silence until they stepped inside the house. She quickly moved past him in the direction of her sitting room. He hesitated, then followed. She pushed open the door, and he put his hand upon her arm, stopping her.

"Wait, Leonore." He lifted her chin with his fingers. "You are unhappy, are you not? Tell me what is wrong."

Her eyes were miserable. "I . . . I can't. I am . . . I shouldn't . . . Oh, Nicholas, I am despicable!" She turned from him, stumbling into the room in her haste. He went after her, shutting the door behind him.

"What is this? You, despicable?" Her back was to him, her head bent. He turned her around and took her in his arms. "What have you done? Nothing criminal, I hope. I refuse to harbor criminals in my house, especially ones who weep upon my cravat."

"I am not weeping."

"No, of course you are not. You never weep. I am sure it is a leak in the roof, which I have neglected to repair." He led her to a sofa and sat down upon it. "Oddly enough, it seems to have followed us, even though we have moved."

She laughed aloud then, and raised her tear-filled eyes to his. "Very well then, I did cry, since you insist."

He kissed her gently. "Tell me why."

"Oh, Nicholas!" She heaved a large sigh and covered her face with her hands. "I . . . I was jealous." He opened his mouth to speak, but Leonore spoke hurriedly. "I know I should not be, for you looked at her—Lady Lazlo—and you danced with her, just as you would anyone else, but she looked at you in *such* a way, I thought she must have been—I should not have thought it, and after all, ours is a marriage of convenience, and I should expect at some time we would do as we pleased, whether apart or together, for people do. . . ."

Patiently, he let her talk on until her voice faded, until the ticking of the clock was the only sound in the room. He had not thought that she would be jealous of the attention he might pay to any woman. He felt absurdly pleased at the idea.

"Well, you need not look so happy about it!" she exclaimed indignantly.

Nicholas kissed her soundly. "Silly Leonore. Yes, Lady Lazlo used to be my mistress, but that was many, many years ago. I do not like her and did not even like her then."

"Do . . . do you like me?" Her voice became breathless as he kissed her just below the ear.

"Of course, sweet one," he said and returned his lips to hers. He parted from her and sighed. "It is late for you, Leonore, and you need to rest after all your work today."

"I don't—"

"No, go. I will come upstairs later. I need to attend to some business I had forgotten in the library."

She looked uncertainly at him, but nodded as they left her sitting room.

After they parted at her chamber door, St. Vire permitted himself to sigh deeply. While he had sat silent in the coach on the way home, he had thought of what he would do, now that Mercia had appeared. It was the middle of the Little Season in London, and he supposed he could remove Leonore and himself to Avebury. But now he was not sure it would be the wisest thing to do. He had implied to Mercia at the ball that he had married Leonore for the sake of convenience. Mercia, of course, would believe he had the same motives as hers—for riches, or at least an easy supply of blood. He sighed and pushed open the library door, and after lighting a fire in the fireplace, he sank into a chair.

To take Leonore away from London would show that she was not just a convenience to him, but rather a necessity. That would be dangerous, both to Leonore and to himself. Mercia wished him to be her consort once again, and she was a difficult woman to convince otherwise once her mind was set on anything. He supposed she still wanted him because he had not turned insane yet. It was useless to speculate on her reasons, for he knew she was insane herself, though her madness was subtle and cunning.

If Mercia knew why he had wed Leonore, how important his wife was to him, she would kill her. That was one of the few predictable things about Mercia. If someone was in her way, she thought nothing of killing and was extremely clever about it. She could even put a glamour upon people and convince them to do the work for her.

If, however, he could convince Mercia that Leonore meant little to him other than something from which he could slake his bloodthirst, that he was at least thinking of becoming Mercia's consort, the chances were good that she would leave Leonore alone. It would give him time to think of how he could rid himself of Mercia forever and make sure she would never be a threat to anyone again.

He thought, then, of how he would go about convincing Mercia of his supposed willingness to become her mate. An ache grew in his chest, and he grimaced. He was becoming very good at identifying these feelings now. It was anger and despondency this time, for he knew he'd have to hurt Leonore, and he did not want to.

She might leave him. Nicholas rose abruptly and cursed under his breath. What would he do, then? Leonore had to stay with him for a year or else he would slide into madness. And yet, if Mercia received even a hint of Leonore's importance to him, Leonore would surely die. He could not even put a glamour upon her to stay—he was riding over rough ground as it was when he used it to make her forget that he took her blood.

If he told her the truth, however . . . No, God no. She would leave him then, most certainly. He suppressed a groan. He'd worked for years trying to reverse his condition . . . and now it could be at the cost of Leonore's life.

Damn Mercia! If she had not come to London, it would have gone smoothly, he was certain. But this excuse did not satisfy him. He pushed away the feelings that rose in him—his anger at Mercia, his fear for himself and Leonore—and forced himself to look at his situation logically.

This time his sigh was very close to the groan he had suppressed earlier. All his actions could turn Leonore away from him, whether from death at Mercia's hand or from her own repugnance at his vampiric nature—if he told her the truth about himself—or because of his supposed infidelity. Regardless of what he did, she would become cold to him, he was sure.

He thought of the way Leonore had looked at him tonight, the way her eyes had told him she cared for him . . . perhaps even loved him, though she never said so. For a moment, he closed his eyes and swallowed. He did not want her to stop caring for him, for he had grown . . . used to it.

Abruptly, he strode from the library. He'd accomplish nothing here; he had only come here to think, and he hadn't even done that well. He wanted . . . he wanted to be with Leonore. Quickly he went down the stairs.

The sound of slow breathing told him she was asleep. Nicholas watched her, the rise and fall of her breasts, her sweet face. The ache he'd felt earlier in his chest expanded, and he let out a long, shaking breath.

None of his gifts would hold her to him, for she did not value the trinkets and dresses he had given her, though she always thanked him gratefully. He had thought the drunkenness and brutishness of Leonore's father would keep her from returning home . . . but he was not sure of that either, for her sister, Susan's, presence gave her some solace.

And because he had to pretend to be enamored of Mercia, he could not even tell Leonore that he loved her.

He closed his eyes against the leaden sensation in his chest. God help him. He had not wanted to love her. It was an awkward emotion, a stumbling block to his plans, a thing that made men into fools. But she had crept into him like a thief in the night, and his heart was lost to her now. He did not even know when she had done it, when his desire for her blood and body had transmuted into desire for her regard, her respect, and her love.

God. Oh God. What was he to do now? If Leonore died, he felt he would die, too. He would go mad immediately, knowing it was because of him that she died, and he'd much prefer to expose himself to the sizzling agony the morning sun would bring than fall into insanity. And if she left him, he would go mad anyway, only perhaps slowly. But then she would be alive, and perhaps . . . perhaps he could find a way to rid himself of Mercia. He would still be a vampire, but Leonore would stay alive.

Nicholas gazed at his wife and touched her cheek gently. Her skin was soft and warm from sleep. He could feel it with more sensitivity than he'd ever had since the beginning of his life as a vampire. He had progressed this far, and now he'd have to give it all up.

He bent and kissed her, running his hand around the fullness of her breast. Slowly Leonore woke and sleepily smiled at him, then reached out her arms for him. Once more he would make love to her, give her everything he could give her of himself now—now that he'd have to give her up, as well.

He would not ask her to watch the dawn with him, to see if he could bear the light of the sun. It would be useless. Regardless of whether his wife chose to stay with him or leave him, she would never again come willingly to his bed or gaze at him with tenderness.

He would stay a creature of the night, and except for when the bloodthirst was upon him, his senses would fade into dullness, and music would be noise in his ears. Tomorrow he would begin to court Mercia, and Leonore would begin to hate him.

And that was a living death, indeed.

Chapter 13

As the maid helped her dress for the masquerade three evenings after Lady Russell's ball, Leonore wondered again that Nicholas had not woken her up at dawn to see the sun rise the day after the ball. She felt relief and disappointment. She would have liked to have seen if his illness had receded; however, if they had stayed up, the sun might have made him ill. It was just as well that they had not, she supposed.

Leonore looked in the mirror, twirling to see how her spangled dress swirled in featherlike waves around her figure. She was dressed as the Elfin Queen Mab, in green silk with thin strips of silver gauze as the overskirt. The light gauze drifted around her as she moved, making her seem as if she floated instead of walked. A white domino draped over her shoulders, and her mask was silver. She smiled at her maid. "You have done very well, Betty. Thank you."

Betty blushed, bobbed a curtsy, and beamed at her mistress. "Thank *you*, my lady. I tries ter—That is, I *try* to do my best."

Leonore's smile grew wider. Her maid had, indeed, improved in the few months she had been in Leonore's employ. She complimented Betty once more and proceeded down the stairs. Nicholas was already waiting for her in the parlor, and he looked upon her dress with approval as he kissed her hand and put it upon his arm. He wore a black mask and domino, but was otherwise dressed in elegant evening clothes.

"You look lovely, as usual," he said and smiled.

"Thank you, Nicholas. I wish you had decided to wear a costume, too. It would have been quite amusing, I think. I wonder you did not."

His eyebrows rose. "But I *am* in costume, my dear."

"Oh, really? What is your disguise, then?" She held up her hand, then put her finger to her temple in thoughtful concentration. "Let me guess. . . . You are dressed all in somber black, except for your gloves, which are white . . . ah hah! I have it. You are a lowly shipping clerk."

Nicholas shuddered theatrically. "If so, then I cannot be all that lowly. Shipping clerks do not wear silk or impeccably tied linen neckcloths."

"What, then?"

He seemed to hesitate, then his smile turned wry.

"But thou, false Infidel! shalt writhe
Beneath avenging Monkir's scythe;
And from its torment 'scape alone
To wander round lost Eblis' throne;
And fire unquench'd, unquenchable,
Around, within, thy heart shall dwell. . . ."

"That is Byron's poem 'The Giaour,' " she said, puzzled. "I do not think you look at all like a Turk."

"Very good, Leonore. Do you remember the next few lines?" He seemed to watch her carefully, and this puzzled her further.

"Only vaguely. I think they say something about the tortures of hell, and then, oh, let's see . . . 'But first, on earth as Vampire sent, Thy corse shall from its tomb be rent—' The rest of it is quite distasteful. I never did care for that part of the poem." She stared at him, then burst into laughter. "Oh, heavens, Nicholas, a vampire? A 'livid living corse'? With 'gnashing tooth and haggard lip'?" Her giggles burst from behind her hand, and she wiped tears of laughter from her eyes beneath her mask. "I think you will have to find a more convincing costume than that. Yes, I admit I have read some gothics, and I am afraid you look nothing like the vampires depicted there."

Nicholas had grinned at her laughter and now smiled at her words. "And can you not conceive of a vampire who looks, well, as tidily dressed as I am?"

"Silly! Vampires are evil, ugly, ravenous creatures. That is the way they are in those stories. I am afraid you will have to resign yourself to either being an exalted sort of shipping clerk, or Nicholas St. Vire with a mask and domino."

His expression became somber. "I am afraid I cannot be the clerk. That, upon thinking of it, would have been very amusing."

"Then you will have to be Nicholas St. Vire with a mask, for you are certainly not evil, ugly, or ravenous."

He smiled again, slightly. "I suppose it makes no difference."

But something in his expression dampened Leonore's spirits, and she gazed into his eyes for a sign of what it was. He glanced away from her. "Shall we go?"

"Of course," Leonore replied. She looked away as well. The fear was there again in his eyes, and a terrible longing. She bit her lip. Just a little, it frightened her.

She did not understand it. She had found no clue to what it was he feared, even though she had perused the books in the attic library for something that would tell her. His books covered the whole scope between the sacred and the profane, with no emphasis on either. Even if he were superstitious enough to try any of the so-called magic in those books, she could not tell whether he practiced good or evil. It was just a comprehensive collection of ancient works. She shrugged to herself. She would question him later. Perhaps as time went by, he would trust her more and tell her.

She conversed easily with him in the coach, making Nicholas laugh a few times. His smiles reached his eyes then, and it seemed his mood lightened. It made their carriage ride short, and Leonore surprised herself by sighing in relief when they reached Lord and Lady Harlowe's house. She glanced at Nicholas. For one moment it seemed he stared angrily at the house, and then his face became smooth and unconcerned.

The Harlowe residence was not as well lit as Leonore would have supposed from their obvious wealth. It gave the rooms an intimate cast that made her feel uncomfortable. She did not know the Harlowes well at all, but Nicholas knew them. She glanced at him, and he smiled down at her. She felt herself blush, for it seemed his smile was seductive in the extreme . . . but perhaps it was only the light.

As soon as she stepped into the room in which the guests gathered, Leonore wished she had not come. She knew some of the people, and those she knew had reputations that bordered upon the scandalous. She looked at Nicholas, wondering why he had brought her here, for he had always escorted her to those events that contained only the most respectable of people.

Heavy drapes hung over the balcony windows, and though some of the windows opened to the air, the rooms were hot and humid. A quartet of musicians diligently played their instruments, and some people danced the waltz in a languid manner, many of them too close for propriety. The guests were lords and ladies—barely masked—and many of them were nowhere near their spouses. She noticed a Sir Jamison whispering in Mrs. Burlingame's ear, his hand caressing her neck as he spoke, while his wife walked out to the balcony with a man who draped his arm around her waist. She thought she saw Lord Eldon, as well, but he was far to the other side of the room and she could not be sure.

She turned to Nicholas to ask that they leave, but he was gone. Her teeth gritted in panicked anger. What could he have been thinking of? How dare he bring her to such a place! She searched the crowded room, but did not find him.

"Perhaps a dance, my Queen?" an unfamiliar voice whispered by her ear, and she turned quickly. A Harlequin leered at her from under his mask, and she took a step back.

"No, thank you, I do not wish to dance," she said.

"A walk out upon the terrace, then?"

"No." She turned away from the man, searching the room once more.

"You are unobliging, pretty one."

She felt a hand slide around her waist. Fury flared within her at the man's actions and at Nicholas's abandonment. Her hands turned into fists, and the sticks of her fan bit into one palm.

"I pray that you unhand me now, sir, or you will certainly

regret it," Leonore said between clenched teeth. The man only laughed and pulled her to him.

She did not think, only acted. Sheer anger propelled her fist around in a circle, and she drove the pointed end of her closed fan into his stomach.

"Oof!" The man fell with a decided thump to the floor.

Horrified at what she had done, she whirled to stare at the man who had fallen. He was gasping for breath and holding his stomach; his mask had come half off, affront writ large upon his face. Laughter broke out around her, and she raised her head with a jerk. Her face flamed hot. A crowd had gathered around her, obviously enjoying the scuffle. Their masked faces—amused Columbines, laughing cavaliers, leering pirates—seemed monstrous to her, and she ran blindly away from them, away from the heat and the suffocating humiliation.

Cool air struck her face and calmed her heated emotions a little as well. Leonore looked about her and found she had run out onto a balcony. She drew her domino close about her shoulders and leaned against the edge of the balcony, breathing deeply of the night air. She would go home as soon as she recovered herself and found Nicholas.

The night sky was black and dotted with the light of stars. Leonore looked up at the moon shining serenely as if nothing had happened only a few minutes before. Some calmness returned to her. She could hear the musicians inside the room still playing relentlessly, and the muted noise of the guests. Relative silence surrounded her, and she was glad of it. The murmur of voices, closer, came to her.

"Nicholas . . ."

Leonore froze, but did not turn around. She was sure the voices came from just below her where the door opened out to the terrace.

"Well, Mercia, you see I have arrived as I promised." Leonore closed her eyes. She knew Nicholas's voice very well.

"You wed her, my dear. I don't know if I can forgive that."

"Oh, come, my dear!" Nicholas said ironically. "Surely you

don't think it is any different from your own . . . marriage to your poor Constantin."

"She is well-born, however. I am sure she could not be living with you without your wedding her in a church. How did you manage it?" Leonore could hear suspicion in Lady Lazlo's voice.

"It was short, believe me. I have lasted longer than any of the others. Why shouldn't I be able to bear this, as well?"

"Then I was right to return here." Lady Lazlo's voice grew eager. "Look you, Nicholas, we shall be a powerful pair should we join together. We could rule here, take what we wish."

"I remember the last time you said that, Mercia. How will I know your indiscretions will not force you to hide once again?"

"I was never indiscreet!"

"So you say. Your depredations amongst society's best were always obvious to me."

"You—" Lady Lazlo's voice had risen, but she stopped herself. "Oh, come now, you know what I am. You are another one of my kind. Of course you'd notice my actions." Her voice was soft and seductive.

Leonore's hands closed into tight fists. *Please, Nicholas, please don't go to her.* She wanted to leave, but moved only to turn and look over the balcony. There she saw Nicholas, not quite facing the balcony; Lady Lazlo was turned toward him.

"Of course I would notice your actions, Mercia," Nicholas replied. "But so did the Parisians."

Lady Lazlo shrugged. "I merely convinced them I was helping their cause. They became very sympathetic after that."

A slow smile came to Nicholas's lips. "How very clever of you, my dear." Lady Lazlo stepped close enough for her to lay her head upon his chest.

"Dear Nicholas, will you join me?" Leonore could see Lady Lazlo's fingers trace a trail from Nicholas's coat lapel to his cheek. He did not move from her, but smiled.

A hot, sharp pain struck Leonore's chest, pushing a short groaning sigh from her. She covered her lips immediately and shrank behind a pillar. For a moment she thought Nicholas's eyes had shot to where she stood, but she could not be sure.

Nicholas was looking at Lady Lázlo now, however. He brought his hand to her shoulder and caressed her neck. "I have yet to hear anything to make it worth my while."

A low, husky laugh floated up from Lady Lazlo. "Kiss me, and perhaps that will convince you."

Don't, don't! cried Leonore inwardly and pressed her hands to her mouth. She watched, numb, while her husband slowly bent and pressed his lips to Lady Lazlo's. Leonore turned then, closing her eyes tightly, and bit her lip to keep herself from crying out. The pain and the taste of blood brought her to a semblance of control, and she swallowed the tears she felt rising within her.

"You will have to convince me more than that. Mercia." Nicholas's voice was smooth, almost emotionless.

This time Lady Lazlo laughed complacently. "Come to me tomorrow. I will do my best to persuade you then."

Leonore's feet unfroze in that instant, and she stumbled from the balcony into the room again. She had to leave—now. She could not stand the idea that Nicholas would go to that woman when only a few days ago he had told Leonore he liked her. Liked. That was not much, was it? Obviously, he felt more than liking for Lady Lazlo.

Her feet sped her past the guests. Tears started to drop from her eyes. She dashed her hand against her mask, dislodging it so that it obscured her sight, and stumbled hard into a firm, male body. Her arms were grasped, and she struggled wildly.

"Let me go! Please let me go!"

"I say, Lady St. Vire, what are you doing here?" came Lord Eldon's voice from above her head. She pushed up her mask and gazed into his concerned eyes. "Not quite the thing, you know."

"Oh, Lord Eldon, please take me home! I—It was a terrible mistake. "I . . . I have the headache, too." She pressed her hand to her temple, for indeed a headache was beginning to form there.

"Where is St. Vire? Surely *he* did not bring you here?" He took her hand and patted it comfortingly.

"No, no, he did not," she lied. "I came with some friends . . . I thought they were friends, but of course they are not." She let out a near-sobbing breath. "Please take me home."

"Of course, of course," said Lord Eldon. His voice was kind, and Leonore nearly burst into tears at the sound of it.

He hailed a hackney and made sure Leonore was comfortable in it before he entered it. Lord Eldon's light, inconsequential chatter calmed her so that by the time they reached the house, she was able to thank him for his assistance in a friendly way.

"Are you sure you do not wish me to see you to the door?" Lord Eldon said.

She smiled at him. "No, I assure you I will be better presently. I *am* much better now that I am gone from that place."

He nodded and tipped his hat to her. "Very well, then. But I shall wait until you have gone into the house."

Leonore waved to him when the footman opened the door, and she watched the carriage start off. Then she turned and entered the house.

Her nod to the footman was automatic, without her customary smile, and her steps to her room mechanical. She thought of the kindly Lord Eldon and wished she had married someone like him. She would not be so confused now, so filled with turbulent emotions that it made her feel ill. From the start Nicholas had confused her, had made her feel things she did not want to feel, and made her want more from this marriage than a marriage of convenience had to offer.

Her maid had stayed up to attend her. The girl smiled uncertainly, and Leonore made herself smile reassuringly.

"You are doing well, Betty. I am tired and have the headache. I only wish to sleep."

A relieved expression lightened Betty's features, and she bobbed a curtsy. "Yes, my lady. I'll be quick, then."

Betty was as good as her word, and Leonore was soon in bed. She gave a last smile at her maid as the door closed.

Then the wracking agony came.

"I will not cry. I will not cry," moaned Leonore into her pillow. It was a chant, a dirge that echoed in her dark, quiet room. She had held off the tears so long they would not come now, and she moaned as if she were gravely ill and in a fever. All her love, her loneliness, and her hopes she whispered into the pillow, all her rage and feelings of abandonment. It did not comfort her.

Above all, the thought that hurt her, that made a rising nausea lie heavy in her belly, was that Nicholas had lied to her. He had said he had not liked Lady Lazlo for years now. It could not be true, not from the way he'd kissed the woman. Leonore had trusted him as she had no one else, for he had never lied to her and had always kept his promises. She had even come to love him.

The thought made her groan aloud, a short, sharp sound. Anger fired her mind, and she was abruptly, fiercely glad she had never told Nicholas of her love. She had told him she cared for him. But she had not, at last, told him she loved him. She held close that thought, as if it were a buoy above her churning emotions. He would never know. She would never let him know.

"I will never let him know," she murmured into the night's silence. She said the words over and over again, and slowly her breath evened out. She was tired, very tired.

"I will never let Nicholas know," she whispered again, and the phrase became a mournful lullaby. At last she breathed a long sigh and fell asleep, her husband's name on her lips.

Nicholas glanced again at the balcony. Leonore had left at last. He gazed at Mercia and smiled at her.

How I hate you. He wished he could rid the world of her, for she was nothing but a monster . . . like himself. He almost grimaced at his newly born sense of ethics. Could he condemn her for the bloodthirst he, himself, had? But then, he never killed his victims unless they were in the process of killing others. Perhaps he could put some ward or spell upon her to render her harmless to those he held dear. He could not be sure he would find one, however. It would take time.

Regardless, she had to be handled carefully. She was dangerous, both to him and to Leonore—to anyone who came in her path, for that matter. Even now, as she twined her arms around his neck and pressed her body against his, he saw the subtle madness in her eyes, an almost animal cunning.

He grasped her arms and moved her away from him. "I thought you said you would try persuading me tomorrow."

Mercia looked at him with heavy-lidded eyes. "Oh, I suppose I could try persuading you now."

Nicholas gauged his words. "You have no sense of finesse, my dear. Everything must be 'now,' and 'soon,' and 'tonight' with you. Where is your sense of anticipation?"

"There is nothing wrong with doing what I want."

"There is, when more pleasure can be had when one waits."

Lady Lazlo seemed to consider this. "Very well. But don't bring your wife. I saw her inside earlier colliding with a Harlequin." She shook her head. "A clumsy wench. How you came to wed her, I do not know. You are so graceful yourself."

Biting back angry words, Nicholas shrugged. "It was convenient. I grew tired of hunting. I am a lazy fellow, after all."

She looked at him slyly. "Or, you could bring her and perhaps we might have some sport with her."

Hot rage and loathing shot through him, and it took all his control to keep from killing her where she stood. He made himself smile and shrug again, feeling ill from the effort. "Perhaps," he said. Even to himself his voice sounded strained. "But I am afraid it would shock the poor creature quite horribly, and she'd be useless for a long time afterward. She is a very good housekeeper. Finding a replacement would be tedious."

"Very well, then. We do not need her." She shot him an indecipherable look. "But you must rid yourself of her at some time, you know. Otherwise I will suspect you are not wholly committed to me."

St. Vire sighed in a bored fashion. "How you harp on that!

So you said during our dance at Lady Russell's ball. I will rid myself of Leonore when I am tired of her. I am not tired of her yet. Besides, I am not as indiscreet as you—*I* do not care to have Bow Street snapping at my heels. Do try to be a little more civilized, Mercia."

"How stupidly particular you are, Nicholas!" she said pettishly. "All these little concerns of yours." She took his face in her hands and pulled him down to a hard kiss. "There! That's to remember me by . . . and remember that if you do not get rid of her in a reasonable amount of time, I'll do it for you."

Fear for Leonore nearly caused him to shudder, but he made himself grin boyishly instead. "But I like my little pet! Can I not keep her a bit longer?"

Mercia burst out laughing. "Oh, very well! But mind what I have said!" She turned and took a few steps away from him, then paused to throw him a kiss before she left the terrace. For one minute he stared at the doorway through which she had gone.

The sharp sound of broken pottery cracked the air. His knuckles hurt, and he looked down at the dirt and shattered clay before him. He'd hit a large plant pot that had been sitting in a niche in the wall, but at least his emotions had calmed a little. For just one moment, it was Mercia who had been in front of him. For just one moment, he had rid the world of her.

St. Vire sighed. He had better look for Leonore. He'd seen her on the balcony. She must have heard most of the conversation between Mercia and himself. It was necessary, he told himself. Better Leonore hate him now. Mercia would then be more easily convinced that the marriage was merely one of convenience.

He entered the assembly room again, but did not find Leonore. Fear shot through him. Had Mercia—no, she couldn't have, not after their conversation. He wished he had never brought Leonore here, but he knew she'd question his absence, and he had not wanted to lie to her in this, at least. He had not realized the sort of people who would be here until after he had stepped into the house. He knew Harlowe was a bit of a rake, but he did not know Lady Harlowe and had assumed it would be a different sort of masquerade because of her presence. He had almost taken Leonore home, but then thought about what he must do. It was better she begin to hate him from tonight; postponing it was futile, for it would make no difference in the end.

Discreetly he questioned a few of the guests he knew and found to his profound relief that Leonore had left with Lord Eldon. He knew he had nothing to fear from his friend, as Eldon was a remarkably kind-hearted young man. He made a mental note to warn him away from Mercia. His friend did not deserve a liaison with her.

His carriage took him swiftly home. When he entered the house, his feet took him up the stairs two at a time. He realized what he was doing and stopped. Of course Leonore must be here; he could trust Eldon to bring her home safely. And yet . . . and yet . . .

Nicholas's hand shook as he opened Leonore's chamber door. The silence in the room was almost unbearable to him . . . surely she was sleeping. He went to her bed. The moon streamed through the window, outlining Leonore's sleeping form. She lay on her side, curled into a tight ball, her knees up to her stomach, her hands crossed over her chest.

A now familiar leaden sensation pressed into him, and the breath that came from him was almost a groan. He had seen people curled in this position before—in Paris when the victims of the Reign of Terror tried to escape the beatings of the mob, in the slums of London when poor drabs tried to protect themselves from a winter's night. He had made Leonore miserable, had hurt her—he who loved her.

St. Vire turned from her, gazing out the window to the moon-silvered street below. It was necessary, he told himself, not for him, but for Leonore. But who had gotten her into this situation in the first place? He had no one to blame but himself.

God, how I despise myself! He almost laughed aloud, bitterly. Leonore had not turned him into a saint, but she had shown him all his sins, shattering his image of himself. He'd been an arrogant fool to think he could simply pluck her from her family and use her for his spell—as if she were some herb in a dish served up for his liking.

"Nicholas . . ."

Turning swiftly, he saw she was still asleep. Even in her dreams she thought of him—no doubt now with misery and grief. He wished he could comfort her. He put out his hand and stroked the hair from her face. She breathed a soft sigh and turned her head so that her cheek fit into the palm of his hand. An ache grew in his chest. Even with the way he had treated her, some part of her seemed to seek his touch.

He removed his coat and neckcloth, draping them over a chair. Just this once he would hold her in his arms and not make love to her. She would not know, for she slept heavily, and he could always move softly on the bed and never rouse her.

The mattress was soft beneath him, and Leonore's form softer still against him. He gathered her to him, her back to his chest, his cheek upon her hair. She sighed, and her body seemed to relax, uncurling slightly from her earlier position.

"I love you, Leonore," he whispered softly, knowing she could not hear him. "You don't know it, but I do." His breath caught in his throat. He wished he could have said it in a clever, witty way . . . but it did not matter, for she was asleep. "Your lovely face and form, your laugh and even the way you tell me I am vain. But God, I must hurt you, and I wish I need not."

He drew her closer, kissing the nape of her neck. She sighed again and nestled into him, and he wished he could weep. But he could not, for vampires had no tears.

"I love you, Leonore. . . ."

She turned and reached for Nicholas, but he was not there in the bed beside her, and she knew it had been only a dream. Leonore opened her eyes. The sunlight that streamed into her room told her it was day; of course he could not be here.

The events of the night before rushed into her then, and she closed her eyes, gasping as if in pain. He would be with Lady Lazlo, most certainly. He had kissed her. Leonore had seen it.

With a low groan she rolled over in her bed and into a depression in the mattress. The faint scent of bay rum arose from the pillow beside her. It was the scent Nicholas always wore, and she was familiar with it.

Why had he come to her last night? He was enamored of Lady Lazlo, she was sure. And yet, he had certainly been in her room. He had not made love to her, but simply lain beside her.

She reached into her memories of last night, hoping to catch perhaps one moment she might have wakened during the night. All she remembered were turbulent dreams that faded into a vague, odd sense of comfort.

And Nicholas's soft whisper, "I love you, Leonore. . . ."

Leonore shook her head fiercely. No. No, he did not love her. She would not believe it, for she had shored up her heart again, and to let the thought in would surely tear her apart.

Pulling on her dressing gown, she rose and rang for her maid. Hers was a marriage of convenience. She had forgotten it and allowed herself to fall in love with Nicholas. It was too late to stop the emotion, but at least she would not let it show.

Betty entered the room and helped Leonore dress. She pushed down the shadows of rage and grief that had obscured her thoughts the night before. A proper wife turned her eyes away from her husband's indiscretions; her own mother had told her that. She would heed the advice, and her marriage would be as any other.

And yet, the soft dreamlike whisper she had remembered entered and nestled in one corner of her heart and stubbornly refused to leave.

Chapter 14

Leonore sat at the window seat, looking down at the London traffic below, her hand folding and unfolding the portion of her skirt she held between her fingers. She was hungry, but she had no appetite; she was thirsty, but she did not care to drink. She did not care about much these days, for a dullness had descended upon her mind, and her heart had frozen into ice.

The March sun shone brightly, doing its best to tempt her into going out. She closed her eyes against the light. She wished Nicholas was with her now, then pushed the wish away. It was daylight, and of course he would not appear. And when the night arrived, he would not be at her side, but would leave her to be with Lady Lazlo. Leonore had tried to bear it for months now.

It would have been bearable if she did not receive speculatives looks and sly questions from those who resented St. Vire's earlier infatuation with her.

The ice around her heart threatened to break, but she would not let it. She would weep if it disappeared. She sighed and rose from her seat at the window. There were things to do about the house, and then she would call upon her sister, Susan.

Leonore busied herself with various tasks, but knew she got in the servants' way. Well, she would go to see Susan and her mother. Her heart lifted, for she was sure of her sister's affectionate reception, and at least a smile from her mother.

She had not even reached the steps to her parents' house when the door burst open and Susan ran to her with her hands outstretched and a beaming smile upon her face.

"Oh, Leo! You must come and look! We have got a new pianoforte!"

Leonore laughed and gave her sister a brief, warm hug. "Only for a pianoforte would you be so excited as to rush out into the cold air without your pelisse." Her sister was beautiful, her guinea gold curls thick and healthy instead of lank and dull as they had been before Leonore had married. The girl's cheeks bloomed with health, no doubt because she had more food and less worry than in the past. "Is Mama in?"

"Oh, how you fuss, Leo! It is only a few steps into the house. And Mama is out shopping for a ribbon. Can you imagine? Her headaches have not been as bad as they used to be."

Susan's blue eyes danced, and she shook her head, making her curls float about her head like a halo. A passing gentleman stopped and stared at her sister before he collected himself and walked by reluctantly. She smiled with pride. Her sister had been attracting several eligible gentlemen's attention lately. Susan had bloomed under the approval she had received from those to whom Leonore had introduced her. Her painful shyness had faded; it became a sweet, innocent manner that, combined with her beauty, gained her popularity even from the sternest of dowagers.

"Do come look, Leo! It's beautiful." Susan seized Leonore's hand and pulled her into the house. Leonore laughed. It warmed her to see Susan so happy. For this, at least, Leonore was glad she had married Nicholas. The thought of him damped her spirits a little, but she dismissed it. No, she had married well. She now only needed to see Susan wed.

The pianoforte was indeed beautiful. It was imported; the workmanship marked it as from one of the finest instrument makers in Germany. Leonore ran her hand over the smooth, lacquered surface, admiring the way some artist had painted intricate gold designs on the edges and singing cherubs and angels on the inside surface of the lid. She looked at Susan's expectant face.

"Well?" Susan said, her voice eager. "What do you think?"

"Beautiful! Have you tried it yet?"

"Yes, of course! I had it tuned immediately when it arrived." Susan sat down upon the bench and laid her hands on the keyboard. A lilting melody—a waltz—sang sweet and pure from the instrument. "When we go to the ball tonight, I must thank Nicholas for buying it for me."

"Nicholas?"

Susan glanced at Leonore, her eyes laughing. "Of course, silly Leo! Who else would have been so generous? Father detests music and would never think of it, and Mama would not know how to go about ordering one."

"Of course," Leonore replied, giving a short laugh. "I suppose I am still not used to Nicholas's generosity." Two months ago she had mentioned in passing that she thought it a pity Susan had to play upon such a poor instrument. St. Vire had nodded absently, and they had talked of other things. And now here was the pianoforte in her parents' home.

Susan had stopped her playing and was looking at her sister anxiously. "Is there something wrong, Leo?"

Leonore shook her head. "No, not at all. I have been gadding about too much, is all, and I am a little tired. I would, however, like to rest and listen to you play a while." The girl smiled and began a sonata.

Leonore listened, but her mind turned to Nicholas again. She did not understand him. Each time they went to a ball or other social function, he would spend a large amount of time with Lady Lazlo if she was there. His attentions were just within the bounds of propriety. And though he was discreet, she noticed they'd disappear together for a short while each time.

Yet, he spent almost equal time with her, Leonore, and would also find time to be private with her. He never initiated conversation about Lady Lazlo. When Leonore would say her name, his lips would harden, and an angry, fearful light would flash in his eyes. Then he would turn the conversation to other things.

And still he would come to her bed at night when she retired, sometimes making love to her. Even when he kept to his room or had gone out with his friends, she could tell the next morning that he had lain at her side for a while. At first she did not want him in her bed at all. Yet, two weeks of his absence had set a yearning fire in her belly, and when he kissed her one evening she had abandoned herself to it and had given him back every kiss and caress. She despised herself for her weakness.

And now this, the gift of the pianoforte to Susan. He still showered gifts upon her and her family, though she told him it was not necessary. She needed only to wish it, and it would appear for her, however whimsical her wish. Once she had told him of a sweet lamb she had seen at a market, and the next day a toy lamb had appeared on her bed. She could almost think he cared for her, for when they were at home, he looked at her as if he desired her. Yet, the whispering about him and Lady Lazlo grew—and with it her own jealousy. She hated herself for it. It made her feel powerless, without control over herself.

The music had stopped, and she looked at Susan to find that her sister was gazing at her with concern.

"What is it, Susie?"

"There is something wrong, I know it. Tell me what it is."

Leonore made herself smile. "Nonsense, Susan! Do continue playing."

Susan frowned and rose from the pianoforte. She sat down next to Leonore and took her hand.

"Leo, there *is* something wrong. You never call me 'Susan' unless there is. Tell me." She hesitated. "I know you are my older sister, and I have confided everything in you since I was a baby. But I am your sister also, and it is not fair that you should carry all the burdens and tell no one."

"Oh, heavens, Susan, there is nothing—"

"Stop, Leonore! I have grown up—can you not see that?" Susan squeezed her hand. "I have always wanted to be like you, strong, brave, and loving. How can I do that if you don't let me? I cannot be protected forever. I do not say much, but I always listen and watch. And since my come-out, I have had many chances to learn." She nodded her head wisely, and Leonore almost wept to see the old look on her young face.

Years of watching for signs of her father's rages had put it there, she was sure.

"You have always been so good to me, Leo," Susan continued. "Perhaps I cannot help you directly, but at least let me know why you are so often sad these days." She gave Leonore a hug. "Please tell me."

A lump in Leonore's throat almost choked her, and she swallowed. She managed to put a smile on her face. "It is nothing. . . . I . . . I, oh Susie, I'm in love with Nicholas, and he is in love with Lady Lazlo!" she blurted. Horrified at her outburst, she covered her mouth with her hand, rose, and walked to the windows. She stared blindly out at the street, trying to control herself and not blather on. She failed. "Oh heavens! Never mind, Susan, it is nothing after all. We have a marriage of convenience. I am content, truly, and I am sure Nicholas is quite satisfied with the way things are. I . . . I am being stupid, for there is nothing anyone can do about it, surely—" She felt Susan's arm come around her in a hug.

"Yes, Leo, I think you *are* being stupid," Susan said gently.

"Susan!"

"Oh, Leonore, you need not look so . . . so older sisterish!" she said with a touch of impatience. "I am not ten years old any longer, but eighteen! I have eyes in my head, after all. I can see for myself that Nicholas is in love with you."

The ice around Leonore's heart threatened to crack. "Nonsense!" she said.

Susan let out an impatient breath. "For goodness sake! Can you deny how generous he is to you—to us, your family—when I know he needn't be? I don't know how many times I have seen him watch you when you were not looking. Or how he must like to touch you, for I have seen him almost reach for you but stop when he recollects he is in company. He takes every excuse to be near you. How can you not think he loves you?"

"But the gossip—Lady Lazlo—"

"Heavens, Leo! I am surprised you listen to such things."

Leonore felt a reluctant laugh bubble up inside of her—how

their roles had reversed! Susan sounded so very grown up. She shook her head, however.

"Susie . . . you will not let this go further, of course—" Leonore began. Her sister gave her a disgusted look, which caused Leonore to laugh. "Stupid of me. Of course you would not." She hesitated and wet her lips. "I saw, many months ago, him kissing her. And they talked as if they were considering a . . . a liaison." Susan's brow furrowed in thought.

"Perhaps that has some significance," Susan said slowly, and Leonore smiled at how grown-up her sister sounded. "But I cannot think it has much, for it seems gentlemen are very fond of kissing." A light blush appeared in Susan's cheeks, and she hurried on. "But still, I cannot think Nicholas is in love with Lady Lazlo, for I believe he quite hates her."

Leonore gave a short, bitter laugh. "How you can say that? I have seen with my own eyes how he dances a little too closely to her for propriety, and how he has disappeared with her from time to time. If he hates her, he would not have kissed her."

Susan shook her head. "I don't know why he kissed Lady Lazlo, but he doesn't like her. He looks angrily at her whenever she looks away from him, and his hands close into fists when she approaches. It is only for a moment, but I have seen it each time. I think if he were like Father, he would probably hit her." Susan sighed. "I've learned it is not right for gentlemen to do that, and I am certain Nicholas is a gentleman."

Her sister had grown up, indeed. Leonore did not know why she thought her protection had kept Susan from understanding what their parents were. It brought a bitter taste to her tongue. She had done Susan a disservice, thinking she could not see what was in front of her, or could be protected from ugliness. What arrogance! She had not protected her from much, it seemed.

"I don't know what to think, Susan, truly I do not. I have tried to broach the subject, but he grows cold and does not wish to speak of it."

Susan patted her hand. "I am certain he loves you, truly."

Leonore's smile was ironic. "Are you, Susie? How can you be certain when you have never been in love yourself?"

"I have so!" cried Susan indignantly. She stopped and blushed a beetroot color.

"Oh, my dear, I did not mean to tease!" Leonore took her sister's hands and squeezed them. "Perhaps you can tell me?"

"It . . . it is Jeremy Fordham, Lord Eldon's younger brother." Susan gazed at Leonore, her face alight. "He is so handsome and so kind to me, Leo! He makes me laugh, for he says the most comical things. And I am sure he loves me, too, for he has told me so, and he looks at me as I have seen Nicholas look at you."

"Oh, Susie! How happy I am for you!" Leonore hugged her tightly. Mr. Fordham did not have the title and wealth she had hoped for her sister, but she knew he was as kind as his brother, and would inherit a sizable legacy from an elderly uncle. Mr. Fordham had appeared at Susan's side nearly every ball or rout. Leonore remembered Susan's earlier words and almost smiled.

"I suppose he kissed you as well?" she said and made her voice somber. She reflected on the quality of her mother's chaperonage—it'd been easy to be alone with Nicholas before they had married. No doubt Mr. Fordham would have had ample opportunity to kiss Susan.

Susan blushed again. "It . . . it is not a bad thing, is it? I have not let anyone else kiss me, for I didn't think it proper, but somehow it seemed different with Jerem—Mr. Fordham. He told me he wishes to speak with Father, that he wishes to marry me. And, oh, when he kissed me I . . . I wanted it to go on forever, but he stopped and said we mustn't go any further until we were wed." She looked miserably down at her slippers. "Cassie Brighthelm looked at me in *such* a way when we came back inside from the gardens. It made me think I should not have, that I was . . ."

Leonore winced at her sister's innocently revealing words, thankful that Mr. Fordham was at least that much of a gentleman. Perhaps all men were easily lured into kissing a pretty woman, although Mr. Fordham meant honorably by Susan. "Never mind, Susie, it is not a terrible thing for him to kiss you. In fact, Nicholas and I—Well, some things are allowed between betrothed couples. Has he spoken with Father yet?"

"He said he would do so today and let me know immediately," Susan said, her expression relieved. She looked curiously at Leonore. "You and Nicholas kissed—"

"Yes, we did," said Leonore hastily, and it was her turn to blush. Heavens, she hoped Susan would not ask questions about what went on between Nicholas and herself before they married.

"And did you—"

A knock on the door interrupted Susan, and Leonore breathed a thankful sigh as the maid Annie opened it.

"It's Mr. Fordham, my lady, Miss Susan."

Leonore smiled. "Please show him in." She glanced at Susan's anxious face. "Don't worry, Susie. I am sure Father must have consented." She hoped Mr. Fordham had offered a large marriage settlement to her father, or else she was not at all sure that he would consent.

A tall young man strode through the door, running his hand through his blond hair and destroying what probably had been a windswept style. He spied Susan and took her hands in his.

"Susan, he said—"

Leonore cleared her throat, and he turned, startled, to her.

"Ah! Lady St. Vire. You must excuse me, I have been remiss. I take it you are well?" he said and bowed.

"Very well, thank you. I see you are looking quite happy." She glanced at Susan, who was anxiously shifting from one foot to another. "I daresay you have something to say to my sister?"

Mr. Fordham grinned. "Yes, I do." He turned to Susan and kissed her hand. "Miss Farleigh, will you marry me?"

"Oh . . . oh, Jeremy! Has he—" Susan's voice trembled, and her eyes suddenly filled with tears. Leonore could feel her own eyes become misty. "Oh, has Father consented?"

"Yes, sweet, silly girl." Mr. Fordham chucked Susan under the chin and looked very much as if he would like to kiss her. "Otherwise I wouldn't be asking you now."

"Yes! Oh, yes, Jeremy!" Susan exclaimed and flung herself into his arms in a fierce embrace.

It would not hurt, thought Leonore, to leave the two alone for they were betrothed now. Mr. Fordham, certainly, was not at all like Nicholas, who had gone out of his way to tell—even show—her that he was a "bad man" as he himself put it. She smiled at the pair, knowing they would not notice that she had left, and left the room, with the door of the drawing room slightly ajar.

She took a hackney back to her house, and once seated, gave a large sigh. Her sister had indeed grown up and would not need her anymore, for Mr. Fordham was fully capable of protecting her now. It would be his duty as Susan's husband.

The thought struck a chord in her. Leonore stared down at her hands in her lap, concentrating so as to bring forth the idea that had been roused in her mind. It seemed an important one, but she could not quite grasp it. She shook her head. Whatever it was, it would come to her in time.

It was an hour and a half to sunset by the time she arrived home. Nicholas would be up soon. She used to step into his room sometimes during the day to watch him sleep; she had not done that since Lady Lazlo had come to London. A strong urge to do so seized her, and she walked quickly up the stairs to her room. If she hurried, she would be able to watch him for a while and leave before he woke. Once in her chamber, she looked for the lamp she used when she went into his room. She could not find it—perhaps it had been taken away to be cleaned. She lit a candle and opened the connecting door to Nicholas's room.

As usual, it was dark, for the curtains were drawn against the light. She drew aside the bed curtains and gazed at her husband. He slept deeply, as he always did, barely breathing. One arm was flung up over his head, which was turned to the side, the lines of his profile like a bas-relief upon his pillow.

A warm, painful ache flowed into her heart, and she knew she would always love him. Perhaps Susan was right. Perhaps he did not like Lady Lazlo at all and had some other reason for kissing her. But that made no sense. A man did not pay large amounts of attention to a lady he did not like, she was certain of that.

She looked at Nicholas, who looked more boyish in repose than he did when he was awake. His lips looked soft in his slumber, and she wanted to kiss them. He was deep asleep; it was not yet dark, and he would not wake just yet. She had not initiated any kisses since Lady Lazlo had entered their lives. If she did it now, she could leave with Nicholas none the wiser.

Leonore leaned over and pressed her lips against Nicholas's. She could feel the slight breath that came from his mouth, soft and lax with sleep, and moved her own lips across his gently. Even in sleep he moved her, causing her to shiver.

She gasped, for hot wax poured from the candle onto her hand. She had forgotten she was carrying an uncovered candle instead of a lamp. Her hand shook from the pain, and more wax spattered from the candle. Another gasp, not her own, made her jerk her head to its source, and a strong hand grasped her wrist.

"What the devil are you doing here?" Cold green eyes stared into her own.

Leonore said nothing, at once frightened and embarrassed, merely staring back at Nicholas. He shifted himself until he sat up, and the bedclothes slid down around his hips. He wore no nightshirt as usual, only his underclothes.

"I hope you were not trying to burn me in my bed, my dear," he said, taking the candle from her hand. "That would be a foolish thing to do, for it would take the house down with me, and then what would you do?"

Anger flared within Leonore. "I . . . I was not trying to burn you at all!"

"No? And what is this?" He peeled a large piece of wax from his shoulder. Beneath it a red welt was forming, and Leonore blushed guiltily.

"I am sorry. I did not mean to do it. I forgot I was holding a candle, and my hand shook and spilled the wax. I spilled some on myself as well," she said and extended her hand.

"I wish you were more careful. It was a stupid thing to do, Leonore. You could have burned the curtains." His words were harsh, yet he took her hand in his. Nicholas peeled the wax quickly away, and she clenched her teeth against the pain. She, too, had red welts upon her hand. He whispered something under his breath as he worked, clearly irritated. Finally, he was done and grasped her hand tightly so that she could not escape.

"Now, tell me. What were you doing in my room?"

"I am your wife, Nicholas. I suppose I can enter your room as I see fit. You are ill with the condition you have, and I believe my duty is to see if you are well." She felt embarrassed that he had caught her here, but she had meant no harm, and he had no cause to question her. The thought brought a spurt of anger to her, which she suppressed.

He looked away from her. "Oh, really? Or was it to cause me more pain? You pushed the curtains away. I told you the sunlight makes me ill." He did not sneer, but his voice came close to it.

"How dare you! How *dare* you accuse me of wanting to hurt you, when it is you—yes, you—who has hurt me!" Leonore gritted her teeth together hard, for angry tears threatened to rise in her, and she would not allow it.

"I? How have I done that? Have I ever lifted my hand to you? Have I not given you every luxury you might want?"

This time it was Leonore who sneered. "And what is that to me? I have had a man's hand lifted against me most of my life—should I lick your boots and be grateful that you refrain? The jewels and the dresses you have given me you can take away, for they are yours by law, not mine."

Her hands clenched into fists, and she tore herself away from Nicholas's grasp. Her mind was afire with rage and humiliation, and she could not stop herself, though she knew her anger twisted her perceptions, whipping her into a rage. The image of Nicholas kissing Lady Lazlo rose in her mind again, and all her suppressed emotions flared into high heat. Her words tasted acid on her tongue, and she spat them out.

"No, Nicholas, it is you who has hurt me, for it is you who has betrayed our marriage."

He tossed the bedclothes from him and swung his legs over

the side of the bed. Leonore moved away from him, but in less than a breath he pulled her into his arms. He pushed up her chin so that she was forced to look at him. His eyes were amused.

"Jealous little cat! You know nothing about it."

She struggled and pushed at him, but he was too strong and she could not move.

"Do not patronize me!" Leonore cried. "I know what I *see*! And don't you think I hear the whispers about you and Lady Lazlo? No, not even whispers—I've been pitied and, yes, *commiserated* with on your new interest!" Her own words humiliated her, for she knew she was losing control, and this humiliated her further. The heat of her rage had melted the ice around her heart, and the pain of it made her want to cry out. She wanted to hurt him, as she had been hurt, and she would push and push at him until she did. If Lady Lazlo was his mistress, she wanted to cut her feelings from him quickly. Their marriage would be one of true convenience, with not even love on her part.

"Thank them for their interest, smile, and say you have nothing for which to be pitied," he said flippantly.

He did not care. That was obvious. Leonore's rage flared hot; she could barely think. "How I hate you!" she said, her voice low and shaking.

Nicholas released her, and instantly she regretted her words. It was not true—she loved him, and that was why she hurt so. She would not have cared otherwise. But she could not tell him, for he had turned his back to her—that and her own sudden fear that she had gone too far. He clutched a bedpost, and for one moment he leaned upon it. Finally, he turned to her, his face smooth and urbane.

"Go change your dress. We are to attend Lady Comstock's masquerade ball and cannot cry off now. Or, if you have the headache, I can make your excuses."

Leonore stared at him, unable to speak.

"Leave. Now," Nicholas said, and anger appeared in his eyes at last.

She turned abruptly and slammed the door after her. She did

not want to go to the ball. If anyone found Nicholas had gone without her, however, the *ton* would talk more than ever, especially if Lady Lazlo attended.

More than anything, she wanted to be alone. Leonore stared at the connecting door, imagining Nicholas intent on dressing for the evening, and a burning defiance made her leave her room. She would not dress right away, but would go to her sitting room.

It comforted her a little to be there. When she opened the door, the warmth from the fireplace and the room's familiar comfort was a balm to the confusion of her thoughts and emotions. She sat in her favorite chair and pressed her hands to her eyes, pressing back the tears she could feel behind them.

God help me. She wanted to leave. She did not want to see Nicholas at that moment, not for the next day at least. But she must keep up appearances.

"I do not want to go, do not want to!" Leonore whispered. She stared out the window, not seeing the sunset above the rooftops of the city. She was tired of the facade she must put up, and never be her own self, her true self, or lose the loneliness the facade must always bring. She seldom discarded that protection around her heart. It happened only when she was caught in the wordless passion of the body, when she and Nicholas discarded their clothes and met flesh to flesh; or when her emotions flared and made her discard words like a foolish gamester at cards.

She felt she did not belong to London society, for she did not know how to laugh lightly, as seemed to be required of all ladies. She wished she could flirt with anyone, not just when Nicholas teased her. She wished he had no effect on her at all.

But Lady St. Vire had an obligation to her station in life and to the name she had taken in church with the vows of her heart and soul. And the former Leonore Farleigh had an obligation to her sister, so that no breath of scandal touch Susan's impending marriage.

Leonore closed her eyes for a moment, then took a deep breath and stood up. She could take up the roles she must play now. It was necessary. She had vented her emotions in an improper way; she should never have done it and could not unsay the words. Now she must go forward as best she could, turning her eyes away from whatever Nicholas chose to do.

A sharp pang went through her heart at the thought, but she suppressed it. She needed to behave with dignity. She'd apologize to Nicholas for her outburst; she should not have done it, regardless of the truth. A niggling voice within her told her that she might be mistaken . . . well, that might be true. Susan had said something of the sort, and she was more perceptive than Leonore had thought.

As she went up the stairs again to her bedchamber, Leonore sighed. She was glad she had come down to her sitting room. It was hard to think around Nicholas, for he always managed to distract her somehow. She knew she had been foolish and had embarrassed herself. She had little excuse for her rage. True, she'd seen Nicholas kiss Lady Lazlo; true, he did spend a great deal of time with her. But it didn't mean she needed to act like a jealous wife . . . though that was precisely what she was, Leonore admitted to herself. She should not have mentioned it at all.

She was glad she had not taken him up on his offer to bring Susan to live with them for a while. Perhaps she could go home. Father was mostly gone from the house, and her mother, with her megrims, hardly ventured forth from her bedroom. There would only be herself and Susan, with Mr. Fordham and other friends calling from time to time.

And yet, as she pulled the bell rope to summon Betty, she knew that it wasn't that Nicholas had kissed Lady Lazlo. He was the only person—aside from Susan—she had allowed herself to trust. She had thought she'd found a firm foundation upon which to set her heart, but now knew she had not. The discovery was like having a leg kicked from under her, and she had stumbled badly this evening. She would not do so again.

Betty arrived with a pair of new gloves. Leonore reflected that it was a good thing the gloves would cover her hands and hide the welts she received from spilling the wax on herself. But as she drew on the gloves, she frowned. The welts had disappeared, and her hands were as smooth, white, and free of pain as if she had never burned them. She shook her head. No doubt she had not burned them as badly as she'd thought, and the pain had been heightened because of her agitation.

Leonore shrugged and focused her mind on the ball she was to attend. She would keep her wits about her and put on an unconcerned face if Nicholas went to Lady Lazlo's side. At least the mask she wore would help hide any slip she might make. She sighed. It was too bad she could not always wear a mask. At times her emotions crowded up within her so she was sure they showed for all to read. She looked in the mirror, then pulled up her gold mask and could see her eyes peering from the slits. She did not look like herself, and it made her feel at once free and oddly frightened. How easy it would be to pretend she was someone else while at the masquerade ball, someone whom Nicholas loved.

Again Leonore shook her head at herself. How nonsensical she was being! She dismissed the idea firmly, and it drifted down into a small, shadowed corner of her mind, convincing Leonore that she had indeed forgotten it.

Chapter 15

Nicholas stared at the door for a moment, then turned and wearily rubbed his hand over his face. Well, he had done it now, hadn't he? Leonore hated him—precisely what he meant for her to feel. And she had thrown his sins in his face once again. It was just as well. Perhaps she would decide to leave him and go back to her parents' house. He shivered and threw a log into the fireplace, not bothering with the tinderbox but summoning a fire-salamander, which he let loose upon the wood. It licked and crawled upon the dry wood until the fire shot up high, then merged with the flames it had created.

He had told Leonore he'd make her excuses if she chose not to go to Lady Comstock's ball, but it was he who wished he did not have to go. Mercia would be there, and she had been getting impatient. Well, he could tell her that Leonore was leaving him, and that should put an end to her impatience.

Pulling on his robe, Nicholas rang for his valet and sighed deeply. He had not been able to find the right spell to protect Leonore or keep Mercia from harming her. It had taken him years to find the one that would turn him mortal again. He was lucky Mercia had little interest in magic, or else she might be more suspicious than she already was . . . although who knew what she might have discovered during the decades she was gone. Certainly, she'd known enough of satanic rituals to create more vampires.

At least the warding he had put upon Leonore had made Mercia overlook her presence. It was not precisely invisibility, but it gave the illusion that he was neglecting Leonore more than he really was.

And that was just it—he could not stay away from her, could not help wanting to touch her and do things for her that would make her smile or laugh or sigh in pleasure. He was a weak coward, to be sure. If he were resolute, he would have made Leonore leave him long ago. Well, he was sure he'd done it now.

When Nicholas finished putting on his costume, he looked in the mirror and could not help laughing. He had selected the mask of a golden dragon, one he had found in China when he had traveled there many years ago. He'd gone to seek the dragon knowledge he'd read about in some of his books. It had been an uncomfortable trip, for his dark red hair and pale skin had frightened many of the people there. They believed him to be a demon . . . and they were not far from wrong, at that.

The only man who had not run from him in fear was an old Taoist priest, who had consented to speak with him of ancient magic. It was he who had shown him how to summon a fire-salamander—the little dragon—and it was he who had given him the mask. St. Vire understood dragons to signify wisdom to the Chinese and so was honored to have received it from the old priest, though he did not know why the man had decided to give it to him, a foreigner. The only thing the priest would say was that for St. Vire, it signified hope.

Perhaps that was why he selected the mask to wear tonight at the masquerade ball. He was not sure of what he hoped . . . or perhaps it was a farewell to hope. He pushed down the persistent despair that threatened to seep into him. Allowing that emotion would do him no good at all.

He certainly looked odd in the mask; it was much smaller than many of the masks he'd seen in China, but it covered most of his face. The long, bright brocade cloth that hung from the top and draped behind him held it in place. He knew it would attract much attention with its exotic design. He did not mind that at all, however, and he rather liked the idea that no one would know who he was underneath it until the unmasking.

Leonore was waiting for him when he arrived at the foyer. He would have laughed if he had not despair just under his surface calm. She, too, wore a golden mask, covering all but her lips and chin. But she was dressed as a medieval Italian princess, with a tall hennin for a hat, the tip of its cone draped with sheer silk. Her dress was as elaborately brocaded as his domino—gold on red velvet, and its long hanging sleeves were edged with ermine. The bodice of her high-waisted gown was low-cut, and her breasts looked white as cream in contrast to the deep red velvet. St. Vire sighed, wishing he did not have to go to the masquerade, but could stay home instead and explore the contours under her costume.

"My goodness," Leonore said when she turned to look at him. "A dragon?"

"Yes, oh Princess." He bowed, feeling at once relieved and frustrated. "It seems our costumes have dovetailed nicely." She had obviously not been so angry that she felt she must leave immediately. Something was keeping her here, despite her hatred of him. He did not want to hurt her more than he had already. What would make her leave? He did not want to kiss Mercia more than he had to, for she disgusted him.

"Yes," Leonore replied, then looked away from him. "Nicholas, I . . . I am sorry for my outburst this evening. It was wrong of me."

"Well, don't do it again," he made himself reply and detested the way he sounded—petulant and rude. He saw her flinch and hated himself even more.

"Of course," Leonore replied, her voice stiff—with anger, he supposed. He could not tell with the mask over her face. He offered his arm as they moved toward the door, but she did not touch him. He shrugged and opened the door.

When they arrived at Lady Comstock's house, Nicholas sensed Mercia's presence and searched the crowd. It was easy to find her; she wore a costume designed to reveal her charms rather than disguise them. She was dressed as Mozart's Queen of the Night—appropriately, he thought. He glanced at Leonore at his side. Lady Comstock, a respectable woman, would not invite people like those who had attended the Harlowe's masquerade; Leonore should be safe from any seducers. He left her to go to Mercia.

She knew who he was immediately—she was of his kind, after all. Her eyes measured him, and her lips widened in a smile.

"A dragon. Does it bite, I wonder?" Mercia murmured.

He bowed and kissed the cool flesh of her hand. "Yes, most definitely," he replied.

"All the time?"

"Surely, you know the fairy tales."

"No, tell me." She took a step closer and briefly touched his chest with her fingers.

"Dragons eat only princesses."

"Ah, I am safe, then, for I am a queen, as you see."

He made himself smile intimately at her. "But queens were often once princesses, so you are not safe at all." He noticed the young Sir Adrian Hambly was not at her side. "Especially when her young knight is not by to guard her."

Mercia shrugged slightly and let out a sad sigh. "Alas, my poor knight is . . . indisposed. He has not been well of late."

Nicholas clenched his teeth. No doubt she had drained the young man to the point of illness—or death. She had not changed at all; she was still the greedy, careless bitch she'd always been. She could use her body like a drug and cast a glamour so that her victims could not leave her. Utter hatred made him bare his teeth, but he turned it into a wide, avaricious grin.

"Then you are wholly unprotected. Beware, oh Queen! Dragons can carry off such ladies and devour them whole."

Mercia laughed. "But I have been known to ride dragons and so cannot be harmed." The musicians at the other end of the room started up their instruments. Nicholas put Mercia's hand on his arm and led her to the dance floor.

He smiled slightly and bent to her ear. "But you do not attend the opera often, yes? Perhaps you don't remember the end of *The Magic Flute*. Fire consumes the Queen and the earth swallows her up."

She cast him a sharp look through her mask. "Is that a warning, Nicholas?"

"For your own benefit, I assure you."

She frowned, but did not speak, for the figures of the dance separated them. Nicholas looked about him and saw that Leonore was dancing as well. She averted her face, and he was sure she had been looking at him. Now she smiled at the gentlemen who passed her in the dance, and a few of them gazed longer at her than necessary.

Angry heat flashed through Nicholas, and he suddenly realized he was jealous. He pulled his gaze away from Leonore. It was a useless emotion, and he should be glad she had some admirers, for then she would not be lonely once they parted. But the thought of Leonore in another man's arms, someone else kissing her and making love to her caused him to misstep. Clumsy fool! He would not think of what Leonore might do when she left him. It had not happened yet. Better he think of what he must do now rather than . . . he would not think of it.

The dance brought him back to Mercia, and she smiled sweetly at him as he took her hand.

"You are truly the gentleman, Nicholas. I appreciate your warning. But let me give you a warning as well: I grow impatient. It has been many months now, and your little pet wife has still not left you. Be warned that I can strike swiftly and close—as you well know."

Nicholas put on a bored expression. "So you've told me. If I dally with the woman, why should it matter to you? You have your little pets, also, and I know you won't give them up. Why should I?"

Mercia's smile grew hard. "Because they mean nothing to me, and I suspect your little wife means more to you than you say."

"Think what you want. As it is, she has informed me today she hates me, and no doubt she will leave soon."

"Will she?" Mercia gave him a shrewd look. "A jealous wife rarely leaves her husband, it seems to me."

"Oh, she will."

"I am not so sure, my dear Nicholas. But if you have any trouble, I can certainly rid you of her. Shall I demonstrate?"

He gave her an ironic look. "I thank you, no. I believe I can manage my affairs quite well." The dance ended, and an improbably mustachioed Turk eagerly asked Mercia for the next one. She nodded her head at the gentleman, then left Nicholas with a last, sly smile.

He stared after her. He was skirting close to the edge; he could hear the angry impatience in Mercia's voice underneath her slyness. Music began again, and he looked away to find Leonore gazing at him. The next dance was a waltz, and he did not want anyone but himself to dance it with Leonore. But when he went to her side, she turned from him and accepted a gaudily dressed cavalier's hand for the dance.

Nicholas's hands turned to fists at this cut direct from his own wife, but he suppressed the urge to tear her away from her partner. Instead, he turned and asked a lady standing next to him for the waltz. She was a plump lady, disastrously costumed as a sylph, but he did not care. Any woman would have done, only so that he could keep an eye on Leonore. But his partner kept up a flow of chatter to which he must at least reply from time to time. Between that and the whirling steps of the dance, he was not able to keep his eye on Leonore at all.

What a fool he was! He made himself respond properly to his dance partner until the dance ended. He looked for Mercia, but she had disappeared. He breathed a sigh of relief. He felt suddenly tired and wanted to go home. But he had not been here very long, and with Mercia's barely veiled threats, it was unsafe to leave Leonore alone at the ball, either. The ballroom, stuffy and hot, seemed to close in on him. At the very least, he wanted fresh air.

A windowed door, slightly ajar, led out onto a balcony. Quickly, Nicholas slipped out and took off his mask and was glad he did. The cold night air brushed his face; he breathed it in and let it out again, and his breath hung in the air, a light mist upon the darkness. No moon shone in the sky, for clouds had gathered, and a faint humidity promised snow. A frozen breeze wafted through his hair, cooling his disordered thoughts, and he was able to think clearly for once.

He leaned against the low balcony wall, his hands rubbing against the smooth stone. His senses had continued to become more finely honed so that the wall's texture came through clearly to his hand and to his mind. Sometimes a passage of music impressed itself upon his ears and surprised him with such emotion that his breath would catch in his throat.

But he'd thought he would become clearer in his mind as well, and he was not. The spell had not said that emotions would spring upon him like a trap so that he did not know how to escape to cool logic and intellect again. It was not the madness, which used to spin him around, taunting him with the merging of reality and illusion. Though he'd yearned for the ability to touch, hear, and see with a fine, sensitive appreciation again, he'd also been proud of his ability to be detached from the foolishness of emotions. He was a scholar and pursued knowledge and pure objectivity. It was not something he thought he'd be giving up when he regained his senses.

Now, however, he'd gone through the gamut of emotions: hatred, jealousy, and yes, love. He had always done what was expedient and logical. This return of his emotions gave him nothing but trouble, for now he needed to sort through them and had no time in which to do so.

And it was a dangerous thing, for it had caused him to become weak and indecisive, delaying his separation from Leonore. Not only did he have to think, but now his emotions demanded that he consider them as well. He was not, admittedly, good at dealing with them. He sighed. Perhaps that was one consequence of becoming human again. Acting from sheer expediency was a far simpler thing to do.

He would have to be vigilant. He could not let his emotions ruin his plans or endanger Leonore. His thoughts turned to Mercia, and he tamped down the anger he immediately felt. Staying a vampire was inevitable. He needed to think like one.

She had not bothered with Leonore so far, but Mercia was clever and impatient and might kill her soon. For all he knew, Sir Adrian was probably dead by now, or close to it, and everyone would assume the boy had died of some wasting disease. After that, who else would fall before Mercia's seduction? Perhaps she would even punish him, enticing his new friends, and he would see them die, one by one. And then, of course there was Leonore.

He would have to kill Mercia.

Relief washed over him. At last he could take some real action, and he could work toward it, however distasteful. There were many ways to kill a vampire—a long knife through the heart, fire, shutting one in a church, and of course, exposure to sunlight. He'd have to choose the most discreet and, if possible, the least dangerous. Mercia was strong, perhaps as strong as he, especially since he'd begun the spell for becoming human again. He would have to be very careful, but he was sure he could do it. Just a little more time, and Mercia would be dead.

Nicholas smiled grimly, put on his dragon mask, and entered the ballroom again.

Leonore refused to watch Nicholas cross the room. She was sure he had recognized Lady Lazlo somehow—perhaps they had arranged an assignation. Her face heated with anger, and she was glad the mask covered her face. If an amalgam of hatred and love could exist in her heart, surely it was a poisonous one, for it made her feel ill. She wished she hadn't apologized to him, wished she had not come to the masquerade at all. *Coward! Have you already forgotten your resolve to turn away your attention from him?* She took a deep breath and smiled at a passing pirate, who responded by asking her to dance.

She made sure to dance every dance that was asked of her, for it kept her occupied and did not allow Nicholas to approach her even if he wanted to. But she could not dance forever, and Leonore's legs finally trembled with fatigue. She sat on a nearby chair and politely refused one gentleman's offer of yet another dance. Unfurling her fan, she began to wave it, but it was taken from her hand and waved for her. She looked up. Nicholas.

He wore his mask still, and he did not smile. Yet, the tension she had sensed about him had lightened somehow. She wished she knew what had occurred to make him so, or even what had caused his strained manner of late. Leonore looked away from him. She should keep herself unconcerned with his affairs. The veil upon her hat stirred, and she felt Nicholas's breath close to her ear.

"Leonore," he said softly. "Let us go home. I do not wish to be here."

Relief washed over her. He had danced only once with Lady Mercia and had not disappeared with her tonight. Perhaps his affair with her was over. She bit her lip. How foolish she was! She should not hope so soon.

"Yes," she replied and rose from her chair.

Snow fell in thick, wet flakes as they stepped out of Lady Comstock's house into the carriage. Leonore was glad she had chosen the costume she wore, for it was heavy velvet and the ermine at her sleeves kept her arms and hands warm. Nicholas sat close to her, and she allowed it, even welcomed it. The barrier that had been between them seemed to have dropped for the moment, though she had all the reason in the world to want to keep it between them. She did not want to be hurt again, after all. Having Nicholas's leg pressed next to hers was comforting somehow, and the lack of tension in his body—tension that had seemed ever-present for the past four months—made her own body relax as well.

Neither of them spoke. Leonore did not know how long this comfort would last and was reluctant to disturb it. She gazed at Nicholas; he glanced at her, then sighed. But he put his arm around her shoulders and pulled her close to him, while his other hand took her hand and held it tightly.

By the time they arrived home, the snow had collected thickly upon the street. Nicholas put his hand under her elbow, steadying her as she stepped down. Carefully watching her feet so that she would not slip, she made her way to the door. But then Nicholas's sharp gasp made her look up and her hand flew to her mouth to suppress a scream.

The snow had covered most of the body that leaned against the door, but it did not cover the blood seeping from Edmonds's neck, or conceal the odd angle of his head and the open, sightless eyes.

Nicholas's arms came around her and pulled her close to him. Leonore burrowed her head into his chest, trying to block out the image still before her eyes. She heard odd, whimpering sounds and realized they were coming from herself. Her breath came fast, and she swallowed the rising nausea in her throat. Nicholas spoke, whispering something harsh, then his voice rose.

"Grimes, take her ladyship around to the back of the house and make sure she is safely inside."

"Y-yes, yer lordship." Leonore could hear the groom clear his throat. "Cor, is 'e dead, then, yer lordship?"

"Yes. Now snap to it, man! Take her ladyship inside." Nicholas pushed Leonore away from him slightly and stared at her. Dread showed clear in his eyes. "Get inside, Leonore. I will attend to this." She did not move. "Go, now." He gave her a push toward the carriage.

Leonore climbed shakily into it. She felt numb, not conscious of cold, and not remembering how she got to her sitting room once she entered the house. She felt a warm cup pressed into her hand and looked up into her maid's frightened eyes.

She took a sip of tea, then made herself sit up straight. Leonore dared not rise, for her shaking legs could not possibly hold her up. She put a firm, confident expression on her face, and pressed Betty's hand.

"You have heard. . . ."

"Yes, my lady. Mr. Edmonds, he . . . He . . ." The maid's voice shook. "Oh, Gawd, my lady, I'm that scared. Are we going to be killed in our beds?"

"No, of course not. I will not tell you to stop being frightened, Betty, for it is a dreadful thing." Leonore squeezed the maid's hand again reassuringly. "But I am certain it was some robber from whom . . . Edmonds . . . successfully defended us with his life. You may be sure his lordship will take care of it. Perhaps we will pay the watch to pass by our house more often, just in case." She had trouble saying the dead man's name, but she forced herself to say it.

Betty looked a little relieved. "Shall I tell the other servants, my lady?"

"Yes, do. I would not want them disturbed any more than they are already. You may tell them they can have every confidence that Lord St. Vire will make sure it does not happen again."

The maid let out a long sigh. "Yes, my lady." She curtsied and hurried out of the room.

Leonore put down her cup, her hand shaking so that the cup rattled on the saucer. She closed her eyes, leaning against the cushioned back of her chair. The heat from the fireplace seeped into her clothing, and her feet and hands ached with returning warmth. She wanted Nicholas here badly now, though she knew he was probably sending for the authorities. Part of her wanted the comfort of his arms around her so that she could press her face into his chest and block out the image of— No. She would scream if she thought of it.

But more than that, she wanted Nicholas to explain what she had heard whispered from his lips. She had thought he had called upon God for mercy upon Edmonds's soul, but he had repeated the word clearly, and she knew he had not spoken of God at all. It was a name, and one she hated.

"Mercia," he had said. "Mercia."

Chapter 16

God. Oh, God. St. Vire pushed open his chamber door and sank down upon the first chair he saw. He pushed his fingers through his hair, then drew his hands down again to press the palms against his eyes. *What have I done? What in God's name have I done?*

It was all his fault, he knew. Oh, he was certain Mercia had killed his valet. The body had her signature upon it—almost emptied of blood and a broken neck. She sometimes liked to do that last thing: It gave her a sense of power. It was her warning, her threat made real. He should have remembered it; he should have done something to have stopped her.

Too late. He'd set the events in motion with his desire to feel, see, and taste clearly again. He'd been arrogant, starting on the spell without thought of the possible consequences. His new friends were no doubt in danger, and his servants. If he hadn't started this course, Edmonds would not be dead now, and the threat of death would not hang over Leonore's head.

But how was he to know? He had little idea that emotions would rise in him to give birth to a damnably awkward conscience. It had confused him, and he had not been able to act in his customary logical, expedient way. Perhaps Mercia had been playing with him all along, slowly showing him her power and bending him to her will. She would kill Leonore. Not now; Mercia was impatient, but she savored the anticipation of the kill. It was her pattern, the way she always behaved. He'd forgotten it in the long space of time since he'd seen her in Paris. He had hesitated—now look at him! Nicholas pulled at his hair and groaned with self-disgust. He was wallowing in his newfound emotions, self-indulgent like a pig in swill.

Leonore. She was no doubt sitting by herself, frightened, and he had left her alone with her fear. At the very least he could go to her and give her what comfort he could. He'd already spoken with the local magistrate, Sir Justin Blake, with whom he had played many a friendly game of whist. Nicholas was certain the man would do everything possible to settle the matter of Edmonds's death. Then he and Leonore would leave this place, leave London for Avebury.

She was not in her bedroom, so he descended the stairs to her sitting room. At first he did not see her, for the chair in which she sat faced away from the door. A slight movement told him she was there, and he went to her. Her hat was on the floor, and her hair tumbled down around her shoulders. She stared blankly at him, her arms crossed across her chest. She breathed in small gasps, shaking as if with a fever, and her lips trembled.

"Nicholas . . ." she whispered. "Nicholas . . ."

He reached for her and she flinched. A sharp pain raked through his heart at her reaction, but he pulled her up out of the chair and into his arms. Her body was stiff and trembling against him.

"Hush, Leonore, sweet. Hush, my love." Nicholas stroked her hair and her back, and gradually she relaxed. Her breath slowed and became even. He led her to the sofa and cradled her in his lap. He kissed her on her forehead, her cheek, and gently on her mouth. "I've taken care of it. You need not worry; I have talked with Sir Justin—he believes it was some footpad who had overtaken Edmonds as he was coming back from his night out."

A large sigh caused Leonore's shoulders to lift and fall. For one moment she leaned into him.

Her body stiffened. She pushed against him and stumbled from his lap. She stared at him, and pain struck him anew, for her eyes were still frightened.

"Is it, Nicholas? Is it truly taken care of?"

He could not look at her. "Of course. Have I not said it?"

"Yes, but you said something else, earlier, when we found—You said her name."

"Her?"

"Mercia. Lady Lazlo. What does she have to do with this?"

"You must be mistaken." Perhaps he had said it—he did not remember. He remembered thinking Mercia's name when he first gazed at Edmonds's body. He made himself shrug.

"Don't lie to me, Nicholas. Don't lie!" Leonore's voice was low and shaking. He looked into her eyes, and they were filled with fear and anger. "I will not have it, not any longer. No facades, no lies. I cannot turn aside my face from what is happening in our marriage. I have tried, and I cannot."

She turned from him, staring into the fire, her hands clenched. "I do not understand you, Nicholas, though I thought I once did. You lavish gifts upon me and my family; you take me in your arms as if I . . . meant something to you. You kiss Lady Lazlo—I saw it!—and pay attention to her so that the gossip about you grows every day. Now Edmonds is dead, and you say her name when you saw his . . . his body. I don't think it was a footpad, Nicholas. What is the truth? What does Lady Lazlo have to do with your valet?" Leonore turned again, her eyes willing him to speak.

He leaned back upon the sofa, tipping his head and staring at the ceiling. What could he say? That he was a vampire? He loved her, but would she believe him? He wanted to tell her what he was; he had hinted and come close to telling her so many times, had almost blurted it out to her. He felt tired, tired to his very soul, and wished she would leave him alone.

"Go away, Leonore. Did I not tell you long ago that I was a bad man? So I am. This is all my damned fault. You would do better not to live with me. You deserve better."

"I cannot believe you killed your valet. That is nonsense. You were at Lady Comstock's ball tonight. I saw you and so did the other guests. Heaven only knows no one could have ignored that costume of yours." Her voice had calmed and grew steady.

He let out a short, angry laugh. "No, of course I did not murder my own valet. That would have been stupid, for I do not know how I will find another who polishes boots to perfection as he did." He lifted his head and gazed at her, watching her reaction to his sneering words. Her lips pressed together in a thin line before she spoke again.

"Stop it, Nicholas! You are not as vain as you make yourself out to be, either. That is yet another facade you wear, is it not? You act and pose, and none of it is really you."

"So you wish to know what the real Nicholas St. Vire is, eh, Leonore?" He sank back on the sofa and gazed at the ceiling again. God, he was tired of it all. A resentful anger burned in him. It did not matter if she knew what he was. Either way she would hate him, and if she made her repugnance clear to everyone, it might give her some safety. He shrugged and felt infinitely old, infinitely weary.

"I will tell you, my dear. I am a vampire. So is Mercia Lazlo. She killed my valet."

Silence, and then: "Nonsense!"

He raised his head and looked at her. "Really? And what do you know about such things?"

"I have read—"

"Nonsense!" Nicholas said, mimicking the same dismissing, angry voice she had used. He stood up and strode toward her.

Leonore took a step backward. He laughed nastily. "Frightened, are you? And so you should be. Do you think me mad? Perhaps I am. But I tell you, there are things you have not seen or experienced that exist in the world. Angels, demons, sprites, and, yes, vampires."

"No." Leonore stared at him, her breath coming short, and shook her head slowly. "No." Not mad, please not mad, she prayed.

"Oh, yes. Shall I show you?" He muttered some words, and a strange lizardlike creature blazed in the palm of his hand. "Can you—or anyone else—do this?" He threw the fiery creature into the fireplace, and the fire blazed high for a moment. "Or this?" He seized a poker and bent it in half, easily. He tossed it away from him, and it clanged upon the floor. She flinched at the sound and closed her eyes. A shudder went through her, and she stared wildly at him again.

"Not real," she whispered. "It is not real." It could not be—she was in a nightmare, she was sure. She swallowed. It was some kind of trick. Or perhaps she, herself, had gone mad. "If you are a vampire as you say, then your teeth—?" she said reasonably. A hysterical giggle almost bubbled from her lips. How ridiculous it sounded. But she looked at the fire and at the bent iron poker still before her, and dread seeped into her.

A frustrated expression crossed Nicholas's face. "So you cannot see them? But I can. Every time I look in the mirror, I can see what I am."

The mirror. Leonore remembered their wedding night when he had "accidentally" broken the mirror, the shards of glass—another mirror, she knew now—in his attic library. And the books in the library, the books of magic. She swallowed the fear that rose in her. No, no, he was teasing her, surely.

She looked into his eyes and saw no teasing there, only anger and despair. Her breath came out in a moan. All the things she had known since she had wed Nicholas—his condition, the way the sunlight hurt him, how he could not go out except at night. . . . And he was pale, more than was fashionable, though with his elegant appearance, all London assumed it was fashion. But surely, surely not . . .

Nicholas laughed again, a short and despairing noise. "Still you do not believe me!" He stepped closer to her, his eyes still angry and now abruptly intent. "You have read gothic novels, Leonore. Shall I show you how vampires use their teeth?"

Sharp fear and trembling shook her, but Leonore breathed deeply and stilled herself. "You will not, Nicholas. You will not, I know it." She did not know what made her say it, but her words were an acceptance of everything: the death of Edmonds, what Nicholas told her, here, now. Reality sank into her, sharp as a knife. She saw everything clearly, then tears obscured her vision. Grief pierced through her—she was dying, surely.

His fingers came up to caress her cheek and feathered down her neck. She shivered with both desire and fear and nearly wept with confusion and growing despair. His hand curved around her throat.

"But I have done it, my dear wife. Most certainly I have. Right here—" He tenderly stroked the hollow above her collarbone. "So soft . . . sweet."

"You will not," she repeated. "Not now." She spoke slowly, feeling her way through her emotions toward something deep within that she could not quite name. Her fear had somehow dissipated, leaving her numb, yet oddly clear-minded.

"How do you know that?" His voice turned sneering. "Did you not accuse me of betraying you?" His hand tightened.

She closed her eyes, then stared at him, at his angry eyes, full of self-loathing. "You care for me. You have said it, you have acted upon it, even when it was not necessary and even after your so-called betrayal." His hand fell from her throat.

"Oh, God. Oh, God, Leonore," he sighed, his breath ragged, and his mouth descended swiftly—to her lips. His lips moved across hers, and he kissed her deeply, sweetly. He parted from her, caressing her hip, bringing her close to him. "I am mad, I have lost all my reason, surely you know that."

She should run from him instead of standing here, letting him hold her. She closed her eyes. Surely she was mad, also. But madman or vampire, she did not care. She let him caress her, let him kiss her mouth, her cheek, her neck. He paused there, and she drew a deep, convulsive breath.

"Do it, Nicholas," she whispered. "If you are a vampire, do it."

A harsh sigh, almost a sob, broke from him, and he brought his lips down swiftly to her throat. She could feel his tongue touch her skin. She trembled, half in fear, half in desire, for the sensations were no different from when he had made love to her. His teeth slowly, sharply, scraped across the flesh of her neck.

A deep groan came from him, and he pushed her, hard, away from him. She stumbled and fell upon her knees.

"Go away. Go away, Leonore, before I hurt you." He raked his fingers through his hair, turning from her. Leonore pulled herself up and stood.

"You are not a vampire."

Nicholas gave a short, breathless laugh. "Oh, yes, I am. You don't know how close I came to drinking your blood this time. You truly don't. I can't wake before sunrise, for the sunlight will kill me, and if I enter a church I will experience an agony so intense that I will wish I were dead. Do you remember? I fainted like a vaporish bride at the wedding."

"Why did you marry me?"

"I did not want to be a vampire anymore."

There, he had said it. Relief flowed over Nicholas, making him feel dizzy. He had told her everything, what he was and why he had married her. She had not run from him, not yet. The leaden feeling that had lodged in his chest almost disappeared, and he felt light. He paced restlessly before the fireplace.

"Do you know what it is like, to have all your senses dulled? It is like seeing through a veil, touching through a glove. I hear, but melodies escape me; I taste, but no flavors stay on my tongue." He glanced at Leonore, who stood beside a chair, clutching it. "That is what it's like, being a vampire . . . except when the bloodthirst comes. Everything becomes sharp for the hunt, and only then. It is a madness. Soon the desire for sensation overcomes you, and you begin to live for the bloodlust, and slowly a vampire becomes mad."

"Of course, you would not want to become deranged," Leonore said, her voice a whisper.

"No, no, I did not," Nicholas said eagerly. Perhaps she understood; perhaps it would not matter to her. "I found a spell, one that would make me human again."

"And I was to be part of it, is that it?"

"Yes, it was necessary, necessary that you come to me willingly. . . ." He stopped, for Leonore was staring at him, her face still and white.

"How I hate you," she said.

Nicholas held out his hand to her, almost touching her, but she flinched from him. "Please, Leonore, I—"

"Don't touch me." She stepped back from him.

His breath left him. Of course. Of course, he could not expect it of her, that she would accept him, the monster that he was.

"I see," he said, swallowing the hope that had risen in him. "I see." The energy his confession had given him fell away, and he felt tired once again. He turned from her, not wanting to look at her. "I suppose it is best that you leave, or I."

He heard only a whisper of her yes before the door shut behind her.

Leonore did not know what she felt as she ran up the stairs to her room. Confusion, certainly; rage, repugnance, grief, horror, betrayal, and loss. And that persistent thing she should not feel: desire. She had told him she hated him, and indeed, she hated how she had been used and manipulated. But it was more a hatred and disgust for herself.

Her desire for him sickened her. She still wanted him even now—he, a creature that preyed upon others for their blood, a monster. When he had taken her in his arms, had kissed her and pressed his lips against her cheek and throat, she had kissed him in return and experienced the beginnings of the melting heat she always felt when he made love to her.

It was not just physical desire. She had looked into Nicholas's eyes, then offered her blood to him. She was a fool, and that sickened her, too. Still she had trusted him, believing he would not take what she offered.

And he had not. He had touched her neck with his tongue and his teeth, had kissed her gently, but that was all. Almost she could make herself believe that it was not true, that he was not a vampire and that magic did not exist. But there was that queer fiery creature he had held in his hand, and the poker he had bent in half. She also remembered the rosebud he had summoned from behind her ear and pinned to her gown. She had taken off the rosebud and put it in water . . . and it had bloomed and stayed fresh for three weeks. She had thought it was a special variety of rose, for no cut rose she had ever seen lasted that long.

Then there was Edmonds. She shuddered at the image that rose before her eyes and shook her head to dispel it. Nicholas blamed himself, but he could not have killed the servant, for Edmonds had been killed tonight—no, last night, for a glance at the clock in her room told her it was long past midnight. Nicholas had been at the ball the whole time; she had seen him except for a few short minutes. It took half an hour by carriage to reach their home. No one could have done the deed so swiftly whatever they might be.

Leonore pressed her hand to her head, wanting to press down her confusion. Nicholas had said Mercia had killed the servant. How could that be? It was true the woman had left before they had, for Leonore had seen Lord Eldon escort her out. But Lady Lazlo was a slight, petite woman, and she could not see how it was possible for her to kill a tall, strapping young man like Edmonds. Perhaps she had hired some ruffians to do the deed, but why she should want to kill a servant, Leonore could not tell. Perhaps the woman was mad. Or a vampire

She shuddered. It was late. Nothing made sense to her. Surely, she would understand better in the morning.

Leonore did not ring for her maid, for she did not want to disturb the servants more than they had been already. They would be near useless with fatigue tomorrow, for they would not be able to sleep well after Edmonds's death. She removed her costume herself, slowly, for it was heavy. But when she touched the white lawn nightgown that lay upon her bed, she dropped her hand from it.

She would not be able to sleep either, for she was sure the image of Edmonds's dead body would rise before her closed eyes and give her nightmares. She gazed at the connecting door to Nicholas's room and wished she did not know what he was so that she could feel comforted if he came to her bed. He would not come to her tonight, not after what she had told him, that she hated him. She shuddered. She did not know how she would react if he did and did not want to find out.

Indeed, she did not know what she would do. Nicholas had said she should leave. He would not want her, not now. A bursting grief rose in her, and Leonore let out a sobbing breath. It was grief for the illusions she had held of him, of course. She reached for her nightgown again. It caught on her elbow as she pulled the sleeve over her arm, for her hand still shook.

She had lost all control and could not stop herself from shaking. At last she had on her gown, and she climbed into her bed. The bedclothes had a slight, residual warmth from the warming pan that Betty had slid between the sheets, but still Leonore shivered. Her feet were freezing, and she shifted them to try and warm them.

She shuddered and shuddered again. Her eyes squeezed tight, and she put her arms around herself, pretending that Nicholas's arms were around her and that he was not a vampire. She craved him still, wanted the comfort of his body, the soothing way he stroked her hair and kissed her. She felt ill. She needed to leave this house, for she did not know what else to do.

Susan. . . . She would talk with Susan. She had grown into a sensible young lady. Of course, Leonore could not tell her that Nicholas was a vampire. But her sister loved her, and she could take comfort in that.

Tomorrow morning she would leave to stay in her parents' house. She didn't know how long . . . perhaps a week, or more. No doubt Nicholas would let it about that her nerves had suffered a severe shock from finding Edmonds murdered upon their doorstep, and that she felt too frightened to sleep at home. Nonsense, of course, and she despised such stratagems. But she supposed one must resort to them to keep up appearances.

Appearances. The curtain was rising once more, and now she must act yet another part. There was no escaping it, was there? She let out a breath and let her muscles ease into the soft mattress.

All the world's a stage, she remembered. But she wished the play would end so that she need not put on another mask.

Chapter 17

"I do not believe you."

"Why not?" Nicholas murmured against Mercia's ear. He trailed his finger along her jaw to her lips. She half closed her eyes and bit his finger, drawing blood. He felt a slight, sharp pain and almost frowned. His senses had not dulled, but stayed the same, though Leonore had been away a week. "My little pet Leonore has run from me and will not return. She told me she hates me and no doubt you, too. How could she not? She is jealous of you, for her own looks cannot compare to yours."

"Almost you convince me, Nicholas." Mercia said his name lingeringly, drawing out the last syllable in her lilting foreign voice. She pulled at the lapels of his coat so that he sat next to her on the chaise longue in her drawing room. "But how do I know you do not go to her when I am not watching?"

He took her hand and brought it to his lips. "You don't. You must trust me, of course." He gave her a wide smile.

Mercia pouted. "But I cannot trust you at all! You killed Louis, after all, and you took a wife not long ago."

"That again! But you must know it was because of sheer jealousy on my part that I disposed of Louis, for you would not leave him. Would you not have done the same?" He ran his hand along her neck, rubbing his thumb just at the base of her throat.

I could kill her now. But that would be a foolish, for her servants knew he was there. Mercia guarded herself well.

"Yes, of course." She nodded, then frowned. "But then there is your wife."

"Really, Mercia, I have told you she has left me," Nicholas

said, making his voice sound bored. "What would you have me do? I will not cause more scandal. Be content with what you have."

"And what do I have?" Lady Lazlo rose from the chaise longue and waved her hand at him in an impatient gesture. "You have not even come to my bed! What am I to think of that?"

St. Vire gave her an ironic smile. "You do not appreciate me, my dear, or my desires. You well know the deliciousness of anticipation. Isn't that how you use your . . . lovers? Slowly, you entice them until they are in your spell, and you draw out the killing to a fine edge until the end. Now why am I not allowed this in something less . . . final?"

"Is that what you are doing now, Nicholas? Drawing me out?"

"Why, yes." He pushed up her chin and kissed her, sliding his hand under her breasts. Her lips were cold as death. He wondered how Leonore could have borne his embrace if she felt the same repugnance for him that he now felt for Mercia.

"Mmm." Mercia gave him a sly smile. "Perhaps I will let you draw it out and let you seduce me. That might be amusing."

"Amusing . . . and tantalizing." He smiled at her and felt a rising nausea in the pit of his stomach. The devil only knew how long he would be able to stand pandering to Mercia's wishes. Long ago he could act out of expediency and occasional lust. But he had changed, and it took all his will to act as he had before.

"But I only said 'perhaps.' " Mercia twisted one curl of her black hair around her finger, her brow furrowed in apparent thought. "The thought of your wife is most distracting to me. The idea of trust—a difficult concept. I need a little security, you see. A show of loyalty. Perhaps if you shared your little pet, or eliminated her entirely, I would be content." She looked at him with cold eyes and smiled softly. "In three days. That would be a good amount of time, yes?"

Fear for Leonore almost choked him. Nicholas let out a long

breath and hoped the sigh sounded bored. That was it, then. Mercia would wait no longer.

"Oh, very well!" he said, making his voice petulant. "But I don't see your doing the same thing. In fact, I am sure you will find yourself another lover in time."

Mercia's smile widened in delight. "You are jealous!"

He took her hand and bit one fingertip. "Yes, of course."

"How wonderful! Will you do it straightaway?"

"Tomorrow," St. Vire replied and took his leave.

"I do not think I have heard you play that sonata before, Susan," said Jeremy Fordham to his betrothed.

"It is new," Susan said, smiling at him as she played. A maid lit a brace of candles against the coming dusk, and it shed a soft light upon Susan, making her hair a golden halo. Leonore could hear Mr. Fordham's sigh clearly from across the room.

Leonore glanced at the couple before her and set another stitch in her embroidery. Mr. Fordham—Jeremy—leaned upon the pianoforte, his eyes going from Susan's hair to her lips and eyes. He had followed her to the instrument, his hand reaching out, but stopping short before he touched her. He was clearly in love with her sister.

Leonore sighed and looked down at her hands in her lap. She missed Nicholas.

After a week had gone by, that was the only sure conclusion to which Leonore could come. She'd gained some objectivity away from him, and so was glad she had come to her father's house for a while. Besides, she needed to help with Susan's wedding arrangements since her mother seldom felt energetic enough to attend to them.

Then, too, she was able to stay away from most of the *ton*'s inquiring eyes. The report of Edmonds's death had spread, and the curious came to call. She played the part of the vaporish wife; Nicholas had let it out that his wife had suffered a tremendous shock from the discovery of the body. Of course she could not think of entering the St. Vire house for some time to come.

But Nicholas had not come once to her during the week she was gone. She was sure the gossips had noticed this, and she was glad for once that her situation gave her the excuse not to venture forth into society.

A week in her father's house reminded her why she had so eagerly left. Jeremy would take care of Susan now that they were betrothed, so she need not worry about her. But her mother still took to her bed with the megrims, and her father still came home intoxicated. She had felt her old stiff wariness return, and the wish that she were back with Nicholas cried clear in her heart.

How could she care for a creature like Nicholas? He was a vampire, impossible and horrifying. He had even taken her blood, though she didn't clearly remember it. Everything had fallen into place when he told her his true nature, and she understood the things she had glimpsed of him since the day she met him.

Laughter came from the couple at the pianoforte, and Leonore watched them, smiling slightly. Jeremy leaned forward and whispered in Susan's ear, and she giggled. He had a confident and elegant air—except when he was around Susan. Leonore almost laughed. He had a reputation as a ladies' man, but his usual grace of manner often fell from him and his speech stumbled a little when he spoke to Susan. It was as if he were so eager to please her that he couldn't decide quite what to do with himself.

It was a charming attribute, actually, Leonore thought. That and his obvious protectiveness over Susan made him an endearing young man. She had seen this protectiveness when her father had passed by them in the park the day after his rage. Jeremy had taken Susan's hand in a reassuring grip. Leonore knew she had little to fear for her sister once Susan was wed.

A familiar chord rang in her, one she had felt before when she had witnessed Jeremy propose to Susan. She thought of what it would mean for Susan to wed him, and how different it was from her own marriage.

But was it? Leonore gazed at her sister and Jeremy, thought of the young man's kindness, of how he had a protective air whenever he was near Susan. Her sister's words about Nicholas suddenly came to her. She had spoken of Nicholas's undeniable generosity and kindness. Leonore had thanked him once for a little toy sheep he had put upon her pillow for her to find. He had said it was a trifle, but he'd looked away from her briefly, as if embarrassed, and his hand's dismissing gesture had seemed awkward. Another laugh from the pianoforte made Leonore look up.

"Oh, Jeremy, how you tease! You know I cannot sing as well as I play. Even you sing better than I do."

"*Even* I? I thank you—I think." Mr. Fordham grinned.

A mischievous smile crossed Susan's lips. "You are welcome. It is the reason I consented to marry you, you see. We shall make a fine duet."

"And that is the only reason?" Jeremy reached over and ran his finger across Susan's cheek and over her lips. Susan blushed brightly, and he laughed.

Leonore bent her head over her needlework to hide her smile. Nicholas had teased her also and seemed to like to touch her face as Jeremy did to Susan. She glanced again at the couple at the pianoforte. She saw Susan's blush turn fiery and Jeremy's too innocent gaze at the ceiling. They must have exchanged a quick kiss when she was not looking. She bit her lip to keep from laughing and bent to her stitching with more diligence. The signs were obvious. He was deeply in love with Susan; Leonore was sure he would be a good, kind husband, like Nicholas.

A quick trembling shot through her, and her needle stabbed the ball of her thumb. She gasped. Susan and Jeremy looked up at the sound.

"It is nothing, really," Leonore said, smiling wryly, and took a handkerchief from her pocket. "I was clumsy and stuck my finger with my needle."

"Shall I get some sticking plaster, Leonore?" Susan asked.

"No, no, it has stopped bleeding already. Please, do play something on the pianoforte, Susan, and never mind me."

Susan raised her eyebrows, but Leonore smiled and shook

her head. Susan turned to the instrument again, drawing forth a light, tinkling melody.

Leonore wound her handkerchief around her thumb and closed her fingers over it tightly. Nicholas *had* been a kind husband. He had said he cared for her. She had not thought it, had not dared think that perhaps he loved her. Was it even possible that a creature like himself could do so? He had lavished gifts upon her, and she remembered seeing a disappointed look in his eyes whenever he thought one of his gifts had not pleased her. He had touched her the way Jeremy touched Susan, tenderly, as if she were precious to him, and more.

Nicholas comforted her a week ago, just after they had found Edmonds upon their doorstep. He had cradled her in his lap and stroked her hair, kissing her gently until her trembling had passed. He had done this before when she had been distressed.

A laugh came from Jeremy this time, making Leonore look up again. She watched Susan shake her head at his teasing. There was no reason why she could not have this with Nicholas, surely.

But he is a vampire, a monster, Leonore, have you forgotten that? said a small voice within her. No, she had not forgotten. But were his kindness and gentleness different because of it? Did she love him any differently now from before she knew what he was? She wet her lips, suddenly dry. No. No, she did not.

But Nicholas admitted that he had sought to marry her—to use her—because he no longer wished to be a vampire. If Lady Lazlo had not come to London, would Nicholas have told her what he was?

Ah, that was the crux of it, was it not? Lady Lazlo, whom Nicholas had said he disliked, but whom he had kissed and paid attention to as if she were his mistress—they had even talked of a liaison between them. What was she to Nicholas?

Somehow, Lady Lazlo had killed Edmonds. She was dangerous. Why did Nicholas pay such attention to her and neglect his own wife for all of London society to see? And yet, he still touched her, Leonore, as if he loved her when they were private at home.

Oh, dear heaven. Abruptly, Leonore rose from her chair, almost upsetting it.

"What is it, Leo?" Susan's voice sounded worried. Leonore focused on her sister's anxious face and Jeremy's concerned one.

"Oh . . . nothing, truly. I . . . I have been thinking it is time I returned to Nicholas . . . I have recovered from my nervousness about the . . . the incident at our house, and believe I should be with my husband now, instead of here. I . . . I should go back."

"If you wish it, Leo," Susan replied, looking at her curiously. "I know I can manage the wedding preparations myself now, for you have arranged it perfectly."

"Yes, yes, of course. If you will excuse me?" Leonore left the drawing room, hurriedly going up the stairs to gather her belongings for her return home—to Nicholas.

It was not quite dusk when she entered Nicholas's room, her lamp held high to guide her to his bed. She drew away the curtains, watching him sleep. She would tell him she understood, that she would not leave him again. Perhaps he would tell her he loved her, for she remembered how he called her his love. What else was he doing but protecting her from Lady Lazlo?

For that was surely what Nicholas had been doing. Leonore hadn't understood why he blew hot and cold upon her, pouring gifts into her hands and lavishing his caresses upon her body in private, and then abandoning her for Lady Lazlo's side in public. Lady Lazlo's languishing looks upon Nicholas clearly told her the woman's feelings. And if she were so dangerous that she killed Nicholas's valet, then it would be nothing to her to kill Nicholas's wife as well.

Nicholas knew Mercia and surely knew what she would do. Was it so improbable that he would send Leonore away from him so that Mercia would think him enamored of her, and leave Leonore alone? She gazed at her husband as he slept, waiting for the night to rouse him.

After what seemed an age, Nicholas stirred and turned toward her. He opened his eyes slowly, then he caught sight of her. Joy and consternation flashed across his face, then he frowned, pushing himself up from his pillows.

"Why have you returned?" he demanded.

His abruptness took her aback, for her mind had been filled with images of a joyous reunion. Foolishness, of course.

"I—I had to come back, Nicholas. I did not want to stay away from you. I don't hate you, truly I don't. I was angry and confused. . . ." Her voice faded away at his despairing look.

"You cannot stay here, Leonore. You must leave."

"Lady Lazlo—"

"Are you thinking she is my mistress? Then I wonder you are here."

"Is she, Nicholas?" Leonore took his face between her hands and gazed at him intently. Nicholas stared at her and said nothing. She drew close to him and pressed her lips to his. "Kiss me, then see if you can tell me. I know you will not lie."

A low groan blew against her lips, and Nicholas pulled her down upon the bed, kissing her deeply. He kissed her as if he could not have enough of her, held her close to him as if he wanted to take her into himself.

"I'm not good for you, Leonore; I have harmed you more than you know," he murmured against her neck.

"Tell me, Nicholas." She pushed back a lock of hair from his forehead. "Tell me."

"I should not have married you— Oh, God. She is mad. She will kill you if she finds you here." His eyes closed tightly as if in pain.

"Edmonds . . ."

His eyes opened wide with desperation. "Yes. Yes, like Edmonds." He moved away from her and sat up, running his fingers through his hair in a tired gesture. "But she wants *me* to kill you—tonight."

Leonore became still as cold ice clamped around her chest. "Does she?"

"Yes, the bit—Yes, she does." Nicholas rose from the bed and paced restlessly in front of the fireplace. "We must leave. She cannot find us together here. I have tried to find a way to get rid of her, but it's risky; she's too well guarded. Perhaps at home, at Avebury, you will be safe for a time, for I have set strong wards upon it." He groaned. "Though whether it will work against Mercia, I do not know."

He could kill me. Then: *No, no he would not. I must trust him.* But she was not used to trusting anyone, and the trust she had developed for Nicholas was too new and too recently shaken. *He could have killed me a long time ago if he were truly enamored of Lady Lazlo. He will not do it, he will not.*

"We must leave now, tonight." Nicholas turned to her and grasped her hands. "Pack quickly."

"But to Avebury! It will take two days! You cannot—"

He gave a short laugh. "Only in easy stages. But not if I drive! I always have horses stabled along the road. It will be uncomfortable for you and will take all night, but we'll arrive there before the dawn." He shoved her gently toward her room. "Go, now!"

Leonore ran to her wardrobe and pulled out dresses at random. She scarcely knew or cared what she put in her bandboxes.

By the time she was done and ready, the strings of her bandboxes held firmly in her hand, Nicholas was at the door. He wore a heavy greatcoat and boots and held a long riding whip. He gazed at her and let out a laugh. "Only two bandboxes?"

"I hurried, as you requested."

"Surely you cannot have many dresses in those. I will be surprised if you have any clothes to wear once we arrive."

"I did not think you would mind that," she snapped. She did not want to talk, for her nerves were on edge. She wanted to leave now.

He laughed again and grinned at her. "No, I suppose I would not mind at all."

They descended the steps of the house, and Leonore glanced at the carriage, then stared.

"A curricle! You must be mad!"

"Perhaps. But it is light and fast, and easier to get two horses changed instead of four. I think it will get us home in good time. You need not worry. I do know how to drive one, though I do not get much of an opportunity since it is a thing one tends to drive during the day."

"But how will you see? There is no lantern."

Nicholas gave her a crooked smile. "I am a vampire. I can see very well in the dark."

Leonore merely nodded and put her foot on the step of the carriage. He helped her into it and jumped up beside her.

"My only concern is that you will become frozen as we drive," he said, wrapping a fur rug around her.

"I shall be quite well, I assure you." She held up a large, heavy cloth bag. "Hot bricks. They heated in the fire while I packed."

Nicholas smiled and brought her gloved hand to his lips. "Admirable. Although I am afraid they won't last the whole journey."

"I will manage." Leonore waved toward the horses. "Let us go."

He gathered up the reins, and with a light flick of the whip the horses went forward.

All the snow of last week had disappeared, and an unseasonably warm sun had dried the streets yesterday. Leonore was thankful for that. Snow would have made their journey more hazardous. They wove their way through the streets and the traffic. The *ton* was out in force, seeking the night's entertainment. She could hear Nicholas muttering impatiently under his breath at the delays. His greatcoat's collar was up around his face, and his hat low upon his head. Only his eyes showed and flashed green when some errant light caught them.

Then they were through, and the road opened. Nicholas flicked his whip, and the horses picked up the pace. Leonore clutched the side of the carriage. She could hardly see in front of them, for though a gibbous moon shone in the sky, thin wisps of clouds obscured it from time to time and dimmed its light. But the whip flicked out again, and the horses began to gallop.

Nicholas let out a breathless, exhilarated laugh. "I have not done this in a long while," he said.

"That does not inspire me with confidence, I assure you,"

Leonore retorted. The wind whipped her hat, and she pushed it firmly upon her head. They were traveling, doing *something* to get away from Lady Lazlo's threats. At least they were taking action, and this lifted Leonore's spirits.

"Try to sleep. It will make the journey seem to go faster." She could hear the smile in Nicholas's voice.

"Sleep? I will be jolted to pieces by the time we arrive in Avebury."

But the curricle was well-sprung and bowled smoothly over the road. Leonore snuggled down into the furs. She did not sleep, but she did drowse, only to awake when they went over a rut in the road or when they stopped to change horses.

One last jolt brought her fully awake. The bricks had gone cold many stops ago as Nicholas had warned her, and her feet felt frozen in her boots. She looked at him, his face relentless in concentration. He stared into the night almost unblinkingly, his lips pressed together in a hard line.

There was no light on the horizon, but Leonore could hear early morning birds chirping above the sound of the carriage wheels. Fear rose in her. If they did not reach his house in time, Nicholas would surely die.

A large, dark shape loomed before them, and she heard him breathe a sigh of relief. "We are home," he said. He drove the carriage around to the back of the house to the stables, where a stable boy stumbled out and stared at them, wide-eyed.

"I am St. Vire. Take the horses and rub them down," Nicholas said to the boy.

"Y-yes, yes, yer lordship!" The boy scurried over to the horses' heads.

Nicholas leaped from the carriage and helped her down. Leonore was glad of his aid; she groaned when she stood up, for her back was sore sitting so long and her legs tingled with cold. She stumbled as she descended, but Nicholas caught her.

"Clumsy of me," she said. "I did not think I would be so tired. I am sorry."

He smiled. "I am sorry, too. Come, let us get some rest." He lifted her easily into his arms.

"Nicholas! Put me down!"

He laughed, and for the first time she thought she heard joy in it. "No. I wish to carry my bride over the threshold of my home. I wish it could be the front door, but I am afraid the door from the stables will have to do." Leonore could feel her face grow warm with blushes. She was glad it was too dark for him to see—and then she blushed even more, for she realized he *could* see in the dark.

"But you must be tired, too," she said.

"Only a little." He pushed open the door with his foot. "I am afraid there are few servants here, only for the stables and for maintaining the house. I don't even think I have a cook here." He set her down again on the other side of the threshold. "Welcome to Avebury." He kissed her.

She smiled at him. "Thank you. Shall you want some tea?"

Nicholas laughed. "Ever practical. No, though if you wish some, feel free to have some yourself. The kitchen is to the right; if you are lucky, you might find a scullery maid to brew you a cup. Please excuse me, however. I need to see to the horses; I hope the hard driving has not harmed them."

"I can manage, I am sure," replied Leonore.

"Of course." He moved toward the stables, then turned. "And ask to have the blue room prepared for you. It's next to mine in the west wing. You'll have to walk a bit; it's on the other side of the house. The servants stay on this side."

The stable boy was rubbing down one of the horses when Nicholas entered the stable. He nodded at the boy and checked the horses. Both were breathing easily now, and both were munching their feed contentedly. He patted one on the back, and the horse flinched and moved away. Nicholas sighed. He liked horses, but they did not like him, for he was sure they sensed his predatory nature.

But St. Vire's heart was light. Leonore had come back to him, and she did not hate him—or so she said. That was something good, even though it was a complication—Mercia would follow them once she understood he had not killed Leonore. There was hope, too. He had returned home, his birthplace, his own territory. Here his strength was greater, his magic more potent. The environs of Avebury was a place of much power, more ancient than his own vampiric nature—older than Mercia, who had lived for more than a hundred years. The closer he was to his home, the stronger he felt, though a fast, hard journey would have tired him greatly, and would have exhausted a human. If it came to a contest of strength, surely he could kill Mercia as easily as she could kill a human. She would be foolish to come here, for she must know he would be the stronger if they fought.

He smiled, his heart lightening even more. He would not mind staying in Avebury with Leonore. He could pursue his studies in magic and have his books brought here from town. The evenings he could spend with Leonore would be comfortable, with no pretence between them. She knew what he was and had come back to him. Perhaps, despite her week's absence, the spell could continue and he could become human once again.

If, of course, Mercia did not come. He would have to study the ways to keep vampires away from his lands, so that if he became human again, she would not come back to overpower him and hurt Leonore. St. Vire sighed. Or kill Mercia.

He gave the stable boy one last approving nod and left the stables. He took the stairs two at a time, eager to see Leonore again. Perhaps she would be in bed already, but he wanted to be sure she was comfortable. Then he would begin his studies.

A brace of candles lit her room, and though a fire flickered in the hearth, he shivered when he strode into the room toward the curtained bed. It was almost as if a cold draft had blown through it, for the back of his neck prickled. . . .

"Nichola-as . . ."

His breath left him, and he froze as fear caught his throat, almost choking him. The voice—low, lilting, and foreign—

"Mercia." Her name came from him in a low, feral hiss. He turned and heard her soft laughter.

"I thought I might come to welcome you . . . and your little *pet* . . . to this most gracious home."

Oh, God, no.

Mercia had one slim hand around Leonore's neck so that her head arched back. Her thumb moved back and forth above the quick pulse at his wife's throat. It would be so easy for Mercia to kill Leonore—one quick movement. . . .

Nicholas made himself smile slightly. "A trifle . . . vulgar . . . don't you think, Mercia—inviting yourself to my little party like this?" He glanced at Leonore. Her arm was twisted behind her, and she was on her knees before Mercia. Leonore's eyes were wide, but she breathed evenly and did not struggle. *Brava, my love. Don't show your fear. Mercia delights in it.*

Mercia looked thoughtfully at him. "But how ungenerous of you to keep me from my entertainment. I thought I would at least come to see how you eliminated your little pet wife."

"You sadden me, my dear. I see you do not trust me at all."

"Of course not," Mercia said conversationally. "I have seen how you fawn upon her. Now you bring her to your ancestral home. Can I truly be sure you haven't more than some fondness for her?"

Nicholas sighed. "Haven't I told you I despise indiscretion? Of course I brought her here! If I killed her in London, do you not think there would be speculation and gossip? Here, there would be fewer eyes and fewer questions."

Despair made Leonore close her eyes, and hope slowly seeped from her. *Please, he does not mean it. He cannot mean it.* She felt Mercia's hand close a little tighter on her throat. Leonore's neck ached with the way it was bent, and her back ached with fatigue. She wanted to cry out, but did not. A wave of defiance, the defenses she had built all of her life against her father's drunken rages, rose up in her, and she angrily decided she would not give Lady Lazlo the satisfaction of a response—even it it meant her death.

And yet: *I am going to die*. Lady Lazlo had come upon her in her chamber, quietly, swiftly, with the strength of a she-wolf. The tea cup in Leonore's hand had fallen and shattered on the floor, and hot tea had scalded her hand. Even now the broken shards of porcelain jabbed her knees through her carriage dress, and the tea, now cold, soaked through the cloth.

"Indiscretion! Always you speak of indiscretion! I am not indiscreet!" said Lady Lazlo sharply.

Leonore opened her eyes again. Her sight seemed sharpened, and everything stood out in clear relief: the bed, the fire, the table with the candles on it. She watched Nicholas, his still, pale, beautiful face, his expression cold as ice. He glanced at her. It was a quick, hooded flicker. She almost thought she saw fear there. Almost. Hope flared again, and she quickly tamped it down. She must wait and watch. Patience, patience.

"If you say so, Mercia." Nicholas shrugged. "I wonder what happened to Sir Adrian? He seemed such a promising young man."

Lady Lazlo made a sound of distaste. "He bored me. I am afraid he did not last long. Some wasting disease, the doctor said." Leonore swallowed and felt the woman's fingers tight against her throat. "Were you jealous?" Lady Lazlo said brightly. "Oh, I hope you were jealous!"

"Of course I was, my dear." Nicholas gave her a slow, seductive smile.

"How marvelous! Perhaps I will release your little pet wife, and we can have a bit of fun with her before you kill her. I would like to see that, you know, see you kill her."

Nicholas kept the smile on his face and shrugged. "If that is what you wish," he said carelessly. He could not let down his guard one moment. How quickly could he move and keep Mercia from killing Leonore? He shifted his feet and saw Mercia's hand tighten on Leonore's neck. Not quickly enough for him to run to her and snatch his wife away. Hope sank in him.

He gazed at Leonore for a moment. She was still, staring at him. It was as if she was trying to tell him something without words. She smiled at him slightly, and he understood clearly, suddenly, that she loved him. Why else had she acted as she had when she knew he had kissed Mercia? Why else had she returned to him? He felt dizzy, and he took a step back, putting his hand upon the mantelpiece to steady himself. Hope, foolish hope, warmed him just as the heat from the fireplace warmed his back.

Hope. Fire. He remembered the old Taoist priest and his gift. He had forgotten the thing that made him different from other vampires. He clasped his hands behind him and breathed a few words within a deep sigh. Heat flared in the palm of his hand. Nicholas gazed at Mercia and smiled sweetly at her.

"You gave me such joy when I saw that the stupid boy was no longer at your side at the masquerade," he said and let his eyes linger upon Mercia's face and breasts. He saw her hand loosen from Leonore's neck, and Mercia's smile turned seductive.

"Did I?" she murmured.

"Oh, yes. You were sublimely beautiful, regal, the Queen of the Night. Remember how I teased you? I admit my words sounded spiteful when I spoke of how the Queen had expired in flames, but the fires of jealousy had consumed my heart."

Mercia's face softened."Oh, Nicholas! I had not thought . . . your wife . . ."

He took a step closer to her; her hand was lax upon Leonore's neck. "I wanted to make you jealous. Tell me I succeeded, lovely, sweet Mercia."

"Oh, let us kill her now, Nicholas. We do not need her at all." Mercia's eyes glowed with incipient bloodlust, and Nicholas's hatred for her flared high.

He grinned fiercely and laughed. "Too late, Mercia." His hand swept from behind him and flung the fire-salamander at her.

Mercia shrieked thin and high, and her hands flew to her hair. Leonore fell to the floor. Nicholas seized her, shoving her away from Mercia.

The little dragon curled around Mercia's hair, dancing down her shoulder to play amongst the folds of her gown. It burned and an acrid stench filled the air. She shrieked again. Leonore pressed her face into Nicholas's chest and shook with horror. He held her tightly, then pulled her farther away.

"We must get out of here, Leonore."

She gazed at him, but he was not looking at her. She followed his stare; the fire had caught onto the rug by the door and climbed quickly up the doorjamb. Lady Lazlo was gone. Burning cloth the color of her gown twisted and fluttered in the air. The fire roared, and the heat nearly scorched Leonore's skin. They would be burned alive if they stayed here.

"Move, Leonore, now!" Nicholas pushed her away from the fire. He went to the bed and stripped off the sheets.

"Where?"

"The window!" He tied the sheets together and secured one end to a bedpost.

Leonore ran and fumbled with the window catch. It opened wide, and she heard a roaring behind her.

"Nicholas!" she screamed. He was standing, looking at the fire. He turned to her. "If you do not come, you will die!"

"If I come, I will die." He nodded toward the window and smiled wryly. "It is nearly dawn."

"Stupid man!" she shouted. "If you do not go with me, I swear I will stay here."

"Damn you, Leonore, go!"

"No! I am afraid of heights."

"*Now* you tell me!" He ran to her and took her hand, almost dragging her to the balcony.

"You go first," she said. "In case I should be frightened and fall." He gave her a penetrating stare, then glanced at the fire in the room. She heard the roar of the fire, closer now.

"Very well," he said and climbed over the balcony wall.

Leonore cast a glance at the room behind her and shivered, despite the heat that poured out the windows.

"Leonore, give me your hand!"

Nicholas stretched his hand out to her, apparently holding onto something underneath the balcony. She grasped his hand, swung her legs over the low wall, and slid down into his arms. Quickly she twined her legs around the bedsheet rope and held tight to it with her hands.

"I have it!" she said. "Go now, Nicholas!"

She heard a thump and looked down. He was on his feet, looking up at her. It was dizzyingly far down, but she closed her eyes and concentrated on descending. Finally, she felt his hands around her waist, and her feet touched the ground. He turned her around, kissed her hard upon the mouth, then cradled her in his arms.

"You little liar," he said into her ear. "You are not at all frightened of heights."

"True," she said. "But you would not have come down with me if I had not said it."

"True." He sighed. He took her hand and led her away from the house.

Leonore gazed back at the mansion. The fire had spread quickly, and she could see flickers of flame curling around the edges of the windows. Nicholas gave another sigh, deeper this time. Leonore turned to him. He had closed his eyes and suddenly swayed on his feet.

"Nicholas!" She put her arms around him, and he leaned against her.

"I am tired, Leonore."

The chirping of birds came to her, and she looked toward the horizon. The sky to the east had lightened. Fear seized Leonore's heart, harder than the fear she felt when Mercia had squeezed her throat and twisted her arm.

"No. No, Nicholas, we will find some shelter." She looked frantically around her, but no place could hide them from the coming dawn. And the house . . . The fire blazed high now; it had spread through more of the west wing. Perhaps if they went to the east—

Nicholas slumped heavily upon her; she stumbled, and he fell to his knees on the grass. She hugged him to her.

"No, please, Nicholas, stand up! We'll go back, the east wing—"

He opened his eyes and gazed at her. "Too tired." His eyes widened. "The dawn. Is that the dawn?"

"Yes, yes it is. Oh, please, Nicholas, don't, don't—"

A small laugh rushed from him. "I have seen the dawn at last," he said. He swayed again and gasped. "It hurts."

She clutched at him, but he was too heavy. He slid to the ground.

"No, oh, dear God, no! Please, Nicholas, don't, don't—" Leonore pulled at the lapels of his coat, but she could not lift him. "No! What have I done? I—I didn't want you to die in the fire—Please, Nicholas, wake up!"

He opened his eyes slowly, focusing upon her. "Never mind, Leonore," he whispered. "It is better. . . . And I have seen the dawn again."

"Stupid man! How can you say it is better?" She leaned over him, trying to shade him. It was useless. She looked over her shoulder at the thin sliver of sun barely painting the clouds above a faint orange. A touch drifted over her cheek.

"I love you, Leonore," Nicholas whispered. He closed his eyes. "I am sorry."

Grief, hard and hot, seized her throat. "No. No. Please, Nicholas. Don't, please don't die." She took his face in her hands and kissed him frantically. No breath came from his lips. "Don't! Don't leave me!" She put her hand upon his chest. Only a faint pulse, and it grew more faint as she tried to feel it.

Leonore stared at him, at the sunlight drifting slowly over his pale, beautiful face, burnishing his hair. "Oh, dear God," she whispered. She hadn't even told Nicholas she loved him. She had meant to, but she hadn't been able to, or found the right time. Now he was dying.

"Please, Nicholas, listen to me. I don't want you to die." Her voice was hoarse, plaintive and pleading all at once. "See, you must not die. Not now. I love you, don't you see? You can't. Please don't—please don't." She lay next to him, her head upon his chest. She closed her eyes. "I love you."

A fire burst in her chest, sending scalding tears coursing over her cheeks. Leonore clutched Nicholas's coat, weeping into the front of it with hard, wracking sobs. She wept all her loneliness, all her love and grief into him, all the terror and agony of fear she had just experienced. But no arms came up around her, and no kisses comforted her.

She did not know now long she lay there, weeping—minutes, hours. The colors of the dawn had disappeared; the morning sky showed gray. It was raining, but she did not know when it began. It soaked her dress, and she shivered with cold—or grief—she knew not which. The rain gradually slackened and ceased, and she could feel the sun's warmth upon her back. She cursed the sun for what it had done to Nicholas and wept again.

"You are ruining my neckcloth."

Leonore jerked up her head. It was barely a whisper. His chest moved beneath her hand.

"Nicholas . . ." She let out a breathless laugh.

"I think you have wept all over my shirt, too."

"You *beast*!" she cried angrily and thumped his chest with her fist. "How can you speak of shirts and neckcloths when I thought you were—when I have been—you stupid, vain, impossible man!" She hit his chest again.

His hand grasped her wrist in a weak grip, then tightened. "Ah, ah! None of that, my love." Leonore stared into Nicholas's green, smiling eyes, then gazed at Nicholas's smiling mouth. "How beautiful you are! Perhaps it is the sun—that is the sun, is it not?—upon your hair. I think you should kiss me, sweet one, and stop staring at me like an idiot."

"No!"

"Yes!" Nicholas rolled over and pinned her to the ground. He gazed at her avidly, as if drinking in the sight of her eyes and lips and hair. "Ah, how beautiful! I never knew, never saw—ahh, Leonore. . . ." He bent his head and kissed her gently, then with more heat. "Your lips, I can feel them . . . soft, sweet, warm," he said against her mouth. "Beautiful, so beautiful . . . I love you, Leonore. God, how I love you."

Leonore breathed a long, sobbing sigh and put her hands behind his head, pulling him down into a fierce kiss. His lips moved upon hers sensuously. A cold drop of water splashed upon her cheek. She pushed him away.

"You are wet," she said, breathing hard. He sat up, gazing at her, an odd, wondering look in his eyes, as if he had just discovered something miraculous and new.

She closed her eyes briefly. "Thank you, thank you," she whispered, the words a prayer. Nicholas was alive—he was alive! A hard trembling shook her, and she felt tears roll down her cheeks. His arms came around her, warm and comforting, despite the dampness of his coat.

"It is no wonder I am wet, with all the weeping you have done over me," Nicholas said, kissing the tears from her cheeks.

"It was the rain."

"Of course it was," he murmured. "Hush, now, my love. You need not cry any longer."

She rested her forehead on his shoulder. "I thought you had died." She raised her head again and looked at him. His eyes became distant, and a frown creased his brow.

"I . . . I think I almost did. I thought I saw . . . heard . . ." He shook his head and returned his gaze to her. "It does not matter now." He looked around him and squinted at the sun that peeked from behind the clouds. "This shouldn't have happened. It has not yet been a year since we married." He shook his head again. "I do not understand it."

"Does it matter?" Leonore said and smiled tremulously at him. "You are alive . . . and I love you."

He gazed at her, his eyes bright. "Do you, Leonore? I had hoped—I was not sure—"

"Yes, and yes, and yes!" Leonore kissed him, fully and deeply. "I have loved you for so long, but I was afraid to say it," she said when they parted. "Will you forgive me for being so foolish?"

"No," Nicholas said, grinning. "You must make it up to me first by telling me you love me—every day will do, I think. And giving me perhaps not less than, oh, five kisses per day. No, six is better, I think. Then I will consider forgiving you."

"It will only puff up your vanity if I do!" Leonore stood up, shaking out her dress. It was damp and clung to her legs. She saw Nicholas staring at her, a seductive smile upon his lips. She blushed. "I suppose I can allow it . . . from time to time."

"Starting today," Nicholas said, then sighed and looked toward the house. No fire burned the west wing now, for it seemed the rain had doused it. A few trails of smoke rose from the broken roof. "But not in the west wing. Our rooms are ruined, and I shall be very lucky if I can retrieve a few books from the library above them. We'll have to stay in the east wing and perhaps share a room."

"I will not mind," said Leonore. "If you do not."

Nicholas smiled at her and kissed her once more. "No. I shall share my life with you. What is one little room added to that, after all?"

Epilogue

The early autumn sun streamed into Nicholas's study. He shook his head, sighed, and shut the ancient *grimoire* he had brought from London. Shoving the notes he had been writing into a drawer of the escritoire, he stood up. He looked out the window at Leonore walking out toward a copse of trees, carrying a bundle under her arm and lazily swinging her hat to and fro in her hand. He really did not want to be indoors any longer today.

He caught up with her in good time, for he ran all the way, enjoying the breeze that sifted through his hair. He marveled again at the blue of the sky, so bright that it hurt his eyes to look at it. Leonore turned to look at him when he touched her shoulder and smiled before she kissed him fully on the mouth. He took her hand when they parted and walked with her to the trees ahead of them.

"I have been foolish, Leonore," he said. "Perhaps even stupid."

"Yes, my love," she replied dutifully.

"*What* an obedient wife!"

"I do try," she said and grinned at him.

He sighed. "I've been impatient and arrogant, also. I discovered it was never necessary to wait a year to regain my humanity."

"Oh?" They came to the trees, which shaded them from the hot sun. Leonore unrolled her bundle—a large blanket—sat down upon it, and took out a book from inside her hat. Nicholas sat beside her.

"The solstices and equinoxes were the important times. It was not just that I had to wed a willing virgin . . . but she had to love me, knowing what I was." He shuddered and closed his eyes. "I almost destroyed you—destroyed both of us. I shouldn't have been so sure of my knowledge; it was wrong—prideful and arrogant. If you hadn't come back to me at the right time—if you had not forced me to climb down from the balcony. . . ." He opened his eyes and saw her watching him. "Can you forgive me?"

"No," she said. "You must make it up to me first by telling me you love me—every day will do, I think. And giving me not less than, oh, six kisses per day. Then I will consider forgiving you."

He laughed huskily. "Is that all?"

"No." Leonore took his hand and placed it on her slightly swelling belly and put aside her book. "I want you to make love to me whenever I ask it."

"Now?"

"Yes," she said and kissed him. Nicholas moved his hands to her breasts, more full than they had been five months ago, pushing away her bodice. She sighed and ran her hands down his thighs.

He loved her then, gently, careful of the new life he had begun in her. He almost forgot himself at the end, gasping and pressing himself deeply into her as Leonore gave a last moan of pleasure.

"I think I will begin forgiving you," she said breathlessly.

"Thank you," Nicholas replied. "Very, very, very much." He felt a slight fluttering pressure where his belly met hers, and he moved reluctantly away. "He—or she—is probably not thanking us at all."

Leonore laughed, then grew silent. "Nicholas . . . do you mind not having your vampire powers?"

"No," he said, smiling at her. He reached over and caressed her cheek. "Some magic is learned, after all." A puff of air burst beside Leonore's cheek, and she started. He opened his hand and a white rosebud lay in his palm. She stared at him, wide-eyed, while he tucked it into her hair.

"Besides, loving you is magic enough," Nicholas said and kissed her once again.

The Devil's Bargain

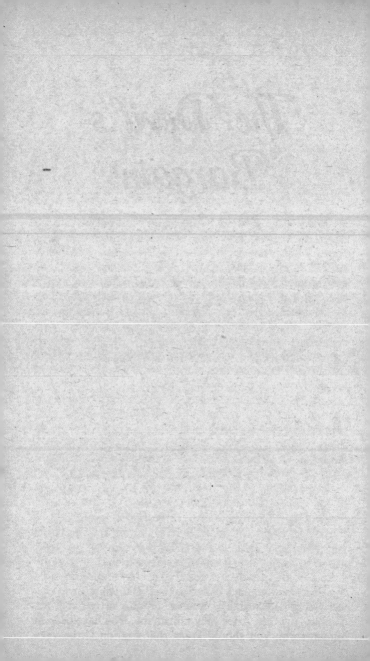

Prologue

It was a place between worlds and times, not yet formed into reality: what Eden was before it was made true. Ariel raised a hand, and an area shimmered and took shape. A field of soft grass rolled to the angel's feet and under, then past. Some blades of grass joined, then fountained into a tree, tall and stately. A few more sprayed their limbs into the newly blue sky, and blossoms quickly transformed to sweet and fragrant apples. A faint rumble sounded from clouds that suddenly covered half the sky, and rain poured into a gentle hollow in the field, filling it until a small lake was born. Then the clouds faded, and the angel surveyed his handwork.

Ariel winked an eye, and a gazebo sparkled into being upon a little hill. It was nothing more than an arched roof supported by slim, elegant columns upon white marble floors, a miniature temple. But a meeting place was needed, though it was only temporary, and the angel admitted to a certain fondness for architecture. He drifted toward it.

Lucifer was already there when Ariel reached it. He bowed gravely and exquisitely to the angel when their eyes met, but Ariel took his hand and pressed it in greeting.

With a wry grin the angel took in Lucifer's attire. "How you affect their raiment, Lucifer! How can you ape their manners, when you say you despise humankind so?"

Lucifer took an elegant pinch of snuff, careful not to let any drift upon his blue superfine coat and white linen cravat. He smiled genially. "I never imitate anyone. On the contrary, my dear Ariel, they imitate me. You have been in human form; you should know that fashion is the very devil." He chuckled, and low thunder vibrated through the ground.

"Extremes always are, as you do know, to your sorrow." Ariel gazed at Lucifer sadly.

When Lucifer smiled again, fiercely, the angel saw that he had also taken on the fashion for filing one's teeth—it was an affectation of sporting coachmen. The contrast between Lucifer's pale, beautiful countenance and the sharpened teeth made Ariel's wings shudder briefly, though his face showed nothing.

Lucifer's sharp eyes noted the disturbance, however. "And to yours, apparently! Do you not like my dental work, then? It is all the rage, and I earned it, you know! I am devilish good at the reins." He laughed aloud, and the skies rumbled, though there were no clouds in the sky at all.

Ariel said nothing, but sat still, watching. Lucifer sneered. "But what do you know of extremes? You were always in the middle, never yea or nay, never for or against—as exciting as a bowl of gruel. And in the heat of my battle, millennia and millennia ago, you could not stand at my side, but turned back like a kicked dog to our Father."

"My brothers and my sisters hoped that because I had once stood at your side, and because I once understood you, that I could persuade you to come back," Ariel said, looking at him steadily.

"I?" Lucifer affected surprise, his eyebrows raised, and his hand spread upon his chest. "Surely, you jest."

"I do not jest, Lucifer," replied Ariel earnestly. "I knew you rebelled because of the creation of humankind—out of love of our Father; it was because I understood and felt that love as fiercely as did you that I first joined you. But then I saw that your hatred and jealousy of humans far outweighed any love you felt. I could not stay with you then, for I saw you acted out of hatred rather than love. We know there is still some love within you, Lucifer. Forget your revenge and your temptations, and come back."

"What, and do penance, as you have done—and still do to a certain extent!—and become a groveling little human worm, to sweat and stink and roll in the mud of his own making?" Lucifer gave a short bark of laughter, and lightning flashed in the sky behind him. "I think not."

The angel smiled reminiscently. "It has been a long time since I was required to live as a human—and yes, even having to resist your temptations, Lucifer. It is not so very bad, you know. They do experience love as we experience it. Sometimes it is of a depth and grace that even we angels aspire to."

Lucifer waved an elegantly manicured and beringed hand. "Oh, I grant you there have been a few saints here and there. But for the rest? Nothing but that sickening nervous affectation they suppose is love, or at most, honest lust. Why, only look—" The Fallen One put up his hand, and a hole glowed hotly in the air. Through it Ariel could see a raging battle; horses charged, swords slashed, and the boom of guns and the dying cries of men and beasts rent the silence of the little temple.

"I do not see it here, my dear Ariel," mocked Lucifer. "Or, wait! Here is a man pierced to the quick—ah, ah, no, alas, it is with a bayonet, not with the look from a lover's eye. And here is one who has lost his heart! No, mistaken again. He has not given it to his sweetheart; it was blasted from him with a cannon-shot."

Grief crossed Ariel's face, but he continued to scan the scene. In the midst of the battle the angel saw a man who leaped in front of another, more tired comrade to save him from a saber thrust, taking the thrust himself.

"There, do you see? Even in the midst of violence, there is self-sacrifice and love."

Lucifer eyed the man, now fallen. "He was merely stupid. Men do stupid things in the heat of battle. Put him in the right circumstances, he would take whatever path I give him."

"I think not."

Smiling, Lucifer turned to Ariel. "I think he would. Most do. Would you, ah, care to wager on that?"

Ariel looked at Lucifer for a long moment, considering. Ariel risked much if he did, for he was still doing penance, and under the conditions of his penance, he was still vulnerable to temptation. Ariel remembered life after life, living as a human: the hardships, the pain, the sorrows, and bodily death. Then, too, the joys, the loves, the laughter. And yet, if he won, perhaps there might be peace for a while, though his fallen brother would not repent. Ariel smiled a little. Living human life had left its mark.

"Perhaps. What are the conditions?" replied the angel.

"I will take that man and put him in such a situation that he cannot but do as I instruct. You cannot influence him directly—his actions must be his own. If he completes the task I set him, his soul is mine, and you must submit to living as a human again—whom I will tempt mercilessly, by the way."

"And if I win?"

"I will not repent, so you might as well forget that," said Lucifer.

"It seems your risk is small. Afraid that I might win?" mocked Ariel gently. Lucifer flashed him an angry look. Little by little, thought Ariel, little by little. "Well, then, that war. I want you to end it. And I have some special social reforms I am sponsoring—I want you to lift any blocks you have put in the way of their success."

Lucifer smiled grimly. "Done." Lightning flashed, thunder rolled again, and he was gone.

Sighing, Ariel turned again to the battle scene and moved closer. The angel's form changed and shifted. A small medical bag appeared in his now quite human-seeming hand, and he straightened his uniform with a smart jerk at the waist. He lifted his hand, widening the hole, and stepped through.

Chapter 1

Sometimes he would wake up to the sound of cannons and the screams of horses and men ringing in his ears. Then he would open his eyes. The reek of blood and dust would fade from his nostrils, and Richard, Viscount Clairmond, would remember once again he was not in Ciudad Rodrigo anymore, but his own sweet England.

Richard lay still, waiting for his heart to stop pounding, and breathed deeply. He focused on the sounds of London's morning traffic, the mundane sounds of people hawking their wares, and the voices of the inn's guests just outside the door of his chamber, until his muscles gradually lost their tension. A small bit of pride grew in him; he was able to lie still upon waking. It was proof that he had a measure of control over some aspect of his life. He smiled grimly to himself. It was a hard-earned control. There had been days that he had awakened and jerked against his splints and bandages and screamed—whether from the pain in his body or in his mind, he knew not.

A knock sounded at his door. "One moment!" he said. Slowly, the viscount eased himself up to a sitting position. His shirt and breeches were within easy grasp, for he had remembered to lay them at the foot of his bed last night. He pulled them on.

"Come!" he called.

The door opened, and a small, neat man appeared. His clothes were shiny at the elbows and faded at the collar, but he wore them with an impeccable air. He peered at Richard with earnest round eyes, and the man's thin mustache twitched. *A squirrel,* thought Richard. *That is what he reminds me of. A squirrel made into a man.*

"Ah! Milord le Capitaine is awake!"

Richard let out an exasperated breath. "What are you doing here in England? I thought I told you I did not need a valet, Lescaux."

The Belgian looked skeptically at some clothing piled upon a chair. "*Certainement*, Milord, but I see you 'ave not recovered all of your wits, for it is with my own eyes I see your clothes in a state most deplorable."

"Milord" put his fist to his mouth and cleared his throat to help suppress a smile. "Yes, well then, if you must know, I have not the money to pay you."

"Bah! What is money to me? The demands of *l'honneur* dictate the actions of Robert Lescaux, not the base coins." Lescaux's lip curled.

"I may not be able to pay you for a long time, and then it would only be a pittance."

The would-be valet frowned terribly, then his face cleared. He shook a finger at Richard. "Ah, hah! Milord is clever, *hein*? Milord seeks to offend Lescaux so that Milord will 'ave no valet. But me, I am clever, too. I 'ave guessed what is in the mind of Milord le Capitaine." He tapped his head with his finger, then strode confidently to the chair. He proceeded to straighten the clothes draped upon it.

Richard gave it up. The man believed Richard had saved his life during battle; perhaps it was so, but Richard could not remember it. But then . . . He closed his eyes for a moment. He remembered leaping, his sword flying from his hand in response to a greater force even as he fell. Then memory faded. Perhaps he had leaped in front of someone, but whether it was Lescaux or not, he could not tell. And how a Belgian had managed to enlist himself in Wellington's Peninsular army was another mystery. Perhaps it was because of Lescaux's facility with languages, despite the danger that he could have been easily mistaken for a Frenchman.

But whatever Lescaux believed, Richard knew one thing: It was the little Belgian's face he first saw when he woke from his delirium, anxiously hovering over him and weeping with joy when Richard opened his eyes at last. It was Lescaux, too, who fed him, put cold cloths on his forehead, and snapped off the head of anyone who dared approach Milord le Capitaine. No, Richard thought, he was mistaken. The man was more like a little terrier than a squirrel.

Whatever brave but foolhardy act Richard might have performed, Lescaux's care was enough to repay him. Without it, he might have died, as so many did in the field hospitals. But Lescaux was adamant. Milord had saved his life. He owed Milord his, or at least his service, for as long as he lived. Richard believed differently, so as soon as the doctor gave him leave to rise, he left half of his quarter's pay in one of Lescaux's boots and used the rest to return to England. Even so, the man had followed.

The viscount shook his head. How he was going to afford to keep himself, much less Lescaux, he did not know. The maintenance of his captaincy cost more than his pay allowed—that is, if he wanted to pay to have a new uniform made, with all its braids and buttons. He was certain he would have to sell his horse, Satan; then he would have to travel eighty miles home to Wiltshire.

Unless he sold out.

Ah, what was the use? Of course he would have to sell out. As soon as he was well enough, he had visited his solicitor in the City. It had been worse than he thought.

He never received word that his father had died, and during his campaign in the Peninsula, his father never wrote to him of the condition of his estates. Why should he? thought Richard bitterly. He never wanted me to enlist. Perhaps Father had been right. Had I been home, perhaps I could have kept him from bringing us to the point of ruin. And Marianne—

"Lescaux, I must shave."

Lescaux beamed. "But of course, Milord." He bustled out the chamber door to order hot water for his master.

Marianne. The last time he had seen his sister, she was fifteen. That was five years ago; she would be a young woman now. Was she married? No. He lived for her letters during his campaigns, and she never mentioned marriage. He must sell out quickly and return home. She must be living all alone—God, he hoped she was all right.

He searched the chamber for paper and ink, and finding it, wrote a letter. There. At least she would know he was alive still, that he was coming home. He included a draft on the bank as well; it was for more than he should have written, but the thought of Marianne living in straitened circumstances horrified him.

It was a simple thing, to sell out of the army. "I'm that sorry, lad," said Colonel Brantham as he pushed forward Richard's prize money. "We could use more good men like yourself. But Lord help me—and no offense meant, my boy—I wouldn't have you the way you are looking now. You aren't well yet. Dashed good thing you thought to bring that—what is he? Netherlander? Belgian?—along with you. You still need someone to look after you, and that's a fact."

Glancing at a mirror near them, Richard ruefully had to agree. His normally wiry frame looked attenuated and graceful, for he had lost a great deal of weight, but it was far from graceful he felt. Under his tan he was pale, and the combination made him look sallow and wan. His skin stretched over the fine bones of his face, and his nose jutted fiercely out of its stark planes. The only softness about him was his mouth, which drooped with weariness, and his eyes, large and tired. He smiled wryly to himself. He looked like the hawk his comrades called him, more than ever now.

He smiled at the colonel. "I'm no beauty, I agree! But I'll recover soon enough. I must look over my affairs, see to my sister, make sure all is well with her. Perhaps I'll volunteer again, in time."

Colonel Brantham shook his hand. "I hope to see it, lad, I hope to see it." He grinned. "The Seventh will miss the Devil's Hawk, no mistake!"

When Richard came back to his room at the inn, he took out the money so that he could pay his fare. He paused. It was much more than he was sure he was supposed to receive upon selling out. A note peeked from under the pile. "A small loan, Clairmond, for your father's sake and for your own. Yrs., Brantham."

He crushed the note. Richard could feel the heat creeping up to his cheeks. So. Brantham knew. Perhaps everyone knew. He was amazed that tradesmen were not already hounding his footsteps. His stomach twisted with shame. If Brantham knew Richard's pockets were all to let, then the colonel must have known that Richard's father had committed suicide. A hunting accident, his solicitor had said. Impossible. Everyone knew how careful the late Viscount Clairmond was with his guns. One does not accidentally point a pistol to one's head and pull the trigger. And as far as Richard was concerned, it was no better than if he had helped his father to the grave.

If he had only been there! But no. No doubt his father would have done himself in sooner, he thought grimly. They'd argued before he'd left for the army.

"Have you no concern for our name, Richard?" his father had roared. "Having mistresses is one thing, but you flaunt them in the *ton*'s face! I could have overlooked it a little, but then you cap it off with that . . . that married whore you ran off with. Good God. I should thank God you were not killed in that duel, but I almost regret it. I doubt they'd let you into Brook's despite any influence I might bring to bear."

Richard had seethed in anger. Who was his father to point fingers? He'd already mortgaged half of the estate to pay for his gambling debts.

"I don't go to Brook's," he had said as coolly as he could. "I go to White's."

"As if you were more than tolerated there!"

"I could always join the army. Then you'd be rid of me for sure."

"You will go nowhere! By God, you will stay here and learn to manage these estates!"

"As you did?" Richard had not sneered, but his father's

face turned red with fury. He'd seized a glass of brandy near his hand and had dashed it in Richard's face.

The brandy had stung his eyes, but Richard merely looked at the old viscount. He bowed briefly. "I will do you the favor of leaving your sight."

The next day Richard had joined the army. Today, he'd left it—and everyone knew why. Visions of throwing his prize money in Brantham's face boiled to his mind, but he knew he could not do this. Brantham had given the money to him out of friendship and kindness, even though he was—had been—Richard's superior officer. Richard could not offend the man so, but the humiliation of others' knowing about Richard's straitened circumstances and the manner of his father's death left a sour taste in his mouth.

Sighing, he gazed around his room. It was small, not the best room in the inn. He should have taken a smaller room at a smaller inn to save on expenses—but enough. He did not know how bad his situation was then, and besides, a few hours more and he would be shut of this place. He left to pay for his room, then he went behind the inn to the mews to see to his horse.

Satan was as black as his name. He had no socks, no stockings—not a speck of white on him except on his forehead. There, a blaze of white shone, curiously shaped. The mark shot upward from the horse's nose and rose to a peak at his forehead. Its distinction was in the two slight marks at the base of the blaze. Together the marks formed a sword. Richard was going to name the stallion Excalibur for it, but the horse had given him such a wild and scornful look when he walked up to him, that he could not help but exclaim: "There's a bit of Satan in you, I see." And so he was named.

When Richard's comrades-in-arms heard it, they laughed. "Aye," said a Captain Sir John Grey, chuckling. "And isn't it right that Satan should be carrying the Devil's Hawk?"

They were a good pair, for the horse was sensitive to Richard's every move. Satan had come to trust Richard through gunfire and never lost heart when his master needed him most. The viscount often wondered if Satan did not have more than a little Lipizzaner in him. For though he was black as sin, he was not the usual hussar's dainty mount. Satan was comparatively small and compact, with a short, thick neck and long back. He was not above using his powerful legs to strike out at enemies, but at the same time carefully tried to avoid fallen comrades.

Richard reached up and scratched the blaze on Satan's forehead. Satan pricked up his ears, then bent his neck to nip his master's pockets.

"Sorry, old chap," said Richard ruefully. "No sugar. My pockets are all to let." He leaned his head against Satan's neck. "Even for you, old boy, even for you."

He patted the horse on the neck and got him saddled. His old friend should bring a good price at Tattersall's. He'd make a good hunter, for his endurance was good and his feet sure. The price would possibly not be what he was worth, for he would be known as "Clairmond's breakdown." Richard clenched his hands, then made himself relax. Brantham knew of his financial condition; once Satan was up for sale, everyone would know.

It's just a horse, Richard told himself. Its price will bring enough money to go home, perhaps last enough to live on frugally until I see what shape the land is in—before I sell that off, too, of course.

That thought depressed him further and threatened to overwhelm him, but he took in a deep breath and straightened himself with a resolute air. First things first, he told himself. I must get Satan to Tattersall's.

Richard then led his horse out of the inn's stable and mounted him. London seemed shrouded; it was late afternoon, and the sun shone weakly through smoky-gray clouds. Few of the fashionable were out, for the clouds threatened wetness. Richard thought wistfully of his room at the inn and pictured a merry fire in its hearth. He was not at all sure he would be back before it started to rain.

"Halloo there! Hawk!"

For a moment he was not certain he had heard his nickname, for the wind had suddenly picked up and whistled in his ears.

"Hawk!"

Grinning, Richard turned. By all that was holy, it was Jack Grey, waving his arms like a bedlamite. His blond hair, bleached by the Spanish sun, blew in the wind, and his cravat was all askew beneath his unbuttoned military greatcoat—but that was Sir John Grey. He never cared for appearances.

"Jack, you madman! What are you doing here?" Richard dismounted from Satan, the better to talk with his friend. "Last time I heard, you were with Wellington in France."

Sir John grinned back. "Last time I heard, you were dead. Thought I was dreaming when I recognized Satan—stood stock-still in the middle of the road, give you my word! Then you turned, and I *couldn't* mistake that beak of yours. Should have known the Devil's Hawk would have the devil's own luck!"

Richard's smile was strained. The devil's luck, indeed.

"Not quite up to form, eh, Hawk?" Sir John eyed him keenly.

"Took some shot in my shoulder, broken ribs, a saber thrust that missed my vital organs." The viscount's smile turned crooked.

His friend looked incredulous. "And you're alive? Good God, man, it's a dashed miracle you aren't even crippled. Whatever doctor took you in should have been sainted! Why, I've known men dead of a broken leg in those field hospitals."

Richard grimaced and shook his head. "More like a guardian angel named Lescaux."

"Lescaux! He here, too? Ingenious fellow, that. Never knew anyone who could cook up stringy jack rabbit as he did."

"*Very* ingenious," Richard said ruefully. "Somehow he got the idea that I was injured while saving his life. Well, I can't remember any of that—" He tensed suddenly at the memory of his dreams. "Not much of it, anyway. But if I did, he's amply paid me back for it. I heard tell he practically bullied me back to life. Can't convince him he's done enough for me, though. Followed me here, determined to be my valet."

Sir John grinned. "That's Lescaux! Persistent."

"Damned stubborn, you mean."

His friend laughed. He looked again at the viscount, noting his civilian clothes, and his face grew sober. "Sold out, have you?"

"Why do you say that?" replied Richard lightly.

"I've got eyes in my head, Hawk. You were always one to live in your uniform. No uniform, no more army. Stands to reason."

Richard shrugged. "I have obligations. I've got a sister to take care of, you see."

"I'd think your father would—"

"Dead."

"Ah." Sir John gave a brief squeeze on Richard's shoulder. "Deuced sorry, old chap."

Richard smiled at his friend—a smile of relief. So Jack did not know yet of his problems. Good. The man was a generous soul as well as a loyal one, and Richard would much rather not have to bear the embarrassment of his generosity. He did not want his—or anyone else's—help. Taking Brantham's charity was bad enough.

"Here we are." Richard looked up. White's Club. It had been a long time since he last passed through its doors. "What say you to a visit?" suggested Sir John.

Richard hesitated. He wondered if he was still "more than tolerated" there.

"For old time's sake?" urged his friend.

Perhaps he could spare a bit from his prize money—and it wouldn't hurt terribly to postpone selling Satan for one day. It would be the last for a long time that he would visit White's. Richard nodded. "Of course."

White's had changed very little. It still smelled of old tobacco and floor wax. Sir John summoned a servant and ordered brandy. Brandy. That was another thing Richard had not had for a while. He sipped it first, savoring the way the liquid seemed to disappear on his tongue, leaving a burning smoky sweetness behind. Then he took a larger taste, letting that same sensation flow over and down his throat. It warmed him, and he allowed himself to relax at last. Just for a little while, he told himself, I need not think of Father, and of ruin. Just for a little while, and then I will take on the burden once again.

"Hawk!"

"Clairmond!"

Richard turned and spied two gentlemen coming toward him. He grinned. "Hobart! Demming! By God, it's good to see you."

"Devil take it, Hawk, you gave me a turn!" exclaimed the Honorable Tom Hobart. He was a tall man, taller than the viscount, and built on much grander lines. He seized Richard's hand in his own hamlike ones, and shook it heartily. "Thought I was seeing a ghost! Had it from the dispatches that you were dead!"

"Almost was, Tom, almost was," replied Richard.

"Cracked ribs, shot in the shoulder, saber cut," said Sir John, jerking his head at Richard.

Edward Demming, also tall, but elegantly thin, raised his quizzing glass and surveyed Richard through it. "By all rights you *should* have been a ghost, Richard. You always did have the devil's luck."

Something flickered at the back of the viscount's mind, but the brandy and the warmth of his friends doused it. "Damned fool luck, more like, my friend."

A deep, lazy voice spoke up. "Care to try that luck at whist, Clairmond?"

Richard looked up. It was the Earl of Wyvern. The earl's land marched with his, but though he was a neighbor, they seldom met. He was a widower, though only five years the viscount's senior, and somewhat reclusive; even in town, he was not known as an open man. When Marianne and Richard were younger, they used to call him the Wicked Earl, and make up all sorts of stories about his supposed evil deeds. It had been easy to make up wild tales about him, for he had a saturnine countenance, with black eyebrows that formed almost a straight line above his eyes.

The planes of his face were severe; but his well-formed lips were sensual. As Richard and Marianne grew older, Richard teased his sister that she was forming a tendre for the earl, for she delighted in making up stories of greater peril, with the Wicked Earl committing crimes of horrendous villainy. Marianne had only curled her lip at him in sisterly scorn.

Yet, here was the Wicked Earl himself, a small smile on his lips, inviting Richard to play a game of whist. How very unwicked, and quite ordinary, thought Richard, smiling to himself. He would have to tell Marianne when he got home.

Richard rose and bowed as well as his recovering body would let him. "I am honored, sir," he replied. Perhaps one game, not very high stakes, he thought.

"And would any of you care to play?" Wyvern looked at the other gentlemen.

Tom bowed out apologetically. "Pockets to let until quarter day, I'm afraid. I'll gladly watch, however." The others joined with alacrity. They called for more brandy, and a servant filled Richard's glass again.

Richard knew a moment's unease at Tom's words, but quashed it. He drank more brandy, readying himself for the game. He had always been lucky at cards before—the devil's own luck, his opponents often said.

It seemed his luck was in this night. He won handily at the first game, and won the second as well. At his friends' urging, he played a third. This one he lost, but not badly, and then made it up in the fourth. By the fifth Richard was doing very well, and the coins piled up before him. He played yet another game.

The earl lost some, gained some, but throughout maintained a cool equanimity. One could tell little from his expression, or from his gray eyes almost hidden beneath those dark brows.

Richard was startled by distant thunder. The storm that threatened earlier that afternoon finally arrived. He looked up and spied a clock, and as he did so, it struck the hour. Was it midnight already? His concentration had been such that he had not noticed the time passing, or the clock striking the other hours. Richard looked at the stake he was wagering. It was quite large, for he lost the last game and hoped to make up the loss.

Suddenly, he shivered. What in God's name had he been doing? He glanced at his companions' faces: Jack gazed at his cards, a small smile curving his mouth; Edward was biting his lower lip. The earl—his expression was the same as ever, unreadable. Richard tried to remember the last—God, had it been five . . . no, six hours? What had he been doing? He had little money, yet he was wagering as if he were as rich as Croesus. It was as if he had played in a haze. It was gone now, but was replaced with an overwhelming fatigue, and his ribs ached. He looked down at his glass of brandy. It was half empty. Richard grimaced and pushed it away.

Wyvern looked up from his cards. "Demming?"

"Fold!" Edward threw down his cards in disgust. He looked at Jack Grey.

Jack's small smile turned rueful. "I'm out." He tossed his cards down. He had lost badly, but it was ever Jack's style to smile even when things went awry.

"Clairmond?" Wyvern looked at him from beneath his brows.

Richard looked at his cards. They were fairly good, but not the best he'd seen either. It was wholly possible for Wyvern to have a better hand. He glanced at the clock again. He shouldn't have stayed so long. Tattersall's had closed long ago. He should have already sold Satan and been on his way home. His head started to ache. He shouldn't be here.

Abruptly, the viscount laid down his cards. Wyvern shot an undecipherable look at him, and let out a small sigh. He put down his own cards.

Richard felt his mouth go dry. He had lost—and lost enormously. He'd be lucky if he had enough money to get himself halfway home. He stood up, and the room wavered around him for a moment. Quickly, he grasped the back of a chair and steadied himself.

"I shall meet with you tomorrow, sir, to settle my account," he said to Wyvern. "If you would kindly give me your direction?" Richard was glad to hear that his voice did not waver at all.

"At your convenience, of course," replied Wyvern. "You may call upon me at Pall Mall; I shall be there for at least a month."

Richard's hand tightened upon the chair back. Wyvern was being entirely too generous. It was usual to settle one's accounts within the week, preferably the next day.

"Tomorrow," he said firmly.

Wyvern inclined his head briefly. "Tomorrow, then."

Richard turned and walked toward the door.

"Hawk, wait!"

The viscount did not hear Jack's voice. He walked swiftly out into the night.

Chapter 2

Chill and heavy rain slashed Richard's face as he rode Satan back to the inn, but he felt nothing. His thoughts jumped about in a confused manner, like mice scampering just beyond his grasp, and he could not catch even one of them to form a comprehensible plan. Finally, one thought came clear, and in his anguish he dropped his reins, groaning loudly. His hands balled up into fists, and he pressed them into his eyes.

He was ruined—even more so than his father had done already. How could he have done it? How could he have wagered what little money he had left? He must have been mad. What the devil had he been thinking of? And Marianne, his sister. How could he face her after this? His stupidity had ruined her, too. He thought of his pistols at the inn. It would be so easy. . . .

No. Richard shook his head fiercely. No. It would be worse for her if he died. Not only would she have no family to protect her, but she would bear a double shame—the suicide of both father and brother. He could not do this to her.

What was he to do? Again the thoughts scampered frantically round and round in his head, until he was nigh dizzy with it. "Oh, God," he whispered desperately, "I would sell my soul just to find a way out of this."

The rain lessened to a drizzle as Richard's horse plodded on, and soon resolved itself to a fine mist. The viscount shivered. He was soaked through and cold and would catch his death of the ague if he did not get to the inn soon. He smiled grimly to himself; at least it would not be suicide.

It took a few minutes before Richard realized he was

lost. The mist had turned into an enveloping fog, and the buildings were vague shadowy shapes in the lamplight. He swore. *Stupid!* He did not remember how long he had been riding; he had just let Satan amble on, directionless, while he tried to restore some order to his emotions. He wondered if he had gone past the inn, or if he had yet to come to it. Perhaps if he knocked at one of the buildings. He hesitated, for it was very late, still in the wee hours of the morning. Catching sight of his sodden clothing, he grimaced. It was more likely that any occupants of a house would have the watch throw him behind bars than give him directions. He could feel his face grow warm with shame. It would be no more than he deserved for his stupidity.

Richard glimpsed a large, dark shape that could have been a house; it was enshrouded by fog and seemed to shift its form. He rode for a few minutes toward it, but he seemed to come no closer to it. More fog rose up and obscured the shape, making a dark gray wall before him. He tugged at Satan's reins then, and the horse obediently turned them around, but the viscount saw nothing but a seamless gray mass of fog surrounding them. Surely they must be near something, he thought. He decided to ride on, for they must come to some building or person—one could not be lost forever in London.

It seemed, however, they could. The fog hinted at shapes, but a steady pace toward the shapes brought them to more fog. Satan's hoofs made only a muffled sound upon the cobblestones, as if there were a carpet between the street and his feet; the mist seemed to absorb all sound. A chill crept up Richard's spine, one that had little to do with the cold and wet. How could it be that he would turn Satan at right angles, and still arrive nowhere? There were houses everywhere around White's Club. He shook his head and rode doggedly on.

After what seemed to be hours, Satan's ears pricked forward. Richard reined to a stop and listened. There—faint and muffled by the thick fog, Richard could hear footsteps. He urged Satan on toward the sound.

The mists parted. An impeccably dressed young man appeared, twirling his silver-headed cane with a jaunty air. Richard's horse started and almost reared. "Hush, old boy! There's nothing to be afraid of. We might just have found our rescuer," he murmured to the animal. Satan settled down, but Richard could feel him twitching nervously under him. The young man came up to the pair and stopped, smiling up at them.

Richard stared. He was not one to notice his fellow man's looks much, but this young man's countenance was extraordinary. If a man could be called beautiful, this one certainly was. His hair was as black as night, his eyes dark in the dim light. The lineaments of his face were noble and sharply defined. His skin was pale, but had a luminous quality about it, almost as if it were lit by some fiery spark within. He wore a fine greatcoat, unbuttoned, and beneath it Richard could glimpse a black-and-silver waistcoat.

"Excuse me, sir, but this fog has confused both myself and my horse, and we are quite lost. Can you tell me how close we might be to Hans Crescent?" Richard asked.

The young man's smile widened, showing white teeth. "Why, as close as around the corner, and as far away as a schoolboy's thoughts at midterm."

Inebriated, thought Richard. He sighed and picked up his reins again.

"But no, not inebriated at all," the man said genially.

"I bet your pardon!" Richard said, feeling his face grow warm. He must have been more tired than he thought to have said his thought aloud. "I did not mean—"

"Of course not," replied the man. "You may be more tired than you thought, but you did not say your thought aloud. You are Richard, Viscount Clairmond, are you not?"

"Yes, but how—"

"Allow me to introduce myself," the man said. He pulled a delicate snuffbox from his pocket and took snuff with an elegant air. "I am . . ." He glanced swiftly at the viscount. "Teufel. Mr. Teufel." He closed the snuffbox with a click.

"Have we met?" The viscount dismounted, uncomfortable looking down on the man.

"Mmmm . . . No, not really. But I have seen you often," Teufel gave another wide, white smile.

Richard did not know whether to be charmed or not. A sense of unease nagged at him, as if there were something he ought to do, but forgot. "Is there something you want of me?" he asked. He did not know why he said that; he felt somehow it was expected of him.

Teufel cocked his head to one side, in a considering manner. "Yes . . . and no. Let us just say that there is something you might want of me."

Richard's smile turned stiff. "I think not." The man may not be inebriated, but he was probably mad. The viscount turned to mount his horse.

"My dear Viscount, how you malign me," Teufel said, his voice mock sorrowful. "I am not at all insane."

Richard stopped. He knew he had not spoken. His uneasiness grew, unfurling into dread. He turned back, facing the man.

The mist behind Teufel shifted gray and black. An indefinable source of light seemed to flicker somewhere within the fog, for a dim glow suffused the area in which they stood. Richard looked at the young man before him. Despite the dimness, he could see Teufel's face as clearly as if they were in sunlight. He fought down his dread and replaced it with anger.

"Who are you?" he snapped.

"Someone who can . . . help you."

"I need no help from the likes of you." Richard turned to his horse again. He could feel Satan's muscles stiffen, as if poised for battle. He patted and spoke softly to him. The horse relaxed a little, but still his ears pricked forward, alert.

"I really think you should listen first. After all, you did ask for help."

Richard leaned his head against Satan's saddle. What had he said? His mind wandered wearily over the last . . . hour . . . hours? He had gone over and over his problems, thoughts of suicide, Marianne . . .

"A little something about your soul . . . ?" prompted Teufel.

Richard turned and looked at the man, incredulous. He must be joking.

"Wrong again, dear Clairmond. I am not joking either."

Closing his eyes, Richard shook his head in disbelief. He had heard tales of this and believed they were only tales. Was this not the nineteenth century? The supernatural had no place in a world where hot-air balloons could send men aloft, or great manufacturies of steel and coal poured forth goods in quantities mankind had never seen before. He opened his eyes once again and looked at Teufel.

"You are not real. I have been ill, and am wet and tired. You are but a sick and tired man's dream."

Teufel smiled. "Oh, but I am quite real. Come, touch me." He held out a beringed hand. Richard hesitated, then grasped the hand firmly. It was warm and dry, and quite real. "You see?"

"What do you want of me?" Richard asked, releasing him quickly.

"Let us say that I can be of great help to you. Your father has died, has he not? And left your estates encumbered with debts. You have no money but what can get you home, and your sister is near destitute. What will you do?"

"I will manage."

"Stupid man!" Teufel suddenly seemed to lose his patience. He spoke sharply. "You have lost your money at gaming—I was there, I saw it!—and you have nothing with which to restore your lands, to feed yourself, or your sister. What occupation will you take, eh? You have been a soldier and are now a gentleman." Teufel almost spat out that last word. "What useful trade have you been trained for?"

Richard had to admit to himself there was nothing he knew, not even how to manage an estate, since his father had jealously held the reins when he was alive.

"Your sister will have to earn her keep. She will make a fine governess. Shall I show you?"

Before Richard could speak, Teufel raised his hand. A small spot in the mist glowed red, then burned away a space to show a perfect likeness of Marianne. There, she was older then he remembered and had shadows of fatigue under her eyes. She wore an old brown dress that had clearly been mended. The likeness seemed to start at a movement that was beyond Richard's line of sight. Then her form was momentarily obscured by another, larger one, that pulled her into its arms in a crushing embrace.

Richard clenched his teeth, and his hands balled into two hard fists.

Teufel seemed to regain some of his geniality. "My, my. It seems she might be having a little trouble, eh?" He gazed meditatively at his fingernails, then took out a small handkerchief and began buffing them.

The image of Marianne seemed to struggle as the man who held her caressed her waist and hip. Finally, she pulled away, her hands flying to her cheeks to hide their redness. Then, Richard could finally see the face of the man who had accosted her. Wyvern!

"I will kill him. I swear I will kill him for what he has done." Richard gazed at the images before him, his body rigid with fury.

"Now, now, my dear sir, no need to be hasty. Your friend Wyvern has done nothing . . . yet." Teufel waved his handkerchief at the hole in the mist. It shrank and disappeared.

"But I have just seen—!"

"The future. What would happen if you left me here by my lonesome self without even considering my offer."

"And what is your offer?" Richard ground out.

"Much better." Teufel smiled. "Simply this: You will do a little favor for me in return for wealth, and then, of course, your soul will be mine after a year."

"Oh, is that all there is to it?" Richard's voice was sarcastic. "No. I think not. I will find a way to manage."

Teufel tapped his teeth with a finger, looking at Richard thoughtfully. "You might, of course. But your sister? I think not. She will want to help you, you know. She, unlike you, has all the necessary skills to earn a living. And if not at Wyvern's house, then another's, more distant from your home. And who is to say how she will fare so far from your protection? She *is* an exceedingly lovely lady, after all."

The despair and pride that had waged a war within Richard's mind and heart so recently threatened to break out again, and wreak havoc with his reason. His head started aching badly, making it even more difficult to think. He pressed a palm against his temple, hoping to still the pain. "I do not accept, but . . . what . . . what is the 'favor' you wish me to do?"

Teufel nodded, as if he took Richard's words quite seriously. "You have had an eye for the ladies, have you not? There is a particularly delectable one, not far from your home. I have heard she is untouched. But then, perhaps it is a matter of the right man to try and—"

"I do not need a pander, Teufel," cut in Richard. His voice was cold, and had an edge of steel.

"My dear Viscount Clairmond! *I* never said—"

"Cut line, Teufel!" His headache pounded now, so that he could scarce see what was in front of him.

"Very well, then." Teufel's voice had grown equally cold. "It is this. You have a choice of sacrificing your sister's virtue, or that of an unknown young woman. If you agree to seduce this woman and abandon her, your sister will be saved. Marianne need not go hungry, nor will she need to earn money for her . . . services. She will even live in luxury. Your choice."

Richard stared at Teufel. He'd known prostitutes and courtesans who had started out much the way Teufel said Marianne would. They were hard women, for they knew that in the end no one would be their protector—they'd have to do the protecting themselves. Some of them dwindled into poverty; some died of an illness contracted from a so-called benefactor. The thought of Marianne, her soft eyes growing hard with cynicism, her body riddled with disease— Richard closed his eyes in anguish.

"This young woman. Does she have a family? A father?"

"Yes, but only a father, and a frail one at that. Consider

it, Clairmond. You have not lived an exemplary life—why else were you forced to join the army? I have watched your depredations amongst the demimondaine quite carefully."

Perhaps it would not be so bad for this young woman. Perhaps her father would make sure she was provided for after Richard . . . He swallowed bile. But not Marianne—not his sister. He had been a disobedient son, a rake and a seducer. He deserved that his soul be damned. But not Marianne. At the very least, he could save her.

"Who is this woman?" Richard said at last.

Teufel smiled, and a hint of triumph lingered on his lips.

A thump on the chamber door roused Lescaux from his chair by the fire, and he rose, rubbing his eyes. The door opened.

"*Mon Dieu*!" he cried. He hurried to the viscount and helped him to the chair he had just vacated. He rubbed his master's hands and gazed anxiously at this face. Milord le Capitaine did not look well. The viscount's face was pale, and his eyes red-rimmed, and he shivered as if in an ague. Lescaux did not know what time it was. There was no clock in the chamber, but he knew it must have been well past midnight, for it was silent in the inn. He pulled his master's coat from him and put a blanket from the bed around him.

"How is this, Milord? You 'ave the cold to the bones, and come so late! Was my care to your health as nothing? Now you 'ave walk about in the bad weather and catch the death of yourself."

Richard sat, gazing at the fire, and let Lescaux pull off his boots. Lescaux glanced at him, worried. Milord looked very much as if he *had* caught his death. To be sure, Milord's face was less drawn and still as when Lescaux had ministered to him in the field hospital, but his eyes—they were as shadowed now with as much pain and anguish as they had been a year ago.

A bitter smile barely lifted the corners of Richard's

mouth. "Caught my death, Lescaux? Indeed. And I have seen the devil, too, and sold my soul to him."

Lescaux shook his head and led the viscount to bed. Milord le Capitaine was very ill, alas.

The Earl of Wyvern was gazing out his study window when a knock sounded at his door. "Enter," he said without turning around.

"Excuse me, my lord, but Lord Clairmond is awaiting you in the parlor," came his butler's voice.

"You may show him in here, Stewart."

"Very good, my lord." The door closed with a soft click.

Wyvern sighed and rubbed his face wearily with one hand. Drat the man. He'd given him a month, but Clairmond's pride was apparently such that he had to come two days later. The viscount could hardly have got the money in this short a time, unless he had received some miraculous windfall. Wyvern shook his head. The Clairmonds—save one—were all very high in the instep. For all that he, Wyvern, was of higher rank than they, the late elder viscount had scarce to do with any neighbor of his that was of later lineage, and whose lineage might have smelled of the shop. As a result, Wyvern had little chance—until lately—to come to know any of the Clairmond family. It seemed on the face of it that the new viscount was of the same stripe. He looked down at the vowels in his hand. Well, he would see what came of their interview.

"The Viscount Clairmond, my lord," announced Stewart.

Wyvern rose and bowed gravely to the viscount. Clairmond returned it, stiffly. The man did not appear well. Wyvern heard Clairmond had been near death from battle wounds. From the looks of his pale, gaunt face and shadowed eyes, he was still not recovered. Wyvern felt a stab of pity for the man, but suppressed it.

"A good morning to you, Clairmond. Please be seated." Clairmond gestured to a chair.

"I prefer to stand," replied Clairmond stiffly.

Wyvern glanced at him and was surprised to see a blaze of anger in his visitor's eyes. "Well, *I* don't prefer to stand, so I would appreciate it if you would take a chair. Damned awkward to have to crane my neck to look at you." The viscount sat reluctantly. Wyvern wondered if Clairmond had got wind of Miss Clairmond's activities. No matter. He had Clairmond's vowels in his hands. They should serve as a lever to forward his desires. He smiled to himself. Desires. Appropriate word, that.

"I would prefer to get to business immediately," Clairmond said abruptly.

Wyvern lifted an eyebrow. "Of course, if that is your wish."

"I cannot give you the money at once," Clairmond said. "It . . . my father left the estate badly in debt. It will take a while before I can repay you. I have a ring, however—it has been in my family for generations—I can give you as collateral." The viscount pulled the ring from his finger and put it on the table before Wyvern. It glinted gold, and the large single emerald in the center sparkled.

Wyvern looked at the ring and then at Clairmond from under his brows. He did not touch the ring. "Keep your ring, I have no need of it." He brought his fingers lightly together and contemplated the viscount over them. "But perhaps we can come to another arrangement."

"My estates, sir?" Clairmond did not take the ring.

The earl's smile was ironic. As stiff-backed as his father, he thought. It would be amusing to see how the viscount would react to his next words. "Another arrangement," he repeated. "I really have no interest in anything of yours. I am willing to forgive your debt to me—to throw these vowels in the fire over there—" and he nodded to the fire burning merrily in the grate close to them "—in return for your sister, Marianne."

"You bloody—" hissed the viscount and rose with such force from his chair that it fell over with a crash.

"Silence!" roared Wyvern.

Clairmond stopped his lunge across the space between them, but his hands clenched into fists, and his face spoke of murder.

"Sit! You insult your sister, not to mention myself,"

Wyvern said sternly, rising. "Miss Clairmond is a lady, and well I do know it, though you seem to have forgotten it with your . . . assumptions." He strode to the fire, then turned to face the viscount. "It came to my ears, after your father died, that your sister was in grave straits. She is prideful—as are all you Clairmonds—and she would not accept my help—the help of a concerned neighbor. However, she would accept employment and has been governess to my two daughters. She has been an excellent governess, and I do not want to . . . lose my investment. I wish to make her my wife. In return, I will burn your vowels and you will owe me nothing."

Clairmond curled his lip. "My sister is not for sale. She marries where she wills, and I will not force her into any sort of . . . arrangement."

"But think, my dear Viscount. How will you live? And do you think your sister will truly be content to hang on your sleeve when she knows what a bad state you are in? I think not. I am offering her a comfortable life and a respectable position in society. She will never lack for the necessities—even the luxuries—of life."

"No. I will find a way."

"Think of the alternative, Clairmond. She is an excellent governess. If not at my home, then she will surely want to earn her keep at another's. And she is a singularly lovely young woman. I am offering her marriage. Some men may not, however much a lady she is. With me, she will live in luxury and respectability."

The viscount seemed to freeze at Wyvern's words. He turned his eyes to the earl, and Wyvern could see a curious emotion just below the surface calm. It was almost as if the viscount were gazing past him into a distant horror. He looked down, and apparently noticing the fallen chair, bent down mechanically and brought it upright. He sat, carefully folded his hands in his lap, and then looked again at the earl.

"It must be by her consent. I will not compel her, and

neither will you." The viscount's voice was almost a whisper.

Wyvern smiled sardonically. "Done. And I know you are a man of your word. It is the pride of the Clairmonds, is it not?" He took Richard's vowels and tossed them in the fire.

Chapter 3

"Now do stop fussing, dear Conny. I shall do well enough!" Eveline looked impatiently at herself in the mirror. Her white round gown with pink piping at the neck and down the front of the skirt was of the latest fashion. Though she was delighted with it when she first saw it, she was never one to dwell on finery much. There was much more to life than that.

"Tch! Sure and I may be only your old nurse, Miss Eveline, but I do know some things that are right and proper at an assembly, and untidiness is not one of them!" Nurse Connor—or Mrs. Connor as she was respectfully known belowstairs—gave a final tug to the ribbon at the back of Eveline's dress. "There, now."

Nurse looked at her charge fondly and sighed. What a fair colleen she is, her face as sweet as the Blessed Virgin's with her dark smooth hair and large eyes—though she'd never seen a picture of Our Lady with sea green eyes. She shook her head at herself. She'd best remember Miss Seton was a lady grown, and not the little child who snuggled in her arms so many years past. She brushed away a sentimental tear and found herself hugged very fiercely.

"Oh, Nurse Conny! Now do be happy! I shall enjoy myself enormously, and you shall hear all about it when I come home. And I am sure Lady Brookland will take good care of me."

Nurse shook her head dolefully. "*That* one! Far be it

from me to say aught against my betters, but she's one that has more hair than wit."

Eveline's grin was mischievous. "And that cannot be much, for she wears a wig, you know."

Nurse's ears almost seemed to prick forward. "Well heaven bless me! Does she, now? I never would have thought, for 'twas a most cleverly done head—" She stopped and eyed her young mistress sternly. "Miss Eveline! I'll wager 'tis all of her ladyship's own hair, and not a wig at all! Haven't I warned you, often and often, of the evils of gossip?"

Eveline smiled demurely. "Oh, yes, *dear* Nurse! But I thought you *might* want to know . . ."

"Tch! '*Dear* Nurse,' indeed! Out with you then! Lady Brookland will be here soon, and I'd not want you to keep her waiting." Nurse made busy shooshing motions.

Eveline kissed her on her plump cheek before she left, for she loved her old Nurse Conny, who had been with her ever since her mother died. She could remember her mother in vignettelike fashion, and felt a warm, loving presence when she thought of her. But after a moment, that presence always receded to vague shimmery memories, whereas Nurse's ample form had always been quite solid and very good at absorbing childish tears. So she didn't mind much not having a mother, for she had her father and Nurse to care for her.

And then, of course, there was the eccentric and kind Dowager Countess of Brookland, who was so gracious as to take her under wing and introduce her—a merchant's daughter—to the fashionable life in Bath. She did not quite know how it had started, but they had fallen into conversation at the circulating library, and Eveline could not help but be charmed by her odd manner and supreme assurance.

She went down the hall to her father's chambers and knocked on the door.

"Enter!"

Eveline opened the door and went to her father's side. The room was lit with a brace of candles near the old oak bed, and a healthy fire was burning in the hearth. A few books were stacked on the table next to the bed, within Mr. Seton's easy reach. He was just marking his page as Eveline came near, and he looked fondly at his daughter over his spectacles.

"Dearest Papa! How are you feeling tonight?" She took his thin hand in hers and lifted it to her cheek.

"Better, much better. And you! All set for gadding about, are you?" Mr. Seton patted her hand.

"Not if you need me, and you mustn't say no if you do! You know I could not leave this house if I knew you were feeling worse. Doctor Stanton said—"

"Stanton is an old woman! He and his remedies. A good claret is all I need—strengthens the blood!" He pushed at his bedclothes fretfully. "As well as getting out of this blasted bedroom and into fresh air."

Eveline smiled at him. His voice was still booming, still authoritative, but he had changed. His accident a few years ago had aged him, and it was frightening at first to see her father, a vigorous man, in so much pain and weakened in his legs. He was a fighter, however, and she was sure one way or another that he would get up and about, despite the doctor's gloomy prognosis.

"To be sure, Papa, when the weather becomes warmer and less wet, you will be able to go about."

"Nothing wrong with a bit of rain! Invigorating!"

"Certainly, Papa. As invigorating as the ague, say, or influenza." Eveline leaned over and kissed her father's cheek.

Mr. Seton tried to look stern, but failed. "Saucy minx! I suppose you are going out with that skitter-wit, Lady Brookland."

"My dear Papa, Lady Brookland is all that is kind and generous."

"She will introduce you to some scoundrel of a half-pay officer, I am sure."

"It does not matter, for I am not at all partial to military men," Eveline said. She cast a mischievous glance at her father.

"No, but they are partial to *you*!" retorted Mr. Seton. He settled himself back in his bed and gazed at his daughter.

"You have a kind heart, my dear, and that encourages them."

Eveline smiled. "But I am also full of common sense, Papa. I well know that none of them would think of offering marriage to a Cit's daughter. I also know the difference between mere flirting and true interest. Besides, I am sure Lady Brookland would not introduce me to anyone inappropriate."

"Humph. Well, I warn you! If you were to run off with one of them, I shall disown you. No half-pay officer will leech off of Augustus Seton, that's what I say!"

"Would you really disown me, Papa?" said Eveline, her eyes wide with mock hurt and innocence.

"No, I would not, and you know it, impudent chit!" growled Mr. Seton.

"I thought so!" Eveline laughed and hugged him. He smiled and tweaked her ear.

"Go on then to your party, or assembly, or whatever it is. I shall do well enough."

"Are you sure, Papa?"

"Yes, I am sure! And you know it also, or you wouldn't be dressed in all your finery and gewgaws. Now get on with you!"

She walked to the door and opened it. "I love you, Papa," she said, and quickly closed the door behind her before he could reply.

"Impudent minx!" muttered Mr. Seton, but smiled.

Eveline stepped slowly down the stairs to the parlor. Her father had not become any worse since his accident, indeed, it seemed he was getting better. The improvement, however, was excruciatingly long in coming. She knew it frustrated her father that he was not able to go about his business in town. He had good managers and employees, and his solicitor, Mr. Crockett, was very competent. When her father became ill, she came to learn much about finances, for business had to continue even though he had been unconscious for a while. Despite her willingness to take on whatever task needed to be done, and her pride in the way she had learned to negotiate with the best businessmen in town, she could not help being glad that she did not have to take them on as heavily as she had been. The double duty of caring for her father and handling his business concerns had been wearing, and she was glad now that she could take some time for pleasure.

"Dear, dear Eveline! How charming you look! You shall put all the young ladies to shame this night, I vow!" Lady Brookland said, as Eveline opened the parlor door. Her ladyship wore an astonishing round gown of striped puce and magenta with an overdress of white gauze. Her turban was of the same puce fabric as her dress, and a large smoky gray plume curled over the top and bobbed at one side of her thin and clever face. The turban covered most of her salt-and-pepper hair which, despite Eveline's teasing of Nurse, was quite her own and still thick. Large diamonds circled her neck, and small ones shone at her wrists and ears. She was never without her thin, silver-topped cane, which she did not really need, for her walk was quick and definitely vigorous.

"And you, my lady, look . . . like a summer storm at twilight," Eveline said and smiled at the lady with genuine affection. "I hope you will forgive me for keeping you waiting! I was just making my farewells to my father and did not heed the time."

"Most proper, my dear. Your father must come first before any pleasure." The countess smiled. "And you dear, sweet child. I know what I really look like is a desperate quiz. But were I to dress as my very dull sons wish me to dress, I would disappear into the wall and attract no notice whatsoever. And what a tedious thing that would be!"

"Society would be the worse off, I am sure," replied Eveline solemnly, though her eyes twinkled.

Lady Brookland chuckled. "I have no doubt of it. But come, child! We must not dawdle!"

"It is that one."

Richard moved a step away from Teufel, even though he knew no one else could see him. Teufel's whisper fell cold on his ear, reminding him of the dank, chill night when they met, and though the assembly room was warm and brightly lit, his presence froze him to the bone. The viscount raised his eyes, then sighed with relief. The young woman he saw was a pretty, sandy-haired chit with a spoiled and arrogant expression on her face. She pushed rudely past a servant, then caught Richard's gaze and tittered behind her fan.

It would be distasteful, but at least it looked as if she might deserve some misfortune.

"No, not that one. The one a foot to the left of her."

This lady's nose had just enough of a lilt to it to keep her profile from being exactly classical. Tiny flowers in her night black hair glowed like stars, and her lashes fluttered long and dark against her cheek. She looked kindly upon a younger girl, and it seemed she introduced her to a young man—thereby earning the girl's obvious gratitude. Then the lady smiled, and Richard caught his breath. She was beautiful. His heart sank.

She bent over a quiz of a lady who looked vaguely familiar to him, and smiled merrily. Looking up briefly, she met his eyes, then turned away. A light blush blossomed across her skin. She looked up again, and then—to Richard's amusement—her chin came up, as if answering a challenge. His amusement did not last, however.

"Yes, that one," came Teufel's voice again.

"God, no," whispered Richard.

"God, yes. Go to it, man! It was your promise. Remember your sister."

"I remember, damn you!"

"Damning me is rather redundant, you know. You must think of something better than that." Teufel chuckled.

Richard felt bile rise in his throat. "Go away, Teufel," he said wearily. "I promised."

Teufel's chuckle faded into the air.

Sometimes Eveline knew when she was being stared at—even when she was not looking at anyone—from a prickling sensation just at the nape of her neck. She searched the crowd in front of her.

The man was tall and handsome, if a bit sallow of complexion. He had a prideful—almost arrogant—face, all angles and severe planes, and a fierce jutting nose. His straight brown hair was just as severe, cut short and neat. She would almost have fancied that his face had been cut from marble, were it not for his mouth. It was well-formed, expressive, but drooped as if with weariness. Eveline looked away, blushing. Goodness, but she was staring just as much as he!

She glanced at him through the corner of her eye. He was still staring at her. Surely, he knew how rude he was being! Well, what is sauce for the goose—! Eveline lifted her chin and stared back. An amused look crossed his face, then he grew somber. He glanced away, and Eveline turned to Lady Brookland.

"He *is* handsome, is he not?" Lady Brookland said, casting a mischievous look at Eveline.

She could feel her face grow warm again. "I should not have stared so. I do not know what came over me."

"Well, were I in my youth again I would be very inclined to stare. He reminds me of . . . Yes, I do believe I remember him—Clairmond. But I had heard he was dead! I am glad to see the reports were exaggerated. I remember his father was quite a charmer—but irresponsible. His son is made of sterner stuff, however. He went off to the Peninsula and distinguished himself there." Lady Brookland smiled at Eveline. "I can introduce you to him if you wish."

"Oh, no really, you needn't . . . I was not at all thinking . . ."

It was already too late. He had come up to them and was already smiling at her. He turned to the Dowager Countess. "Lady Brookland, I believe? How do you do?"

"Very well, Clairmond, thank you. I am sorry to hear of your father's passing. Charming man, most charming."

Clairmond's face seemed to freeze for a moment, but then he said genially, "So I have understood. He had many friends." His gaze moved to Eveline, who was standing with downcast eyes beside Lady Brookland.

The countess's lips twitched upward in a barely suppressed smile. "Pray allow me to introduce you to my dear friend Miss Seton. Miss Seton, the Viscount Clairmond."

"My lord." Eveline curtsied, then lifted her eyes to his. She drew in her breath. His eyes. They were large and dark—so very dark! She felt almost as if she could see into his soul. It was as if a deep sadness lived there, and almost a sort of resignation. Eveline wondered what it was that hurt him so, and then shook herself mentally. Really! She was becoming quite fanciful.

"Miss Seton." The viscount glanced at the musicians at the end of the room. "If you would do me the honor of a dance . . . ?"

Eveline let out her breath. "Oh, yes, please! That is, I would be most delighted." A blush rose furiously to her cheeks, and she felt annoyed. She was acting in a stupidly missish way—all for a simple little dance, and—oh dear, it was a waltz.

He took one of her hands in his, and his other hand went to her waist. Eveline could feel them, warm and firm, through the cloth of her gown and clasping her gloved fingers. She felt herself blush again and looked down at her feet as if to concentrate on the steps.

"You dance superbly for someone who has just learned." Eveline heard amusement in Lord Clairmond's voice and raised her eyes to his face. He was smiling, and one corner of his mouth quirked higher than the other. It was an intimate smile, almost as if he was sharing a little secret with her. Eveline felt a little breathless. She gathered her scattered thoughts together.

"If you must know, I learned to dance the waltz more than two years ago, even before it was much heard of in England."

The viscount's eyebrows went up. "I understand it was considered a rather, ah, fast dance at that time. How daring of you."

Eveline lifted her chin. "I was not committing an impropriety, for I danced it only with my schoolmates. One cannot say I was fast for doing *that*."

"And I suppose your schoolmistress knew all about it."

"Well, no, she did not." Eveline cast him a roguish look.

The viscount burst out laughing. "You are enchanting!"

"Oh, please don't!" she blurted. He smiled at her quizzically. "I really am not enchanting at all. And I do feel so very uncomfortable when you . . . when gentlemen say such things."

His smile grew wider. "Then you will just have to learn to become comfortable with it, for it is true, you know."

Eveline looked steadily and a little sternly into his eyes. "Is it?"

Her eyes demanded honesty. Richard's smile faded, and he gazed back at her, considering. "Yes," he said.

Her mouth formed a silent "Oh" as she stared at him, then blushed in embarrassment. "How brazen I must sound, as if I *wanted* to be complimented—and I don't really—that is to say, I am not trying to fish for . . ." She broke off in confusion and looked away.

He gazed at her profile and thought of a cameo inlaid with ivory and carnelian. She could very well have been a model for one. Her lips looked soft and pink, and suddenly he wanted to touch them with his own, in spite of himself. He wondered if they would taste as sweet as they looked. "Have you been long in Bath, Miss Seton?"

Eveline cast him a grateful look for this change in subject. "Only for a year. My father has been quite ill, so we came to Bath so that he could take the waters."

The viscount's brow creased. "Have you no other protectors, then?"

"Of course I do! There is dear Lady Brookland, who takes me to all manner of amusements, and my Nurse Conny, who takes care of me at home."

"I mean male protectors—a brother or uncle."

"Why, no. I do well enough, I assure you! I have even managed a little of Papa's business."

"Business?"

"My father is a merchant, sir." Eveline looked at him straightly, as if watching for some reaction.

"He is fortunate to have you to help him," Richard replied and smiled widely. He breathed a mental sigh of relief. So, she was not a lady born. At least there would be less of a scandal; trouble enough, but the *ton* cared little for the reputation of an untitled nobody. He relaxed. Cit's daughters were notoriously eager for a title. If she were such, then all he need do would be to wait for her to make an advance toward him to secure a title for herself. Then she would be justly punished if she let her greed for a viscountess's title lead her to ruin.

Richard let himself enjoy the rest of the dance: the feel of her small waist against his hand, the brush of her gown against his legs as they twirled around the room. He looked again at her green eyes, her lips that invited kisses. The task before him would not be without its rewards—and he might as well take them, since he had no other choice. He knew what he would do now. He'd flirt with her lightly, tease, and disappear—only to double his attentions toward her when he saw her again. That was what he had done with that married woman so long ago, and it had served his purpose. He did not fool himself that Miss Seton would part from him as easily as that woman did. But he doubted anyone would pursue him once he left her—there was only her invalid father, after all.

Conscience rose in his heart, but the viscount suppressed it. Between the still possible ruin of his sister, Marianne, or the ruin of Miss Seton, there was no choice. More scandal would attach itself to Marianne than to Miss Seton, he was certain. Further, did not Miss Seton say her father was a merchant? She would be very well provided for, no doubt, regardless of what happened. Marianne, on the other hand, would have nothing if he did not fulfill Teufel's agreement.

"Would you do me the honor of going into supper with

me?" he asked when the dance ended. He still held her hand and carried it gently to his lips.

Miss Seton blushed adorably. "Oh, yes! That is to say, if Lady Brookland approves."

"Of course." Richard smiled at her, and he led her to the Dowager Countess.

"Why, of course you may!" cried her ladyship when she heard Richard's request, which included herself. "But I have been claimed by my dear friend Admiral Roxsley, so you will have to be content with Miss Seton, Clairmond." Lady Brookland cast an arch look at Eveline.

"I will do my poor best, my lady," said Miss Seton demurely. She peeked up at the viscount through her lashes and a dimple appeared in her cheek.

"Your poor best, Miss Seton, is more than riches," he replied, and bowed.

Chapter 4

There was one pause, one frozen moment, while the young woman paled and pressed a shaking hand over her mouth. Then she rose hastily and drew in a sobbing breath.

"Richard! Oh, dear God, Richard!" Marianne stumbled forward, and her brother caught her. She buried her face into his neckcloth, weeping, and cast her arms around his neck as if she would never let him go.

"Hush, hush, little girl," Richard murmured into her hair, patting her back. He moved her to the sofa and sat her down, giving her a handkerchief from his pocket. She took it gratefully and dabbed her eyes and nose. He smiled. "Or I should say, big girl; you have grown since I last saw you."

"They said . . . they said you had died," Marianne murmured, and the tears threatened to fall again. Straightening her back, she swallowed and smiled instead. "But then your letter came, and the money . . . I thought at first it was a cruel joke, or perhaps one of our neighbors . . . You must know, Richard, that our neighbors have been more than kind; I would never, never take charity. But then, I saw it was in your own hand, and your own signature, and I knew it must be you, and that you would come home again." She stood up and turned to the window. Richard could see her tears falling, reflected in the glass.

He came to her and put a comforting arm around her shoulders—thin shoulders, he noted. He mentally cursed his father and himself again. Thoughtless! Well, he would make it up to her and gladly forfeit his soul.

"There now, Marianne, sweeting. I am home, and you are not alone any longer. I will take care of you."

She turned and smiled up at him. "Oh, I would not blame you if you think I am a silly, useless thing! I have become quite a watering-pot, have I not? But I assure you, I have made myself quite useful! You need not fear I will hang on your sleeve."

"You may hang on my sleeve as much as you please."

"No, no! I would detest that. I know we are . . . are in the basket, you see," she said, looking at him with dark, grave eyes. She sat down again on the sofa.

"And where did you hear that vulgar phrase, dear sister?" Richard's smile was wry.

"From the stable boy, of course!" Marianne grinned. She bit her lip, her expression sobering, and cast an uncertain look at him. "I hope you do not mind it, but I have had to sell off Papa's horses, you see, although I did keep Jupiter for my own transportation. I didn't want to be beholden to so many . . ."

"No, of course not. It is well that you did. I was going to do so myself when I returned, so it is just as well." He had not sold Satan, himself; it cost little to travel by horseback, especially if he slept in haylofts from time to time.

Marianne smiled another uncertain smile at him, then looked down at her hands, fiddling with his handkerchief in her lap.

"But you are not pleased."

"It is not fit that you should have anything to do with selling horses, my dear."

"Should I have sold off our paintings instead?" she asked, puzzled. "Flour and tea, I have found, cost quite a bit more than I would have thought, you see."

Richard burst out laughing. "No, not that, either. But I suppose I cannot blame you if you are not up to snuff. It is not as if you have had any opportunity to gain some town bronze, after all."

"Oh, pooh! *That* is nothing! I have heard it is quite noisy and dirty in London!"

"You would not say that if you had had a chance at a Season, Marianne."

His sister put a comforting hand on his arm.

"You mustn't think I would miss that sort of thing, truly! Why, I have heard that London dandies will rudely ogle a lady with their quizzing glasses, just like horrid Mr. Candle in town! I think I should feel quite uncomfortable with dozens of Mr. Candles staring at me, to be sure."

Richard gazed at Marianne and saw that despite his teasing that she had grown up into a big girl—she had indeed grown into a singularly lovely young lady. She was tall, achingly thin, and her clothes hung ill upon her. But her dark gray eyes were large in her sculptured face, and her nose had escaped his own aquiline shape into something quite straight and elegant, while her lips were delicately curved. Her hair, light brown and thickly curling, formed a halo about her head. It was short, he noted, and he last remembered it as long.

She saw his gaze rest upon her hair, and her hand flew to her head in a guilty gesture. She smiled at him, but he could tell it was strained, and her eyes avoided him.

"Oh, I see you have noticed my new crop. I saw it in *Ackermann's Repository* only the other day, and thought I should look quite à la mode. So I had Susan cut it—she is quite good at dressing hair, you know—and I like it so much better than when it was long."

"You sold it, didn't you?"

"No, I—"

"Don't lie to me, Marianne. I know you have had a horrible time of it. I can tell. We are . . . poor," he made himself say, though his tongue almost stumbled over the words.

"If you must know, yes. I did sell it. I thought you would be pleased."

"Pleased! That my sister was in such straits that she had to sell her hair? Good God, Marianne, what sort of bas—

what sort of man do you think I am to be pleased that you had to sell your hair to live?"

"Don't! Just don't, Richard! It was not for food, but for a little thing that I wanted to buy," she snapped at him. She looked at him and sighed. "I though you would have been proud of my economy, Richard. Oh, don't let's argue! You are just come home and should receive a better welcome than this."

Richard gazed at Marianne's distressed face and relented. Time enough to talk of finances, and how to go on. Indeed, he would much rather not think of it—or the future. He smiled at her.

"You are quite right. We should not argue. And I do think you have done admirably in my absence. As for welcomes, I suppose if dampness is any measure, I have been welcomed quite well." That brought a merry smile to his sister's face.

"Oh, I knew you would tease me about being a watering-pot. Well, I shall tell you that I am not at all a feeble little thing anymore! I think I have managed quite well after Papa died; why, I have even been able to buy some new sheets for the beds, and our servants' wages are only a few months in arrears!"

"And I should be grateful for the latter?" Richard said.

Marianne's lips twisted briefly in a hard little smile. "Oh, yes. When Papa died, our servants—the ones we had left—had not been paid for a year."

"I see. And our tenants?"

"They are desperately poor, Richard." Her mouth trembled as if she were going to weep again, but she pressed her fingers to her lips as though to still her feelings. "They . . . have very little. I have gone out every day with food and what clothes I can find, but it is not enough. I do not even know if they have enough to move to a better estate than this one." Closing her eyes briefly, she shook her head. "You will have to see for yourself."

Her brother nodded in agreement and gazed at her, at the fleeting cynicism and sorrow that looked so foreign on her generous mouth. He had never remembered her so when she was a young girl, and before he had left for the army. He almost felt that he did not know her any longer. It had been four years; she had changed from a cheerful little girl to a grown woman who was trying to manage a household on almost nothing. He thought of the other young ladies her age, and knew she was far more mature than they. Hardship had made her so, he was sure.

"As far as the servants' wages go, I think they will be able to be paid in full. I regret to say I must leave again for Bath—" He held up a hand at Marianne's anxious look. "In a week's time. I have . . . business there. Meanwhile, we do have a week, do we not?" He smiled. "You will have to let me know of the changes since I was last here," he continued. "In fact, I am surprised that our cousin Wendle is not here. Did he not try to claim my title?"

Marianne grinned mischievously. "Oh, yes."

Richard lifted his brows.

"He did indeed come. But I am afraid he left quite hurriedly."

"Oh?"

"I shot him, you see. Papa taught me how to use a pistol—and a hunting rifle, too—before he died. I am quite good at it."

"Good God." He gazed at her in consternation. "Did he try to . . ."

Marianne blushed and looked away.

"By God, I knew he was a slimy little weasel, but I never thought he'd—" Richard gritted his teeth. "I will strangle him the next time I see him. He'll not dare come near you or this house again, I swear it."

She let out a little bubble of laughter. "Oh, you need not worry, truly! He thinks me an absolute witch, an irredeemable hoyden. I took great care that he would remember I dislike him so—every time he sits down. I used rock salt, for I was so very angry that I was sure I would do him a great injury if I used shot."

Richard stared at her, uncomprehending, then a slow grin

grew on his face. His shoulders shook with silent laughter. "You *are* a little witch!"

Marianne pressed her lips together in a prim line, but her eyes danced merrily. "I am not. I was merely disposing myself of an unwelcome suitor." Her brows creased thoughtfully. "It was unfortunate that he chose to travel here on horseback, too."

Richard burst out laughing, unable to contain himself, and she joined him. After a few moments they subsided, and he grinned at her.

"You cannot dismiss all your suitors that way, you know."

She smiled. "Oh, I don't have any suitors, so that is neither here nor there, is it? I have enough to occupy myself, after all, without silly boys coming to call."

There was silence, and then: "I understand Wyvern has called from time to time?"

Marianne glanced at him, blushing. "Oh, I daresay you have heard that I have gone to his house. But it is quite proper, I assure you! He is always sure to have a maid present if I cannot bring my own. I am governess to his two daughters, at an exorbitant wage, too! I thought at first it was charity on his part, but he pointed out he'd never been able to keep a governess on for more than a month. The girls are quite high-spirited, and I imagine an older governess would not do for them. And there are very few that want to stay at such a stark place, he says."

"If he paid an exorbitant wage, I would imagine more than a few would risk it." Richard's lips twisted in a cynical smile.

She shook her head. "No, for Sarah and Stephanie are quite mischievous. They even set fire to one poor lady's wig—although I am sure it was an accident, and not at all malicious."

Richard's smile turned amused. "And you are not daunted by them at all?"

"Oh, no. I can see how they might have made such a mistake in setting the wig afire. As for their tricks, why, they are precisely the ones you used to play on our governess, so I always know what to expect." She smiled and shook her head fondly. "They really are the most darling girls."

"I? I never set our governesses' wigs on fire."

"No, for none of them had wigs, but you did other things. I remember them all," Marianne said, grinning. "So you see, it is not at all charity on Lord Wyvern's part. I am simply the best one to keep the girls in proper order, and teach them, too." Marianne said this with simple pride, and Richard could not bring himself to persuade her to cease her teaching, especially after he had railed at her for selling her hair.

"And how does Wyvern . . . treat you?" he could not help asking.

"Oh, well enough," she said calmly, but blushed. "He is all that is proper and is most gentlemanly; he comes only to see how the girls are doing in their studies and their deportment and leaves soon after."

"Does he? And that is why you are blushing now?"

"Oh, for goodness' sake, Richard! As if there was anything in his behavior to blush about! It is just that I was thinking . . ." She smiled at him mischievously. "I was thinking he is nothing like the stories I used to make up about the Wicked Earl. He is quite ordinary, and very correct in his behavior. Quite the opposite from the way I had imagined him when I was a girl. Do you remember the stories we made up of him?"

Recalling them, Richard thought how he, too, had believed Wyvern quite ordinary when he invited him to play whist at White's. He turned away to gaze out the window and made his voice as cheerful as possible. "Oh, yes, I remember. But people are rarely as one imagines them to be." He turned back to her, hoping he had composed his expression to a sufficient calmness. Marianne smiled and took his arm, then leaned her cheek against his shoulder.

"Yes. Lord Wyvern is more pleasant than we had ever thought the Wicked Earl would be."

Richard's hand trembled on the edge of making a fist.

"Yes. I suppose he is," he replied.

The neglect and decay of his estate was worse than he had thought. Richard now understood why his solicitors would not meet his eyes when they told him into how much debt his father had driven the estate.

Richard sat on his horse and gazed at the huddled family before him. They were his tenants, but their clothes were almost as threadbare as a London beggar's. He did not need to go into their hovel of a home to imagine its disrepair; it was clear from the random boards nailed ineffectively over holes that must have let in the cold and damp of a winter's night. It was a pitiful attempt at holding their home together, but no doubt the man could do little else.

The man—Richard remembered his bailiff had said the man's name was Wardle—cleared his throat and looked down at the ground. "My lord, I know 'tis past time for the rent . . . I know I told the bailiff I'd have it. But the crops warn't so good this time, and my foot was broken this past spring, so I couldn't put in as many crops. I swear, maybe a sen'night—"

"Good God, did you think I'd come here to collect the rent?" exclaimed Richard, aghast. He got down from his horse.

Wardle dared lift his eyes. It was a beaten look, as if he'd been threshed against poverty as hard as wheat against stone. "The bailiff, he said—"

"The bailiff's a fool!" Richard said furiously. He stared at the babe wailing weakly at its mother's breast—at the woman's frightened, almost feral gaze. All the children had a listless manner, and their faces were pale and thin. He had never remembered the tenants like this, not before he had left for the army. What must his father have been thinking of? His breath went short with anger. Not of his tenants, certainly. "How long has it been like this? Your house, the lack of repairs?"

"T'warnt long, yer lordship, and not bad, beggin' yer

pardon, till maybe a year ago. Miss Marianne, she comes by to help, but with young 'uns the victuals goes quick, like."

"A year!" The man's words were like the blow of a hammer to Richard's gut, leaving him breathless. These people had lived a year in this condition. He pushed his hand in his pocket, drawing out what coins he had in it. "Here, take this, and buy some food."

The man stared at Richard's out-thrust hand. "Why, why, that's a whole five pound, yer lordship!" He did not touch the money.

Richard grasped the man's rough hand and pressed the coins in to it. "Take it. I will not have people starving on my estate."

Wardle stared at the money in his hands, as if it were some foreign thing. A shiver went through his thin frame, and a few coins clinked to the ground. With a sob the woman beside him bent and scrabbled for them, then clutched them as tightly to her breast as she did her own babe, and stared wildly at the viscount.

"Yer lordship . . . ," the man said faintly. "I, I . . . thank you m'lord! Thank you!" Richard turned away, not wanting to see the tears he heard in Wardle's voice.

He climbed on his horse and rode off. Something must be done, and if it meant his soul was lost in exchange for the lives of his tenants, so be it.

Chapter 5

"Dreaming, my dear?"

Eveline gave a little start. "Oh, I am sorry, Papa! I was not attending—how rude of me!" She turned from her seat by the parlor window and gave him all her attention. The bright sun and blue sky had beckoned her outside, but there was not anyone with whom she wished to go on an outing, really. So she sat in the parlor instead, listening to her father read from a newly purchased novel. Or rather, not listening, for her mind had clearly wandered.

"It is nothing, Evie." Mr. Seton smiled. "I suppose you are thinking of some rascally young man who has caught your eye, eh?" He shifted himself in his Bath chair and wished he did not feel so uncomfortable. He did not come downstairs very often, but there had been something in his daughter's expression, a sort of abstraction, that had caught his notice of late. He was not a successful merchant by mere chance; he prided himself on his ability to pick up another's intent or mood from the person's telltale countenance.

His daughter blushed, but grinned mischievously. "Oh, no, dear Papa, much worse. He is all of a half-pay officer, just returned from the Peninsula."

Mr. Seton's eyebrows rose. "Is he, then? And I suppose this rogue is paying you extravagant compliments?" He pulled his wool blanket closer about him.

"Well, of course! Do not all rogues pay in Spanish coin?"

"Minx!" her father growled affectionately, but knew a moment's uneasiness nevertheless. For all that Eveline teased, there was a certain light in her eyes when she talked of her admirer. Mr. Seton had always been proud of his daughter's looks, her intelligence, and common sense. She had his own acute sense of the essentials of any situation, so much so that she handled with relative ease his business affairs when he had been so ill. But love, now. That was a different kind of cat altogether. It turned many a man's wits to mush, and as for women . . .

"So tell me of your admirer, then. Especially his name."

"Well, he is Richard, Viscount Clairmond. He was a captain in the Peninsular army."

"A viscount, is he?" Mr. Seton's gaze turned wary. "Better to stay with your own kind, Evie. Oh, I wouldn't say nay to a title for you, and it would have been your mother's dear wish. But a nobleman's ways are different from ours." A niggling uneasiness flowered in the back of the merchant's mind. There was something about the name Clairmond . . . but he let it go. It would come to him in time.

"How different?" Eveline crossed the parlor to the mantelpiece, her steps impatient. She picked up a delicate porcelain Limoges egg without looking at it, and rolled it around in the palm of her hand. "Are noblemen without feelings? Are not morals and right behavior the same for all?"

"Yes, and yes." Mr. Seton sighed. "But few of them know the struggle with life that most of our class have gone through, and as for their morals . . . Let us say, my dear, that they take them less seriously than we do."

"Surely not all!" his daughter protested.

"No, of course not. But theirs is a rich and idle existence, full of privilege, and often without consideration for those not in their circle."

Eveline stopped rolling the little egg about and held it tightly instead. "So are you telling me that he is trifling with me because I am not of his class?"

"Do get off your high horse, daughter! Did I say that?"

"No, but I think you were leading up to it."

Her father laughed. "In a way, I suppose I was."

"How complimentary you are to me today, dear, dear

Papa!" She tossed the ornament in the air and caught it neatly, then put it back on the mantelpiece with a decided snap. "I am your daughter, Papa! Would I be such a fool? True, Lady Brookland takes me about to all the routs and balls and assemblies in Bath. True, I do have admirers. But do any of them call at this house? I think not. Do any of them mean marriage? Most certainly not." Eveline's smile was wry.

An ache grew in Mr. Seton's heart. His daughter was no wide-eyed innocent who saw nothing in people's actions but good. She, like him, could weigh a man's heart against his words. And yet, he wished that it had never been necessary for her to be so. He sighed. Certainly, there were many promising young men of business he had asked to his house, and introduced them to Eveline. But she had never shown any interest in any man until now.

"Then how is this one different?"

Hesitation showed plainly on Eveline's face. She glanced at her father, then said: "I do not know that he is different."

The merchant wished he could stop his questioning at this point, that he could say, "Well, then, that is that." He could not, however. Eveline had a clear-reasoning mind—more sharp than many men he knew. Logically, of course she would state the facts: that objectively she did not know this admirer was any different from any other. Yet, clearly, this viscount *was* different in some way essential to her. Mr. Seton sighed again.

"Is there one thing he does that other men do not?"

Eveline hesitated again. "He listens to me."

"Eh?"

She blushed, then laughed slightly. "Perhaps it sounds silly, but he listens to me, to what I have to say . . . as if it were important."

"I should hope so!" Mr. Seton tugged at the shawl across his legs, pulling it closer to him.

"No, really, Papa. Most men will listen to me—to most women—with an indulgent air, as if they know better no matter what I say. I declare, some come close to patting me on the head as if I were a little dog! But Lord Clairmond . . . he listens, and takes my words quite seriously—unless I am not serious, that is, and then he responds in kind." Eveline put her hand on her father's arm. "Do you see what I mean, Papa?" she asked earnestly.

"Yes, I do, child." He did indeed see. It almost made him regret the education he had given Eveline. He'd educated her for a position far higher than a merchant's daughter would normally aspire to, yet her birth would never tempt anyone from the *ton*. But what else could he have done? She was his only child, and when her mind proved to be as sharp as his, how could he not give the girl all the lessons that would hone that mind to a fine edge? And with that sort of mind came the knowledge that Eveline would never be content with the usual life of a merchant's wife. Though she never spoke of it, she must know it. She never was more than civil in a friendly manner toward the young men that called upon them. To tell the truth, once they'd found how much more astute a mind she had than theirs, they soon left for less daunting ladies.

Was this viscount worthy? Certainly his title would be, thought Mr. Seton. But he wanted someone right for Eveline, not just a title. He patted Eveline's hand gently. "Well, my dear, if he wishes to call on you, I would like to meet him."

"Yes, *if* he wishes to call on me," sighed Eveline.

The house was in a fashionable part of town, which Richard expected. What he did not expect was that it was also well-appointed, decorated with elegance and good taste. Perhaps he should not have been surprised. Miss Seton never dressed vulgarly, nor was her conversation simpering or banal. It seemed fitting that her home reflect her character. The viscount gave his hat and coat to the butler, and a mocking smile briefly touched his lips. What, really, did he know of her? He had danced attendance on her for two weeks, stayed away for another two, and now he was back. That was not much time in which to know anyone. Better he should rely on what he knew of merchant's daughters in general: women who thought only of titles and estates, with little refinement or elegance of mind.

But it was difficult to keep in mind. The Setons' butler announced him, and Miss Seton looked up, surprise writ large on her face—and that was the difficulty. For when he looked upon her face, Richard could not believe there was anything grasping or vulgar behind those large and intelligent eyes, the kind smile of welcome, or the soft, impulsive, brief touch of her hand on his own. He made himself remember the faces and the poverty of his tenants instead, and Miss Seton's attributes faded in comparison.

"How good of you to call, my lord!" she said. Richard had meant to bow over her hand only in the usual way, but somehow the feel of her long tapered fingers in his own made him bring them up to his lips. He noticed she hesitated slightly before pulling away. He smiled, and when he rose, he saw she was blushing slightly. "I have not seen you in a while."

"Not for two weeks, that is so, ma'am. I had business to attend to." That was true, although he also meant to stay out of sight to pique her interest. Miraculously, his solicitor had found an investment that had somehow been overlooked and had sent for him immediately. Miraculous, indeed. The viscount could sense the hand of Teufel in this. An advance on the contract, no doubt. But it gave him enough to send to Marianne, to keep the duns at bay for a while.

"Is there something amiss?"

Richard looked up, startled. Miss Seton's face wore a look of concern. "No, not at all. Last week's business was tedious; I was merely reflecting that I am glad to be shut of it." He must keep better control over revealing his feelings—the lovely Miss Seton was too perceptive by half.

She nodded as she rang the bell for a servant. "It can be tedious, I know. My father says I have a good head for business, but I cannot see it. One would think a talent for a certain thing would make one fond of it. But I, alas, do not care for sums at all."

"It takes more than sums, I would think, to make up a talent for business," Richard said lightly.

"That is what Papa says, but I am sure that sums are the greater part of it." She paused as the maidservant entered, and she looked up at him. "Would you be pleased to take some refreshment, my lord?"

He smiled and shook his head. "No, I thank you. I have come only to call and ask if you would be willing to take a short ride in my curricle with me."

"Now?" Her eyebrows rose briefly at his nod, and she hesitated. "I . . . would be very pleased to do so, my lord. I shall have to tell my father."

"You seem surprised, Miss Seton."

"I rarely go on carriage rides with gentlemen."

"Do you not like to do so?" he asked, curious.

A wry smile touched her lips. "I am rarely asked." She glanced at a watch pinned to the bodice of her dress. "I shall be ready in a quarter hour; is that soon enough?" He smiled and bowed in assent, and she walked gracefully out the room.

As soon as Eveline left the parlor, she all but ran up the stairs to her room. Her cheeks were flushed when she spied her nurse, who was startled out of arranging flowers on one of the side tables.

"Oh, Conny, he is here!" Eveline pulled hard on the bell rope. "Oh, yes, my maid. I must have Janie to help me change to a carriage dress. I must hurry!"

"Whisht! Now what is all this, Miss Eveline?"

"Lord Clairmond! He has invited me for a carriage ride in his curricle." Eveline flung open the wardrobe door and pushed aside one dress after another in a distracted manner. "No, no, not that one. Oh, that jonquil makes me look positively ill! I should never have bought it! Where is my cherry merino?"

"Oh, Lord Clairmond, is it? Well, he may be a lord, Miss Evie, but crushing your clothes like a heathen because you're in such a hurry I will not have." Nurse clicked her tongue in disapproval and went to the wardrobe, pulling out the cherry carriage dress at once. "Sure and it's in less time I found it, for all your scrambling!"

"*Thank* you, Conny!" Eveline smiled brilliantly upon her.

"My, you are in a tizzy, Miss Evie, which—if I may be so bold to speak—won't bring you downstairs any faster than if you dressed with more care as a lady should."

Eveline stilled herself and looked at her nurse gravely. "Of course, Nurse Connor, you are quite right." She stopped and waited until the maid entered to help with the tiny buttons on the back of her dress.

But Nurse did not miss the little spark of mischief in her charge's eye. She shook her head and frowned. "Eh, and there you stand as if butter wouldn't melt in your mouth." Her expression softened, and she said: "Well, then, excepting he's a lord and all, what is there about the man that has got you so shatter-brained, child? Taken a bit of your heart, has he?"

"Oh, nonsense, Conny! You know I have no interest in titles, and besides, it is only a carriage ride, after all."

"Which is why you rushed in here like a besom from a fishmarket, flinging your clothes about, is it now?"

Eveline's lips trembled upward in a half-suppressed smile, though she blushed. "I am sorry for crushing my dresses, but I have been so dull lately, staying indoors because of the rain. I would have been eager for any outing, I daresay." She moved away from the maid when the last button was hooked, and gazed into the mirror. She smoothed back her hair, and Nurse began to tidy it.

"Humph!" said Nurse. She noticed her mistress had not precisely answered her question; she'd only said that she had no interest in titles, and not if her heart were engaged. Well, it was early days yet. She'd kept note of her young lady's talk of this viscount, and it had been but a few weeks he'd come to her notice. Miss Eveline had a practical head on her shoulders, and was too good, beside. Little chance she'd be carried away by a handsome face and a title.

And it was true. Eveline was not at all carried away by

Lord Clairmond's face or his title. As she entered the parlor again, he took her gloved hand to his lips, and the sun cast its rays through the windows and across his face, showing every feature. She reflected that he was not a beautiful man or wonderfully handsome. The lineaments of his face were too angled for that, his skin sallow beneath its brownness—certainly not the classical looks fashion favored so. It was a manly, strong face, stern in repose; but it could soften, as it did now while he looked at her.

He smiled. And that, thought Eveline, feeling breathless, was his attraction. For when he smiled at her, a warmth grew in his eyes, dispelling the darkness she sometimes fancied dwelt there. His gaze might wander, but it never wandered to other ladies' faces when he talked to her, but lingered on each of her features until it returned to her eyes again in clear appreciation. It seemed as if, during the time the viscount was with her, she had the whole of his attention; none of it grudged, or impatient, or patronizing; and certainly it was admiring. How could she be proof against that?

But she knew little of him. Only a few weeks' worth of his presence, and that was not knowledge enough of anyone for—Eveline stopped her thoughts firmly. She knew little of him, and perhaps she would come to know more, but that was all. She was a merchant's daughter, after all, and perhaps presentable enough to dance with him or ride in a carriage with him, but not more than that. She would enjoy what she had and not expect anything else.

And yet, and yet . . . A little tendril of joy crept in, and she allowed it, even letting it grow. A bit of happiness *must* be permitted her, surely. She had worked so hard this past year, with Papa's illness, and the business!

"I thought we might drive down Great Pultney Street and then to Sydney Gardens," Lord Clairmond said. "Unless, of course, you wish to go elsewhere?"

Ah, there it was again: his eyes caressing her face, smiling almost intimately. Eveline shook herself mentally, then nodded. "Oh, yes, the gardens would be delightful, thank you." She wondered briefly if his manner toward her were simply the way he was around all ladies. She supposed it must be true, if any of Lady Brookland's gossip were also true. All the Clairmonds, had said the Dowager Countess, were charmers. Well, then! To succumb to his looks and his smile was folly, for they meant nothing.

But the afternoon conspired against her. For it was a warm day for spring, warmer than she'd expected. All that remained of the clouds that had obscured the sun and sky for weeks on end were small white wisps, too fragile-looking to survive such warmth. The sky was a blue that only spring could bring; so bright and deep it almost hurt her eyes to look at it. It made all things stand out sharp and clear, and whenever Eveline looked at the viscount's not classically handsome countenance, the clarity of her vision etched his eyes, his mouth, the lean lines of cheek and jaw painfully into her heart.

"I suppose you have seen Sydney Gardens many times already," he said as they approached.

Eveline looked at him, a little surprised. His voice had sounded diffident, almost apologetic. Somehow the emotion did not fit with her perception of him, for he seemed a proud man. But she smiled and said, "Yes, I have. We have lived here, my father and I, for two years, after all. But I never tire of it; it is pretty and I am always finding something new in the gardens."

"New?"

"Shrubbery, flowers, trees. It is different than in London, somehow. Perhaps it is because the gardeners are always changing something, planting new flowers and such every year." She turned to him, smiling in a comforting manner. "I daresay it is all very new to you as you are only recently come back from the Continent."

"Yes." His voice sounded odd, as if he were holding in his breath as he spoke. She saw his jaw stiffen and his body tense as if he were readying himself for an assault. She remembered suddenly that Lady Brookland had said he'd been thought dead, for his injuries had been severe. An aching warmth flooded her heart, and she put her hand on his arm.

"I am sorry. It must be . . . difficult for you coming back to England. I should not have even hinted at the . . . the unpleasantness you must have experienced there."

He turned an astonished gaze on her. "*Unpleasantness?* Is that what dirt and blood and death are to you civilians? Good God."

Eveline could feel her face grow warm. "I . . . I am sorry. How could I know? And since I do not know, how can I find the right word to describe it?" She looked away, at once angry and ashamed. How could she know? Yes, she'd heard the reports, but the numbers of dead and wounded had been so high as to be incomprehensible. She had tried, but her mind had refused to take it in, for at that time she had been deep in her father's business during the day, deep in worry over his unconscious state, and nursing him at night. "I only meant after living in different countries and fighting for so long, that coming back to England must seem almost foreign to you."

Lord Clairmond gazed at her with angry, yet assessing, eyes. He blinked, and it seemed a mask came over his face, smoothing it of expression. "Yes. I am sorry. I have been inexcusably rude, have I not?" he said, his voice civil once more.

"Don't. Just don't," blurted Eveline.

He raised his eyebrows in question.

"You . . . you disappeared, you see," she said. "I would much rather have you angry at me for my thoughtlessness than have you pretend you are not."

His smile was amused. "Disappeared? But I am here, as you see." Flicking a glance at the approaching gardens, he slowed the horses, then stopped. As he stepped down and helped her out of the curricle, his smile broadened. "And I am not at all angry at you, believe me."

Eveline bit back a sigh and fell back to common civility, returning his smile and saying, "It was only an odd expression of mine. Silly, actually." It was not really an explanation, but Lord Clairmond only smiled again and nodded almost absently.

She regretted her outburst. The day was still crisp and clear, and yet their outing felt clouded to her now, as if a mist separated them. An ache grew where she had felt joy just minutes before, and as she looked up at Lord Clairmond's face once more, she knew a thing she wished she did not: She was falling in love with him.

It was not, as she had thought, truly because of his smile, although it was one of the most attractive things about him. It was the air of singularity, of aloneness, of apartness; as if he were not a part of this civilized, ordinary town of Bath, but as if he belonged somewhere else—dark, wild, and even cold. It was something she, herself, knew, for though she was educated and raised as a lady, her education went far and above what most young ladies received. It set her apart, set her mind raging with a wild passion, wanting to be out of the ordinary, but knowing her birth would hardly let her do so. But cold . . . . She was not that, she was sure, and that element she perceived in Clairmond intrigued her.

The viscount said something about the gardens; she had not heard the whole of it, she realized, for she had not been attending. She turned her face away from him to hide the blush suffusing her cheeks. She replied something—she was sure it was inane, though her confusion did not let her remember what she said—and blushed more fiercely at the thought of her inanity. She hoped at least it was adequate enough to turn the subject and continue the conversation in a more conventional vein.

It was; or at least enough for the viscount's easy address to make it so. As they strolled the gardens, a crisp breeze cooled Eveline's warm face so that she could gaze at him once again and smile. She saw an assessing, intimate expression in his eyes then, and fearing she would blush once more, she looked away and caught sight of a squirrel looking at them quizzically from a tree. A laugh broke through her discomfort, and she pointed at the little animal. "Do look! Is he not the most odd little creature? He looks for all the world as if he wishes desperately to talk to us," she said.

Lord Clairmond's lips twisted in a wry smile. "More likely he wishes we had a piece of bread to feed him." She glanced at him, half reproachfully at his commonsensical reply, and he laughed at her look, and comfort returned.

And yet, Eveline was dissatisfied. The day continued to be bright and clear, but though he smiled and talked so easily, she could see just as clearly the fleeting shadows in Lord Clairmond's eyes.

Chapter 6

Richard, Viscount Clairmond, however, was quite satisfied. Slowly, surely, he was pulling Miss Seton in, like a fish on a line. He had heard her hurried steps as soon as she left the parlor: She had been eager to ride in the carriage with him earlier this afternoon. All for a title, he was certain.

He sighed, sitting on the inn's bed, trying to tug his boot off. Lescaux cleared his throat in a meaningful way, but Richard ignored him. He bent his attention to thoughts of Miss Seton instead, smiling a little in relief. She was a creature of little compassion, surely. He'd seen other women weep at the mention of all the men dead in the war, but not a tear filled Miss Seton's eyes. She was pretty, and had no heart—and he was thankful for it. It would make the seduction and eventual abandonment much, much easier; for all his depredations amongst the demimondaine and high-born light-skirts, he had never seduced a young woman innocent of fleshly delights. Well, he thought, she was certainly not a lady of birth. Perhaps she knew nothing of respectable behavior, whom she should entertain or not. Was she not nearly unchaperoned in that house, with her father an invalid?

Richard's conscience rebuked him for this last thought, for he had heard nothing disreputable of her, but he turned a deaf ear to his conscience. So what if Lady Brookland had introduced Miss Seton to him? He only knew Lady Brookland as an old acquaintance of his father's, and nothing about the lady herself. Perhaps she was faulty in her judgment of dressmakers.

He absently tugged at his boot again. This time he could not ignore the louder throat-clearing from Lescaux, for the valet stood directly in front of him. Richard glanced at his supremely disapproving expression and laughed.

"Oh, very well, you old fraud!" he said, extending his foot. Lescaux sniffed—as haughtily as any patron of Almack's—and flicked out a handkerchief from his sleeve.

"For God's sake, Lescaux, get on with it!"

His valet eyed him sternly, the handkerchief delicately poised in midair between his thumb and index finger. "Milord le Capitaine, there is a wrong way of removing a boot, and a right way, *n'est-ce pas?* I, Lescaux, cannot do anything but what is right. It would be a . . . a smarch upon the reputation of Milord."

" 'Smirch,' Lescaux."

"Bah!"

The little man tenderly wrapped the handkerchief around the heel and pulled. It came off easily. He smiled in obvious satisfaction.

Richard rolled his eyes to the ceiling. "Very well, I admit it, you are correct. I am incapable of pulling off my own boots." He stood up and walked to the washstand to wash his face.

"I did not say *that*, Milord." Lescaux's expression was still complacent, however. "You are, of course, capable of it. But a man who is thinking of *l'amour* cannot be responsible for looking at his boot, when he would prefer to look at a lady, particularly one such as Mademoiselle Seton, eh?"

The cloth in Richard's hand dropped into the washbasin. "I am *not* thinking of *l'amour,* I assure you."

The valet's smile was skeptical.

"Lescaux! For God's sake!"

"Of course not, Milord. What do I, a valet, comprehend of these things?" He shrugged his shoulders expressively. The knowing look still remained, however.

Richard did not know whether to laugh or snap at his servant. He'd known when he agreed to have Lescaux as his valet that the man would barely respect the boundaries between master and man; he'd never stood on ceremony with anyone when they were in the army, yet even Wellington himself had overlooked it and laughed at the Belgian's outspokenness.

Lescaux sighed. "English! They appreciate only horses. Were such a one as Miss Seton to come upon a Belgian . . . ah!" He kissed his fingers to the air. "Such grace, such beauty—*et très douceur!*"

"She is, I assure you, merely a flirtation."

The valet pursed his lips thoughtfully. "Ah? And so she thinks it, eh?"

"No doubt," said Richard lightly. He removed the rest of his clothes, readying himself for bed.

Lescaux sighed sentimentally. "And many opportunities for the flirtation, *oui?* The assembly, the musicale, the ride in the park, the masquerade, and tomorrow the alfresco luncheon in the country." He ticked off each item on his fingers.

"For God's sake, have done!" Richard snapped. "If she thinks my attentions are anything more than trivial, then it is she who is at fault, not I!" He flung aside the bedclothes and moved between them, turning his back to Lescaux.

The valet stared at his master for one moment, then shook his head. He had not spoken of fault at all; it was Milord who had spoken of it. Lescaux sighed again, not sentimentally at all, and removed himself from the viscount's chambers.

Richard was lost again, but this time he did not have his horse, Satan. He could feel mist, as he had the last time—cold and clinging to the skin of his face. A chill presence grew behind his back, and he turned. Teufel.

"What do you want?"

Teufel looked thoughtfully at him and swung his diamond-topped walking stick slowly to and fro.

"Well?" Richard clenched his teeth in impatience.

"You are taking your time about seducing Miss Seton's virtue, are you not?"

"And you are taking your time about your promise of wealth, are you not?"

Teufel raised his brows. "I will deliver it *after* you have done your task."

"Pardon me," Richard replied sarcastically. "That is not how I remember our bargain."

"I thought you a gentleman and an officer, bound by your word, and here you are trying to squeeze out of our agreement." Teufel shook his head sorrowfully.

Anger boiled within Richard at the insult. "I would meet you for that, were you human, Teufel."

"But I am not, and there is nothing you can do about that, can you?" Teufel replied kindly. "I forgive you, however. You were quite ill when we met, as I recall. I cannot really blame you if you do not remember exactly the way I phrased the terms."

Richard gazed at Teufel in frustration. Briefly, he had hoped his recollection had been as he remembered it. But it was true he had been ill, having contracted influenza as Lescaux later informed him. It was also true that his memory was elusive on exact wording of the agreement, for the thing that dominated his mind was the wracking pain of fever he had felt at the time. If he was, however, no longer an officer, certainly he was a gentleman and had made a gentleman's agreement. He was bound by his word, no matter how Teufel spoke mockingly of it.

"Your creditors grow impatient, I think," Teufel said.

For a moment the viscount averted his face. "They can wait. Besides, you must know seduction is best done slowly." There was a sneer in his voice.

Teufel grinned. "Of course. But you could have had it done and over with, oh, yesterday. You could have suggested a longer ride to the lovely Miss Seton, taken her off to one of the abandoned cottages on your estate, and have ruined her quite successfully, I am sure. It is only a two-hour ride there, after all."

Richard's hands almost curled into fists, but he made them relax. He smiled coolly. "How crude. You must know I prefer the elegance of slow seduction to the vulgarity of rape." His voice was heavily ironic.

"Of course." Teufel gave an equally ironic bow. "But I grow impatient. Surely your charm is such that you can accomplish a seduction within a month?"

"You flatter me."

"Not at all, my dear Clairmond. How many women have you seduced in the past, hmmm? In far less time? Shall I name them for you?"

Richard felt nauseated. For all that Miss Seton was a grasping merchant's daughter, she was an innocent compared to the women he had lusted after in the years before the war. They had known what lovemaking would entail and were experienced in it; Miss Seton no doubt was not experienced at all. If she struggled, it would be little better than the rape he detested.

"And how is the lovely Miss Seton so very different? These merchant's daughters—they are far more earthy, however virginal, than the ladies of your own rank, shall we say?"

The viscount stared at Teufel in barely concealed disgust. "I will do it in my own time. You need not remind me."

"Oh, but I must, I must!" replied Teufel. He gently tapped the diamond end of his walking stick against his smiling mouth. "I think you forgot yourself yesterday—forgot your purpose in pursuing Miss Seton."

"Not at all," replied Richard, keeping his voice cool with an effort. "But I merely thought I'd take some pleasure in the process, you see."

"Of course. And I am sure you shall." Teufel chuckled. "Tomorrow."

Richard's lip curled in distaste for his vulgarity.

"Oh, oh, so high!" mocked Teufel. "I do admire pride, you know."

"Go away. I will do it in my own time. I cannot guarantee it will be tomorrow."

"Of course," Teufel said. He saluted Richard with his walking stick, and the mist enveloped him.

Richard stared into the dimness where Teufel had disappeared. He unloosed his clenched fists and pressed his palms into his eyes with weariness.

When he removed them, it was day, and he was sitting up in his bed, chill sweat trickling down his face. *A dream.* Of course. It was a dream, and he had been asleep . . . but Richard did not feel rested at all.

He closed his eyes again, but sleep eluded him. He shivered violently. Cold—he felt cold. He looked at the low fire in the fireplace across the room from the bed, and pulling on his robe as he arose out of bed, he threw some logs upon the fire, scattering ashes in his haste. The fire sank, then flared higher as the flames licked at the dry wood. He pulled a footstool to him and sat on it, holding out his hands and moving his feet toward the heat. Slowly, slowly, the warmth returned to his limbs, his fingers and toes aching with the blood now coursing through them. A knock sounded on the door.

"Come!" called Richard.

It was Lescaux, carrying carefully ironed neckcloths. The little man glanced at the fireplace and the roaring fire, and feeling the tremendous heat coming from it, looked curiously at his master. The sun was streaming through the windows, bright and warm, but it seemed the viscount did not feel it or see it. The room was almost suffocating in its heat.

The valet reverently laid the neckcloths over the back of a chair. "I think Milord le Capitaine has need of his sleep, so I did not disturb him, *oui?* But the time, she passes, and I think also you do not want to miss the alfresco luncheon with Miss Seton."

The viscount looked at the old clock above the mantelpiece. "Good God. I should have left here already to hire the curricle." He rubbed his face wearily. "I shall depend on you, Lescaux, to help get me ready as soon as possible."

"Of course, Milord." And yet, Milord le Capitaine did not move as fast as one would when looking forward to an appointment with a lovely young lady.

Eveline awoke with a warm sense of anticipation, feeling as if she were a child promised a treat on Christmas Day. She opened her eyes and chuckled to herself. It was the wrong season for Christmas, for the bright spring sun flung its rays through her window and the singing of sparrows told her it was quite otherwise.

Ah, but the treat, however, was soon to be given her, for was she not to go out into the country with the Viscount Clairmond today? She stretched her arms joyfully, then tossed back the bedclothes and rose from her bed.

She did not take long to dress, for she had already chosen the clothes she would wear. The slight dissatisfaction she had felt upon the close of her carriage ride with the viscount was totally routed when she had later received, not two hours later, a missive writ in his large, dark handwriting, requesting her company on an outing to an alfresco luncheon. It would be with a few of his friends, perhaps two hours out to his estate. It would take nearly the whole day, but she was sure she could not find the length of the event tedious at all.

For she fully acknowledged that she was in love with the viscount, and though she did not know whether he felt the same toward her or not, she felt she could not, should not, put a stop to her feelings.

It had come to her in the night, in dreams of light and shadow. Eveline had dreamt of the sleepless nights when she did not know if her father would live or die, the fatiguing travels to her father's house of business, made even more wearying by wondering if he would be alive when she returned. She remembered, even before her father's accident, the halfhearted morning calls of young men who clearly believed young ladies should read nothing more than descriptions of the newest fashions in Ackermann's

Repository. She did not want to become a bored matron filled with trivial thoughts and petty gossip, as she had seen many of these young men's wives become, though she thought wistfully of marriage as well.

She could never marry the viscount, of course. He would find someone of his own station to wed. But here now was love, and though she might die a spinster, she'd seize the experience and it would warm her as a cold and tedious marriage would never do.

How could such an emotion be wrong? It filled her heart with light, and she told herself she did not care whether he returned her affections. She knew it was an impossible thing—that he could want to marry her, a merchant's daughter. Time and time again she had reminded herself that he was merely looking for amiable company, perhaps a flirtation, but never, never marriage. He was a viscount, and of an old family, she had heard. And so, the most she could hope for was to love, and take what joy she could from his company.

She knew he would probably leave at one point, never to see her again, perhaps to marry another, better-born lady. The thought brought a sharp, hot pain to her; but she knew also that if she did not take what she could of love, she would regret it all her life.

She took her pink round gown that Nurse had set out the night before and put it against herself, swinging around in a little waltz. She would think only of now, and when Clairmond came for her, she'd gaze and gaze at him as many times as she dared, so that she could remember him always.

The door opened to let in Nurse, who also carried in Eveline's breakfast. The woman gazed sternly at her mistress and put down the breakfast tray. "As if I hadn't taken great care to take all the wrinkles out of that lovely dress, here you go crushing it, Miss Eveline!"

Eveline put down the dress hastily on the bed, spreading and smoothing the skirts. She smiled demurely at her nurse.

"Oh, no, Nurse Conny! I was not crushing it, truly! Only . . . only seeing if it fit as it should."

Nurse eyed her skeptically. "And it's a grand number of inches you have grown in the last month, I'll warrant."

Eveline burst out laughing. "Of course!"

Nurse's lips twitched, and a twinkle grew in her eye, but she tried to keep her face stern. A chuckle broke out instead. "Aye, and well do I know you've taken a fancy to that Lord Clairmond!" Her face sobered, and she looked keenly at her charge. "But you'll not be losing your heart to the gentleman now, I hope. That one may be all of a lord, but I've heard he might look higher for a wife, Miss Evie—and I mean no disrespect to you or Mr. Seton."

Eveline's eyes grew grave. "Of course I know that, Conny." She turned away, gazing out of the window. "It is a flirtation only, I am sure." She looked at her nurse again, giving her a brilliant smile. "Meanwhile, I shall enjoy every minute of it."

Nurse Connor sighed quietly and picked up the dress. There was no telling her young lady anything; she'd taken the bit between her teeth and run. She was sure Miss Evie would never do anything disreputable; but she feared she'd break her heart instead.

Chapter 7

The Earl of Wyvern turned over the invitation card meditatively. He was certain it did not come from Clairmond himself. The man disliked him, possibly for the same reason the late viscount had refused to associate with the earl's family, and very probably because Wyvern had forced Richard Clairmond's hand regarding Miss Clairmond's fate.

The card was, most likely, from Miss Clairmond herself. He was sure she would be going to the alfresco luncheon; no doubt Clairmond had told her to invite what friends she wished. Wyvern's hand tightened, creasing the card, and his lip curled at the thought. Did he not know Marianne had no friends to invite? She had had no time for frivolous pursuits, no time for calling on friends too far away to travel safely in her decrepit little gig. She'd had to use what time she could squeeze from the day to attend to estate affairs, and spend a few hours with his daughters for the frankly meager salary he gave her.

He'd wanted to give her a higher wage, for he well knew she and her servants had barely enough to manage both the estate and their stomachs; but he knew if he had, she'd grow suspicious of his charity and would not take the extra money if she found out how much more she was already being paid than the usual governess's wage.

The earl turned the little card over and over again in his fingers, then flicked it down on the silver salver his butler had left on his escritoire. If Clairmond knew nothing of Marianne's friendless state, it would serve Wyvern's purposes just as well. He would go. If he did not, Miss Clairmond's pride would surely suffer. He smiled a slight, ironic smile. Her image grew in his mind's eye, and he could see her back stiffening in defiance if he were not there. He could not do it to her, of course. Life had dealt her pride severe blows, not the least of which was a thoughtless brother, but she had bravely held up her head through it all.

A dull ache went through the earl's heart at the thought; he had fought against the feeling for a long time, but he had finally acknowledged that he loved Miss Clairmond—Marianne. His interest had been sparked when he had found her fishing in the brook that separated their estates. It was in a part of the brook that had been claimed both by his father and the late viscount, her father. He had questioned her right to fish in it, and she had defied him. He argued, and she threw her fishing rod in the brook in a rage. When he laughed, she stormed off, leaving brook, fish, and rod behind.

Of course he had to return the fishing rod; and when he did, she had received him with chill formality, worthy of a dowager duchess. He had also noticed the faded furniture and curtains, her dowdy dress, and how she had worn her pride like a royal robe.

He rose and pulled the bell rope for his valet, and when the servant entered, he readied himself for the luncheon. He smiled to himself, remembering. He had presented the fishing rod to her, and she had taken it in a grand manner, looking very much like a rather shabby queen with an overly thin scepter. And then, seeing the picture she made when she happened to glance at a nearby mirror, she had burst into laughter. And for the first time since his wife's death, he had laughed as well.

He did not know how it had happened, but during the course of his call, he had acceded to her all rights to that portion of the brook his father and hers had argued over for decades. He had noticed the poor repair of her house, and it irked him. He had sent a carpenter to work on it. She sent the man back. She would take no charity, thank you, her note had said. But each time he called upon her, the quality of her life vexed him more and more until he ached to do something, anything, to help her.

When the last governess had fled from his house, her wig still ablaze in the fireplace—his daughters had tied a string to the wig while the woman had dozed, and when she rose from her chair, it had fallen off into the hearth—he had hit upon the idea of hiring Miss Clairmond to care for his daughters during the time he sought another governess. So he had written a pleading note, and Marianne had come to his aid, as—she said—a neighbor should. Yes, he had calculated it correctly: He could depend on a Clairmond's sense of duty, if not pride, to spur Marianne into coming to him, if not her need for money.

Each day the earl saw her—for he made sure to look into the nursery-schoolroom from time to time—he could not help wishing there was more he could do. He caught himself staring at her, at her slim, oval face and pale, clear complexion. He'd look away, but his gaze would move back again to linger upon the long line of thigh and leg as she sat, and upon her form outlined by the thin, worn muslin dress she usually wore.

The earl had not thought of marriage for a long time after his wife had died, but he thought of it now. Would Miss Clairmond come to him without a dowry? He well knew her pride would not allow her to come to him without bringing something. It was a damnable obstacle, her pride.

Well, he had got Clairmond's consent—however unwilling—to his courtship of Marianne, and having gained her friendship, he would begin to woo her in earnest. No doubt the viscount believed the earl thought of her only as a substitute mother for his children at best. At worst . . . A cynical smile crossed Wyvern's lips. No doubt Clairmond thought him a satyr lusting after an innocent maiden, from whom it was his brotherly duty to save her. If so, perhaps he would allow the viscount to continue thinking it. His smile grew wider. If it made Clairmond agonize over Marianne a little, and drive him to bettering his estate and his sister's life in general, then most certainly he would allow him to think it.

How entertaining it would be! He could be virtuous and pursue a pleasurable courtship at the same time. Wyvern chuckled to himself and with a last little tug on his neckcloth put on his hat at a definitely rakish angle and left the room.

The sun was hot on Eveline's face as she lifted her gaze to the sky. Were it not for the breeze that blew steadily upon her as Lord Clairmond's curricle bowled over the road, she would have felt quite uncomfortable. Though the sky was mostly clear with a few gray clouds in the distance, the air felt thick and heavy with moist heat. Another guest's barouche bowling along in front of them showed the occupants chatting to each other; Eveline could see the fluttering of handkerchiefs from time to time, so she supposed they, too, were feeling the heat. She looked surreptitiously at the viscount. He seemed cool and composed despite the energy needed to guide two fresh horses.

Clairmond's eyes met hers and he smiled; but now she was conscious of a subtle, new disturbance. The shadows she had seen in his eyes before seemed to have deepened, and though he smiled at her intimately, it was of a sort that made her feel suddenly uneasy. Eveline wondered why he had sought out her company. Flirtation, she had thought. However, there were many other ladies with whom he could do that—ladies of greater birth, of comely and beautiful looks who had actively sought out his company. She had seen it in the assembly rooms, and in the pump room. And yet, he had responded to them with smiling civility and flirted with them not at all. Her nurse's cautionary words came to her again, and her father's as well. A little trepidation crept into her. . . . Could it be that because of her lower birth, he thought her more likely to be seduced, for example?

Eveline shook her head and smiled at herself. *Of course not*. He had always acted the gentleman, and she had often experienced the sort of approach from so-called gentlemen who were interested in nothing but seduction. He had always treated her as if she were a lady born, rather than the practical merchant's daughter she actually was. Regardless, she was no fool to fall for anyone's blandishments. She was firmly resolved to enjoy the rest of the day, and no thoughts of wrongdoing would mar it.

They soon arrived at their destination, a small park of grass and trees near a lake, with the rest of the party. Lord Clairmond had told her it was on the outskirts of his property, and so it was; it was only a little way from the main road from Bath. There were three carriages in all: the one she was in and the other two with Lord Clairmond's friends.

With a smile the viscount introduced her to his friend, Sir John Grey, and his sister Miss Lavinia Grey. Sir John was a tall blond man, a little unkempt in his dress. His sister was also tall for a woman, but she was as neat as her brother was untidy, and her merry face was heart-shaped rather than long.

Sir John bowed over Eveline's hand and threw a laughing glance at Lord Clairmond. "So this is what has been keeping you from the delights of London, eh, Hawk?"

Eveline blushed, then suppressed a smile as she looked at the viscount. It hadn't occurred to her, but he did indeed look like a hawk, with his aquiline nose and large piercing dark eyes.

Clairmond rolled his eyes. "Good Lord. I see I may depend on my friends to make fun of my poor face. Why I ever decided to invite you, Jack, is beyond me."

"To keep you humble—the Clairmonds' pride is legendary, and pride is a sin, you know." Sir John turned to Eveline. "I swear to you, Miss Seton, that the Clairmonds' insteps are so high that their bootmakers have to make a miniature bridge inside their shoes to keep them supported." Eveline chuckled at the image.

"Oh, Jack!" Miss Grey chimed in. "I do not know how you can say that. Why, if it were so, how is it that he has consented to be the friend of such an untidily dressed person as yourself?"

Clairmond put his hand over his heart. "I thank you, Miss Grey, for coming to my defense." He gazed at his friend mockingly. "Yes, do tell me why it is I am your friend, oh unkempt one."

Jack looked innocently at them all. "Why, Hawk, you must know it's to make you shine all the brighter by contrast."

Eveline's suppressed giggle burst forth in a laugh. "I wonder that you can call each other friends the way you insult each other so!"

"Surely you must know, Miss Seton, that it is a curious habit men have of insulting their dearest friends!" replied Miss Grey, also laughing.

The occupants of the last coach stepped down, and then Eveline knew Miss Grey's words must be true. For as soon as a tall, dark figure descended from his carriage, Lord Clairmond's face turned from laughing ease to cool civility. The viscount's face softened when he looked at the young lady next to the man, but not by much.

"Wyvern." The viscount's bow to the man was as exacting and formal as the most stringent etiquette book might require.

"Clairmond," returned the earl, his voice holding just a hint of irony.

The young lady by Wyvern's side moved to place her hand on Clairmond's arm. "You did say I might bring a friend, Richard." She looked uncertainly from one man to another.

There was a short silence, and Eveline became conscious of the heavy, humid heat of the air around them.

The viscount's face unfroze just enough to give a polite smile. "Of course. You are welcome, Lord Wyvern." The earl bowed.

Clairmond took the young lady's hand and turned to Eveline. "Miss Seton, may I present to you my sister, Miss Marianne Clairmond?"

Miss Clairmond smiled at her and held out her hand, and

when Eveline took it in greeting, she liked her immediately. There was a forthrightness about Miss Clairmond's bearing, with which the merchant's daughter felt quite comfortable; she herself was far more used to dealing with frankness than with the exacting behavior often demanded in polite circles.

"I am pleased to meet you, Miss Clairmond," Eveline said. "Lord Clairmond has mentioned to me that he has a sister." She hesitated only a little; she realized the viscount had said little of his family and only mentioned that he had a sister once or twice. But then he seemed to be a private man, and perhaps he was simply not wont to talk of family matters much.

"And I, you, Miss Seton." Miss Clairmond gave her a warm smile and then looking teasingly at her brother. "And I think Sir John is in the right of it. You were never so fond of Bath before."

Eveline blushed and shook her head in denial, unable to speak out of discomfort at the attention she was receiving. Lord Clairmond came to her rescue.

"Marianne, you minx, you are putting Miss Seton to the blush! Quite an ill-mannered way of receiving our guests, I believe."

His sister only opened her eyes in wide innocence. "Why, how can that be? It cannot be ill-mannered to compliment one's guests!"

Eveline laughed, clasped Miss Clairmond's hand briefly, and looked quickly at the viscount. "No, Lord Clairmond, how can it be rude? I declare, I have not been given so much Spanish coin in all my life! How can I dislike it?"

"Spanish coin! Richard, have you not complimented her at all?" cried his sister.

"Shameful!" exclaimed Miss Grey at once, her eyes twinkling.

"Hawk! You have been shamefully behindhand, man!" Sir John said at the same time.

They all burst out laughing, including the viscount. "Well, then! I will shower Miss Seton with flowery compliments all day to make up for it, shall I?" The group laughed again and then set off toward the luncheon that Eveline could see the servants had laid out near the lake.

Through it all, however, she had noted the Earl of Wyvern's silence. He had said nothing through the company's banter, but the slight twinkling in his eyes told her he had been amused. Yet, there was still that distance, the chill formality between him and the viscount, and the slight unease of the rest of the group toward the earl. She did not know the cause of the coldness between the earl and his host. However, Miss Clairmond seemed to be on good terms with Wyvern—she had even named him friend—and Eveline could not think that the forthright Miss Clairmond would not quickly find a defect of character in her escort had it existed.

Indeed, it seemed Miss Clairmond found no defects at all in the earl, for when she looked up at him, her smile was warmly friendly . . . and perhaps there was a little more. Certainly Lord Wyvern was very attentive to the viscount's sister. It seemed to Eveline that the earl was wont to accede to Miss Clairmond's every wish, and when his gaze fell upon her, the stern cast of his face softened a little. Eveline smiled to herself. Perhaps it was because she, herself, loved Lord Clairmond that she believed she saw the emotion in every glance between other ladies and gentlemen. Whatever the case, it was a pleasant fancy, and she was not adverse to indulging in it for a while.

Lord Clairmond's expression, however, was a little more difficult to decipher. He poured her a little wine, then looked into her eyes for a long moment afterward, his expression serious. Then he smiled, but she could not decide whether it was warm, friendly, or civil. It seemed to be all of these, and she knew it was part of his charm, and an alluring trait. She smiled at the thought.

The viscount's brows rose, and he said, "And what has caused that wry little smile?"

"Oh, only that it is not always easy to tell what you are thinking from your expression."

"I see I have improved. It means I have become a better cardplayer, and can hope to win the next time."

"Hmm. Rather like negotiating a sale of property. You cannot reveal what you know or have guessed of the deal or the property, lest your opponent gain the advantage."

"Very like *vingt et un*." Clairmond chuckled. "It is a card game," he said in response to her questioning look.

Eveline looked at him curiously. "Do you play much at cards?"

This time there was no mistaking the look on his face: grim. "I used to. I do so rarely now."

This was clearly an unpleasant subject for him, so she went on smoothly. "I have not played cards much, perhaps silver-loo at most. I think making investments is safer. It has risks also, but these are well-informed, calculated ones. It is far easier to know the history of a company or business and base your decision on that than it is to discern the cards in a game."

"True." He smiled again. "You sound knowledgeable. I suppose your father has spoken of such things to you many times."

Eveline smiled. "That is what most people would think, is it not? But my father has spoken only of general business principles; I assure you, much of my knowledge is from experience."

"From experience?" The viscount's brows rose again. "He has allowed you to decide on investments for him?"

"He had no choice." She made her voice light. "He was seriously ill at the time."

"I am sorry."

She cast him a quick look from under her eyelashes. "You need not be. He is much better now, and I believe it was a valuable thing for me to do. I learned much, I think, about whom to trust, and how to assess a man's character." She chuckled. "I have found it to be an advantage to be a woman in such negotiations. Few men assume a woman knowledgeable or well-advised in her dealings." She widened her eyes mock innocently. " 'Oh, dear sir, I simply am *not* conversant with such matters as *you* are. Perhaps you can enlighten me?' "

"Is that what you say?" The corners of Clairmond's lips quivered upward.

"Oh, yes! And I am ever so grateful when they give me the information I need to buy and sell at an excellent profit."

He let out a shout of laughter. "You are a minx, Miss Seton!"

Eveline cast down her eyes. "You are *so* kind, my lord," she said demurely.

He laughed again and took her hand to his lips. She looked up at him then and saw the shadows had fled his eyes, replaced by laughter and a definite warmth. She felt an answering warmth through the hand he held, and it flowed into her heart and became joy. *This is why it is worth it. It matters not if he marries me; it is enough that I have made him laugh for a time and for me to remember it.* A whole loaf was impossible; did she not hear for herself how proud the Clairmonds were of their lineage? But she could make do with the half and be happy with it, for if there was anything *she* prided herself on, it was her practicality.

She glanced away briefly and caught sight of Miss Clairmond's and Miss Grey's interested eyes. Hastily, Eveline pulled her hand from the viscount's grasp. She wondered if they could discern her feelings for him and resolved to put a stronger control over her features, just in case it were so. They talked of other things then, and occasionally the other guests would drift by and contribute to the conversation, fanning their faces lazily in the heat.

Sir John sauntered over, his collar wilting, and looking even more untidy than ever. He caught Lord Clairmond's eye and jerked his head toward the western sky.

"Ought to pack it in, Hawk, in my humble opinion. Those clouds look deuced nasty. A bad thing to have the ladies drenched by rain, eh?" His mischievous grin, however, somehow gave Eveline the idea that he wouldn't think it a bad thing at all if it did happen.

Eveline looked up at the sky, and her smile faded, for the clouds did indeed look very large, very black, and very threatening. Good heavens! She wondered if it would be possible to get back to Bath without ruining her dress.

The viscount gazed at the sky as well, then nodded decisively. "Quite right, Jack." Quickly, he signaled to the servants and ordered the luncheon remains to be taken away. None of the guests protested, for they, too, could see the dark clouds and feel the increasing humidity that signaled rain in no uncertain terms.

The first to leave were Miss Clairmond and the earl; it seemed Wyvern had been very aware of the impending storm for quite some time and had ordered his horses to be ready. Sir John and Miss Grey were next, as Clairmond still had to shout a last few orders to his servants.

At last Eveline was seated in the curricle. A gust of wind nearly blew her hat from her head, and she looked anxiously at the sky again. Though the wind was a welcome relief from the earlier still heat, it also clearly pushed the clouds closer overhead. The viscount took the reins, and they were off.

The wind turned more fierce as they went on and kicked up the dust of the road so that the carriages ahead were obscured from Eveline's view. The air was damp now, though no drops of rain yet fell upon them. She saw Lord Clairmond squint his eyes against the dust, as if to discern the direction of the road and the carriages ahead. His lips tightened, and she knew that he saw as much as she did: nothing but the road ahead. They had lost the others.

Thunder rolled in the distance, and the horses tossed their heads nervously. The viscount muttered something, and Eveline smiled to herself. She was sure he had uttered a curse. She could understand his frustration. It had been a most pleasant luncheon, but for the impending rain and haste to leave. She did not mind it, although she felt uneasy at losing sight of the rest of the carriages. It left her relatively unchaperoned, but she comforted herself with the idea that the other guests knew when they had departed, and if the viscount returned her home in an adequate amount of time, there could be no scandal attached to it.

And then the rain poured. An especially large gust of

wind tore at her bonnet, but failed to dislodge it; in revenge it threw large drops of rain upon her face. She wiped the wet from her eyes with a handkerchief, but it was useless; the wind only flung the rain more fiercely onto her. She glanced at Lord Clairmond and caught his aggravated gaze before he returned his attention to his horses.

"Damn!" The rain was falling in sheets now. Clairmond urged his horses to a faster pace.

Eveline did not reprove him for his oath, for it reflected her own sentiments. At least there was no dust obscuring the road now. She smiled in spite of herself. "You need not worry, my lord. I will not melt."

A quick grin crossed his lips before it turned down in frustration again. "At the risk of seeming a graceless boor, I will say that not only do I believe you, but it is for another reason I wish to hurry. There is a stream nearby that often washes over the road in weather like this; I wish to get beyond it before it floods." A flash of light covered half the sky, and thunder sounded again. The horses shied, but he subdued them, his arms straining against the reins.

"Surely it is not so dangerous that we cannot cross it?"

"Normally not, but it depends on the conditions. I have seen too many carriages overturned into the ditch in stormy weather because of it; it is not something I would care to experience, believe me."

"No, not I, either." Eveline held on tighter to the side of the carriage while the viscount drove it faster than ever.

"Deuced rain!" He pushed aside a straggling lock of hair that had dropped in front of his eyes. "I can hardly see in front of me. I shall have to slow down; I don't want to come to the stream before I can see it."

It was too late. Lightning seared the air in front of them, and the horses reared. The curricle lurched suddenly to one side and seemed to slide. Eveline grabbed desperately for the upper side of the carriage toward Lord Clairmond, but her hands were slippery with rain, and she could not get hold of it. She felt a further sliding, and her side of the carriage moved downward. A strong arm came around her waist.

"Steady, now! I have you. There is a pocket on the side of the door. Use it as a handhold until you can get some purchase with your feet."

She felt along the side of the door, for her hair had come down into her eyes and she could not see. She found the pocket and wedged her hands securely.

"I have it!"

"Then move, quickly!" He still held her.

"Mind the horses!" she ordered.

With a crack of laughter he released her. Eveline moved one foot about until she came into contact with something solid—the side of the carriage she was sure. Shifting her feet as quickly as she could, she was able to move herself to what looked like the sloping side of the ditch. She put her foot down from the carriage, found an out-thrust rock, and stepped firmly on it. From it she leaped to the road into ankle-deep, muddy water. She ignored it, pushed her hair from her eyes, and turned to see Lord Clairmond struggling to keep the horses from bucking the carriage to pieces. It was useless; she could already see protruding splinters of wood on the inside of the coach where the horses had kicked it.

Suddenly, the carriage gave a groan, and she jumped quickly away from it, landing in still more mud. She watched the curricle slowly slide downward into what seemed more like a river than a ditch.

"Devil take the damn thing!" Clairmond was still trying to get the horses loose from the curricle. Eveline looked up at him, at the grim line of his mouth as he fought to undo the traces.

Finally, he undid them—but all for naught. Lightning struck again, but this time much closer than before; the horses reared and bolted. Eveline cried out, for she was sure that the viscount would be dragged away with them. But the rain and mud did him a service at last: The reins were so slippery with wet that they slid through his hands.

"How could I have been so stupid?" He grimaced and

took off his glove, opening and closing his hand gingerly. Eveline saw that his hand had been rubbed raw right through the gloves. "I should have seen the clouds forming sooner than I did." He looked around and shivered. She could see he was as soaked as she was, and she remembered that he had been ill not long ago.

Gently touching his sleeve, she smiled at him. "You could not have known—I certainly did not. But that is past. I think our first objective should be to find shelter. Neither one of us should be out in this rain."

He stared at her, then nodded. "You are right." He sighed. "I wish we were closer to my home; I could lodge you in my house, and Marianne would be there to accompany you. But we are too far away for that." He looked again at the land around him. "If I am not mistaken, we are on the far edges of Sir Anthony Malworth's property; there should be something nearby for shelter."

The rain decreased to a drizzle, but it did little good. Eveline could feel her wet dress adhering to her body. Now that the threatened rain had burst from the clouds, the heat of the day had disappeared, and she shivered.

The viscount must have noticed it, for he said, "Definitely, we must find shelter." He held out his hand to her. "Come, please."

Like an obedient child she took his hand and trudged forward, pushing her legs against her sodden skirts. She and Lord Clairmond did not talk, for it was effort enough to slog through the mud, and Eveline felt she must clench her teeth to keep them from chattering. The daylight was waning, and the thick clouds would make the evening come sooner. They had to find shelter quickly; she hoped they would find aid as well.

It seemed an age before Lord Clairmond exclaimed, "There!"

She could not see anything, except . . . Yes, there was a dark shape in the encroaching dimness ahead. She quickened her steps and almost slipped in the mud, but for the viscount's strong grasp on her hand.

"Thank you."

"It was the least I could do," he replied.

She parted the hair that had fallen across her eyes and looked at him, and saw his hair was also plastered across his brow, and a wry smile on his face. Eveline chuckled.

"Yes, I suppose it was." She held her sodden skirts away from her and grimaced. "We are a mess, are we not?"

"Quite." His smile widened to a grin, and he nodded his head toward the shape that now showed itself to be a small cottage. "I am afraid we shall have to beg the mercy of whoever lives there."

"Do let's," Eveline said primly, as if she were taking tea in a drawing room. She could joke a little now, for it seemed help was near.

Clairmond's grin turned into a chuckle. "Thank heavens you are not the type to go off into the vapors."

"Thank heavens, indeed! Then where would we be?"

"Not at this cottage, to be sure!"

He stepped up to the door and knocked. There was no answer. He knocked again. Nothing. He peered into the window, then sighed. "There is no one here. There seem to be holland covers over the furniture. I think it is untenanted."

Eveline's heart sank. She glanced behind her, at the deepening gloom and the muddy tracks she and the viscount had made to the cottage door. She looked at him and saw him gazing at her uncertainly. He also looked behind them, and then seemed to come to a decision. "Stay here. I will see if there is a way to enter it without breaking in. Making you walk any farther than this would be folly." He turned and began trying the windows before she could protest.

He turned the corner of the cottage, and after a few minutes she was startled when the door in front of her opened. "How . . . ?"

Grinning, he jerked his head toward the inside of the house. "An open window, conveniently left unlocked." He bowed grandly—as much as his sodden clothes allowed—

and Eveline laughed despite her nervousness. "If my lady would enter . . . ?"

"I thank you, sir," she said mock haughtily and stepped in.

The cottage was almost as cold as the outside had been, except, of course, there was no wind to make it more chilly. Holland covers were indeed draped over the furniture, and a fine layer of dust clung to the mantelpiece. She sneezed and shivered.

"You will catch your death of cold." Lord Clairmond drew her to the hearth, found a tinderbox there, and threw a log into the fireplace. "I only hope the wood is not green."

Luck favored them in this, if not in their past circumstances. A few minutes passed before a flicker grew in the grating and then caught the rest of the wood. Eveline shivered again and drew near, holding out her hands to the fire.

It did little to relieve the cold. Her dress was soaked through, and she felt chilled to the bone. She gazed at the viscount, and he looked as pale and miserable as she felt. Compassion moved her, and she laid a comforting hand on his arm.

"It is not so dreadful, truly! I am sure we shall become warm quite soon, and then perhaps we can go in search of some aid, or perhaps someone may find us before that."

Lord Clairmond looked at her, and the shadows were in his eyes again. His lips twisted in a smile half-wretched and half-ironic. "My dear Miss Seton, it is truly far worse than you seem to think."

She looked at him, confused, and then a trickle of realization grew in her mind.

"Yes, I see you are beginning to understand," he said, his voice grim. "Your reputation is quite irrevocably ruined, your virtue altogether compromised."

Chapter 8

Miss Seton stared at him, a lost look in her eyes, and shivered violently, as if in an ague. Richard thought she looked like a waif, hair trailing across her face and dripping water on the floor. Her dress was ruined and clung to her form, showing a figure that was far from waiflike. Desire flared in him, and he could hear a chill voice in his ear: "Now, Clairmond, now is the time." He looked away from her, clenching his hands, and sharply cut off the voice.

"No."

Startled at the answer that seemed an echo of his own mental one, he turned to her again. "What?"

"No. I cannot be ruined. We have not been together for that long, have we?"

"It matters not how long we have been together so far! Your reputation would suffer even if went we went walking back to Bath at this moment. Certainly, by the time we warm ourselves and leave this place, it will be long enough and your reputation will be in shreds."

"No. I did not want . . . I did not think . . ." Her hand crept to her mouth, as if suppressing a cry.

"Neither did I, frankly." Something in his chest suddenly ached at the bewildered, frightened look in her eyes. He took her hand and pressed it. "Let us not think of it at this moment, my dear. What we must first do is become warm; it would do us no good at all to die of cold before we ever have a chance to look for help."

Miss Seton looked at him, her expression less frightened. "Thank you, my lord. What you say is very sensible." She gazed about her. "Do you think there may be a comforter somewhere in this cottage? I do not want to use the holland covers for fear of ruining the furniture."

He tried to smile encouragingly at her. "Perhaps. Shall we look?"

She returned his smile, seemingly eager to do something to keep herself occupied. They searched this cupboard and that, and found a large, somewhat worn quilt stored away in a cedar chest. Bringing it near the fire, Richard wrapped it around her.

A concerned look crossed her face. "But what of you, sir? You must be as chilled as I, I am sure."

He shook his head. "No, I shall do well enough." He was beginning to feel more cold than he had before they had first come into the cottage, but was sure it would pass.

The chill did not seem to pass for Miss Seton, however. She still shivered under the quilt, her teeth still chattered. Richard let out an impatient breath.

"I did not want to suggest it earlier to save your blushes, but you are shivering as if with an ague. That quilt does you no good when you have a rain-soaked dress beneath it." He paused at the uncomprehending look on her face. "You will need to take off your dress and dry it," he continued.

If her face had been pale, it was bright red now, easily seen in the firelight. "Oh, heavens," she said.

"I will not look, I promise you."

She continued to blush and shook her head. "No, really, I cannot."

"My dear Miss Seton," Richard said, his voice impatient. "While I take full responsibility for our situation here—it was stupid of me to set out toward Bath when I suspected the road would be bad—I will *not* take responsibility for your death from a chill. Do me the favor of using the common sense I have seen in you and do as I say. I think you must acknowledge that you have not become any warmer in the past fifteen minutes or so, despite the fire and the quilt about your shoulders."

This time the pink in her cheeks was that of anger at his

tone, he was sure, rather than embarrassment. She gave him a level look, then nodded stiffly.

"Very well. If you will turn your back, my lord. . . ."

"Of course, Miss Seton." His voice was equally as stiff as he turned away, but when he was sure she could not see him, he smiled a little. She sounded as haughty as his father used to sound, and it was an odd thing, he thought, to come from a merchant's daughter.

Richard heard her move and then the sound of wet cloth slapping the floor. It made him more conscious of the water dripping from his own coat and shirt underneath. He should take his own advice and remove his coat. He hesitated, then took it off and draped it across a chair near the fire, careful not to turn in Miss Seton's direction.

It was well that he did; he could feel the fire—warner now—immediately through his shirt, except where his sodden neckcloth dripped down the front of his waistcoat. He sighed, and took the neckcloth and waistcoat off, too.

"You may turn around now." Her voice was still stiff, and he grinned before he turned to face her.

She was once again wrapped in the quilt, holding it tightly around her. He smiled at her, and her eyes widened as she turned away, blushing. Richard's smile turned once more into a grin. Apparently, she was more modest than he had thought.

"Come now, Miss Seton. Have you never seen a man in shirtsleeves before?" he teased.

"No, I have not!" she said firmly and brought her gaze back to him with what seemed to be resolution. His grin became wider. She looked him in the eyes, then frowned. "You are teasing me!"

"Yes, and I am sorry. I suppose . . . I must confess, Miss Seton, I do not like our situation, and I was trying to make light of it."

"Well, it was not very kind of you, but I shall overlook it this time," she said and smiled nervously. Richard released a large exaggerated sigh.

"I am so very relieved, ma'am."

Miss Seton laughed, but the respite from the pressure of

their predicament was small. The uneasiness between them returned, and it could not even be enlivened by halfhearted attempts at conversation on either of their parts. Finally, they gave it up, and only the crackling fire made any sound.

Richard moved restlessly and looked at Miss Seton. She sat on a footstool, staring into the fire, apparently lost in the contemplation of the flickers of flame before her. She no longer shivered. He was glad of it. She had looked extremely uncomfortable, but that had disappeared. However, there was a sad cast to her face—lost and even miserable. Miserable. And it was his fault. He wished, suddenly, that he could make it up to her, to recompense her in some manner for their current predicament, and for the certain seduction he must inflict upon her.

The honorable thing to do now would be to marry her—but that was not in the agreement, was it? According to Teufel, he had to seduce and abandon her. But there must be something . . . something he could do so that she could go on and perhaps still retain one small bit of pride.

Then it came to him: He would make her hate him. He stood and looked out of the window at the rain, feeling more chilled than ever. He was fairly certain he could seduce her without a promise of marriage, but then she'd hate herself for giving herself away to a seducer when he left her. It would be the way he'd feel were their situations reversed. But if he proposed marriage, it would be clear to everyone that he had purposely seduced her, and that he was a vile betrayer, and that she, an innocent, could not be totally at fault. He would be shunned, of course. No man could promise marriage, lie with his betrothed, jilt her, and escape extreme censure. But at least she would be an object of pity, rather than condemnation. Perhaps some good man would be able to see her superior qualities of heart and mind, and marry her regardless of her lost virtue. But seduction without promise of marriage would ruin her chances at marriage for life.

Bile rose to his throat at the thought of using that stratagem. It was like an overused part in an old French farce. But it would at least be an excuse on which she could hang her pride. He'd be considered a lying bastard by everyone, and it would be no less than he deserved. He would be banned from White's Club as well, for his reputation would be tarnished. He suppressed a bitter laugh. That should be no burden. He had been banned from Brook's before his army days; he should be used to being shunned by now. But at least it would be seen that the fault was more on his side than hers. Well, then. Richard hesitated, then cleared his throat.

"Miss Seton."

She started, then looked up at him, all attention.

"Miss Seton, will you do me the honor of becoming my wife?"

She stared at him in astonishment. "Y-your wife?"

"Yes. It is needful, is it not, so that your reputation will be salvaged?"

"No. No! I cannot force you to marry me because of a stupid carriage accident! Surely, someone will come soon."

"It is over an hour, my dear, since the time you should have returned home. Your good name has been thoroughly, most definitely compromised."

Miss Seton jumped up and paced the floor, the quilt dragging behind her. "Oh, this is stupid! Surely there must be another way out of this predicament."

"I assure you, ma'am, there is no other way."

"You can't want to marry me!"

He smiled. "And how do you know that?"

She stopped her pacing and stared at him, suddenly, keenly. "Do you?" she said.

He moved toward her until he was but a hand's length away. He put up his hand to cup her chin and stared for a long moment into her eyes.

"Yes," he said and knew he did not lie, however much he knew he could not fulfill his wish.

Miss Seton was still for a moment, then a soft sigh escaped her. The quilt slid from her suddenly relaxed shoulders, and she shivered and hurriedly pulled it around her neck again, blushing.

Reluctantly, he moved away. He had come very close to

kissing her. He did not want to seduce her yet, if for no other reason than he did not want to do exactly as Teufel bid—he would do this his own way, slowly.

"I . . . I need to think," she said.

Richard shook his head. "No, Eveline, it is past time for thinking. You must admit it is the only answer if you are to retain any bit of respectability."

She looked at him sharply. "I did not give you permission to use my name."

He knew it was a ruse, a way for her not to give him an answer. He admired her for it; it showed a bit of pride, the way she tried to retain some semblance of control of their situation.

"True, you did not," he replied. "My name, however, is Richard, and I will allow you to use it all you like."

Her lips quivered upward, and a twinkle appeared in her eyes. "I suppose it *is* rather late for formalities, is it not?" She sighed. "You may call me Eveline, or Evie if you wish."

"Eveline, then, until we become more accustomed to each other." He looked away from her then, not able to meet her eyes. She was too perceptive, and if his plans were to work, he could not let her suspect one bit of insincerity. He heard her move away from him, and he watched her return to her footstool by the hearth, pulling her quilt close around her. Silence fell between them again.

The initial warmth he had felt upon removing his wet coat was gone now, though the fire on the grate was still burning strongly. His hands and feet felt numb with cold. His shirt was only slightly damp in places now, and his trousers were almost dry. He sat on a bench close to the fire, and yet he continued to feel colder. He shivered. Perhaps if he were to walk about a bit, he could retain a measure of warmth.

He rose and paced twice around the room, then went back to the cottage window and looked out of it. Rain poured furiously in sheetlike waves against the cottage walls, and thunder still roared in the distance. It was dark, and no one would venture out to look for them for some time. An angry fire burned in his chest, and he returned to walking a bit faster before the hearth. *Teufel!* Their accident had to have been Teufel's doing. Well, he would not be forced into seducing Miss Seton before he was ready.

And yet, he could not deny the fact that it did not matter if he seduced her or not at this time; her reputation would be in tatters regardless of what he did to her. What did it matter, and who would know the difference then? He could seduce her now, and either way the tongues would tattle in Bath when they returned. His stomach clenched at the thought.

I would know the difference. She would, also. He grimaced. Good God, it was humiliating! He felt like a bull bought to service a farmer's livestock.

Richard shivered more violently and rubbed his hands hard over his shoulders to warm both hands and arms. He wished there were a way out of this, a way he could claim his side of the bargain, and not ruin Miss Seton. But she was ruined already! Yet, he felt he could not seduce her—not now, at least. Later, another day—perhaps he would have another opportunity. He shook his head as if to shake the confused thoughts from his mind.

"My lord . . ."

He stopped his pacing and turned to see Miss Seton gazing at him uncertainly, a blush suffusing her cheeks.

"Richard, I am quite warm now, and I can see you are not any warmer than when you started. Perhaps . . ." Her face grew more red. "This quilt is quite large. Perhaps you would care to share it?" Her gaze fell to her hands clutched tightly together in her lap. "I understand our . . . our situation, how bad it is for both of us. It cannot be any worse than it is now. Certainly, it will be no worse if this quilt covered you as well. Lady Brookland has told me of your past illness; I could not feel comfortable if you were to become ill again because of my selfishness. You need not sit very close. . . ." She looked up at him again, biting her lower lip, modesty and anxious concern clearly at war in her expression.

He stared at her, considering her invitation. From any

other woman he'd know it to be an invitation to further intimacy, but with Miss Seton, abruptly, he felt unsure. All he knew was that he felt tired, his teeth chattered, and his fingers and feet were frozen. What difference did it make, indeed? He nodded curtly.

She opened the quilt, and he caught a glimpse of smooth shoulder and white shift before he moved to sit beside her. He stumbled a little as he sat and involuntarily grasped her arm.

"God heavens! Your hand—it is like ice!" she gasped.

He felt his hand taken and chafed between her own. He looked down at her, at the quilt tucked firmly under her chin. She caught his gaze and blushed, but went on with her rubbing.

"Let me have your other hand—Oh, dear, this one is just as cold. I cannot help thinking your illness must have affected you more than it appears. You seem to be healthy, my lord, but your constitution cannot be strong when your blood runs so cold!"

He did indeed feel warmer, now that he was covered with the quilt and sitting beside her. Her hands upon his seemed to radiate warmth. He smiled and closed his fingers over her hand and brought it to his lips.

"You are very kind, ma'am."

Miss Seton gazed at him, her hands suddenly still. He had never been so close that he could see into her eyes. They reminded him of a meadow, of home, of shifting shades of green upon lake and grass on a summer's day. They drew him in, and Richard raised his hand to touch her face. She turned her head slightly, so that her cheek fit into his palm, and closed her eyes. But now her lips trembled, tempting him with the possibility of kisses, and he smoothed his thumb gently across them. They moved, and he felt her breath, quick, upon the ball of his thumb. Then her eyes opened again, warm and full of light, and he was lost. He lowered his head and pressed his lips to hers.

Her lips were sweet, as sweet as he thought they'd be whenever he had looked at her. She gasped, and he deepened his kiss. He'd been so cold—cold as winter, as a deep dark pit. But Miss Seton—Miss Eveline, Eveline, Evie—was warm and soft and he needed her. He moved his hand to her waist and drew her gently to him. She wore no corset, perhaps because of the earlier heat of the day; he could feel the dip of her waist through her shift, the rise of her ribs, her breasts' fullness.

"Marry me, Eveline," he murmured against her lips.

"I . . . no, this is not right . . . I cannot . . ." Her voice was breathless.

He did not know if she protested his proposal or his actions. He moved her so that she sat upon his lap, then slipped his hand inside her shift. She stiffened, and he kissed her again, softly, then firmly, then softly again. Her breath came more quickly, and she relaxed. Slowly, tentatively, her hands moved up his chest to his neck, exploring him.

Ah, God, she was sweet. Richard pulled her down to the rug, and the quilt tangled around them. The thought came to him that he was seducing her now, and it made him pull away briefly. No, he could not do this, not now. But he gazed into her eyes, heavy with passion and confusion, and he felt he must kiss away the confusion and make her feel a passion to match his. All the practiced techniques he had planned fled his mind, and he only wanted her to feel as he felt, touch as he touched. He wanted to give her pleasure, not as a trade for his own as he had done with other women, but for her own self and for him.

He moved his lips down her cheek to the long column of her neck. Her breath quickened, but no protest came from her. He pushed her shift from her shoulder and kissed the path he made. Her skin tasted of salt, and of woman.

"My lord . . ."

"Richard. My name is Richard. Say it," he murmured against her skin. "Ah, you are beautiful." He needed to be close to her; he was so cold and she warmed him, and he wanted to be in her, to be enveloped in the heat he knew was there. He moved to kiss her lips again and pulled her shift farther down.

"Richard . . . I don't . . ."

"My God, Eveline, I have wanted you for so long. Tell me you will marry me." He kissed her deeply and cupped her breast with one hand, stroking gently. "Please."

"I . . . Oh, Richard!" Her voice was something between a gasp and a sob. "Oh, Richard, yes, yes!" And she pressed herself against him and kissed him with fierce passion, her lips imitating what his own had done just moments before.

Eveline did not resist him. She could not. From his first kiss she knew this, knew it was hopeless. She loved him, and he wanted her, wanted to marry her. She felt her heart was full of fire and light and a joy that spread throughout her whole self. Her mind conspired with her heart, and she told herself that it did not matter; she was ruined anyway, her reputation would be in shreds when she returned home. The supposition would be that she had given up her virtue, regardless of her actions. She would be unmarriageable to anyone else, for even what money her father could gather together for a dowry would not make up for her fallen state.

But *he* wanted her, wanted to marry her. He had said so with his words, and now his lips and his hands. It would not matter, no, nothing mattered but this, the heat and the joy.

His hands touched her face, her hair, her body, and it was fire, it was wind, it was deep water. She loved him, and she would seize what there was in his kisses and caresses, to hold to her heart when she became old someday.

She knew a moment of doubt when he moved away from her to gaze upon her breasts and watch his own hands moving upon her flesh. Eveline shivered with an odd chilled feeling. She had seen the misery behind his eyes when he first proposed, and though she could sense his sincerity when he said he wanted to marry her, she did not know if it were truly duty or love.

And yet, now he kissed and caressed and there was a fire in her body. Did her kisses inflame him as well? She did not know much about men, and she had had no opportunity to learn this side of them. Perhaps . . . perhaps he did care for her after all.

Tentatively, Eveline's hand moved up to his neck as he

kissed her. He smelled of damp hair and of lemons, and the faint taste of wine was in his kiss. She touched the nape of his neck hesitantly and felt the curls there, softer than she thought they'd be. Then, daringly, she moved her hand downward to his chest, beneath the open shirt. He let out a breath like a moan and caught her hand, but did not move it. He kissed her more passionately, moving down her throat. Eveline twisted her hand from his grasp and boldly pushed her fingers through the light mat of curling hair upon his chest. But Richard seized her hand again and laced his fingers with hers as he continued to kiss a trail that shimmered like trickling champagne on her body. She started to protest at the unfamiliar sensation, but her voice came out only as a sighing moan. It did not matter. Nothing mattered but this.

She felt him move a little above her, and his fingers played over her, raising her shift from below, up to her secret places. She clutched his shoulders, but he kissed her and she relaxed once again, closing her eyes.

Richard touched her again more intimately, moving slow and quick and slow again. Eveline tensed uncontrollably at the pleasurable ache that grew within her. She wanted . . . wanted something, something more than the pleasure his hand was giving her, and yet she did not want him to stop. She felt him move over her, spreading her legs widely, and something hard and warm rubbed back and forth over where his hand had touched her. She pushed her hips against him urgently and wrapped her arms around his neck, sighing and moaning at the hot intensity coursing through her.

Then he moved a little lower, and the hardness entered her body. A sharp pain made her open her eyes, and the breath she released was a whimper.

He kissed her again, tenderly. "I am sorry . . . sorry . . ." he murmured and moved back a little, touching her with his hand. "It will be better, I promise you. . . ."

The pain eased, and she relaxed again. He did not move his body except to touch her where he was joined to her, and then, slowly, he pushed in. She ached, but it was a different sort of ache now, and as he moved in her the pain faded and became an urgent scintillation, just on the edge, the edge of—

A burst of fire and ice spread from where he moved within her, and her breath came from her in a long moan.

Richard heard it and felt the pulse within her. He could hold off no longer, and he kissed her full on the mouth, moving quickly, fervently. She cried out again, and he poured his life, his soul, his heart into her. "Eveline, Evie, love . . ."

He sank down upon her, then pulled her to her side, holding her close, kissing her eyes, her cheek, her lips. An odd feeling, secure and sure, came over him. He felt as if he had come home at last, something he had not felt before even though it was now four months since his return to England. "Beautiful, so beautiful . . ." he murmured against her throat.

He felt her hand caressing the nape of his neck. He opened his eyes and looked into hers. She was smiling, but there were tears just at the corners of her eyes. Richard's heart twisted with pain. He had hurt her, he knew, but he could not help himself, she was so warm and he had been so cold. He kissed her gently.

"I am sorry, my love, that I hurt you," he said.

Then he realized what he said and knew it was true: He loved her. Ah, God, no.

"It . . . it is all right, Richard, truly. It does not ache much now." She blushed and hid her face on his chest. "I did not mind it . . . afterward." She raised her head again, smiled tremulously, and traced the line of his jaw with her fingertips. "I love you."

He held her close, pressing a kiss on the hair that curled on her forehead. He closed his eyes in despair. He loved her and now he had to leave her, and it was almost more than he could bear. My home, my estates, he told himself. Marianne. I must save them. But the words were ashes in his mouth, dry and bitter.

Chapter 9

Sunlight stroked Eveline's eyelids, and she opened them, momentarily disoriented. Her bedchamber did not have faded wallpaper, nor did it have a cracked mirror on one wall. Then a sigh beside her wakened her memories, and she blushed.

After their intimacies of the evening before, Richard had carried her to the cottage's small bed and had lain with her there to sleep. But his caressing hands had wakened her in the night, and he had loved her again, less painfully and more joyfully than the first time. She remembered his eyes in the flickering firelight, full of light instead of shadows. He had called her "love," murmured endearments in her ear, and kissed her tenderly, and she knew in her heart he truly loved her. He had asked again that she marry him, and she had said yes, and yes again.

Not wanting to disturb him, she turned carefully and gazed at his still sleeping face. The angled planes of his face softened in repose, and he looked younger than his years. She wanted to touch his face, but feared to wake him. Sunlight shifted over his face, and she contented herself with watching him and listening to the silence of the morning.

A slight snore issued from his lips, and Eveline giggled, putting her hand over her mouth to suppress it. With a jerk Richard opened his eyes. He saw her, then smiled.

"Good morning, Eveline." Pressing a gentle kiss on her lips, he pulled her close to him.

"Good morning," she said, smiling. He gazed at her intently; she wondered what he was thinking, but did not feel like asking. It was too comfortable in his arms, and she did not really want to disturb the moment. Eveline moved her fingers over his face, tracing the line of jaw and temple. He was a miracle to her; handsome and gentle, with a well-informed mind—and he loved her. Had he not said it, time and time again, as he kissed her and moved upon her last night? And they were to be married. Her heart swelled to bursting with joy and love for him. Practicality nagged at her mind again, however, and she sighed and pushed him gently from her.

"However, it *is* morning, my lord, and we must be on our way, I believe."

"Call me by my name, and then kiss me again. Then, perhaps, I shall think of it."

Eveline blushed. "Oh, heavens. Very well, then . . . Richard." She pursed her lips.

He grinned. "None of that, my dear. You did not kiss that way earlier." He ignored her further blushes and kissed her deeply, thoroughly, and gently trailed his fingers over her breast. The tingling began again, and she sighed and relaxed. But once again a certain urgency pushed insistently at her mind for attention.

"Oh, Richard, please . . . I want . . . but I think we must go home and, oh, dear, what must Papa be thinking?" The thought banished the sensations that were beginning to course through her. Richard released her, and she sat up. "Oh, how selfish I have been!" Eveline pressed her hands to her cheeks and closed her eyes in shame. "I did not even think—Papa must be ill with worry for me, and I cannot have him upset. If only there had been a way to tell him I was safe! Please, we must go away from here as soon as possible." She stood up off the bed and clutched the quilt to her chest.

Richard gazed at her, and she thought she saw the shadows in his eyes again where there had been light the night before.

"Of course," he said. He did not move for a moment, looking at her somberly, then leaned toward her and lifted a curl of hair from her shoulder. He dropped the curl, then turned away. "I believe your clothes are still by the fire. I shall bring them to you."

"Thank you." She looked away from him as he rose from the bed and pulled on his trousers. She shook her head at herself. He was the same this morning as he was last night—lean of limb, but with well-sculpted muscles—and she had gazed her fill at him then. She loved the way he looked, so different from herself; he was like an adventure in a foreign land, filled with breathless sights and sensations. Yet, the night's darkness and his embrace had surrounded her reason like a hot mist, and now in the cool morning light she felt . . . alone, adrift. Eveline shook her head at her thoughts and firmly dismissed them. What was done was done. She bent to pick up her shift, which had fallen onto the floor during the night. She dared to glance toward him again when she rose, but he had silently left the room.

Richard shut the chamber door quietly behind him and leaned upon it, closing his eyes. He opened them again immediately. It was useless. All he could see was Eveline, her green eyes full of light and joy, her soft lips, her body slim and pliant. Images came to him of her face in the night, eyes half closed in passion, tender and soft in the morning; and the way the quilt had draped over her bosom when she rose from the bed, revealing part of one curving hip. Even now he wanted her.

He despised himself.

He had forgotten his intention not to seduce her, to defy Teufel's edict by at least another day. But he had not. His own lust for her had moved him, and he had done it, and quite thoroughly. She was now "damaged goods." And he, Richard, Viscount Clairmond, had done this to her. He, who loved her.

Shame and agony shot through him, as intense as the pain that had wracked his body when he had been in the field hospital. He clenched his teeth over the groan that almost escaped him. He had pushed away all thought of what he had done until this morning when she had mentioned her father. The cottage had seemed a protective shelter for them, from the elements, from the world. Eveline had been a surcease from the chill that seemed to permeate his body often these days. He had woken to her joyful eyes and suppressed laughter and had wanted to love her again.

Then her words had slapped reality into him, and he had to move away from her. For even though she was now a ruined woman, he knew he was, in truth, the defiled, the one whose soul was soiled. He had looked at her, her skin like pure cream, and felt he should not touch her, lest he somehow stain her.

Nonsense. Nonsense, he told himself. He was the same as before—Richard, Lord Clairmond. He shook his head, for the words seemed almost meaningless to him, somehow.

He sighed and pushed himself away from the closed door. *Enough.* As the most sensible Miss Eveline Seton said, they had to return home. Both of them had to face the world and its certain censure; he might have sold his soul, but he was not, at least, a coward.

His shirt was thoroughly dry now, as was her dress. Both were ruined by the wet, hers more so than his. Mud streaked the hem of her dress, and the rain had made the color run into a mottled pattern. His blue superfine coat was not much better. He put on his shirt, then draped the dress over his arm.

"Come in," came Eveline's voice in answer to his knock. He pushed the door open. He caught his breath. The sunlight shone through the window and laced its rays through her shining dark hair. Light touched her forehead and her cheek and outlined her softly smiling lips. Her green eyes were partly in shadow, seeming larger somehow because of it. One sleeve of her shift had fallen off her shoulder and made the line of her throat long and elegant. God, she was beautiful.

Richard pulled his gaze from her with an effort and brought her dress to her. "I'm afraid your dress is quite ruined."

"It will have to do, however." Her voice was brisk, and

he looked at her again. Her lips were pressed together in a firm line, but her eyes were anxious.

He could not help it; he touched her cheek and kissed her. "There was nothing we could do, Eveline."

"I know," she said.

But he knew there was; he did not have to seduce her last night. He wondered if she regretted it. No doubt she did; perhaps that was the source of her anxiety. What's done is done, he thought. I must go on. He did not want to think of what he had to go on to next.

A silence settled between them as they dressed and tidied themselves and the cottage the best they could. Occasionally, Richard would glance at Eveline and see her teeth worrying her lower lip. She moved with haste; he could tell she was anxious to go.

Finally, they were done, and Richard opened the cottage door. The sun was bright, and the sky mocked them with its cloudless blue, as if the thunderstorm of the night before had never happened. He found Eveline gazing at him, her expression uncertain. He smiled at her in reassurance, and she seemed to relax. They stepped out of the cottage.

The road was wet and slick with mud. Lescaux would grumble at the state of Richard's Hessians once he returned home, he knew. Eveline's half boots were no doubt in worse shape. She stumbled and slipped, and he pulled her upright.

"Take my hand," he said, holding it out.

She did, and he laced his fingers with hers. He noticed her blush and the trembling smile upon her lips. He remembered he had held her hands thus last night when he had made love to her. A little warmth grew in his heart. Perhaps she did not regret all of it. That, at least, was something he had done for her, as small as it was, and however much it would not last.

They walked for about an hour before Richard heard a splash and a rumble behind them. He turned to see a farmer's cart trundling at a fairly good pace through the puddles on the road. He hailed the farmer and when the man stopped, pressed some coins into the man's hand at his skeptical look. The man's expression lightened at this largesse, and he cheerily welcomed them onto the cart. Richard lifted Eveline onto the soft hay within, which they shared with two sweet-faced, newborn lambs, much to her delight; she was city-bred and apparently had never been close to such young animals before.

Richard sighed and leaned against the side of the cart. It would not get them to Bath much faster, but it would at least relieve them from another two hours' walking. He grimaced. He would take whatever respite he could get. God only knew he would get little of it later.

A flood of relief entered Eveline when they reached her house at last, and it was echoed in her butler's eyes.

"Thank goodness you're well, Miss Eveline! Your father, Mr. Seton—"

She looked at him sharply, anxiously. "What has happened to him, Laidlaw?" She walked quickly up the steps, conscious of Richard following her into the house, despite her worry for her father. Please, God, Papa cannot be ill now.

"No, no, you need not worry, miss," replied the butler. "He is not ill, precisely. He has merely overexerted himself, or so the doctor says."

"Doctor?" Fear clutched at her heart, and Eveline's steps quickened even more. "Oh, heavens!" She felt a hand grasp her arm, and she paused. She turned to see Richard gazing at her gravely.

"My dear, stop. It would do him little good to see you in this state. You may want to look at yourself before you go."

She turned to look at a tall mirror in the hall. She gasped.

"Oh, heavens!" she said again. Her dress was spattered with mud, and one streak of it smeared her cheek. The mud had acted as a sort of glue and had stuck hay on her skirt. Her hair was straggling from out her bonnet. She looked a fright, and if her father saw her, it would do nothing to lessen his anxiety. "You are right. I must wash and tidy myself, to be sure."

"Is . . . there anything I can do Ev—Miss Seton?"

She shook her head. "No. No, it is better that you leave now and look to your own clothes." She smiled mischievously. "You do not look much better than I, I assure you!"

Richard grimaced. "No doubt you are correct. I dare not even look in the mirror, or all the way home I shall be thinking of the scolds I shall receive from my valet." He lifted her hand to his lips. "I shall call upon you later."

Shyness suddenly overcame her and she looked away. "Y-yes, of course."

He took her hand and pressed it. "Good-bye," he said. He seemed to hesitate, but after staring into her eyes for one long moment, he left.

She hurried up the stairs to her room, impatient to see her father. All she needed was to change her clothes, wash her face and hands, and then go to him. She was halfway to her chamber when the door to her room burst open and her nurse bustled out of it.

"By the blessed saints!" cried Nurse Connor. "Oh, my lamb, my precious! Are you hurt? Oh, your dress! It's a bath for you, then, to be sure, and some fresh clean clothes." Nurse bustled into the room again and rang for a maid. "And then some victuals—I'll warrant you have not had one bite to eat since yesterday! Ah, I knew that Lord Clairmond was a bad 'un!"

"Nonsense! He is no such thing!" Eveline said impatiently. "And I have no time for food, Nurse! I need nothing but to see Papa." Nurse fell abruptly silent. Eveline felt a pang of remorse and took the woman's hand in her own, squeezing it affectionately. "Oh, Conny, I'm sorry! I am tired and I have been so very worried about Papa. Lord Clairmond has been all that is . . . kind to me." She saw Nurse's expression soften. "If you please, Conny, will you help me? I look positively frightful, and my dress is ruined. I cannot see Papa, looking like this."

A martial light grew in Nurse Connor's eyes as she gazed at the mess that was Eveline's clothes.

"I should say not, Miss Evie! And how you got yourself so dirty I cannot imagine!"

"I walked in the rain and mud."

"Walked in the—My word! And where was his lordship and his carriage, pray?" Nurse pulled the bell rope for a maid, clucking her tongue disapprovingly.

Eveline grinned. "He was walking in the rain and mud beside me, Conny. Our carriage broke, you see, and then the horses bolted when lightning struck nearby."

The older woman shook her head and pulled a screen toward the fire. "Thank heaven you were not killed outright! Although if you catch a chill from it all and die from lung fever, I should not be surprised. Not that I think it will happen, mind you, now that you are home, but it would not be an unlikely thing! Why, my very own niece, God bless her innocent soul . . ."

Eveline let her nurse ramble on as a servant came in with the bath and warm steaming water was poured into it. She took off her clothes—which Nurse gingerly picked up between thumb and index finger—and sank thankfully into the bath.

A sudden gasp brought her attention back to her nurse. "Conny, what is it?"

"Your shift . . ."

Eveline turned in her bath and gazed at the shift Nurse Connor was holding in her hand. It was stained, but not with mud; it was a brownish red, like blood.

Eveline looked at her nurse's pale, worried face, and she blushed. "It . . . it must be my monthly courses. I felt so miserable with cold, I must not have noticed."

Nurse's face grew more anxious still. "Miss Evie, you had your courses but a week ago."

Uneasiness crept into Eveline at the older woman's expression, though she did not know what her nurse was implying.

"Miss Evie, what did his lordship do to you?"

She remembered, suddenly, the pain when he had pressed into her last night for the first time. She remembered, too, at the Young Ladies' School in London years ago, the schoolgirls' whisperings about beaus, of scandal, and confused reports of what occurred in the marriage bed.

She had paid no heed to them, for it all sounded like nonsense. Now she could not avoid making connections in her mind between those rumors and the intimacies she had shared with Lord Clairmond. A tightness grew in her stomach, and she looked away. "Nothing. I have told you, he was all kindness and—"

"Ah, no, my poor lamb! I *knew* he should not have been trusted! Oh, dear—"

"Stop! Stop," Eveline said fiercely. "He loves me! He told me so!"

Nurse shook her head, beginning to weep. "Oh, Miss Evie, that's what they all say to get their way with a maid."

A wild fear caught hold of Eveline's heart. "No. He asked me to marry him, before . . . before it happened. He is an honorable man, truly, I know it! Listen, listen to me—" She grasped Nurse's arm, heedless of the water that dripped from the bath onto the floor. "My reputation was as nothing by the time we reached the cottage—we had been too long absent. He asked me to marry him, to save me from ruin. If he were truly a dishonorable man, he would not have asked me. He could have ravished me then and there, without asking me to marry him. But he did not, do you see?"

Grief still crossed Nurse's face. "But he should not have taken advantage of you, whatever he might have said!"

Eveline looked away. "It was not all his fault. I love him. I did not say no."

"Mary and Joseph save you!" The tears slid down Nurse's cheeks once more. "Eh, I knew you had taken the bit between your teeth, and nothing I could say would stop you, for I know your stubbornness, Miss Evie, that I do!"

Eveline made herself sit back in her bath. "Not a word to Papa, promise me! Not until Lord Clairmond has spoken to him." She picked up some lavender soap and began to wash.

"Miss Eveline! I can't be telling half truths to your father now! Why I never—"

"Conny, please! It would do no good, and he must have

been worried about me already for him to have overexerted himself. I will tell him myself, if you please!"

Nurse stopped her blustering and sighed again. "Very well, miss! Sure and your father was in a rare taking when you did not appear when you should have."

Eveline looked at her nurse anxiously. "Conny, is Father . . . very ill?"

The older woman hesitated. "No, I don't think—" She threw up her hands in exasperation. "It is hard to say, Miss Evie. He is very tired, that is all I know. He was very upset when you did not return home yesterday."

Relief washed over her. Surely Papa could not be feeling so poorly if Nurse was exasperated rather than worried.

Eveline finished bathing and dressed hastily. She almost ran to her father's chambers. His valet, Simpson, let her in, and she gazed at her father propped up in his bed. She tried to discern any problems from his expression. There was little to tell. Simpson seemed calm, but there was an uncertain air about him, as if there were developments he could not quite comprehend as yet. She touched his sleeve.

"Simpson, how is my father?" she whispered.

The valet hesitated. "Just the same, and better, I think in some ways . . . but I do not want to hope. . . ." He sighed. "I don't know, Miss Eveline, and that's the truth of it." He nodded toward the bed. "Best ask Mr. Seton. He'll be glad to see you, that's for sure."

She smiled at him reassuringly and turned to her father. He was a little pale, his eyes closed, but when she came to his bedside, he opened them. A relieved joy spread itself across his face, and Eveline took his hand and squeezed it affectionately.

"You see, Papa, I am here."

"Thank God, my dear. I was very worried."

"You need not have been, I assure you. But I have been worried about you! What is this that Simpson tells me? That you overexerted yourself?" Eveline knew she was postponing the inevitable, but she felt she must know how her father fared first.

"Oh, do stop fussing, girl! Simpson is an old woman, as

is my doctor! Indeed, I am much better—better than I have been since my accident."

"Oh, really, Papa? Which is why you are now in your bed, and not in your Bath chair, I suppose?" She made her voice light, though she could see that weariness made his eyes heavy.

Mr. Seton let out a short laugh. "Oh, very well, yes, I did overexert myself. But hear this: I rose from my chair yesterday—without the footman's help! My foot moved, Eveline!"

Eveline clasped her father's hand tightly, and tears came to her eyes. "Oh, Papa! This is wonderful! What . . . what does your doctor say about this?"

He snorted and waved his hand dismissively. "Ah, what does he know? He is cautious—as all doctors are, to be sure!—and does not want to say a recovery is on its way. But no one keeps a Seton down, eh?" His face sobered, and he looked at her keenly. "However, you will not keep me from what needs to be said, my dear. A valiant effort on your part to avoid the subject, but I have seen more years than you, Eveline."

She smiled at him, but her eyes avoided him. "Lord Clairmond took care of me very well."

"Forgive me if I doubt it, my dear!" Mr. Seton said with a heavy sarcasm that was rare in him. "I will be blunt with you—you must know your reputation is in shreds. Unless . . . he lodged you with respectable folk."

Her words clearly deserved the sarcasm. Eveline was glad of her father's forthrightness, nevertheless. "And well do I know that I have little reputation left, Papa! It could not be helped, however. The rainstorm was very bad, and our carriage slid into the ditch because of it. If we had not found shelter, I am sure I would be deathly ill with the ague, and Lord Clairmond as well!"

"With respectable folk, of course," Mr. Seton repeated. His voice was hard, as if he hoped the tone of his words would make his statement true.

His daughter looked away from him briefly. "No, I am afraid it was in an untenanted cottage."

There was silence.

She took his hands and pressed them reassuringly. "But Papa, it is not as bad as it seems. Lord Clairmond is . . . a most honorable man. He has asked me—no, urged me to marry him. I did not want to at first, for I did not want to accept him on such terms, but"—she gave a little, breathless laugh—"he loves me."

Mr. Seton let out a small groan. Eveline stared at him.

"What is it, Papa? Are you not feeling well?"

"God! If I were capable of walking from this room, I would take a whip to him in a manner he would not soon forget!" He closed his eyes again, and his fists clenched in impotent rage.

Eveline suddenly felt cold. "No! Papa, he loves me, he told me so."

He opened his eyes again, and his gaze was a mix of anger and sorrow. "My dear, dear Evie girl. You have ever been a good judge of character, but I think your heart misled you. I wish to heavens I had talked with you earlier, but you had seemed so sensible! I have looked into the affairs of your viscount—"

"Papa!"

"Granted, it was sooner than I would for any of your suitors, but I would have done it at some time, be he titled or not—and well you know it! But Clairmond is an impoverished man. His estates are mortgaged to the hilt. I do not know if there is enough substance to the man to get him out of his troubles."

Eveline was silent. She looked out of the window at the blue sky, ironically untroubled by clouds. She turned back to her father and smiled. "I do not see the problem, Papa. We live quietly and without ostentation. How could he know how well off we are or not?"

"You know better than that, my dear. The man has solicitors, just as I do."

She lifted her chin stubbornly. "If he is indeed as impoverished as you say, then perhaps I can help him."

"That is precisely my point, Eveline. How do you know

that your viscount did not propose to you—indeed, compromise your reputation—with that aim in mind?"

Eveline's heart sank, and she fell silent once again. She had indeed considered the possibility. Her mind roamed back to their time in the cottage, and she could not believe it. Whatever his motives, whatever his actions, she knew in her heart that he loved her. It was in his touch, his kisses, his tender looks and gentleness. But then she remembered the shadows in his eyes, the flickers of anger and sadness she had seen on his face, and she did not feel so confident. She wondered if it were possible for someone to not know their own feelings of love for another. Surely it was impossible! She had known, almost instantly, when her emotions had changed from attraction, to liking, and then to love.

She shook her head. "No. I will admit the possibility—I can be as practical as you, believe me! But I *know* it, Papa. I *know*! Have you not felt this yourself, that you know a thing so well it seems a part of you?"

Mr. Seton pressed his lips together repressively. "Yes, Eveline, I have known it in various business dealings, and you and I both know my instincts have always been proved true. But love is a different thing, and I have seen too many people swayed by emotion and make disastrous choices."

"Ah, Papa, do you not trust me? Am I not your daughter and inherited your abilities?"

He sighed and smiled at her. "Yes, I do, in general, and you are my daughter. But I wish to tell you, Evie, that though you may be compromised, you need not marry him. We can go elsewhere, away from the scandal. I can well provide for you, and perhaps in time when the scandal subsides, we can look about us for a good husband for you."

She stared at him in surprise. She had not expected this; she had thought her reputation, regardless of her actions or intent, would have made this impossible.

"I do not want you to marry a man who cares only for your money and will no doubt make your life miserable. Certainly you can marry someone else if you are not totally ruined."

Eveline felt her cheeks grow warm, and she looked down

at her clasped hands in her lap. "No, Papa, I wish to marry Lord Clairmond." Her voice was firm and left no room for argument.

After a brief silence she heard her father blurt, "Did he . . . take advantage of you, Eveline?"

A struggle took place in her heart, then she said bluntly, "Do you mean, did he seduce me? No, of course not, Papa!" She made herself look squarely into her father's eyes. *That is the truth*, she told herself. *It was no seduction, for he took only what I offered him freely. I loved him and would have given him my soul if he had needed it.*

Mr. Seton gazed at her, his eyes disturbed. He sighed again and said: "Very well, then, my dear. I shall expect to hear from him soon."

Eveline smiled at him affectionately and with relief. "Of course you will. He had offered to support me here today, but I told him he needed to change his clothes first." She laughed. "He was as sodden and muddy as I, and not fit to be seen."

Mr. Seton smiled and relaxed against his pillows.

But Lord Clairmond did not call the next day, or the next. Or the day after that. When Eveline sent a hesitant note to the inn at which he was staying, she was told his rooms were empty and he had left Bath.

Chapter 10

Young Adrian Hartley was not feeling very well. He did not know why he had come to the gaming hell—or rather he did, for it was his friend Tom Stamps who had convinced him to come. It was a lark, something he had not ever done. But now, it was no longer a lark. For he had lost two hundred pounds, and he did not know how he was to get it back.

Adrian looked about him and shuddered. The main gambling room was vulgarly decorated; scarlet curtains clashed with the blue-and-green patterned wallpaper, and the chairs were a sickly yellow. The rooms smelled of port and anxious sweat, and the low murmur of conversation ebbed and flowed like a muddy wash. He wished he had not come. He could see now it was not the sort of place his father would have approved. Indeed, the senior Mr. Hartley would not have approved his suspension from Cambridge, or his travel to London, let alone to a gaming hell. He thought again of the two hundred pounds he had lost and almost groaned.

He would get no help from anyone, he was sure. He could see Tom slumped against one wall of the room in a drunken stupor. Adrian himself had been bosky as well when he had entered the place, but faro had soon driven the spirits from his mind. For he had been caught in gambling fever, and no drink was as sweet as that.

But now there was only a bitter taste in his mouth, for he did not know what he was going to do. Adrian saw a man curse and slap his cards down on a table, only to start another game. Perhaps . . . perhaps if he played another game he would win his money back—and then some. Adrian moved to a table and volunteered to be a fourth at whist. A dark-haired man, impeccably dressed, looked at him up and down. The man smiled wryly and shook his head.

"Better you should go home, boy. The play's too deep for halflings," he said.

Adrian felt his face flush warmly. He bowed and turned to another table. Again, he was refused, and at another, yet again. His former opponent—to whom he had lost his money—smiled welcomingly at him across the room, but Adrian was sure by this time the man had cheated, although he could not prove it. He did not want to play the man again and lose even more. Yet, table after table refused his offer to play.

His stomach contracted in painful anxiety. He could not go home, two hundred pounds in debt! He wet his dry lips and ordered a glass of brandy, which he swallowed quickly though it choked him. The drink flared warmly within him, and he felt once again that he must challenge the next stranger to a game of faro. His eyes lit upon a man near him who seemed about to leave the room.

Adrian did not mean to do it, but he grasped the stranger's sleeve. The man turned and stared at him, eyebrows lifted. His face was lean and spare, but his expression kind, though sad. He gently pushed away Adrian's hand.

A wild despair coursed through him, and he almost wept. "You!" he whispered hoarsely. "No one will try their skill against me. *You* shall do so!"

The man frowned and shook his head. "You are drunk. I suggest you put your head under a pump. Good night to you." He turned to leave.

"You must!" Adrian heard his own voice take on a pleading tone and cringed inwardly at the sound, but could not stop himself. "Just one more game. . . . one more."

The murmur of the gamesters near them grew a little louder, and Adrian noticed with embarrassment that a few were frowning at the interruption to their game. He returned his gaze to the stranger before him.

"No," the man said, but paused. "I assume you have lost money?"

Adrian felt ill at the question. "I . . . I will win it back, I am sure!"

"I doubt it," the man replied dryly. "What is your name?"

"Adrian. Adrian Hartley."

"I would advise you, Mr. Hartley, to go home and raise what money you can."

The young Mr. Hartley paled even more. "My father will kill me."

"Be glad you have a father." Again the man turned to leave.

"No, please! If my father finds out, I swear I'll kill myself," Adrian cried passionately.

The stranger froze. He turned back once more.

"Very well, then."

Adrian Hartley choked out a sob of relief and sat at the nearest empty table. A pack of cards was already set in the middle. The man picked them up. "Your game?"

"Faro, Mister . . ."

"Clairmond. Richard, Viscount Clairmond." The viscount shuffled the cards. He gave Adrian a curious look, half angry and half mocking, but he paid little heed. He eagerly snatched up the cards that the viscount laid before him. The youth stared at his cards—not bad, but not good either. Perhaps, the next draw . . .

Adrian glanced quickly at the clock and saw an hour had passed. All his attention had been focused on the game, and he had not noticed the time. He gnawed his lip, feeling the anxious hope rise in his chest again, for he had good cards this time. Surely he would win! He looked at his opponent, who seemed to come to a decision. Lord Clairmond put down his cards.

Hope died, and despair replaced it.

"Another game?"

Adrian looked up, feeling half frightened, half eager.

"Yes. Yes, of course." The words were out of his mouth before he could stop them.

"Very well." Lord Clairmond dealt again.

The viscount won again, and then the next one. Adrian's stomach clenched again, and his playing became mechanical. By the fifth game he felt he could not look at anything but the growing number of vowels in front of Lord Clairmond.

Once more the viscount took the cards and shuffled them. A low moan forced itself from Adrian's lips.

"What was that, Mr. Hartley?"

"No more. I cannot . . ." Adrian could feel himself turn hot and cold at once, and shame filled his gut.

The youth looked at the pile of vowels before him. He did not count them, but he was sure the amount must come to over five thousand pounds. He looked once more at Lord Clairmond, who put out his hand to gather the pieces of paper. The viscount paused.

"How much did you lose before you came to me, Mr. Hartley?"

Anger flared within Adrian's heart, then faded to dull despair. "Two hundred pounds."

"And how old are you?"

"I . . . I am just turned twenty."

"You are a fool." Lord Clairmond gathered the vowels together and rose. "Come with me."

Adrian looked at him, puzzled.

"Come! There is nothing for you here."

The youth rose slowly; he would not have questioned the man even if he had thought of it, for his mind felt as if a fog engulfed it, and his limbs as if they moved through mud. He followed the viscount out of the gaming house.

Mist shrouded the night, and Adrian shivered. Lord Clairmond walked in front of him, away from the gaming house, and did not look back, as if he expected Adrian to follow him. The youth dully followed—where else had he to go, after all? At last they stopped at a lamppost, and the viscount turned and stared at Adrian.

"What are you going to do now?" he asked.

Mr. Hartley gazed at him, uncomprehending.

"You have lost over five thousand pounds. What are you going to do?"

A low groan wrenched itself from Adrian, and he covered his face with his hands. "I don't know! I don't know!"

Two hands jerked Adrian forward by the lapels.

"You stupid fool!" He shook Adrian roughly, like a terrier with a rat. "You lost two hundred pounds, and then went on to lose *five thousand!*! What the *devil* did you think you were doing?"

"I . . . It started out as a lark—"

"A lark! God!" Lord Clairmond shook Adrian one last time, then thrust him away. The youth stumbled backward and fell. "You were a pigeon easily plucked! You could have lost far, far more than five thousand pounds!"

Adrian felt faint hearing the amount. "I would have won it back . . ." he began, but his voice faltered at the obvious foolishness of the remark.

The viscount sneered and stepped closer. Adrian moved back until he was up against the lamppost.

"Do you know how deeply dipped you could have got?"

Adrian shook his head, wide-eyed. Lord Clairmond moved closer so that he was eye to eye with him. "Enough so that you'd sell your soul to get it all back. Do you know what it's *like* to sell your soul?" he asked softly.

Fear lanced through Adrian. "You . . . You must be mad!" He moved back from the viscount.

Lord Clairmond gave a bitter laugh. "You lose your soul, and there is nothing you have left after that, do you see? Your pride's only a facade, and your good name means nothing. You tell yourself you're doing it for your family and your lands, but that turns hollow, too. And there is nothing left in you." His eyes closed briefly, then he opened them. Adrian froze and crouched closer to the lamppost. The man's eyes were dark and lost, as if he were staring at an abyss.

"All for this!" the viscount cried and thrust the vowels he'd won under Adrian's nose. "The turn of a card, and some stupid pieces of paper that mean nothing compared with all you have lost!"

Lord Clairmond stared at the stack in his hand for one moment, and then with fury-fed strength, tore it in half. He threw the torn pieces with such force that they fluttered across the street and around them.

The emotions in Adrian churned and changed from stupefaction to joy to consternation.

"You can't . . . you can't . . . debt of honor. . . ."

"Honor?" Lord Clairmond spat the word. "There was no honor in winning this from you, boy." He shivered, passed a hand over his eyes, then stared hard at Adrian. "Go home. Go home to your father and tell him you lost two hundred pounds. Then remember how you could have lost five thousand, and be grateful."

Adrian stood and gazed, bewildered, at the scattered pieces of paper around them. He, too, shivered. Perhaps he could go to the lodging he and Tom had acquired and borrow some money from his friends on the morrow so that he could go home. Suddenly, his father did not seem the ogre he had thought him, and he remembered all the times the senior Mr. Hartley had easily forgiven him his mistakes, after a hard lecture. Adrian drew a deep breath and finally looked up. "I . . . I thank you, sir."

But the viscount had already turned and walked away into the mist.

Richard strode through the chill night toward home. He would not go out again this night. There was no place where he could occupy his mind, to keep out thoughts of— No.

He thought of the bills he had found in his father's room before he had left the estate. Five thousand pounds. His stomach clenched at the thought. He could have taken those vowels and made the boy pay. He could restore a good deal of his estate with that amount. Marianne would not feel the need to be the governess to Wyvern's daughters, and Richard could thumb his nose at the earl's proposal.

But there had been something in the youth's eyes, a desperation that had suddenly brought the room, the cards, the people into sharp focus. Richard had been in a similar situation when this bargain had started with Teufel, and he despised where he was now. He saw the boy, Hartley, imagined him meeting Teufel in the dark of night and soul, and could not let it happen. Richard would not be the instrument of an innocent's fall—once again.

The viscount groaned at the thought and looked up thankfully to see he had arrived at his town house. The house was dark when he entered and his servants asleep, but he took one of the few burning candles from its sconce to light his way to his study. There, he lit a fire, saw the brandy bottle he had left on a side table, and poured himself a glass.

This was not the first time a raw young man ready to be fleeced had been put in front of him at a gaming hell. He had gone the night before and had been challenged to a game, which he had refused. Not once, but twice. Was this Teufel's way of coming through with his side of the bargain?

Richard saw in his mind's eye countless years ahead of him, where he led young men into poverty and hopelessness, winning game after game from them. A wave of nausea filled his stomach, and he hurled his glass into the fireplace. The smell of burned brandy came to him, and it stung like brimstone in his nose.

He could not live with that. He had never dreamed of himself as a cardsharp, an ivory turner. He was skilled at games of chance, but the thought of his sucking out the life of ones like the young Mr. Hartley filled him with disgust. Richard had come so close to utter hopelessness himself; each time these naive boys approached him, he lived the hopelessness again.

Misery surged through him, overwhelming him, so that he moaned aloud and clutched his hair in his hands. No. No, he could not do this, could not be the cause of corrupting those who had done him no harm. Who knew how far it would go, how far Teufel would go in presenting him with so-called opportunities for further debasement? Would there be other innocents, others like Hartley, and . . . Eveline?

Eveline. Her face rose up before his eyes, her face full of light and love. Surely, he had ruined her. It was all of seven days since he had last seen her, and she haunted his dreams, not with expressions of sadness, but with the joy and love he had thrown away. He was a fool—an utter, stupid, useless fool. He shook his head. At least he did not take advantage of the young fools he had encountered since he had returned to London.

This last thought stopped him, and an odd, elusive feeling he could not identify settled in his mind. How was it that he could refuse to take advantage of Mr. Hartley and not have Teufel appear to chide him? Was Teufel not so perceptive as Richard had thought? He remembered, vaguely, stories he had heard as a child of bargains with the devil, and how some of the victims had escaped their bargains. Perhaps . . . perhaps there was a way he could fulfill his bargain with Teufel, yet not totally destroy the things he valued.

Richard wet his dry lips, and his heart beat faster. He had done as Teufel requested, had seduced, then abandoned Eveline. Yet, Teufel had not said how long he was to do so. There was no time limit, no agreement had been made about it. If . . . *if* he went back to Bath, presented himself to Mr. Seton, and asked for Eveline's hand in marriage—married her, in fact, would that not make amends? And he *had* abandoned her—for a time. Surely that would fulfill the terms of the bargain.

Perhaps, also, the bargain was as he remembered it, and not as Teufel had said it was in their conversation. He shook his head. There was no way he could prove it, or show he was right. It was a useless hope, he was sure.

He winced at the probable reception he would receive. Who could blame Eveline if she could not feel any tender emotion toward him for the way he had treated her. At the very least he could marry her and restore her reputation in that way. No doubt she despised him, but it was the least he

could do. She could do as she wished, and he would not come near her if that was what she wanted.

A new energy came into him, and he rose restlessly from his chair. He had come to London to sell his town house, but his supervision of the sale was unnecessary. That had merely been an excuse to leave Eveline, he knew. Surely she would see, however much she must despise him now, that accepting his proposal would give her at least a modicum of respectability. Richard grimaced. It was probably the only thing he could give her.

Thoughts of her face, her form in the shifting shadows of that night when they had lain together in the cottage, came to him. He pushed them away. He would not defile that memory with regrets, but do what he could to make it right. To the world she was a ruined woman, but he knew in reality that it was he who was not worthy of touching her. At the very least, he could make the world look upon her with approval again.

He would leave tomorrow for Bath.

Chapter 11

Eveline sat in her chamber, looking out of the window. Her hands were folded in her lap, her whole aspect calm—the calm of quiet anger and despair.

He did not come. It had been a week since the day of the storm, and no bad weather could have prevented Richard from calling upon her. Indeed, she thought bitterly, it was not bad weather that kept any of her usual visitors from calling on her.

For she had soon discovered that news traveled quickly in Bath. She had made a few friends in the two years she and her father had resided in the town. Now, other than one or two visits from the curious, no one came to their house.

She was ruined. The idea was not foreign to her, but she had not quite understood the real consequences of her seclusion overnight with Lord Clairmond. She had never known anyone who had been compromised, and rarely paid any attention to gossip. At the cottage Richard had told her her reputation was in shreds, and while she had acknowledged it, it seemed oddly without meaning to her.

Now, it meant a great deal. She was not used to slights or insults; the first time an acquaintance had stared at her, pulling her skirts away from Eveline's shadow and passing without speaking, Eveline had gazed at the woman in astonishment. Then the whispers, the speculative looks came every day after that, in increasing numbers. Only one person had acknowledged her; a man whom she had met at one of the assemblies. Eveline had been in the circulating library, and he had looked at her and smiled. She returned his smile, glad that there was someone who did not think ill of her. But she had been quite wrong; he had come to her and whispered a foul suggestion into her ear. It was all she could do to clench her hands to keep from slapping his leering face in front of the library patrons. She had stalked from the building, leaving her selected books behind her.

Then there was Papa. He spoke little to her; she doubted it was wholly from anger at *her*, but from anger at Lord Clairmond. Papa was pleasant to her, but would not meet her eyes. She had shamed him, and that was worse to her than any anger he could express.

Leaving her room was an effort for her. She knew it was cowardly, but there was only so much of sneers, whispers, and snubs she could stand. Oh, she would go out again tomorrow to defy them all, but more than once a day made an angry heat seize her limbs, and she was not sure if she could keep herself from doing someone violence. She smiled grimly to herself. Of course she would not, but oh, she had come close to it.

A knock sounded on the door. " 'Tis Lady Brookland to see you, Miss Eveline," came Laidlaw's voice.

Eveline froze. Lady Brookland! She wondered why the dowager countess had come. To castigate her? Eveline had not done the countess's patronage justice. Lady Brookland had been everything that was kind and generous, but Eveline did not feel confident after being shunned by everyone she had known. She had not seen Lady Brookland since before the alfresco luncheon. She sighed. She did not want to face any more slights, not today. Going out once this afternoon had been enough.

"Miss Eveline?" questioned Laidlaw. His voice sounded worried.

She came to a sudden decision. "I shall be down directly; you may tell Lady Brookland it will be but a few minutes."

Quickly she tidied herself. She would look her best and take no insult from anyone, not even Lady Brookland. Eveline walked steadily down the stairs to the parlor, then paused at the door. She took a deep breath, put on her haughtiest expression, and entered the room.

Lady Brookland stood near the window; Eveline could not tell her expression, for the countess's back was to the sun, and her face was obscured in shadow. Eveline curtsied formally and gazed at the old woman with as much calmness as possible.

"My lady, you are welcome."

The countess rushed forward and held out her hands. "Oh, you poor child!" She came out from the shadows, and Eveline saw Lady Brookland's face, full of kind concern. Eveline could only shake her head, for she could not trust herself to speak without weeping. The older woman's kindness struck Eveline's heart harder than any of the sneers and snubs she'd received so far. Grasping Eveline's hands, the countess pulled her to a chair. "Why did you not tell me? Oh, I wish I had been in town when it had happened!" She pressed her lips together in vexation.

"There . . . was nothing anyone could do, my lady," Eveline replied, glad that her voice shook a only little. "The carriage had gone into a ditch, and it was all we could do to find shelter."

Lady Brookland pressed Eveline's hands again between her own. "I am sure there was no avoiding it." She looked at Eveline carefully. "Of course, he is doing all that is proper."

Eveline turned her face away. "As soon as we found the cottage, he asked me to marry him."

"Well, then, I shall make sure that fact is well known, and soon!"

"No, please, I . . . Not yet—"

"Not yet!"

Eveline looked up to see Lady Brookland's astonished face.

"No, ma'am. I . . . I am waiting to hear from him."

"Waiting! Surely he has talked with you and your father since that time."

"He has not. He left Bath the day after the luncheon a week ago."

Lady Brookland gazed at Eveline in consternation. "Impossible! Why, I knew Clairmond's father since he was a youth, and Clairmond as well! Both of them had wild reputations, but neither of them have ever forsaken a duty. There must be some explanation for it."

"Perhaps duty does not extend to merchant's daughters," Eveline said lightly.

"Nonsense!"

Doubt clouded Lady Brookland's sharp and clever features; clearly she was disturbed. Eveline opened her mouth to reply, but was interrupted by Laidlaw's entrance.

"Miss Seton, 'tis Lord Clairmond to see you."

The room suddenly seemed to spin in front of Eveline's eyes, making her breathless, and she closed her eyes to gain some composure. *He has come*, she said to herself, and the relief she felt in those words was a pain almost too much to bear. She had thought she had borne her humiliation well, that she could shoulder her ruined reputation with a good grace. But the lifting of her heart at the sound of Lord Clairmond's name told her it was not so; the crushing weight of her disgrace had made her think she felt nothing for him after he had left her.

"Miss Seton?"

Eveline opened her eyes and smiled at Laidlaw's anxious expression. "Do bring him up to this room, Laidlaw."

"It was as I thought!" said the countess, clearly relieved. "Surely it was something of great urgency that took him from your side so abruptly." She frowned. "However, there is little excuse for Clairmond not to have given you notice of it."

Eveline found herself wringing her hands and firmly stilled them. She did not know what she would say when Lord Clairmond came in; she clearly did not understand him as she had thought. He had said he would come to her again, and she expected it would be the next day; and now it was more than a week since their stay in the untenanted cottage. She had felt anger, then an aching grief, then confusion, and finally a dead calm. But now he had come to see her, and she did not know what she felt except relief, perhaps more, perhaps less. Did she not love him anymore? She did not know.

The door opened, and she looked up. It was indeed Clairmond; she had not dreamed Laidlaw's announcement, and she was not dreaming now. Something had changed in him; he had a grim expression, and his face was haggard with weariness. And yet, there was a feeling of unrest about him, as if there was some emotion barely suppressed beneath his surface calm. Eveline stood, and Clairmond came forward. He held his hand half outstretched, then dropped it.

"Eveline . . ." he whispered, and there was such an ache of longing and hopelessness in his voice and eyes that Eveline felt a sharp pain lance through her chest. A pronounced clearing of the throat issued from Lady Brookland, and he turned toward the countess. He looked startled as if he had just noticed her presence, then bowed gravely, first to her then to Eveline. "Lady Brookland, Miss Seton."

The countess inclined her head coolly. "So you have returned, I see. I suppose you have come to rectify the harm you have done Miss Seton?" Her blunt words were clearly an insult.

"Lady Brookland! I am sure I can deal with—" Eveline exclaimed, but Lady Brookland held up an imperious hand.

The expression on Lord Clairmond's face grew stiff. "Of course."

"Good." She turned to Eveline, her expression softening. "You may be sure, my dear, that I shall do all I can to scotch any rumors about you and young Clairmond here." She transferred her gaze to the viscount. "I shall expect to see the announcement of your engagement in the *Gazette*. Soon."

Lord Clairmond said nothing, but nodded curtly. He looked at Eveline, then said: "Is it possible to see your father, Miss Seton?"

"Yes. Yes, of course, he has been expecting you for . . . That is to say, he is available at the moment." Eveline could feel her face flame, and she hurriedly pulled the bell rope for a servant. "Laidlaw will take you to him."

"Thank you."

It was but a minute before the butler arrived, but to Eveline it seemed an age. She felt she could not look at Lord Clairmond, though she more than once felt his gaze upon her. How else could she keep from blurting out words she was sure would be disastrous? Eveline was glad of Lady Brookland's presence; it gave her a measure of control over her riotous emotions.

Then the door opened, and the viscount turned to leave. Eveline looked up at last and met his eyes. He smiled hesitantly at her, but there was an odd look of hope and defiance in his gaze. He bowed, and before she could speak, he left the room.

Richard wished the butler would hurry, but of course that was probably not within the old servant's ability. He reined in his impatience and acknowledged that though Laidlaw's slowness did not suit his eagerness, it suited his trepidation quite well. For Richard well knew that the interview between himself and Mr. Seton would be unpleasant—and deservedly so.

The butler halted before a door at the end of the hall and knocked.

"You may enter."

"Lord Clairmond, sir," Laidlaw announced, opening the door.

Richard had expected a dim room with drawn curtains, as befit the room of an invalid. He stepped into an extremely large chamber instead, the windows clearly open to the sunlit sky. It seemed Mr. Seton's chamber served two functions: At one end was a canopied bed; at the other a huge desk with quills sprouting from one of the boxes set into it, and papers scattered across the desk's surface. As with the parts of the house Richard had seen, it was well-appointed: A clock of polished oak ticked the minutes away upon the mantelpiece; the curtains were of an elegant drape and color; nothing was out of place or ostentatious.

Mr. Seton apparently noticed his gaze, for he said: "You must excuse the informality of my seeing you here; as you see, I have limited access to most places in this house—or out of it, for that matter—and find having my office and my bedroom combined most convenient." Mr. Seton sat in a Bath chair at the desk, a quill in his hand. His tone was cordial, but Richard could hear an undercurrent of anger in it.

Richard felt there was little he could say to this. He bowed, then said abruptly: "I have come to ask for Miss Seton's hand in marriage."

Mr. Seton raised his brows. "I see you wish to come to the point quickly. Very well then." He set down his quill and pushed himself away from the desk. "Where were you a week ago?"

"London."

"Which you deemed more important than my daughter's reputation, or indeed, your honor," Mr. Seton said coldly.

Richard looked levelly at the merchant. "No, sir, I did not."

"You did not! Then I wonder why you are here so late as to have my daughter suffer as she has this past week! You damned bastard! Do you know what you have done to her?"

Richard could feel his face grow cold, and he closed his eyes briefly. "I can guess."

"You guess!"

There was silence, and Richard could see the rage and sorrow struggling on the merchant's face.

Richard clenched his teeth, then said: "You are right to be angry, sir, and I deserve any insult you care to give. However, I am trying to make reparations—as poor as they are."

"Poor . . . Yes, that is it, is it not? I know of your financial condition; did you think to force my daughter to marry you so that you could extort money from us?"

Rage and insult flared within him at Mr. Seton's words. "I don't want your money!" To his horror Richard found his hands closing into fists. He turned away from the older man and relaxed his hands. "Do you not think I would have returned long since if that were so?"

"Then perhaps you could not swallow the thought of having a merchant's daughter as your viscountess?"

"No!" Richard stopped, and knew it was not true. He remembered his thoughts upon meeting Eveline, how he had tried to justify his seduction of her. He took a deep breath and turned back to Mr. Seton.

"Yes," he said. "I did, when I first met your daughter. And yes, I meant to seduce her." He laughed bitterly at the surprised look on Mr. Seton's face. "Did your sources not tell you that I was a rake?"

"No." Mr. Seton looked thoughtful. "My solicitors are more versed in financial matters than in society gossip."

"It is no wonder you are astonished."

Mr. Seton cast him a keen glance. "No. I am surprised that you would admit it." He picked up his quill again, but only held it in his two hands.

"At least you know I do not lie."

"I do not know anything of the sort," the merchant said sharply. "What made you return?"

"I love her."

"Don't insult my intelligence, Lord Clairmond." Mr. Seton sat back in his chair and ran the feathered end of the quill through his fingers.

Again anger flared within Richard, but it faded to weariness. "Since you will not believe anything I say, what does it matter?" He sighed. "The fact remains that Miss Eveline's reputation can only be redeemed if I marry her."

"He is quite right, Papa."

Richard turned quickly. Eveline had entered the room so quietly that he had not heard her. He glanced at Mr. Seton.

Apparently, he had not heard either, for there was a look of surprised chagrin on his face.

"Eveline!" her father exclaimed.

"You have needled him quite enough. He has come back, and whatever his reasons for doing so, he wishes to make some reparation to my reputation. He has asked to marry me. Is that not enough?" Eveline did not look at Richard, but at her father. Her face showed only calm, but her hands were clasped together tightly.

"No, it is not enough!" Mr. Seton cast her an angry look. "I tell you, Eveline, he will not see one penny of my money if he marries you!"

Eveline gave a little gasp, but said: "Casting me off, are you?"

The clock ticked too loudly in the quiet that reigned in Mr. Seton's chambers, while Richard watched father and daughter warring silently with each other. Finally, Mr. Seton slapped his hand down on the desk, in an impatient gesture.

"No, I am *not* casting you off, and well do you know it!"

Eveline smiled slightly. "I thought not."

"However, I will not finance the rebuilding of his estates or any of his property if you marry him. You will have to live in his house, and I can guarantee you, my dear, it will not be in the style you are used to."

Eveline opened her mouth to reply, but Richard cut in: "I have said, Mr. Seton, that I do not want your money."

"So you say!" retorted the merchant.

"So I say and so it will be!" Richard said impatiently. "You may talk with my solicitors and tell them to tie up any funds, property, what have you, so that I may not touch it."

"Stop!" Eveline cried out. Arms akimbo, she gazed angrily at both Richard and her father. "Will you stop this wrangling? It is nonsensical, and nothing to the point." She turned to her father. "Papa, I know you are angry, but the fact remains there is nothing that can be done to save my reputation except for me to marry Lord Clairmond. He asked me to marry him at the cottage, and I accepted. If it means I shall be living in circumstances that I am not used to, so be it. I shall adapt, believe me."

Mr. Seton stared at his daughter for a moment, then let out a crack of wry laughter. He shook his head. "Your mother always said you took your stubbornness from me, and so it is! Very well, then!" He turned and gave Richard an ironic look. "I give you my permission, Lord Clairmond. You may marry my daughter." He sighed, then put aside his quill, rubbing his forehead. "Go now. I must write a letter to my solicitors and yours, so as to arrange matters."

"As you wish," Richard replied and bowed. He turned to leave and discovered that Eveline had silently left the room.

He stepped out of the room just in time to see Eveline hurry down the hall, and he lengthened his steps to catch up with her.

"Eveline!" He reached out and seized her arm.

She stopped immediately and looked pointedly at his hand on her arm. Then her eyes, full of anger and confusion, met his.

"Yes?" she said coolly.

Richard released her. "I must talk to you."

"I have agreed to marry you. Papa has consented to it. What else is there to discuss?" She pressed her lips together, as if to stop herself from saying more, and proceeded down the hall to the parlor.

He did not know what to say. He wanted her to understand that he had taken a very large risk in coming back to her, but that he had to come back. But it was not something he could tell her, and looking at her defiant eyes and remembering Mr. Seton's patent disbelief, he also did not know whether she would believe him. All he could do was marry her, redeem her good name, and hope that she would forgive him someday.

"I had to come back to you," he could not help saying.

"Oh, really? When did you come to believe that?" she retorted. "When you realized perhaps there was more to me than what I gave you at the cottage?" Eveline thrust open the parlor door and went through, and he caught the door before she could slam it after her. He closed it quietly behind him.

"Yes, I admit it." She spat the words behind her. "I know now that I acted the harlot for you, though I did not know it then." She went to the mantlepiece and leaned her forehead against it. Her hand curled around a small Limoges egg that sat near the ledge. "And yes, am I not vulgar for even mentioning it? But I am only a merchant's daughter, after all!" There was an agony of shame and self-mockery in her voice, a thing he had not ever heard from her in the weeks before their seclusion in the cottage. "I am surprised that you bothered to come back! Why, what difference could any of it make to the common-born Miss Seton?"

In two swift strides Richard had crossed the space between them and seized Eveline by the shoulders. She glanced at him, and then looked away, but he captured her chin with one hand and made her look at him. Glaring at him, she tried to pull away.

"Look at me, Eveline!"

She stilled, and then reluctantly met his eyes.

"You no doubt will not believe me, and I would not blame you for it. If you hate me for leaving you to your humiliation, then do so—I admit I deserve it. Yes, I admit I stupidly thought of you as 'only' a merchant's daughter at first, but as I came to know you, it did not matter. Yes, I even admit I had set myself out to seduce you. I did tell myself yet again when I left that you were not of my class. *But it did not matter!* Every day I saw you in my mind's eye, and I hated myself. Every night I dreamed of you, and I despised what I had done."

Her lip curled. "Oh, you came to desire me *despite* my lowly state, did you? Or was it your honor that pricked you so?"

"Listen to me!" Anger flared high in him, and he shook her slightly. "I care nothing that you are a merchant's daughter, and as for honor, if I said it was for that reason, you would not believe me, though it's also true. It was for *you*, Eveline, though I was too stupid to realize how much you meant to me when I left."

She stared at him, still defiant, the look of disbelief still in her eyes, but there was uncertainty in her face as well. "How can I mean anything to you at all?"

"Oh, God." Richard let out a despairing laugh. She was his lifeline, his road to self-respect, and he could not tell her. "Oh, God, you can't know, can you?" He pulled her closer and leaned his forehead against her hair. "Will it mean anything to you if I told you I love you?"

"I—"

He cut her answer off with a kiss, fierce and demanding. He did not want to know what she felt before he convinced her, and he must have that chance. She was stiff in his arms at first, and he could feel the porcelain egg still in her hand hard against his chest. She softened against him, and he heard something fall to the floor between them with a sharp cracking sound, and her hand uncurled and flattened. Slowly, her arms came around his neck. Profound relief surged within him, and he, too, relaxed, his kiss becoming gentle and searching. Her lips responded, and she moved closer to him. He had his answer, he believed. And yet, when they parted, she still looked uncertain.

"Eveline, it is true . . ." Richard said earnestly, cupping her chin and kissing her once more.

She moved away from him, reluctantly, it seemed. "It is not that I don't think you love me, Richard. It is just that I am no longer confident of what I know of people. I had thought I could get a sense of people better than I had apparently done." She paused, then looked up at him. "Why did you do it, Richard? Set out to seduce me, that is?"

Richard closed his eyes briefly. "I cannot tell you now. Later, perhaps. But not now. Please believe me when I tell you I cannot."

"I see."

There was no censure in her voice, not even disappointment; she spoke in a considering, thoughtful manner. But somehow Richard felt that he had fallen short, perhaps because her voice seemed withdrawn. A sense of dissatisfaction grew in him. She smiled a puzzled smile at him, and the dissatisfaction turned to resolution. It seemed so far that by marrying her he would escape one horrible consequence of the task Teufel had set him—Eveline's ruin. Perhaps . . . perhaps he had escaped even more than he had thought. A tendril of hope pushed itself to the surface of his thoughts, and he smiled down at his betrothed. He would make it up to her somehow, show her that he was more than the wastrel and rake her father thought him, that she no doubt thought him. Perhaps he was not all that she thought him before he seduced her, but surely there was something she had seen in him that was true.

Chapter 12

Eveline fingered the white silk lace veil, a confection made of thread so fine it seemed it was made of spider-silk. She held it up between herself and the mirror and could still see, as if through a mist, her reflection twice as pale as she looked this morning. Setting down the veil on her lap, she stared at herself in the mirror. She should look happier than she did. It was her wedding day, after all, and that made everything right with the world.

Did not all her Bath friends return to call upon her once the announcement of the betrothal and wedding date appeared in the newspaper? And did she not receive a nervous apology from the man who had accosted her in the library? Did she not now go to all the assemblies and balls—except that she was received with more respect and friendliness than before? Why, she should be ecstatic at the profound difference in her social state, now that her reputation had been so brilliantly retrieved!

Nevertheless, she was not. Oh, she had smiled and danced and chatted cheerfully at all the functions she had attended in the past month, but though everyone had acted as if nothing had occurred to her except for her brilliant—that was their word—brilliant match, though she was showered with approval, it seemed oddly unreal to her. Her feet would be tired, her face aching with smiles, her throat sore with talking—these things were real. But the sudden change from pariah to the latest peeress-to-be, the welcoming smiles where there had been only drawn-away skirts, made her feel that she had gone from real life to acting in a play.

Eveline sighed. She should be grateful. Lady Brookland had done a great deal of work spreading the news of her betrothal. The countess had made it known the betrothal was a long-standing one and kept quite secret, which of course made Bath society nod their heads wisely and say they had known it all along. However, it did not set well with Eveline at all. Her former disgrace had suddenly stripped the mask from those she thought she had known, and she did not feel the confidence she once had in her powers of perception. Not even with Richard.

She pushed aside the thought and steeled her mind to the wedding that was to come in the next few hours. There were the last minute things to be done, of course, as there was with any large event. She carefully folded the veil, and put an apron upon her dress in preparation for descending into the kitchens. She had arranged the wedding feast, and she needed to make sure Cook had all she needed in help and supplies. Thankfully, Lady Brookland had taken over writing out the invitations—Eveline had protested at first, but the countess had insisted, and Eveline had relented, acknowledging Lady Brookland's superior knowledge of the *ton* and society ways.

There was a knock at the door, and at Eveline's bid to enter, the door burst open, and Nurse Connor came in, eyeing Eveline sternly.

"What is this? An apron! Good heavens, Miss Eveline! Is it the housekeeping you're doing now? And you to be wed in the next few hours!"

"Oh, Conny, you know it is not housework! I must go down to the kitchens to make sure Cook has all she needs to finish preparing the wedding feast."

"Sure and it's a bad set of servants your father has hired, that you must make sure they are doing their duty!" Nurse said disbelievingly. "Laidlaw will take care of it, and well you should know it!" Clicking her tongue in disapproval, Nurse rang the bell for a maid. "Keep your mind on looking as a bride should, miss! It will take at least an hour to put on the gown, and to do your hair up properly—no doubt more. So it's best you start preparing now."

Eveline smiled wryly. "I wish I could feel more useful than a dressmaker's doll at this moment."

Nurse frowned. "There's nothing more useful you can do than to get that dress put on you." A slight knock announced the maid, and her eyes were shining with excitement when she entered.

"Oh, Mrs. Connor, Laidlaw said I might 'elp Miss with the dressin'—it's true, ain't it?"

Nurse looked over the maid with a grim expression while the maid shifted anxiously from one foot to the other. Nurse nodded her head. "Very well! But mind you do as I say, Susan!"

"Oh, *thank* you, Mrs. Connor! I won't fail yer, truly I won't!"

Eveline suppressed a smile at the maid's enthusiasm. She knew the whole household was excited about her impending marriage to Lord Clairmond, and it would be a wretched thing indeed if she were to spoil their enjoyment by seeming to have doubts about it. So she allowed herself to be pushed and pulled about for the next two hours until her two attendants stepped back to view their handiwork.

The dress was cut low, but the same spider-silk lace fabric that made up her veil covered her bosom to her throat. It was a pretty conceit, for it was so sheer that it could make no claim to modesty. Her arms were covered by the lace, also, indeed, lace covered the whole dress, except for the front of it, where the shimmer of silk satin was allowed to peek through. Eveline looked into the mirror and was glad that pink piping edged the dress; the unrelieved white would have made her look more pale than she was.

Nurse nodded to Eveline's reflection in approval. "Now there's a lady fit to be seen at a wedding." Her brow creased for a moment. "Eh, but you'll be wanting a bit of pink in those cheeks, Miss Evie, for all that the white suits you." She pinched Eveline's cheeks lightly, but the color subsided quickly. Nurse frowned.

"Oh, Conny, never mind! I am merely nervous; you know I never have any color when I am so."

"You can pinken 'em summat if you wet a red ribbon and rub it on yer cheeks, miss," Susan volunteered.

Nurse turned on the maid in an instant. "Is it paint you're suggesting to Miss Eveline, now? And I suppose I should get some lampblack for her brows next, so she can look like one of those besoms that prance about on the stage?"

"Oh, no, Mrs. Connor! I never . . . !" cried the maid.

"Hmph! Well, see that you don't!" Nurse turned and gazed assessingly at Eveline's face. "Howsomever, 'twouldn't hurt to have a little bit of color. . . ." She went to Eveline's dresser and rummaged about in a top drawer.

"Conny! I am shocked!" Eveline said and threw a laughing, conspiratory look at the little maid. "Are you suggesting that I should . . . *color* my cheeks?"

"Well, and nobody said it was a sin to paint the face on a waxwork, which is what your wedding guests will think is coming up the church aisle if we don't do something for your cheeks. And that's the truth of it, Miss Evie!" Nurse pounced on something in the drawer with a triumphant cry and drew out a deep pink ribbon. "I think that will do; what do you think, Susan?"

The maid nodded her head vigorously. "Oh, yes, Mrs. Connor, 'twas what me own sister used when she—" She gave a guilty look at Nurse, and Eveline remembered Susan had a sister who was lady's maid to an actress. Eveline smiled reassuringly at the maid, and Susan continued: "That is, 'tis a very pretty pink, Mrs. Connor."

Nurse wet the ribbon and rubbed it upon Eveline's cheek.

Eveline surveyed herself in the mirror. "My goodness, Conny, it does make me look less pale." She did indeed look better. She shook her head mock sorrowfully. "But I never did think you would stoop to using paint, Nurse!"

"Now it's not as if I stooped to anything, miss! Not ever would I—" Nurse caught Eveline's laughing look and chuckled. "You were ever a teasing one, Miss Eveline!" She turned to the maid. "Get on with you, Susan, and be sure you change into your best frock!"

"O' course, Mrs. Connor!" The maid gave a little curtsey, and almost ran out of the room in her eagerness to be part of the wedding preparations.

Nurse gazed fondly at Eveline. "I've thought of your marrying often, Miss Evie, but never did I think to see you look like a princess, just like I'd imagined it." She sighed sentimentally and dabbed at the tears at the corners of her eyes. "Well, now! It's time I should get myself tidied up! Lord only knows I wouldn't want to shame Mr. Seton by looking like a fishwife!" She gave one last adjusting tweak to Eveline's veil, then left the room.

Eveline sighed, and gazed at her reflection again. She looked quite well, she thought, and Papa should be pleased. Would Richard, though? Perhaps. She wondered what he would look like at the church. Would he be as uncertain as she?

If only he had not left Bath after their stay at the cottage! She had been so sure of him, so sure of his basic goodness. Even now a part of her could not believe what he had admitted—that he had set out to seduce her from the very start. It was a long time ago—before he had gone to the army—that he had been called a rake, and every report afterward had shown he'd changed his ways. It was what Papa's solicitors had found out about him, too, not just from the rumors amongst the *ton*. Richard had been horribly wounded while trying to defend a fallen friend, and it had been only the strength of his will and the devotion of his valet that had kept him alive and whole. He had never been known to have cheated or tell a lie, and his family heritage had always upheld extreme honor as their standard. How could it be that someone of such reported integrity purposely would have set out to ruin her?

But he had not, after all, had he? came her mind's voice, and Eveline had to admit it was true. He could not, at the end, abandon her, and surely that was to the good? And yet it puzzled her. Why had he done it at all?

It was a piece of the puzzle that did not fit, a maze that had only dead ends, and an ache in her heart that would not go away. The only other answer was that her perceptions were at fault, her usual good judgment gone awry. Papa had said that love often got in the way of a man's judgment, and apparently it had happened to her. And yet . . . and yet there was the persistent niggling idea that something was missing.

Eveline shook her head. She was to be married, and that solved the problem of her ruined reputation. For now, it was enough. Perhaps, once they married, she would find out. She smiled at herself. There was no perhaps about it. Her Papa had always said that there was never a problem she left alone until she solved it. He had been right. She would not leave this puzzle about Richard alone, until she knew. He would not tell her why he had done what he had done; that did not matter. She would find out in other ways.

A knock sounded on the door, and Eveline jumped, startled out of her thoughts.

"Miss Eveline!" called her nurse's voice. " 'Tis time!"

An odd sensation of heat and cold at once went through her, and her stomach tightened. She made herself relax and breathe deeply. "I am coming!"

Eveline opened the door and went down the stairs, Nurse hovering around her all the while. The coach was waiting, and when she stepped into it, she gasped in surprise.

"Papa! What are you doing here? I thought you would go ahead of me to the church!"

Her father smiled broadly. "Now how could I not walk beside my daughter at her wedding?"

"Walk? Papa, do not joke with me, please!"

He laughed. "But no, I do not. You shall see!"

She looked at him and noticed for the first time that he no longer looked as thin and worn as he had in the past two years. His face had filled out, and there was a certain vitality she had not seen in him for a long time. What had she been doing that she had not noticed it? Hope rose within her, and her mouth became suddenly dry. Could it be . . . ? No, really, he could not have recovered fully, she shouldn't think it. And yet, here he was in the coach, and saying he would walk down the church aisle with her.

"I . . . I suppose we shall see," was all that she could reply.

The coach ride was short, and they soon came to the church steps. A footman opened the carriage door, and slowly Mr. Seton stepped down, holding the footman's arm firmly, then grasping the cane held out to him. *Stepped* down! Eveline pressed her fingers tightly against her lips to keep them from trembling. She put her hand out to him and he grasped it.

"Papa! I . . . How . . ."

He grinned at her. "Surprised you, eh? I have been trying to walk for a long time, but never did tell you—Dr. Stanton disapproved, you see, and I did not want to make you anxious. Then my foot moved, and I knew I was doing the right thing! So I have been practicing with Charles here." He nodded to the footman, who broke out in a wide smile. "And thought to surprise you one day."

"Well, you certainly did!" A surge of joy flooded Eveline's heart as she looked *up* at her father. She found herself smiling at him, and descended from the carriage, taking his arm as they walked up the church steps. Mr. Seton's steps were unsteady and halting, but he leaned more on his cane than on his daughter's arm.

Richard looked up when the door opened, and his breath stopped in midinhalation. The sun beamed down through the windows of the church, and as Eveline entered, she was bathed in its light. It was no earthly woman who walked slowly toward him upon her father's arm, but a fairy, an angel, a queen. As she came closer, the sun filtered through the misty veil, and her face looked as if it were alight from within. There was joy in her eyes, and Richard's heart rose with hope, hope that the joy was because of him.

Perhaps it was; the joy did not change when she looked upon him, but there was also doubt when she released her father's arm and came to Richard's side. He suddenly noticed her father, that he was not in a Bath chair, and his eyebrows rose as he bowed respectfully to Mr. Seton, who merely bowed and smiled in return. Richard looked a question at Eveline, but she shook her head, her smile growing wider, dissipating the doubt he had seen in her eyes. He was happy for her, but his hope died. No doubt her joy had been because of her father's recovery, not because she was to wed and become Lady Clairmond.

With an effort, Richard brought his gaze to the vicar, and the ceremony began. The words rolled over him, and he responded in a firm voice, and he was not sure how, but it was over before he realized it. He looked at Eveline, and she smiled shyly at him. He raised her veil, drew her toward him, and kissed her gently.

Eveline trembled in his arms, for the kiss was warm and inviting, and she almost forgot herself in her wish to have it last longer. He had looked upon her with such hope as she came up the aisle. What was it that he hoped? She could not tell. She had wished to reassure him nevertheless. He looked so impeccably handsome—and calm. She, certainly, was not calm at all

Turning toward the congregation, she saw their smiling faces. The church suddenly came into sharp focus, and, startled, she glanced at Richard, and then at the congregation again. Oh, heavens, she was married! She remembered the clergyman saying the words, and that she had replied, but it was as if she had done so in a dream. An odd bubbling urge to laugh came to her, and she swallowed. She took a deep breath and put her hand upon his sleeve.

She accepted the congratulations in a daze, glad of the support of Richard's arm, for her knees felt weak and her mind bewildered. Eveline knew she smiled and chatted with the guests, but for all she knew she could have spouted inanities. She was married! She looked at her new husband, and suddenly he seemed a stranger. What did she know of him, after all? She had known him but two months, had been betrothed for only one of those two months—a short betrothal, in truth; most of the betrothals of her friends had been at least a year. It was an odd thing: Two weeks into their acquaintance, and she had felt she had known him down to his heart. Now, two months had passed, and she believed she did not know him at all. And now . . . now she was married to him and must live with him in a place she had never been.

Richard led her to the carriage, helped her up into it, then climbed in himself. She sat and folded her hands in her lap, then found she was wringing them, twisting the ring upon her finger. Quickly, she pressed her hands into her lap.

A warm hand covered hers, and she looked up at Richard. She smiled a nervous smile at him. He raised his brows in question.

"It is a foolish thing, my lord—"

"Richard." He smiled at her. "We are married now, and it has been an age since we agreed to use our Christian names."

"Yes. Richard." Eveline cleared her throat and looked down at her lap. "Richard, I am . . . a little afraid."

He lifted her hand and pressed it between his own. "I, too."

"You?"

"Oh, yes. I have many fears; I wonder if you will despise my home, if you will miss your life in Bath, for instance. I cannot support you in the style to which you are accustomed, you know."

"Well, I can make do and become used to it, I am sure."

Richard pressed his lips together as if suppressing a grimace and looked away. "You have not seen my home. It is large, to be sure, larger than the house in which you have been living. But half of it is in extreme disrepair, and the rest is drafty. The grounds are ill-kept, half wild with brambles. And my tenants . . ." His expression hardened and pain flickered over his face. "Well, you shall see."

"It cannot be so bad that—" But then the carriage stopped, and they had arrived at her house—her father's house now. They descended from the carriage, and as they entered, Eveline glanced at Richard. He had a resolute expression on his face, and she dismissed her fears from her mind. She would deal with them as they came; it was not time to think of possible troubles now.

Marianne, Richard's sister, was the first to greet them, having left the church as soon as the ceremony ended, so as to be part of the welcoming party. Eveline was glad of Marianne's presence, for her eyes lighted up when she saw Eveline, and extended her hands in welcome.

"It will be lovely to have you for a sister, Eveline! Oh, I knew you were just the sort of wife for Richard, and I told Wyvern so after our luncheon, did I not?" Marianne turned, smiling, to the tall man beside her.

"Indeed, you did!" He seemed to transfer his gaze from Marianne to Eveline with an effort. He smiled at Eveline and bowed over her hand. "Please accept my congratulations, Lady Clairmond."

"Thank you." Eveline felt Richard's arm stiffen under her hand. She glanced up at him. He smiled cordially, but his eyes were cool as they gazed at Wyvern. Here was another mystery; she had seen this before at the luncheon, this animosity between the two. It puzzled her, for Marianne was allowed to call Wyvern friend, and yet Richard clearly did not like him. If Richard knew of something that did not do Wyvern credit, should he not have told it to his sister? And yet, it seemed he had not, for Marianne clearly did not think ill of the earl at all.

The earl bowed briefly to Richard. "And to you, as well, Clairmond."

Richard inclined his head slightly, still smiling. "Thank you." Eveline glanced at Marianne, who looked from Richard to Wyvern with a puzzled expression on her face. It seemed she did not know what to think of their behavior, either. Eveline reflected that she had been extremely naive to think it possible to know much of people at all. Ever since she had met Richard, she was seeing that it took more than a few conversations to assess a person properly—at least in society. Business was quite different than *ton* ways.

The wedding feast was all that Eveline had planned, but it, too, passed quickly for her. There was an abundance of guests; it seemed to her that they passed in a blur. She could remember Sir John Grey and his sister, Lavinia, of course; the Earl and Countess of Rothwick, who were newly married themselves; Mr. Hobart and Mr. Demming, two of Richard's particular friends. The health of the bride and groom was drunk, speeches were made that caused Eveline to blush, and then, suddenly, it was done. Toward the end, she finally felt less nervous, less unlike herself. Perhaps it was the company of friends. More likely it was the combination of champagne and sheer tiredness, she thought, smiling wryly.

A hand touched her shoulder lightly, and Eveline turned to see Richard smiling down at her.

"Shall we go?"

A sudden fluttering of her stomach made her draw in a breath, but she released it quickly. "Yes. Yes, of course." She smiled nervously at him and took his hand.

They climbed into the coach again, now one for traveling and piled with trunks of clothes on the top. Again they were in a carriage, again private, but this time Eveline did not voice her fears, but chatted of inconsequential things. The time was past for that; as she looked upon Richard's tired face, she decided that she would keep her thoughts to herself for a while. Perhaps she would not mention them at all. From the way Richard pressed his hands to his eyes when he thought she was not looking, he had more than enough to think about without her own small worries burdening him.

A bit of hope rose in her. Perhaps, if it were business matters, she would be able to help him. She had helped her father and had done well—even made considerable profit in the business; there was no reason why she could not do this for Richard as well.

Chapter 13

The carriage passed green hills and flowing brooks on the way to the Clairmond estates, but Richard scarcely noticed. He had seen the scenery before, and all it meant to him at the moment was that they were approaching his home, and that he felt an increasing dread the closer they came. He glanced at Eveline from time to time as they conversed, at her calm face and composed manner, and wondered at what point of their arrival her composure would change. How much would her good manners cover the dismay she would no doubt feel when she saw the state of his house and his lands?

It was an odd emotion for him, he realized suddenly. He had never cared one way or another about people's thoughts or opinions of him, his family, or his estate. It was enough that he was a Clairmond, landed, with a title and money. He smiled wryly to himself. He was more like his father than he would have liked to admit. The Clairmond name was all that had mattered to his father—well, not all, or else he would not have committed suicide. Richard pushed the thought aside. It was an ache that would be best healed if left alone.

But now he had little money, and that seemed to make a great deal of difference. First, he had not wanted it revealed to his friends, and now, though Eveline must know of it from her father, he did not want her to see how poor she had become in marrying him. It was a stupid wish, for of course she would see it, if not now, then later. He repressed one more sigh that threatened to arise. At least no one could say that he was a fortune-hunter. He had let his solicitors handle the marriage contracts, but was certain Eveline brought no fortune to him. He could not see signs of a great fortune in her family's style of living, for though they had good taste, they had no excesses clearly manifest in most wealthy merchants he had had the chance to meet.

The carriage rumbled past the gates of his estate, and Richard was sure the neglect was apparent to anyone. The trees in the orchard they passed were full of dead wood and had not been pruned since before he had gone to war, he was sure. No sheep kept down the high grass on the grounds, for he owned few cattle, or even servants to scythe the grass. The gatekeeper's cottage was old and in need of repair—abandoned, in fact, for he had no gatekeeper.

Then there was Clairmond Hall itself in front of them. It was a large, rambling construction, and would have been an imposing one, if the broken-down condition of the west wing were not clearly visible from the drive. Ivy clambered over a quarter of it, and covered, thankfully, the cracks in the windows Richard was sure were underneath the vines. He glanced at Eveline and was relieved to see her expression was one of interest and curiosity rather than distaste. Perhaps she would not mind it much.

Richard sighed aloud then and castigated himself for a fool. If she did not mind the neglect of the outside of his home, most certainly she would mind the neglect of the inside of it. As they entered the house, Richard looked upon the interior as if with a stranger's eyes. How had he not noticed when he returned from the Peninsula that the drapes were so faded, and even in spots, worn? How had he not noticed the scuffed rugs and the moldings so badly in need of repair? The full force of the lack of money hit him again, and shame quickly followed.

He did not look at her when he said, "We are home." He reflected with a wry twist of his lips that it was an inane statement. Of course they were home.

Eveline turned around in a circle, looking her full at the old hall. She drew in her breath and turned to Richard.

"How old is it?" Her voice was full of awe.

He smiled, relieved. "Old."

She raised one eyebrow and put her hands on her hips. "Oh, really?"

He laughed. "Yes, really." He clasped his hands behind his back and surveyed the walls and beams of the hall. "If I am not mistaken, this part of the hall was built about forty years before the Conqueror came."

"Then there have been Clairmonds since that time?"

"No. My ancestor was an upstart Norman baron who obliged William I by razing the Saxon castle to the ground—except for this hall, of course. Then he built his own house around it."

Eveline shook her head and smiled. "One would have thought he would have kept the castle as it was and built what he wanted onto it."

"A terrible waste, I agree!" Richard replied. "But perhaps it was not to his taste. His descendants seem to have followed his example—a little less drastically, to be sure. You can see the differences as we go through the house."

As they turned toward one door of the hall, it opened and Marianne came in, full of smiles and holding out her hands to both of them.

"Oh, I am so sorry I was not here right away to greet you! But Cook had some difficulty down in the kitchens, and I spent more time than I had thought I would helping—that is, solving the problem." She gave an apologetic look at Richard.

He took her hand and pulled her into a hug. "I see you are becoming quite the housekeeper. And do not worry, Marianne. Eveline can easily see we do not stand on ceremony here."

Marianne turned to Eveline and pressed her hand in greeting. "I do think you will like your room, Eveline. It is the blue room right next to Richard's . . ." Her voice faded off as she blushed furiously.

Eveline felt herself blush also at the thought, but smiled at her sister-in-law. "I am sure I will like it, thank you! The room, that is. The way it is decorated, of course." Marianne turned more red than before, and Eveline put her hand on her brow and grimaced. "Oh, dear, I am making it worse, am I not?"

"Never mind, Marianne," Richard said, a tremor of laughter in his voice.

"Oh!" Marianne said, blushing still. She looked at Eveline, and then they both burst out laughing. "Oh, dear. This is not a very good welcome for you, is it? I had hoped we could do it in some style," she said, wiping the laughter from her eyes, "but I did seem to have botched it." She pressed her hand to her lips, suppressing another giggle.

"No, no! Not at all," replied Eveline, and then impulsively hugged Marianne. "I am so glad to have you for a sister-in-law. I had always wished for a sister when I was growing up."

Marianne blushed again, this time from pleasure at the compliment.

"Perhaps you should show her to her room," Richard said to his sister. He looked apologetically at Eveline. "There are a few things I need to attend to."

"Oh, of course." Eveline looked uncertainly at him, then turned to his sister. Marianne had a surprised expression on her face, but she smiled back and moved to the door, motioning Eveline to follow her.

The room was indeed blue; deep blue drapes were at the window and matched the blue canopy on her bed. The chamber was light and airy, for it had large windows, and pale blue wallpaper with cream stripes and a pink floral pattern. Eveline felt cheered immediately. Though she had thought the outside of Clairmond Hall very distinguished and old—quite romantic, in fact, with all the ivy draped over it—she thought the great hall quite dark and overwhelming. Perhaps it was because of the lack of candles; she would have to see about buying more, if possible. But her room, now! This was quite delightful, not much different than the way she had her own room decorated.

"Do you like it?" came Marianne's hesitant voice from behind her.

Eveline turned to her and smiled. "Oh, yes! It is very pretty, just the sort of colors I like."

A relieved smile spread across Marianne's face. "I am glad! The drapes were faded, but I made sure to wash them properly, and even tried a little dye, too. I have become quite good at supervising the laundry, you know!" The pride suddenly faded, and Marianne looked self-conscious at her words.

Eveline nodded. "I have done that most all my life—my mother died when I was young. So I well know how time-consuming and what a dead bore it is, too!"

"Isn't it!" Marianne again looked relieved, her smile becoming brighter. "I never knew how much work it was until our housekeeper left two years ago." The look of relief turned to frustration, and she pressed her lips together, as if to keep herself from saying anything else.

Eveline came to her and pressed Marianne's hands between her own. "My dear, you need not keep me from knowing what is needed in this household. I am well aware that you and Richard are not as well off as you used to be. If there is anything I can do to help, I would be glad to do so. I have kept house for my father ever since I turned fifteen; this cannot be so different. And knowing is so much better than being in ignorance, is it not?"

Marianne sighed and looked gratefully at her. "Oh, you do not know what it has been like! I do not like to admit it, but what is the good of keeping one's stupid pride when it comes to practical things? I have had to scrape and save and do all I could to keep everything as it should be, and that is not enough, I know."

Eveline bade her to sit down on a chair, while she herself curled up on the bed.

"And Richard! He has changed so since coming home," Marianne continued. "He was used to be so merry! But I am sure it is the shame of Father committing suicide—there, I have shocked you, have I not?" She paused and gazed at Eveline, as if waiting for a reaction.

"Yes, a little," Eveline replied calmly. She was shocked, but compassion stirred her as well, and her heart went out to Marianne—and to Richard. It could not be easy to live with such a thing; many people thought it a disgrace and a blot on one's family's reputation. "But that is past now, and you must go on as best you can."

Marianne relaxed in her chair. "Yes, that is what I think also. Richard does not know I know about Father, but how could I not hear it? And Father rarely spoke to me those last few days. Do you suppose it must have been some reverses on the 'Change? I do not know much about such things," she said in reply to Eveline's surprised look. "But since he mentioned something about not being able to sell out of funds or some such, I suppose our accounts have not done well."

"No, it seems not." The London Stock Exchange had been volatile, reflected Eveline; fortunes were made and lost on a retreat or advance of an army. "It has not been wise to speculate in the past years, unless one has a large fund of money to start with."

"Father never had, it seems to me." Marianne shook her head. "And now we have come to measuring out tea with a scale, and using it over and over again until the taste of it is gone out altogether." She smiled resolutely and lifted her chin in an unconscious, defiant manner. "But I have done very well, though Richard does not like it. I am actually a very superior governess, did he tell you?"

"No, he did not."

Marianne looked disgusted. "He wouldn't! He has become so stuffily prideful since he came back from the Peninsula—almost as much as Papa had been! But the Earl of Wyvern is paying me a wonderful wage to teach his daughters. I do not know why they have had such difficulties retaining governesses in the past. Sarah and Stephanie are such sweet girls, and very lively and spirited."

Eveline smiled widely. She suspected that their liveliness was exactly what had made it so difficult.

"No doubt they have seen the error of their ways under your tutelage," she said, keeping her voice carefully neutral.

Marianne gave her a suspicious look, and then laughed aloud. "I do like you! It is such a relief to have someone to tease and joke with again."

"Well, I am sure you are a very good governess and Lord

Wyvern must think you fully deserve the wage you receive."

A blush grew on Marianne's cheeks, and she averted her face.

Eveline smiled. "He is a very gentlemanly sort of person, it seems to me. Indeed, he was most pleasant both times we have met," she said.

Marianne gazed at her eagerly. "Oh, do you think so? He has been all that is amiable and kind to me. I sometimes think . . . No, I am sure he must have offered me this position as governess from kindness, although he couched it in such terms so as to save me from any embarrassment. And you must not think he has any designs on me! He always has a maid stay in the schoolroom with me, even though I am sure the girls are company enough. The maid rarely leaves me alone with him, and then it is only for a minute or so. He has my own footman wait for me so that I may be escorted home safely, as well. So you see it is quite proper, and done from the kindness of his heart."

Eveline agreed gravely, although she turned her face away to hide a smile. It was clear from Marianne's artless speech that Wyvern was not without tender feelings toward the governess he had hired. Why else would he have extended such an invitation to Marianne, who, she was sure, had little experience in the teaching of children, regardless of how well she was doing with the girls now? And why else was he taking such special pains to ensure that no opportunity for scandal touch the young woman? A grin threatened to spread across Eveline's face. He must be thoroughly frustrated now, however, if he had any wish to court Marianne! There was no way he could do so while she was under his roof and his employee.

A sigh from Marianne made Eveline look at her again.

"But Richard does not like him. I do not know why! We have been neighbors forever, and though we never saw much of him when we were growing up, he has never done us wrong." Marianne shrugged carelessly, though a frustrated frown crossed her face. "Perhaps it is because of that old dispute over the south stream Father used to have with

Wyvern's father, but Wyvern acceded that to us after I talked with him about it last year. Richard has not been the same. I suppose I have changed, too, since our circumstances are now different."

Looking at the young woman's discontented face, Eveline wondered if there was some way she could promote a match between the two. She would have to think on it. She smiled to herself. Perhaps there was some way she could accompany Marianne to Wyvern's estate and give them some opportunity to meet away from the schoolroom.

The clock struck, and Marianne jumped. "Oh, dear, it is near suppertime, and I must prepare for it." She went to the door and turned to Eveline with a smile. "I will send Jeanie up to you to help you change."

"Thank you," Eveline said, and Marianne left. Eveline stared at the closed door, pondering her situation. She was used to taking on challenges, as she had when her father had been so ill. She was sure there was something she could do to help Richard and Marianne. Looking about her room, she noticed a little desk with paper and writing implements upon it. She would write to her father's solicitors and request a copy of the settlements agreed upon between her father and Richard's solicitors. They were used to such requests for information from her, and they would send them, she was sure. That, however, could wait until tomorrow. Perhaps it would even be a good idea to survey the estate as well as the house and see the totality of what needed to be done.

The maid knocked and entered the room, and Eveline carefully chose a dress from the wardrobe; she was thankful she had thought to send at least a few of her clothes before her to Clairmond Hall. She sighed. Most of the clothes she had brought were of a design that was more fashionable than what she was sure Marianne owned. Eveline selected a round gown of simple cut, hoping that it would be plain enough not to put Marianne to the blush.

But when she descended for supper, she saw that her efforts were as naught. For though Marianne had clearly put on what was the least worn, the least faded of her dresses, it looked shabby next to Eveline's. She saw Marianne look at her own dress and surreptitiously glance at Eveline's, and a wistful expression came over her face. Eveline's heart ached for her, but she did not want to draw any notice to their differences, so she said nothing of it.

She asked questions of the estate, instead—innocuous questions about their childhoods, and where they had roamed. It was not just for politeness' sake, either. Since she had never lived in the country, but always in town, the descriptions of their antics, their pranks and wanderings upon the estate fascinated her.

"Could you show me these places?" she asked. "The oak tree you climbed, Richard, and the lake in which you swam and got nipped by the turtle, Marianne? I would so much like to see them."

Marianne threw Richard a disgusted look. "You have got for yourself the best wife possible, Richard! See how she agrees with you it was a turtle, and not your fingers that pinched my leg!"

Richard gave her an innocent look. "Well, of course."

Eveline laughed, glad she could, for a moment, make them forget their worries. They removed to the parlor afterward, dispensing with the formality of Richard enjoying his port by himself. He went with them instead, and they continued their jokes and banter until Marianne abruptly yawned.

"Oh, my, but I do feel tired." She gave another yawn and looked from her brother to Eveline and back again, and seemed to come to some decision. "I, for one, have much to do tomorrow, and must get my sleep. I hope you will excuse me if I seek my bed." Before they could murmur more than brief good nights she went quickly to the door—but not without a last laughing look at her brother.

Richard gazed at the door closing behind his sister, a speculative expression on his face. Eveline raised her brows at him, and he said, "I am merely thinking that my dear little sister is having some romantical notions." He rose from his chair and took her hand. "*Are* you tired? Shall I escort you to your room?"

Eveline blushed lightly. "A little tired, perhaps. If it would not inconvenience you, I would like your company. I am not at all sure I would be able to find my way to my room quite yet." She stood up, and he put her hand on his arm. Suddenly nervous, she felt she could not look at him and looked instead at the floor in front of her as she walked.

"You must excuse my sister's abrupt departure. She is a mischievous minx." His voice held a suggestion of laughter.

"Of course," Eveline replied. "She is no doubt thinking our marriage is quite romantic, and I think perhaps she might have a tendre toward someone herself." She managed to look up at him briefly.

He had a concerned look in his eyes. "Do you think so? That she has an interest in someone?"

"Perhaps. Most young ladies fancy a young gentleman from time to time." Eveline looked away, remembering the expression she had seen in Marianne's eyes whenever she had gazed upon the Earl of Wyvern, and how the earl had been so careful of her reputation. She considered the undercurrents of animosity between Richard and Wyvern and thought it politic not to speak of the state of Marianne's emotions just then.

"Did you? Fancy a gentleman from time to time, that is?" Richard asked. They had stopped before a door, and Eveline recognized it as the one to her chambers. He opened the door for her.

Eveline felt compelled to look up at him again. There was a question in his eyes, beyond the words he had spoken.

"Once," she said. He lifted his hand, and she felt it touch her cheek gently. She closed her eyes at the caress.

"Was it I?"

"Yes."

"Why?"

She opened her eyes again. "I believed there was more

worth of character in you than there were in other men I had met. And . . . you seemed to care for me."

Pain appeared to cross his features for a moment, then he pressed his lips upon hers. "I swear I will prove my worth to you once again, Eveline. I swear it."

And your love? she thought, but could say nothing, for he kissed her again; his kisses were intoxicating, and she lost herself in them. It was not she, therefore, who drew away at last, but Richard. He looked at her, and he drew in a breath.

"I think . . . I think it is time for us to retire." He almost pushed himself away from her to the door next to hers.

Eveline looked at him, bewildered. "Of course," was all she could say. She moved into her room automatically, and Nurse Conny, who had come before her, and who had laid out her nightgown, was there waiting to help her undress. Nurse chattered away, congratulating her on her wedding, and commenting on how fine a day it had been for it, but Eveline paid little heed.

Would he come to her tonight? Eveline felt her face become warm at the thought. She slipped into her bed and drew the covers over her thin lawn gown. Of course he would, she thought. They were married now, and it was right and proper that she submit to her husband's embraces. Nurse had told her all about it the night before at her father's house, and though Eveline blushed remembering the last time she had submitted to Richard's embraces, she admitted it would not be something she'd find unwelcome. And yet, she still felt awkward and nervous, unready for a married life.

"Conny, tell me a story." The words slipped from her before she could think, but she knew it was the right thing to ask. It would be a last farewell of her old life, before she would fit herself into the title of viscountess.

Nurse looked at her in surprise. "A story, Miss Evie? My lady, I should say!"

"No, no, Conny, just for now at least I can be Evie. I feel

. . . nervous. You know how one of your stories always comforted me."

"But 'tis your wedding night! I cannot be here when Lord Clairmond . . . That is to say . . . Oh, heavens, Miss Evie!" Nurse blustered, and a blush reddened her cheeks as she glanced at the connecting door.

Eveline blushed also, but laughed. "You needn't worry. I am sure he will knock before he enters, and I will give you plenty of time to leave before he opens the door." She extended her hand to her old nurse and clasped her hand tightly. "Just this once, and then you may save your stories for the future."

Nurse gave one last glance at the connecting door and gingerly sat herself down on the chair next to the bed. "Sure and it's a silly thing to ask me, for all you're a lady grown now, and not a child!" She sighed. "But I'm that foolish, Miss Evie, to want to tell you tales one last time."

Smilingly gratefully, Eveline settled herself down into the pillows and listened to the rise and fall of Nurse Connor's hushed voice. She told more than one story, tales of the wee folk, of saints and the devil, of promises kept and broken, and souls lost and won. They were the tales of Nurse's childhood, and now they were the tales Eveline would always remember from her own. At last Eveline's eyes drooped, as they used to when she was a little girl with Nurse by her side.

"There you are, drowsing as you always did when you were a child!" Nurse Conny said, glancing at the clock and rising hastily to her feet. "That's enough of stories—I'm ashamed I let myself tell such childish things to you, Miss Eveline, and that's a fact!"

Eveline opened her eyes wide again and smiled. "Thank you, Conny. I'm glad you did. I just wanted to remember one last time how you told them."

"Eh, and you'll be telling your own wee ones, some day soon, I'll warrant you," Nurse said, smiling mistily at her former charge. "Well! I'll be wishing you a good night, miss—my lady!" Dabbing sentimentally at her eyes, Nurse doused the candles before she left, except for one by Eveline's bed.

The candle dimly lit the connecting door. The warm spell Nurse had woven over Eveline with her stories faded. The new Lady Clairmond waited, wondering if Richard would come, deciding he would not, and hoping that he would. But as the night grew longer, and as the candle burned down, she laid her head upon her pillow and wept, certain he would not.

Chapter 14

Richard shifted this way and that in his bed, tangling his bedclothes and then sitting up to untwist them, only to lie down and wind them around himself once more. He thought of Eveline next door, thought of her lips when he kissed them, and remembered how soft her skin had been when he had touched her at the cottage. The cottage. It seemed an age since they had been there, kissed, tangled themselves in the old quilt just as he now tangled himself up in his own bed, empty but for himself alone.

He could not get his thoughts away from her, thoughts of how she was his wife now, how he by the laws of land and church was permitted to touch her all he wanted. And yet he was not worthy of even the kiss he had taken before he left her at her door. He winced at the thought, twisting the sheets once more around him.

But she had not resisted at all and had given him a kiss for each of his own. He would have thought she'd feel repulsed by him, that somehow she must sense the chill of Teufel's influence over him. Certainly the cloying unease had been tangible to himself, having manifested itself as an icy block of tightness in the pit of his stomach. But Eveline had acted as if there was nothing at all but his own self, whole, within her arms, and not a man whose soul would not ever be hers, much less his own.

Perhaps there was nothing to sense. The thought flared in his mind like a fire in the night. He had heard nothing, sensed nothing from Teufel since the seduction of Eveline. Richard had married her, and still there was nothing. Perhaps . . . perhaps in defying Teufel and marrying her, he had voided their bargain.

His body eased into the mattress again, shifting only slightly so that he was comfortable. Indeed, he had received no money from Teufel, not as he had promised so as to improve the estate at all. The unnatural cold he had felt was gone; it had not come over him since he had decided to come back to Eveline.

He sighed, and hope flowed into him. He would find some way on his own to improve the estate, even if it meant he had to work in the dirt at the side of his tenants to do so. Eveline had not disdained his home when she entered it, despite its run-down state, and she had not been embarrassed at Marianne's admission that she helped in the kitchens. She was a merchant's daughter; work and trade were not scandalous words to her. He smiled to himself. Marianne had been correct; he had wed the right woman, indeed.

Richard rose then, determined to go to Eveline, to tell her he was grateful for her acceptance. He paused, for the light of the fire in the grate reflected on the face of the clock on the wall and showed him it was quite late. No doubt Eveline was already asleep. And yet, he felt he must see her, if only to know she slept quietly, and was not turbulently awake as he had been.

The connecting door opened smoothly and quietly. Richard could see her slight form within the bed, for one side of the canopy was drawn back. It seemed she slept, for one slim arm rested upon her forehead and her eyes were closed. Sighing, he decided he would not disturb her even with a kiss, but then the light of his candle caught a line of gleaming wetness upon her cheek. He drew in a breath, as if from a sudden sharp pain. She had been weeping. He hoped it was not because of him or their marriage; he hoped it was only homesickness. But he could not help touching the trail of the tear down her cheek gently with his thumb. And when she opened her eyes, startled at first, and then full of the light of gladness, he could not help kissing first those eyes, then her cheek on which he had found the trail of tears, and then her delectable mouth, which moved upon his own with a fierce eagerness he had only once experienced, more than a month ago at the abandoned cottage.

Hot wax dripped upon his hand, but Richard only laughed softly at the sting of it, for he had forgotten he was still holding the candle as he kissed her. Setting it aside on the table beside the bed, he blew out the flame, and removed his robe even as he slipped into the bed beside her.

He could see nothing of her except what the fire in the hearth and the moonlight streaming through the windows revealed; but the darkness and the brief glimpses of shoulder and breast and thigh were as erotic as the half-remembered dreams of his adolescence. He touched her body and kissed her, and it was as if it was before the war, before he had known he had lived under his father's disapproving eye. He remembered instances of joy long ago, and here it was again, magnified, as he moved upon her and felt her hands move upon him in tentative innocence. No trembling chill shook him as it had when he had seduced her, but only the hot trembling of leashed passion. He moved, he touched, he stopped and started, only to hear her sighs and moans of pleasure.

It was almost too much for her, the pleasure—an elixir of sensation and happiness that he had come to her and wakened her from her drowse. In their intimacies Eveline knew the barrier between them had disappeared. This was what and who he was: as tender and strong and gentle as his caresses were upon her body, a laughing man, who tickled and nibbled until she did not know if she convulsed from laughter or ecstasy. He murmured her name and called her "sweet" and "love" as he touched each part of her. Then she knew the ecstasy, the flash of heat and light that made her cry out involuntarily, and made him kiss her fiercely as he moved deep and quick to the finish.

Richard rolled to his side, holding her close and carrying her with him, kissing her eyes and lips and cheek while he did so. Eveline waited for the wall to rise between them again, the slow tensing and withdrawal she had felt the first time they had bedded. He made no movement from her, but his body relaxed even more except for his arms, which held her closer than ever. Eveline sighed in relief and laid her head upon his chest. For now, she thought drowsily, now he was here with her, and not disappeared beneath his cool civility or obscured by the shadow she had sensed in him from time to time.

His arms loosened from around her little by little, and he, too, drowsed. But Eveline did not notice, for she was fast asleep, dreaming of soft touches and laughter.

The chirping of birds woke Richard, and he opened his eyes, momentarily disoriented. This was not his bed or his room . . . it was Eveline's. He recalled the night before, and smiling, turned in the bed toward her. She was asleep and still, but he remembered when she was not, last night, how warm and sinuous her movements had been against him. He let his gaze wander over her face, her uncovered breasts, and hot desire surged through him again. Softly he lowered the bedsheets from her, following the course of its removal with his hand. Eveline shifted, stirred, and opened her eyes. A smile warmed her face when her eyes met his, and she held out her arms to him in frank affection and invitation. Happily he sighed and accepted.

Again they kissed and caressed and loved, and when they both reached the height of their pleasure, Richard felt cleansed, emptied of the guilt and free of the snare in which Teufel had kept him. He was married to Eveline, his wife, whom he loved. There was nothing better than this, even the possible redemption of his estates, for hope had come upon him again, and the feeling that he could restore all by his own efforts grew as well. He had defied Teufel, and nothing had come of it. He could defy the situation in which his father had left the estates and learn to do something to restore them.

Richard moved reluctantly apart from Eveline, and he grinned at her sound of protest. He could not resist kissing her again, but that warmed him to thinking of more pleasure, when he really knew he should get on his way to learning what he could do with his lands. He moved away from her again.

"Enough, Eveline."

She looked at him in surprise.

"No, you did not do anything, except look so beautiful and inviting that I wanted to love you again."

She blushed, but said, "Well, that is not my fault! I cannot change how you see me, to be sure." Her stomach growled suddenly and loudly, and she pressed her hands upon it as if to suppress the sound. "My! I am *very* hungry. How odd!" she said, amazed. "I never feel hungry in the morning. I wonder why I am now?"

Richard looked at her disheveled hair, her love-flushed face, and well-kissed lips and laughed. He did not wonder at her hunger at all.

"What is so humorous?"

He merely shook his head and chuckled, rummaging amongst the bedsheets for the robe he was sure was there.

"Tell me!"

He grinned mischievously at her. "No." He pulled up a sheet and looked under it. Ah, there it was. He drew on one sleeve of the robe over his arm, but it was all for naught, for a pillow hit him over his head and the sleeve slid off again.

"Minx!" Richard growled. He grabbed the pillow and pulled back his arm to throw.

Eveline ducked and grinned. "Not fair! You would not tell me why you laughed at me, and so you thoroughly deserved a pillow in your face."

"And *you* deserve it for making me lose my robe again in the bed." He threw the pillow but missed, for Eveline dodged it.

"Ha!" she cried triumphantly, but her glee was short-lived. Richard leaped at her and pulled her down on the remaining pillow.

"You must give in now, my love, for I have caught you and will not let you go until you cede to me."

"No."

"Yes! Or else I will . . ."

"What?" she challenged.

"Tickle you!" And he suited the deed to his words.

"No!" she shrieked, laughing, but he held her firm and wiggled his fingers against her ribs. "No, don't! Stop!"

"Don't stop? Very well, my lady, I will continue." His fingers found all her ticklish spots—her ribs, her neck, the backs of her knees. She pushed him away, laughing, but he moved himself atop her to hold her firm. His fingers found her neck again. She convulsed with laughter and tried to wriggle out from under him. His fingers stilled then, and his hands' movements became a caress.

"Ah, God, Eveline . . ." He sighed and kissed her on the sensitive part of her neck he had just tickled.

"Ahh . . ." she whispered, but then her stomach growled loudly, and she began to laugh again. Richard raised his head and cast an affronted look at her, but his lips quivered upward and she could feel him shake with suppressed laughter. He rolled away from her and rose from the bed, draping his robe around him as he did so.

"I suppose I should take pity on your starving state and allow you your breakfast." His stomach rumbled noisily then, too, and Eveline burst into giggles.

"And you!"

Richard gazed mournfully down at his stomach. "Traitor!" he said. This made Eveline laugh again, quite helplessly.

"Oh, do go, Richard! I shall die laughing if you stay here," she gasped.

"Very well." He kissed her once more, lingeringly, until her laughter died away, replaced by sighs. With a last grin he went to the connecting door and left the room.

Eveline sighed again, happily, and clasped her arms around her knees. She had not known quite what to expect after the wedding day; she had hoped she and Richard would brush along amiably after the disastrous start of their betrothal. This, however, this laughing Richard, whom she had only glimpsed before their marriage was more than she had dreamed. For he was all that she thought he was the few months after they had met—droll, intelligent, kind, and gentle. But then it seemed a cloud had descended upon him from time to time, chilling his expression when he did not look upon her, and when he thought she did not look upon him. She did not know what had changed, but she wished it would continue. No, she would make sure it continued. For once she had seen Richard as she believed he could be, and indeed was; she would not let that part of him disappear again.

Sighing, she rose from her bed and pulled on her robe, which Nurse had draped over a chair the night before. Eveline rang the bell for a servant and thought of the day ahead. If it were the estate's problems that made Richard grow cool in his manner, then perhaps there was something she could do to help. She went to her little desk and trimmed a quill. She would write the letter she had been thinking about last night, and ask for a copy of the marriage contracts and agreements. She did not remember all of the funds that were to come to her at her marriage, but there was one she thought she might be able to use for the estate's purposes. Or, if not that, to use in other ways. . . . Eveline smiled to herself, thinking of Marianne and the Earl of Wyvern. Perhaps there was a way Wyvern could lose his most estimable governess, so that the only way he could see Marianne again was as his betrothed. Her smile grew wider at the thought, and she dipped the quill in the ink and began to write.

Chapter 15

If the wedding night and the month after were the pattern card for the rest of a married couple's days, then, Eveline felt, all of her days afterward would be a life in near paradise. And so it seemed to her. There was not one day that passed without laughter or stolen kisses, and her happiness flowed outward to touch Richard and bring him closer to her.

It was not that Eveline did not see the poverty of Richard's, and her, tenants. They had gone riding across the property, Richard on his horse, Satan, and she on Marianne's gelding, Jupiter. He had reluctantly shown her around the estate and would have avoided the tenants' cottages, but she insisted.

"I am your wife, Richard," she had said. "What you must bear, I will also."

His face had tightened with shame, but he nodded. "Then be prepared for the most abject poverty you have seen outside of the London slums," he'd said grimly, and he had thundered off on his horse toward the first set of houses huddled around a well, not waiting for her reply.

If the tenant farmers were not as wretched as the people she had seen when passing the London slums, they were not far from it. The children were thin and hollow-eyed, the parents not much better. The buildings in which they lived were run-down things, worse maintained than the stables in which the Clairmonds' horses were kept. Eveline had bit her lip to keep from weeping at the despondency in the people's eyes. Yet, as they gazed upon the viscount, their eyes lightened with a faint elusive hope. She did not know what inspired them to feel so, or come to Richard to bow and shake his hand, for objectively he had done little to ease their hardship. But perhaps they saw the same thing she had; the kindness in him, and the sincere wish to do something for them.

Her heart ached for them, too, and so she made sure her hands ached for them as well. She was a fine needlewoman, and so she raided the attics of Clairmond Hall to see if there was anything that could be used to clothe some of the people. She found a trunk full of old clothes, not moth-eaten at all, for the trunk was fortunately made of cedar. They were out of fashion, and a few were worn at the elbows, but that would matter little to those who had no clothes at all. She mended what needed to be mended, took some bolts of plain cloth that had been laid away by an unknown Clairmond relative, and cut and pieced them together. There were also some very fine pieces of cambric and lawn, a bit yellowed, but enough for a few shirts and shifts; some deep blue muslin and cherry cotton as well. At the very bottom of the trunk, however, lay a length of silk satin of a pale peach color—it would not look well on her at all, but she knew the warm color would suit Marianne to perfection. Her sister-in-law was of a similar shape to herself, except Marianne was perhaps a few inches taller. Eveline smiled and thought how she would secretly make this dress, and then invite Wyvern to dinner with them to see the result. She remembered Richard's cool civility toward the earl, but shrugged it off. If Richard did not wish to discuss his animosity toward his perfectly amiable neighbor, how could she justifiably shun the earl? She could not, especially since she was sure it meant Marianne's happiness.

Richard encountered Eveline after her sojourn in the attics and grinned at her dusty dress and cobwebbed hair.

"Look, Richard! I do believe these old clothes are just the thing for the Wardles, and some for the Johnsons as well. I will just mend some of them and perhaps in a sennight I can bring the clothes when next we see them."

"The Lady Bountiful, I see," he said, then grimaced. "Not that there is much bounty on this estate to distribute.

But certainly we can spare the clothes. I hope." His slight smile lessened the import of the last two words, but it was enough to sober Eveline a little.

"I found some other cloth as well, good enough to make you some shirts and some dresses for Marianne and myself."

Richard's brows raised. "Treasures in the attics. Well, perhaps after I see what the latest accounts are, after quarter day, you can seek out a seamstress to make them up for you."

"Oh, no, I mean to do them myself." At Richard's skeptical look, she said, "I have always been handy with the needle. Indeed, I know how to make a pattern and set a sleeve as well. You shall see."

He smiled and kissed her. "Very well, then. I am sorry that you have to do this at all, though."

Eveline merely smiled in return. She expected to receive her father's solicitor's reply to her letter any day now, perhaps tomorrow. If she remembered correctly, there would be cause to clear the lines of worry from Richard's brow.

She suddenly noted that he wore no jacket; indeed, he was wearing what looked like a rough shirt that a farmer would wear. He wore old boots, well worn at the toes. She looked at him quizzically.

"Irrigation," he said and smiled wryly. "A ditch needs to be widened, and our bailiff said we were short of hands. I therefore offered my own."

"Ah, yes," she said and nodded, as if this were a common thing for viscounts and the rest of the nobility to do.

"Scandalous," Marianne said, who had come up behind Richard. "We have come down in the world, Eveline." Her smile matched his.

Eveline grinned at her. "I do not know what *you* have to complain about, Marianne. Richard has turned into a ditchdigger, and I a seamstress. You, however, are a most superior governess, and outrank either of us." Both Richard and Marianne burst out laughing.

"You mustn't say that, Eveline," Richard said. "She will

get ideas above her station, and there will be no talking with her at all, then."

"Seamstress?" Marianne raised her eyebrows at Eveline. "I thought you were the consummate housekeeper, unrivaled in six counties. Surely you must acknowledge that a housekeeper is at least of a class with a governess."

"You are right." Eveline turned to Richard, eyeing him up and down, and linked her arm with Marianne's. "I do not know what we are about, associating with a common fellow like Clairmond, here." She haughtily raised her nose in the air, and Marianne giggled.

Richard grinned, bowed very low, and shuffled his feet. "Yes, milady, only wanting to oblige, milady, beggin' yer pardon."

"Very well, then!" Eveline said and proceeded to move past him, but he grabbed her and gave her a loud kiss on her mouth. "Richard! Really!" she cried, blushing, and threw a shirt at his head from the pile she had under her arm. He threw the shirt back at her. Marianne shrieked with laughter, then seized a piece of clothing from Eveline and threw it at Richard.

By the time Richard surrendered, clothes were scattered along the hall in which they stood, and they were gasping with laughter. They gathered up the clothes again, and each went on their way.

But it was this sort of thing, Eveline thought afterward, that happened every day despite their difficulties, although the difficulties had eased, to be sure. She had found she could contribute in a large way to the maintenance of the household, for she was shrewd and knew how to economize and bargain. Food became a little more plentiful, and Marianne gained a pleasing roundness to her figure. Eveline did not blame her sister-in-law for not knowing how to economize as she, Eveline, did, nor did she blame Richard for that matter. They were not raised to account for every penny as she was. She was glad, then, that she was able to do something they had not known how to do, and to help in her own way.

She thought also that perhaps there might be a way she

could look at more than the household accounts. Had she not conducted Papa's business for him when he had been so ill? Surely, the accounts for the estate could not be so very different.

Approaching Richard was not easy, however, not as much as she thought it'd be. For as she went to the library a few days later where Marianne had told her he was, an image of his face, becoming cool as she spoke to him of her ideas, came before her. She made a moue of impatience. It would not be so easy to broach this subject with him, worse than with Papa, for Papa knew well what her abilities were, and Richard did not. Further, she was not at all sure that her stubbornness—which her father knew too well to stand against unless it was extremely important—would work against her husband. His face would turn polite, his manner elusive, and he would coolly retreat; she did not know how to apply her persistence to this, whereas it was easy to do so with her father's blunt words and heated arguments.

Upon entering the library, she found, both to her disappointment and relief, Richard's valet, Lescaux, there instead. She rarely saw him, for he mostly attended to Richard's clothes, and the rest of the time he seemed to disappear, only to appear again at Richard's side when the valet was needed. He was quick and efficient, and she appreciated this in a servant. He also, it seemed from the household accounts, drew extremely small wages for a valet. She knew Lescaux had served under Richard in the army; she supposed there must be some loyalty that remained that the little man still stayed with his master despite the wages.

She smiled, and Lescaux bowed. He had been taking down a book when she entered, and he placed it on a table when she entered the room. Then his face brightened in a smile.

"Ah, milady! It is a fortunate thing you 'ave come. I 'ave letters for you."

Eveline raised her brows. "I thought it Tilton's duty to bring the mail." She did not really mind, but her impression of Richard's valet was that the little man was very precise and strict about the servants' hierarchy.

Lescaux smiled gently. "The so honorable butler is very old, no? He has heavy duties. It is but a little thing for me to bring up the letters." He snapped his heels together and with great precision and elegance held out a silver salver to her.

Eveline chuckled. "And very well you do it, too, Lescaux." There were two letters, and she took both. She looked at the first one. It was written in a hand unknown to her, black letters on stark white paper. She put it back down on the salver. The second one was from her father's solicitors, and she hastily opened it. She scanned it, her heart pounding with excitement.

"Good news, madame?" Lescaux inquired. It would have been an impertinent question from a servant, but Eveline in her joy did not mind it. Then, too, Lescaux's respectful manner was such that she felt somehow she could not take offense at his query.

"Yes, yes, it is! It seems I have come into funds—funds that were not tied up. I must tell Richard!" She moved toward the door and stopped, realizing she did not know where he was. "Oh, dear. Lescaux, Miss Clairmond told me his lordship would be here, but he is not. Do you know where I may reach him?"

"I saw Milord but a quarter hour ago with the bailiff. Me, I believe he will come soon."

"Oh, very good. I shall await him then." Eveline sat upon a chair for a few moments, but then stood up again, pacing restlessly.

Lescaux watched her for a moment, then said, "He is a proud man, Milord le Capitaine is."

"Yes, he is, but what is that to say to anything? Especially when I am sure I have the answer to the problems he has been having with the estate." She went to the window, her steps impatient, and looked out of it, as if she could perhaps see her husband and make him come into the library by the sheer force of her will.

"He is also a man of a stubbornness extreme. It is possible you will not convince him."

Eveline looked at the valet in astonishment. "Whyever not? Surely, he cannot wish to have his lands remain as they are, and his tenants so very poor."

Lescaux smiled. "Of course not. However . . ." He paused, his ears seeming to perk up. "Ah, I believe Milord is here."

Footsteps neared the library door; it opened, and Richard entered. He looked tired, but his face brightened with a smile when he saw Eveline. He came to her, then noted Lescaux waiting patiently behind her. He took Eveline's hands in his own, but looked at his valet.

"Yes, Lescaux?"

The little man came forward with the salver. "Merely a letter, Milord."

Richard smiled and took the letter. "Taking over Tilton's duties, are you?"

Lescaux smiled politely. "Not at all, Milord. I make myself useful, and the poor Tilton, he weeps on my shoulder when I offer my service."

His master laughed, and the thought of the staid and wooden-faced butler expressing such emotion made Eveline smile. Lescaux's eyes twinkled at them, he nodded, and excused himself from the room.

The door closed, and Eveline turned eagerly to Richard, only to find him perusing the letter he had received. He had grown quite pale, and his lips were pressed together tightly, as if he were suppressing an oath.

"What is it, Richard?"

He looked up at her, a bewildered look in his eyes, as if he had suddenly grown aware she was before him.

"Is . . . is it bad news?"

He seemed to shake himself, then said, "No. It is nothing, really, a . . . debt I had overlooked." He smiled at her slightly, but it did not reach his eyes.

"Oh, but you need not worry about such a thing now. I have wonderful news, Richard! I know you had agreed with Papa that he should tie up whatever I would inherit from him, but I knew there was something else—not as much as I would ever inherit, but enough to help."

Richard's smile faded, and he looked at her steadily. "Eveline, I am sure you are mistaken. My solicitors are very careful; they would have made sure that it would all be yours—or at least our heirs'."

Eveline blushed at the thought of children, for they had not talked of this before, and she was momentarily distracted. She recollected herself, however, and waved the letter she had received in front of him. "Only look here!" she said triumphantly. "I remembered something that my father once said about a great-aunt of mine on my mother's side, and I remembered a letter she sent me long ago when I was too young to understand such things. But she had set aside a fund, to be given me when I married, and Papa's solicitors confirmed it."

His face stiffened, but he said quietly: "How much is it?"

"Ten thousand pounds, Richard!" she said, clasping his arm eagerly. "Ten thousand! Only think of what can be done with it! The west field can be drained, new irrigation put in the south, more seed, more cattle! And the tenants' cottages, why, at the very least we could repair them so that they are livable, and no doubt more."

"Ten thousand!" Richard's face grew tight with anger. "Ten thousand! Why did you not tell me this before?"

Eveline stared at him, then let go of his arm. "I . . . I had forgotten. No doubt Papa had forgotten, too. You need not be angry! I did not want to tell you until I knew for certain. It is but a small part of the inheritance I was to receive."

"Small!" Richard seized her shoulders in a painful grip. "What do you mean—small?"

She looked up at him, frightened at the dread shadowing his eyes. "Why . . . why, did you not know?"

He searched her face and said hoarsely, "I left myself out of the negotiations between your father and my solicitors. I wished the advantage to be yours, not mine!" He shook her a little. "How much?"

"Sixty thousand pounds."

"Sixty thousand!" He released her, almost pushing her

away. "Do you mean to say you had a dowry of sixty thousand pounds?"

"No. Not exactly."

He sighed and seemed to relax a little. Eveline could not look at him, but honesty compelled her to speak over the lump in her throat. "It is sixty thousand a year. In income. In my name."

There was silence, and Eveline dared look up. Richard's mouth was a straight white line, his eyes dark with anger and frustration. He looked at her as if she were some strange, dreadful creature, and the pain of seeing it sliced into her heart. She moved a step away from him, confused. What had she done? After an initial reluctance and resistance on his part, she thought he would understand and welcome a chance to repair his fortunes. Frustration, she could understand; anger, perhaps. But dread? She held out a tentative hand toward him.

"Richard, please . . . what . . . Is it something I have done? Said?"

"No."

She ran the short distance to him, and it was her turn to shake him, to grow angry at his stony silence. "Tell me! Why do you look at me like this? I deserve that you tell me—now!"

His expression changed. It seemed to soften as he looked at her, and indecision warred with something else. . . . Almost she would have said it was fear, except she had never known him by report, or in her short experience of him, to have feared anything. Then his countenance became smooth and cool, and she felt somehow that she had lost a gamble, had played a game of chance and lost. He smiled at her, and touched her face in a gentle caress. His fingers were cold, and she shivered.

"Foolishness, my dear. An upsurge of foolish pride—no, vanity—that is and has been useless, which I had thought I had largely excised from my character. It seems I had not."

Eveline stared at him, searching his face, trying to discern the truth or meaning behind his words. But his countenance was still and composed, even pleasant.

"Pride, is it?" she said. She did not know what else to say, how to bring *her* Richard back, the one who laughed and whose touch was warm and drew an answering warmth from her.

"I dislike being seen as a fortune-hunter, which is what anyone would think, you see. Your father, for instance." He looked away from her briefly, his expression still coolly pleasant.

"My father must know by now that you are nothing of the kind. His solicitors have told me that you would accept nothing from him—or from me."

"Well, let us just say I do not like the idea of battening on my wife."

Eveline let out an impatient breath. "If that is all, then you may pay me back when the estate starts showing a profit. No one can say you were battening on me then. It would be a purely financial exchange. Or, you could use it for collateral. You may even deal with it through your solicitors and my father's if you wish."

"I would prefer not to do so," he replied.

"Pride, in other words."

Richard looked her in the eyes. "Pride," he said.

"I do not believe it."

"You may believe what you wish. It is what I say." His voice and face turned cold. He sketched a bow, then strode from the room.

Hot anger closed her hands into fists, and Eveline sank down upon a chair. How dare he! How dare he lie to her and treat her as if she were nothing but a stupid ninny, who knew nothing of financial arrangements or, indeed, of a person's character? And he had intentionally lied, she could tell. All the reasons he had put forward were not true, or at least he must know it would not matter to her, or to those who cared for him. Pride! How could he say that, when not a few days ago he had donned the clothes of a peasant and labored side by side with his tenants?

She put her hand upon the table beside her as she rose

from her chair and touched a book instead of the table surface. Lescaux had left it there. She suddenly remembered the valet's words about his master, that Richard was prideful—and stubborn. What was there to be stubborn about? She had offered a loan; it was not charity. Why, even her father told her he had borrowed against her mother's expectations long ago, when they had little money for investments. It had prospered, and Eveline's family had become wealthy. What she proposed was nothing compared with that, for she had the money already. She remembered then, that Lady Brookland had told her that a man did not borrow money from a woman—it was not done. Eveline bit her lip. Well, there. She had hurt his pride then, perhaps. It was a silly thing, but it was the way of those born to title, she supposed. She grimaced. Heaven only knew the number of impractical rules there were in any society, those of the titled, or those of the merchant class.

But if Richard did not want to borrow her money, he could put it up as collateral. She had told him so, and surely he could see it. Yet, he did not even want to do that.

Why? It made no sense. It made no sense! And she was sure she could ask, beg, nag at Richard every day, and he would not tell her. There had to be another way to find out what it was he would not say, indeed, why he had looked upon her for a moment as if there were something repugnant about her, when there had been none of that since the day of their wedding.

Marianne. Perhaps she would know. Eveline looked at the clock above the mantelpiece. It was still morning; Marianne would be at Wyvern's house, teaching his daughters. It would be four hours before she returned. Eveline frowned impatiently. She would not wait. She would go to her sister-in-law now and talk with her during the midday meal.

Chapter 16

Eveline went over her encounter with Richard in the library again as she walked to Wyvern's estate. It would take an hour to get there, and she could have taken the carriage, but she needed to think, needed to let the exercise wear away her anger and her confusion.

She still thought Richard's reaction to her announcement of her wealth more than it should have been. Of course, she had expected some opposition, but not the reaction of anger and horror she had read in his face. Indeed, he had never bent a look of anger upon her but once, when she had talked of the war and inadvertently touched a soreness there. There was, must be, something else. And then it was as if two puzzle pieces slid together: She had seen the same dread, the same anger darken his eyes before they were married, and the morning after their lovemaking in the cottage. There was much she did not know of his life before she met him. She had been foolish not to have found out more before she had fallen in love with him; Papa had been right about that. The course of events would not have changed, and she would have been just as much in love with him, but she was certain she would have seen her way more clearly now if she had known more of his past. Regretting the past was also foolish, however; bending her mind and efforts to the present and future was more important.

Her eyes gazed at the path to Wyvern's estate before her, but her mind's eye focused on the library where she and Richard had been just a few minutes ago. She went over the clues to his behavior again. She had seen his expression of dread before their marriage and then today. What had changed? She thought of the events just past, remembered when the first hint of change had occurred.

The letter. Eveline stumbled upon a root she had not seen and gained her balance with an out-thrust hand upon the topmost beam of a stile. Not her letter, but the one he had received. His face had paled, and that was when the dread and, yes, the despair had first flickered in his eyes. And then she had told him of her news, and the despair had overcome him. She stared, unseeing, clutching the hard wood in front of her. What was in the letter? He said it was an old debt he had overlooked, but she had seen him find his father's old debts—quite large ones, at that—and his expression had changed to nothing more than a disgusted grimace. If it was a debt, she was sure she would have seen at least a little relief in his face when she had told him of her news. There had been no relief at all, not for even a moment, but the despair and dread had grown.

Anger flared up within her. He had not told her the truth about the letter, either! She supposed it was because he thought she, a woman, should not know of such financial matters. But he *knew* she was used to such things, dealt with them, in fact. And had she not told him she was his wife, that she would bear what he must also? Her anger faded, and uneasiness took its place. There must be something else about that letter. Something that would prohibit him from telling her. A debt of honor? She searched her inner sense of him, what she knew of gentlemen's honor and loyalties. Eveline shook her head. No. There must be something else.

She must see that letter. Eveline turned around sharply and went back the way she came. Yet again she went over the events in the library. Did he take it away with him when he left? Mentally, she viewed him taking the letter, looking at it, then turning to her when she told him her news. He had seized her shoulders and . . . she had not felt the paper in his hands. She would have felt it against her shoulder if he had still held it. He had not put it on the table or his pocket, or anywhere else for that matter. It must, therefore, be in the library still.

Eveline ran the last few feet into the house and up the stairs to the library. She thrust open the door, and her eyes searched the tables, the chairs, the floor. A slip of white caught her gaze. There, behind a chair leg! She bent and picked up the crumpled bit of paper, smoothed it out, and read.

> My dear Clairmond, I felicitate you: you will soon be able to redeem your estates and keep your sister from ruin. I would not be surprised if you received the good news directly after this letter.
>
> Oh, and one thing: Our bargain is not yet finished. Or at least, not on your part. You must admit that, yes? We did not agree that you would marry the chit, after all. But I am generous. I will let you do a few other tasks for me instead, and then we will call it even, shall we? The next time you are in London, do look for me. Soon. I have been frequenting Vauxhall lately—an amusing place. Your servant, Teufel. P.S. Your nights have been a bit too occupied for me to do anything but contact you by letter rather than in my usual manner. My, my.

The room took a quick spin around Eveline, and she sat down abruptly on a chair, staring at the words in front of her. Bile rose in her throat. Richard had intended to seduce her that day at the cottage. Not because he was enamored of her, not even because of her fortune, but because someone had told him to do it. Someone who knew what she and Richard did each night, perhaps even spied on them. She pressed her hand to her mouth, painfully, to stop the sick feeling she had inside her, but a low moan escaped her.

Desperately, she read the letter again, looking for something in it that would bring her world, her mind, back in balance again. The words blurred in front of her, and she angrily wiped away her tears with the back of her hand.

Think! Think! she told herself fiercely, and once again made herself read.

The estates. Ruin. Marianne. A bargain. Eveline took in a deep breath and let it out again, focused her mind on the problem, and forced herself into objectivity. She would make no excuses for him, nor for herself. That was useless. She scanned the letter again. The seduction was part of the bargain; it was a task Richard was required to do to save what he had loved most, and all that he had left to him at the time. Richard's father had chosen a way out of his predicament by committing suicide—a thing that benefited no one, and caused more hardship than ever for his son and daughter. But Richard had chosen a dishonorable path as well. Eveline closed her eyes as a momentary pain struck her heart, then shook her head to clear it. She would not give in to it, not now.

But why did Richard choose it? Eveline stared out of the library window as if to take the clarity of the sky into her own mind. Marianne. Ruin. She remembered when she had first seen Marianne at the luncheon, much thinner than she was now. It was for Marianne, and to save her from some ruin this Teufel had threatened, and the tenants on the estate. It had not been for Richard, himself, at all.

Eveline imagined herself in Richard's place, imagined the choice between the ruin of a stranger and that of a beloved younger sister and the poverty of one's tenants. He had not known her when he had made the choice. Given that choice, she, too, would have gone down the same road he had, she was sure. Then he had married her—and that was not in the bargain; she assumed he was supposed to abandon her.

But he had not. He *had* married her, and because of that was apparently still tied to Mr. Teufel. Richard could not, at the very last, do something that would ruin her life.

And who was this Teufel, who apparently hated her or her father so much that he plotted her downfall? Eveline's brows drew together. She knew of no enemies she might have who wished her ill. Her father, while having many business rivals, had no enemies she knew of, for the rivalry between him and other merchants had always been friendly, though highly competitive.

Eveline stood up, clutching the piece of paper. She would confront Richard with this letter. Then she crossed the library threshold and stopped. If she went to him with the letter, what would he do? Despite the letter, she knew, knew with every part of her heart and soul, that he loved her. It was in his gaze, his kisses, his touches, and his words. But though he spoke of the things he felt for her, he did not tell her of other things, the things that pained him most. If there was any danger to her from this Teufel, she could not expect him to tell her of it. Just as he had protected his sister, and just as he had tried to protect Eveline by making her his wife, he would try to protect her now with some misguided gentleman's code of honor she would rather not have to deal with. It would be useless for her to confront him about this, for he would not tell her.

It would be useless, also, for if she tried to find out, he would know what she was about and stop her. Eveline pulled in her lips to a straight, hard line. She would not, then. If Richard felt he could not share his concerns with her, she would not air hers, either. She would go to London and find out for herself, leaving a note to be given him later in the day. Her father kept a town house there in which she could stay and there was always a staff ready, so coming unannounced would cause a small stir, but not a horrible inconvenience. She would go soon. If not today, then tomorrow.

She needed an escort. Going over her acquaintances in her mind, she settled on the only ones available: Wyvern and Marianne. She would go to them now.

This time she took Marianne's horse, for Wyvern always sent his carriage for his governess, or provided Marianne with a horse from his own stables. The stable boy goggled at her as she spat out orders to have the gelding saddled. She did not want to waste any time. Quickly she mounted and spurred the horse to Wyvern's estate.

The earl's butler was clearly startled at her appearance. In her haste she no doubt looked a fright, but she did not care. "Miss Clairmond," she said to him. "Where is she? Is she still in the schoolroom?"

"Y-yes, my lady, but I think—"

"Thank you. I know my way." Eveline moved past him and up the stairs.

She turned a corner, then stopped, startled. She could see the long sweep of Marianne's old brown dress she had mended but two days ago. But the rest of Marianne was hidden by a large masculine form that had her in its arms in a crushing embrace. Marianne seemed to struggle a little, but it was only to pull her arm out from under his and curl it around the back of his neck, while the man who held her caressed her waist and hip.

"Marianne! Wyvern!"

Marianne pulled away, her hands flying to her cheeks to hide their redness. Wyvern turned, a frown crossing his brow, but when he saw Eveline, it was replaced with an obviously embarrassed look. Despite the anxiety Eveline had felt on the way here, she had to suppress a smile at the red that appeared high on Wyvern's cheekbones and at his definite discomfort.

"It . . . it is not what you think, Eveline!" blurted Marianne. "Truly!"

"I am sure you do not know what I think," said Eveline, making her voice cool. She turned to the earl. "And you, sir! What do you have to say for yourself? If either Lord Clairmond or I had known the way you treat your employees, and that employee his sister—"

"She is not my employee," Wyvern said abruptly. "That is to say, I discharged her today." He looked more uncomfortable than ever.

"Oh? And for what reason?"

"Because I want her for my wife, dash it all!" Wyvern replied, obviously goaded.

"He proposed, you see," Marianne said. "And I accepted."

Eveline nodded. "I thought that was it. Congratulations."

Both Wyvern and Marianne stared at her, then Marianne burst into laughter and Wyvern grinned widely. "Oh, Eveline, you are a terrible tease! I am so happy! I have loved Wyvern—"

"Anthony," the earl said. Marianne beamed at him.

"Anthony," she said, and her voice was a caress. She looked at Eveline shyly. "I have loved him ever so long! And then I found he loved me, too! But he had to dismiss me, for he could not properly ask me to wed him when I was his employee."

Eveline took their hands in hers and smiled at them. "I have known it for quite a while, you know. You have been smelling of April and May since I came to Clairmond Hall. I am happy for you." She released their hands, and Marianne grew solemn.

"Eveline, do you think Richard . . . would approve? He does not seem to like Anthony at all."

"I think, my dear, that I shall deal with your brother." A closed look crossed Wyvern's features.

Eveline's impatience suddenly exploded from her. "Oh, for heaven's sake! Richard will not talk, and now you! If someone does not tell me what the dispute is between you two, I swear I shall burst!"

Marianne glanced up at the earl. "You see, I said it would not serve." She turned to Eveline. "Anthony was not very pleasant to Richard. He won a great deal of money from my brother, but threw the vowels away when he had Richard's permission to pay his addresses to me. Anthony thought if he lost to my brother, perhaps Richard would use the money to make me more comfortable. But he won instead and thought then to ask to court me." She smiled. "I think it was excessively noble of Anthony to do so, but he was *not* right in allowing Richard to think he cared nothing for me."

"I still think I—" began Wyvern, but Marianne put her hand to his lips.

"No, you were *not* right. You should have discerned the true situation between Richard and myself before you assumed he had neglected me."

"I am older than he is, Marianne, and a widower. He must have thought to have you marry someone more eligible than I. I admit I was selfish enough not to want him to do that." Marianne opened her mouth to reply, but he held up his hand. "And no, I do not want to argue about it. That is the past. If I have erred, then I shall make up for it." He smiled at Marianne, and she sent him a look so full of love that Eveline looked down and adjusted her pelisse over her dress, so as to give them some measure of privacy.

Eveline wondered if she should tell them of Richard's predicament. Would it put a burden on them, knowing all that he had done for Marianne and the estate? She had gone to them, thinking to ask for their help, but now she felt she could not—not now. But perhaps there was another way she could get an escort.

She looked up at the earl and said, "I . . . was wondering if I could ask a favor of you, my lord. I shall need escort to London. There is some extremely urgent business I must transact for my father, who has been quite ill. It is a long way, and I do not think I should ask Richard, for he needs to attend to crucial estate matters daily. But while I have transacted business in Bath by myself, I know well it is not seemly for me to do so in London. So I was wondering . . ." Eveline wet her lips, for they were suddenly dry. "I was wondering if you could accompany me, and Marianne, as well." She smiled at her sister-in-law. "I do not want it to be altogether a business trip. I thought perhaps we could go to Vauxhall, and such, as well."

Marianne clasped her hands, and her eyes glowed with pleasure. "Oh, Eveline, yes! When?"

Eveline looked uncertainly at Wyvern. "Well, I was hoping it would be tomorrow."

Wyvern raised his brows, but said, "Of course. However, perhaps you could do me a favor in return, and let your nurse stay with my daughters while I am gone. They no longer have a governess, you see." He smiled down at Marianne, and she beamed at him.

"Yes, of course. Tomorrow?" Eveline said. Wyvern bowed in assent.

Both Eveline and Marianne went home, then Eveline rang for a maid to pack up her clothes. She had wanted to go today, but saw that it was not wise. Better she present it to Richard just as she had done to Wyvern and Marianne, and then leave an explanatory note for him to read later.

Richard was cordial to her at dinner and throughout the evening, but his restraint was almost tangible. Marianne looked to and from each of them, obviously wondering what was afoot, but neither Richard nor Eveline enlightened her. It was while Marianne entertained them at the pianoforte in the parlor that Eveline broached the business trip to him.

He gazed at her and his lips pressed together before he said, "I suppose it is to settle your inheritance."

Eveline lowered her eyes. "Yes. I have been used to dealing with Papa's solicitors, and you mentioned you did not want to be involved with any dealings with them, so I thought I might go myself. And I thought Marianne might like to accompany me as well, perhaps to see a few sights." She hesitated. "It would be such a treat for her, I am sure, Richard! You cannot begrudge her some pleasure after all her hard work, even if it means using my own funds for it."

Indecision flickered across Richard's face, and then he nodded shortly. "No, I cannot deny her that. Perhaps," he said, and he looked away from her to Marianne, his expression harsh. "Perhaps it would not be amiss if she were to procure bride-clothes as well. I will, of course, reimburse you when you return." Marianne had told him of her acceptance of Wyvern's marriage proposal during dinner, and though he smiled and congratulated her on her good fortune, his smile did not reach his eyes.

"Of course," Eveline replied, and she, too, looked away. She went up to her chambers not long after, and when Richard did not come to her that night, she did not know whether to be relieved or sorry.

Chapter 17

Richard sat in his study, slumped in his chair, and stared at the pile of bills upon his escritoire. More bills. He had found them stashed in a cupboard in his father's room and did not know which had been paid and which had not. He pressed the palms of his hands to his eyes, then gave a short bitter laugh. Teufel's letter had solved it all for him, didn't it? He did not need to reread it to remember what it said. The bold, stark handwriting blazed in front of him every time he closed his eyes.

The letter had sniggered at him and put a tawdry cast upon the gilt-edged days he had spent with Eveline. A month of joy, more than he had ever known before, and of hope. *Eveline*. He missed her already, though she was gone only yesterday. It would be a good thing for Marianne, he had to admit, however, and he could not deny his wife's request that Marianne go with her.

He had hoped to be free of Teufel; he had hoped perhaps to make something of his estate by his own efforts. He had begun to do so—oh, in small increments, to be sure, for he was still learning—but he had begun. And now this filth of a letter from Teufel. Richard felt ill. He could not even think to touch Eveline that night after he had read it.

He rose, rang for a servant, and ordered brandy from the maid who appeared. He let out a short laugh. His father could not pay the bills, but the cellar was full of the best brandy that could be smuggled during wartime. Despair threatened to overwhelm him, but he pushed it away. Not now. Not now when he had to think of a way to solve his problems.

A light, sharp knock sounded.

"Come!"

The door opened, and it was not the butler who came in with his tray, but Lescaux. Moreover, he carried no brandy but a light repast of tea, jam, and scones. The little man placed the tray on a side table and poured hot tea into a large cup.

"Lescaux, I ordered brandy."

The valet gazed at his master in disapproval. "Milord, you 'ave had no meals since this morning. The sun, he is dropping down the horizon. Also, I 'ave looked upon the brandy—and it is of a sort inferior." He curled his lip slightly. "Tea is preferable."

The corners of Richard's mouth twitched upward. "And why are you the one to bring me up my dinner?"

Lescaux's face brightened. "Ah, it is dinner you wish? Eh, *bien!* I shall go and procure the ham."

"No, Lescaux. This will do quite well. And answer my question if you please!"

The man shrugged. "Eh, what can I say? The so good Tilton is old and has heavy duties. Your footman has many things to do, also."

"You surprise me, Lescaux! I would have thought it beneath you to do a footman's duty."

The valet gave him a quick look and said smoothly, "My pride does not suffer in doing what is right, Milord."

There was a short silence, then Richard burst out, "Damn it, Lescaux, I do not know how I put up with your impertinence!"

Lescaux smiled benignly upon his master. "Why, Milord, it is because you know I am right."

"More like I could not afford another one, you should say!"

The man looked at his master with eyes full of hurt.

"Oh, for God's sake, cut line! I know you better than

that, and you can't come over me with your cozening looks."

Lescaux grinned widely. "As ever, Milord, you know me well."

Richard could not help grinning back. Then he looked once again at the pile of bills before him and sobered. He sighed, almost groaning.

"That let—these deuced bills. Good Lord, Lescaux, what am I to do?" Richard drew in his breath and let it out slowly. He had almost spoken of the letter.

The little man frowned thoughtfully. "There is always something one can do, good or bad, *n'est-ce pas?* What else can you do? You have done more good than your father, I think." He shrugged.

The viscount grimaced. "And that is little enough!" He rubbed his hand wearily over his face, then took a sip of tea. It was strong and the hot astringency felt good going down his throat. He took a few more sips, felt revived, and eyed the scones with a little more attention. He looked up to see Lescaux gazing at him in an interested manner.

"Perhaps a little ham, Milord?" ventured the servant.

Richard thought on it and shook his head. The staff needed to be fed as well, and if there was a ham in the kitchens, he'd much rather his servants ate it. Lord knew they had more work to do than he did.

"I think, Milord, perhaps Madame le Vicomtesse or her father could well advise you on such matters."

The viscount stiffened, and the scone he had bitten off felt dry in his mouth. He swallowed and stared hard at the other man. "That is enough, Lescaux," he said softly.

The valet sighed, shrugged his shoulders, and left the study.

Richard cursed softly to himself. Lescaux never said much directly, but what he did say was like a thorn in Richard's side. He did not need it, not with Teufel's letter whose words were like a chain around his neck. And for what?

To save his estates and to save his sister. Richard felt nauseated again and pushed the plate of scones away, groaning softly. But there was nothing else, not even the Clairmond pride. Pride! Good God. He had none, despite the lie he had told Eveline. Teufel had made him all too aware of that; Richard was nothing more than his slave. He had thought to save his home and Marianne, but now he wondered if he could bear to look at his sister or his wife, with the knowledge of his own degradation hot in his mind for the rest of his life.

Eveline! Richard cringed inwardly. He had at the very least bewildered her with his rejection of her help. Yet, at the moment she had told him of her fortune, he had seen Teufel's side of the bargain come to fruition at last, and knew he was not free, had not ever been free of his damned influence at all.

There is always something one can do, good or bad. Lescaux's words came back to him, and he pulled up his shoulders as if to ward them off. Certainly, he had done the bad. But the good? Was there any good to be had of his situation?

Richard pushed aside the pile of bills and absently picked up the tea cup once again. The tea was less hot now, but a large swallow warmed him and stirred his thoughts to more activity. He felt, suddenly, that there had been something missing, that perhaps there might be something he could do that he had not thought of. He went over the past year, the initial agony of mind he had suffered upon notice of his father's death, and the despair he had felt when he found how impoverished his estates were, and how his tenants were near to starving. Now these were old pains, more like an old ache rather than the sharp persistent agony that permeated his mind at first. Perhaps it was because of the promise of release from ruin by his own efforts, small as they were. He felt, somehow, he could think more clearly now. He thought of the letter again and clenched his teeth. No. No, he was *not* going to London. Not after all that he had established here at Clairmond Hall from his own efforts. He would not touch any of Eveline's money, which was actually Teufel's, he felt sure—it was the last thing he could hold on to and still retain what little pride he had left.

An odd warmth crept in his heart; it felt a little like hope again.

And then the hope burst into a flaring thought: the land by the brook. Marianne had said that Wyvern had acknowledged it as Clairmond land—and it was the only land not entailed. He could sell it, perhaps, to Wyvern. Their fathers had disputed the ownership of it; Wyvern could not deny it would be a good addition to his estate. It would bring in just the amount of money, he was sure, that would enable Richard to make the repairs on his estate so sorely needed. His solicitors would be scandalized at his selling off the last of his unentailed land, but what did that matter if it meant the rest of his estate would suffer if he did not sell it?

Richard's hand shook. Quickly, awkwardly, he put down his cup on the edge of the table, and it tipped and fell to the floor with a crash. He ignored it. Yes. His soul would still be lost, but it was something he could live with, live with himself. *Eveline*. He must tell Eveline.

He rose from his chair and then stopped. Eveline had gone to London. A sense of chagrin came over him, but he shook it off, and smiled. When she returned, he would give her back any money she spent on Marianne, and perhaps even buy a little trinket for her.

Well, the next thing to do then was to call upon Wyvern and see if he would be open to such an offer. Hurriedly, he rose from his chair and rang for Lescaux.

"I need a change of clothes," he said when the valet entered the room. "I must call on the Earl of Wyvern . . . business matters."

Lescaux looked at him curiously, then raised his eyebrows at the broken teacup. Richard followed his gaze.

"Oh, that! I am sorry," he said, giving a breathless laugh. "Clumsy of me." He felt impatient now. "I will go to Wyvern now—or as soon as I am ready."

The valet hesitated. "There is another thing, Milord. Madame le Vicomtesse has given me this for you." He held out a folded piece of paper.

Richard waved it away. "Not now, Lescaux. I think it can wait." He walked swiftly to the door. "Oh, and have the carriage waiting for me within the next half hour, Lescaux."

"Half the hour!" cried Lescaux, aghast. "And you expect to look *comme il faut* in such a time! No, no! It must be an hour!"

"Half an hour, Lescaux! No more." Richard left the study, ignoring his valet's violent imprecations on the impossibility of his master.

But when Richard went to Wyvern's house, it was to find the earl had gone to London—with Eveline and Marianne, Wyvern's butler said. Richard frowned. Eveline had not told him that the earl was to accompany them. Uneasiness unfurled within him, but he pushed it aside.

The butler cleared his throat. "I believe, my lord, that he wished to accompany Miss Clairmond."

"Ah, of course." The better to keep an eye on his acquisition, thought Richard sourly. He wished his sister well, however, and she, certainly, was in alt over her betrothal. That was something to be glad about, however temporary she might find that happiness. He nodded to the butler and left.

Richard entered the great hall of his home and paused, looking around the room. It seemed very empty to him, for he knew that Eveline would not come through one of the doors, or that he would hear her voice before a fortnight passed. He sighed, then remembered the letter she had left behind for him. He smiled to himself. Perhaps it was a note, wishing him well while she was away. He would go back up to his study and read it.

The note was still there on the table on which his scones and tea had once sat. He picked it up and opened the seal. A crumpled piece of paper fell out. He retrieved it, and his breath left him as if he'd been hit in the stomach. It was Teufel's letter tucked in Eveline's note. With trembling hands he read her note. *Oh, God.* She'd gone to confront Teufel; she didn't know who he was, but she was sure he was some enemy of her father or of hers. *Teufel. And Eve-*

line. He crushed the letter in his hand. Oh, God, not Eveline. Not Eveline!

Violently he rang the bell, and both Tilton and Lescaux came at his summons. "Tilton, have Dickon saddle Satan for me! Now!" he barked. "Lescaux, my greatcoat! I want you to pack my clothes and follow me to London, Grosvenor Square, the Seton town house."

"Yes, yes, my lord!" gasped Tilton, clearly alarmed, and hurried off again.

Lescaux cast the viscount a sharp glance. "Madame la Vicomtesse, Milord?"

"Yes, damn it! She's in trouble. I've go to go *now*!" Richard strode to the door.

Satan was saddled and ready by the time Richard came down by the stables. Lescaux was also there, sitting on Marianne's Jupiter.

"Damnation, Lescaux! I told you to pack my clothes and follow me!" Richard shouted.

"But I did, Milord!" The valet pointed to two large saddlebags attached to his saddle. "*La voilà!* Your clothes and all the necessary accoutrements for the journey."

Richard could not help the brief grin he gave Lescaux. "You amaze me! I did not think you would be content with crushed clothes in a bag."

Lescaux raised his brows haughtily. "I have been in the army, *oui*? I have learned to live with what is given to me."

The viscount nodded. "Of course."

"Besides which," the valet continued, "the footman follows with the coach and remains of the clothes."

Richard grinned. "Remaining clothes, you mean." He gave Lescaux a challenging look. "I warn you, however: I will not wait if you lag behind!"

Lescaux looked offended. "Not I, Milord le Capitaine!"

Satan's ears pricked forward at Richard's approach, and the horse nickered softly. Richard mounted, gathered the reins, and patted the horse's neck.

"You've got to give me everything you've got, old boy," he said. Satan reared his head as if to acknowledge his words, and at Richard's nudge leaped into a gallop.

Lescaux gazed at his master for one moment, gave a firm nod, and spurred his horse after him.

Eveline had settled her affairs with her father's solicitors quite easily. It was as she had thought: Her great-aunt had left her a legacy of ten thousand pounds to do with as she wished upon her marriage. This had not been part of her inheritance from her father at all, and as such, had not been tied up when he had negotiated the marriage settlements with Richard's solicitors. She was surprised that her father had forgotten this legacy. She smiled. It could very well be that he had overlooked it on purpose, for though he had often promised her retribution whenever she had misbehaved as a child, he never did follow through as harshly as he had said he would. She was sure it was thus, now. Well, she would *not* tie it up with the rest of her inheritance, and she *would* do with it as she wished.

Her first wish was to help Richard on the estate, to bring some measure of comfort, especially to his tenants. Perhaps she would put it to him as her duty as mistress of Clairmond Hall. Was it not the responsibility, after all, for the lady of the land to take care of the ills of her own people? Surely he would understand it in this light and not object when she used her money for this purpose.

But she could do nothing about that until she returned to Clairmond Hall. She could, however, have her second wish immediately. Indeed, she had already secretly taken one of Marianne's dresses and sent it to a dressmaker's shop as a pattern for other dresses. There was one shop that featured dresses ready-made in different sizes; all that was needed was to take in or let out the seams according to the size of a lady if one wanted a dress or two quickly. And that she did, for Marianne would accompany her to Vauxhall.

Immediately upon her arrival in London, Eveline had penned a note to the address in Whitechapel from whence Mr. Teufel's letter had come. As soon as she sent it off, however, unease overcame her. She castigated herself for not thinking of it sooner: If this Mr. Teufel was so powerful that he had the ability to threaten Richard with Marianne's ruin, most certainly he could be a threat to Eveline. She wished she knew how to use a pistol, but neither she nor her father ever thought she'd have an opportunity to use it. She was sure it was because she had been so ill with anger and anxiety that she had not thought of protecting herself earlier. And yet, she could not have asked Richard to come with her, for it seemed Teufel had some hold over him from which he could not escape.

There was, however, one man who would perhaps help her—the Earl of Wyvern. Eveline did not like to confide in someone who to her was a relative stranger. She smiled. However, he would soon become a relative, and not a stranger at all. And if she told him this Teufel was someone who had threatened Marianne, then most certainly he would wish to help.

So she wrote another note, this time to the earl, who was staying at a lodging nearby. He came promptly, and so did Marianne's dresses at the same time—very opportunely, indeed, for it meant Marianne was upstairs in her room excitedly trying them on, which allowed Eveline to talk privately with Wyvern.

She directed him to sit on a comfortable chair, and then she, too, sat, trying to think of how to broach the subject; but the earl was a keen man, and so spoke first.

"There is something troubling you, Lady Clairmond?" he asked. His voice was kind, but not curious, and his deep-set eyes seemed sympathetic. Eveline was grateful for that. She smiled at him.

"Yes . . . yes, there is. There was another reason I requested you come with Marianne and me to London." She hesitated and decided on bluntness. "There is a man, Teufel by name, who apparently seems to have a hold upon Lord Clairmond. I came upon a letter from this Teufel the other day, which threatened my husband with Marianne's ruin because he married me."

Wyvern raised his eyebrows. "I would think Lord Clairmond would be more than capable of handling such a person."

"Of course he is!" Eveline said instantly. "But it must be

that this Teufel is some enemy of mine or my father's—why else would he try to do Marianne harm because of me? And think! Now there is not only the threat to Marianne, but also to me! How is Richard to keep an eye on both of us?"

"I think you have been very foolish, Lady Clairmond." Wyvern pursed his lips briefly in disapproval. "If this Mr. Teufel is one who wishes both you and Marianne harm, what is the sense of coming here, where he is? It would have been better had you stayed home, and Marianne, too."

"No, it would not have been!" Eveline rose from her chair and paced the room impatiently. "It also seemed from his letter that either he or some accomplice was spying upon us at Clairmond Hall, as well. So it would not have made much difference, do you see?" The earl gave a reluctant nod.

She clasped her hands tightly in front of her. "Richard could not do anything without either myself or Marianne coming to harm. What choice did I have? I could not wait, knowing that at any time someone at the Hall might do us some harm, while we waited passively for it. At the very least, I had to come and confront the man, here, in London. But then—not being as foolish as you might think"—she smiled ruefully at him—"I did not want to come to harm at the same time. So I asked you here. You, after all, have a stake in this, do you not?"

Wyvern smiled wryly. "Yes, indeed I do. However, I should rightfully send both you and Marianne packing for home."

Eveline gazed at him assessingly, the corners of her lips lifting upward briefly. "But you will not, will you? For you cannot bear the thought that there is someone who means to harm Marianne, and in fact would much rather deal with him now than later."

The earl's smile fell away. "You are very perceptive, Lady Clairmond; uncomfortably so. How much more do you know of me?"

"That you have been in love with Marianne for a very long time; that you have taken great precautions for her reputation, not as if she were a governess, but a lady you intended to wed; and that you are obliged to go with me if you wish to further protect her, for you do not have Teufel's direction nor can you identify him." Her smile became broader. "Among other things."

Wyvern grimaced. "Perceptive indeed. I am thankful that your husband is not so." He sighed. "It seems I have little choice but to help you. What do you propose to do?"

Profound relief flooded through Eveline. "Thank you, my lord. I have requested that Mr. Teufel meet me at Vauxhall tonight, as it seems it is one of his haunts. He has replied and has said he will find me. I would be pleased if you and Marianne could accompany me to Vauxhall."

"Marianne? I think not, if you believe she also may be in danger."

"And she would think it most peculiar if you went with me to Vauxhall without her. Besides, if she stayed here, how easy it would be for Teufel or his associates to strike at her at this house while you and I went to Vauxhall."

A frustrated expression crossed Wyvern's face, then he nodded. "You are right, of course. It is better that I keep an eye on both of you. Or, better yet, ask an acquaintance along. I have in mind my cousin, Sir John Grey, who is also in town."

"He is your cousin?" Eveline said, surprised, for she remembered him as one of Richard's closest friends.

Wyvern grinned. "Yes, a very distant one, which is why your husband doesn't know it, and Sir John keeps forgetting it. But he's a valiant sort, with a ready wit, a boon companion to ladies and gentlemen alike. He will, of course, be your escort—at first. After which we shall contrive to lose both him and Marianne, so that both of us can seek Teufel."

Eveline hesitated. "I think it better if I confronted him alone."

Wyvern's grin twisted into a grimace. "Both brave and foolish, I see. I do not think it better at all."

"And how forthcoming do you think he'll be with you glowering next to me?" Eveline retorted.

"Very well! I will, at least, stay at a distance, close enough to hear what is said, easily at hand should trouble occur."

Eveline pressed her lips together, then nodded. "Agreed."

Marianne walked in then, lovely in her new dress, and Wyvern's expression lightened.

"Marianne," Eveline said immediately, "Wyvern and I were discussing an outing to Vauxhall this evening. Sir John Grey may be accompanying us. Would you like to go?"

"Ohhh!" Marianne's eyes glowed. "Oh, Eveline! I don't know what to say!"

"Say yes, my dear, and we shall go," Wyvern said with a chuckle.

"Yes, oh, yes!" Marianne cried.

"It is done, then." Eveline smiled at Marianne's excitement. She looked at the earl. "I shall send an invitation to Sir John straightaway."

Eveline rose to leave and so as to write her note, as well as to let the betrothed couple have a little time to themselves. But before she left the room, Wyvern turned to her and murmured with a smile, "Does Lord Clairmond know what a troublesome lady he has married?"

Eveline sighed. "If he did not, he does now."

Chapter 18

Satan was fast—as fast as a fire through dry brush—but Richard knew the horse was only flesh and blood, and not the lord of the fiery realms himself, despite the animal's name. And because he could not afford changing horses, Richard had to pace his old friend and hope that he'd make it to London before Eveline encountered Teufel.

Lescaux stayed with him as Richard expected; he'd ever been that way on the Spanish Peninsula. They slept at inns and in haylofts, depending on what was available when they were too weary to go on. The valet did not speak as much as usual, however, and his face was serious and solemn. Perhaps it was that he could clearly see Richard's mood, and so knew it would disturb his master rather than divert him. For Richard paid little attention to his surroundings; eating, sleeping, and riding only for the purpose of getting closer to London and to Eveline.

Eveline. Every time her name sounded in his mind, he could see her, smiling, laughing, or her eyes half closed in passion. And on the heels of those images were the ones he could imagine: fear, horror, dread upon her face—all the emotions he had felt in every encounter with Teufel. It was his fault. He should have told her when she had asked about the dread that must have shown on his face when he received Teufel's letter; but he had wanted to keep her from the degradation that had already touched him. He could not bear that it touch her, and if truth be told, he could not bear that she think him so debased and degraded that he'd acceded to Teufel's wishes. He had; what was done was done, and he regretted it. It did not matter; she was in danger now, and he must keep her from it.

Night had fallen, and the light in the windows were dim when Richard and Lescaux came to the Seton town house in Grosvenor Square. *Please,* thought Richard. *Please let them be here still.* He pounded on the door and was answered by a startled footman.

"I am Richard, Lord Clairmond," Richard said. "I believe my wife and my sister are here."

"Yes, that is—"

"Take me up to them," Richard snapped.

"I cannot, your lordship! That is, they have gone out."

Fear lanced through Richard, and he seized the footman by the lapels. "Where? Where did they go?"

"Vauxhall, my lord, with Lord Wyvern and Sir John Grey."

Richard released the footman and swore loudly. He turned to Lescaux. "Let's go." He strode back to his horse.

The valet's hand held him back. "No, Milord. You must wash and change your clothes first."

"I don't have time for that, damn it!"

"You will 'ave less time if they throw you out, Milord. You look like you 'ave come from *une maison de fou*! The Bedlam!"

Richard looked down at his clothes, streaked with dirt and dust; there could be no doubt his face was just as dirty. "Very well!" he snapped and turned to the footman. "A room, and quickly, man!"

Once they gained a chamber upstairs, Lescaux pulled from the saddlebags a complete set of clothes, wrinkled to be sure, but at least not dirty. Richard washed quickly, then donned the clothes. The valet gave a moue of distaste when he gazed at his newly dressed master, but shrugged his shoulders. "Eh, *bien*! There is nothing more I can do."

Richard cast an impatient look in the mirror. "Good enough. At worst they'll think I've slept off a debauch in my clothes. Shouldn't be any different from half the people there, I'm sure." He strode to the door, then turned to look at his valet. "Wish me luck, Lescaux."

"*Bonne chance,* Milord le Capitaine," Lescaux replied, but the viscount was already out the door.

Fantastic masks, like creatures from an unknown land, flashed past Eveline as their owners danced and laughed and drank. The heat was oppressive, and Eveline waved a fan at herself. She wished she could take her mask off as well, for it pressed against the bridge of her nose, irritating her, but she felt it was wise to keep it on. She was not used to such revelry—she had gone only to the balls and assemblies in Bath, chaperoned by Lady Brookland, all highly respectable. But Wyvern, indeed Sir John, assured her and Marianne that the gaiety here was not unusual for London, although they also assured them that it was best if they stayed with their escorts. Eveline could easily see that not all the people came to dance and talk, but to take shocking liberties with each other as well.

In truth, she wished she were gone from this place, for she did not want to meet this Teufel who threatened her husband and herself. But it seemed that she'd meet him sooner or later, and she'd reasoned sooner was better, so that she could get a good measure of her enemy before much time went by.

She looked at her sister-in-law and envied her unconscious enjoyment. Marianne looked lovely in her new peach-pink dress and matching domino, and her eyes sparkled with merriment behind her mask, enchanting her betrothed all over again—and more than a few other gentlemen who looked on as well. Eveline sighed and fanned herself, then looked at the watch pinned to the bodice of her dress. It wanted but ten minutes until she was to meet Teufel. She moved restlessly and then touched Marianne's arm.

"It is so oppressively warm here, do you not think? How refreshing it would be if we could walk in the gardens!" she said, smiling.

"Oh, yes, do let's!" Marianne said. She glanced up at

Wyvern at her side. "I have never been to Vauxhall, you know, and have heard much about the gardens."

The earl smiled at her, but shot a quick look at Eveline. "I have heard much, as well, which is why it is a good thing both Jack and I are escorting you ladies."

"What have *you* heard?" Marianne asked, her eyes wide with interest.

Wyvern turned eyes equally wide with innocence. "Why, nothing, of course."

She tapped her closed fan smartly upon his arm. "Odious, provoking man! If it is something scandalous, why do you let us go out at all?"

"To see how red you become when you blush, of course," Wyvern replied. Marianne's cheeks turned pink.

Eveline laughed. "You are right, Marianne! He is odious. Are you sure you wish to marry him?"

Sir John leaned toward Marianne. "Say no, Miss Clairmond. You cannot let such a wicked man as Wyvern keep you away from more virtuous fellows—such as myself."

Marianne cast a provocative look at her betrothed. "I shall not say no, but I will teach him a lesson and not go out into the gardens with him. If you would be so kind, Sir John—" and here she smiled prettily upon him. "If you would be so kind as to escort me instead, I think he might mend his ways."

"Alas, Wyvern, you are left with me," Eveline said. "Small consolation, indeed!"

"Not at all, Lady Clairmond," the earl replied. "However, I shall find out if it is true that absence makes the heart grow fonder—or whether it's out of sight, out of mind." He gave Marianne a wicked look from under his dark brows that made her cheeks grow more pink than ever, though a smile trembled on her lips. Marianne lifted her chin defiantly and took Sir John's arm, leaving their box before Wyvern and Eveline.

It had turned out quite well, thought Eveline. She was with Wyvern as she had wanted, and Marianne was with

Sir John. She glanced ahead of her. It should be easy to lose them. She slowed her steps and looked up at Wyvern.

"The Dark Walk, he said in his letter."

Wyvern grimaced. "Of course. It would be. It is an odd path, with a few twists and turns, and an easy place to be private with someone. Confusing, also; there are some paintings on the walls that lead you to think it is yet another path."

A sense of unease came over her. "Will there be somewhere you can hide so that you can hear me?"

"Yes. As I said, there are plenty of places in which to be private and conceal one's self." Wyvern glanced to the right. "This way, if you please."

Eveline nodded and looked ahead for Marianne and Sir John. They were gone. She felt more nervous than ever and looked up at her companion. Even in the dim light, she could see Wyvern's saturnine face turn even more stern as they progressed toward the Dark Walk.

The day had been warm, and Vauxhall's ballroom even warmer, but here in the gardens it was quite cool. Eveline drew her shawl closer around her. Indeed, though it was early summer, the night air chilled her as if it were early spring instead. She looked above at the sky and saw the stars did not twinkle brightly at all, nor could she see the moon shining as she had seen upon her arrival at Vauxhall. A mist had descended instead, and soon the Dark Walk was shrouded in uniform grayness instead of the varying shades and shapes of shrubbery, earth, and architecture. The grayness seemed to absorb everything: light, dark, sound. Eveline could no longer hear the music and voices from the ballroom. All sound was damped, although she was sure they could not be that far from the ballroom. The air was still cool, cold, in fact, and yet it was oppressive, as if it were pushing down upon her.

"Deuce take it!" exclaimed the earl. His voice sounded as if he spoke in a small, closed room. "We must be at the place Teufel had said he'd meet you, but I cannot tell because of this mist." He released her hand from his arm. "I am sure there must be a hedge here." He reached out his hand to the side of him and moved a little away from her.

The mist enveloped him, and suddenly he was gone. Eveline froze. "Wyvern! Come back this instant!" There was no sound, not even a footstep, though she strained her ears to hear. "Wyvern!"

She turned around, her arms outstretched, but she could see nothing, feel nothing. Fear curled up around her heart, pressing upon it and making it beat harder than before. "Wyvern!" she called again, but there was no sound, no movement in the unvarying grayness around her. Finally, there was a sound, a shifting in the mist. Footsteps. She sighed with relief. No doubt the earl had turned back from his exploring. She frowned. She would give him the scolding of his life for scaring her so!

The footsteps grew closer, light and quick, and the mist stirred. But it was not Wyvern at all who appeared, but a young man dressed impeccably in black, carrying a diamond-topped walking stick. Eveline drew back, then stared. She had seen handsome men before, but this man was beautiful. His hair was as black as his coat, and he was tall and well-built. His pale skin seemed translucent, almost as if a light glowed through it from within. Eyebrows, thin and straight, slanted above eyes that were extraordinarily fine and large and dark. He gave her a smile, and she was almost charmed, for his lips were finely molded as if carved by a master sculptor. And yet that smile did not reach his beautiful eyes—eyes that were bottomless pools of ancient rage and despair.

He is old—fundamentally so, she thought, then shook her head, for surely he could be no more than five-and-twenty. No doubt he was old in debauchery. She looked away from him, and her breath came out in a sound that was almost a moan, for the oppressive mist around her seemed to sink into her heart and press upon it unbearably. She forced her gaze back up again and stared defiantly at him.

The young man bowed elegantly. "Lady Clairmond, I presume?"

"Yes." It was all she could say. She took a large breath and let it out again.

"I am Teufel. You summoned me, and I am here, at your command." He bowed again elegantly and mockingly.

"I found your letter to my husband—a foul letter that threatened him and my sister-in-law." Eveline let the outrage and anger boil up within her. It warmed her and forced out the creeping chill that had insinuated itself into her flesh.

Teufel shook his head sadly. "Foul? Oh, dear. And I had worked so very hard over it, too."

"Yes, I can tell," Eveline said coolly. "Just the right amount of slyness, a pinch of arrogance, a touch of vulgarity, and enough cowardice to threaten two ladies who have done you no harm."

Affront and fury flickered on Teufel's face, and then he smiled an appreciative smile that actually reached his eyes. "Touché. Do you know, my lady, I do think your cleverness is wasted in marriage—a horribly dull and overrated institution, in my opinion. You should be a courtesan, instead, and hold salons. You would be feted for your intelligence and admired for your undeniable beauty." His smile widened, and his gaze wandered down her body and back up again to her face.

Eveline gritted her teeth. "Answer me!" she cried. "Who are you, and why do you threaten me? Are you an enemy of mine, or my father?"

"Really! Such emotionalism." Teufel took out a small snuffbox and took snuff. "How can I be an enemy, when I have brought you and Clairmond together? My, my, my." He shook his head musingly. "Such . . . passion."

Eveline could feel her face grow hot with embarrassment and anger. She took a step forward. "You *told* him to seduce me and the intent was that he abandon me as well, though he did not. I think that is enough to tell me that you wish me ill!"

"Oh, that. Just our little bargain. He was in dire straits,

you know. I thought it a good thing to help him a little—charitable of me, was it not?"

"He should bring you in front of the magistrates. What blackmail have you put upon him?" she demanded. The oppressive chill of the mist seemed to press upon her more, dulling her thoughts. She shook her head to clear it.

Teufel threw back his head and laughed out loud. "Blackmail! Oh, my dear Lady Clairmond! How could it be blackmail if *I* saved his estates and his sister from ruin?"

"Then why? Why did you direct him to ruin me? And why threaten Marianne?"

The young man stared at her speculatively for a moment, then said with a charming smile, "I wanted his soul, of course."

The chill finally penetrated her heart, becoming a seeping dread. No, he could not mean that, of course, she thought. He mocks me.

Anger returned to her. "Nonsense! Speak to me plainly, if you please! Lord Clairmond's soul, indeed!" She pressed her lips together in disgust.

"Oh, don't do that, Lady Clairmond! It ruins the line of those lovely lips." Teufel came forward, and the mist swirled away from him. He took her chin in his hand, but she turned her face away. "Such haughtiness! But one often gains that with a title, yes?"

"Tell me what you forced upon my husband." Eveline's voice was low with controlled anger—and fear. She could feel the oppressiveness more now when he came close to her. It was almost as if it emanated from him.

"I?" Teufel's voice sounded hurt. "I forced him into nothing. It was an agreement. He would give me his soul and do a few tasks for me, in return for the restoration of his estates and keeping his sister from ruin."

Eveline did not bother to hide her fear now; she could not. It rolled over her like a wave, and she felt she could not breathe. She stared at Teufel. "Who . . . are you?"

He smiled tenderly at her and ran his finger down her cheek and neck and the tops of her breasts, leaving a cold pain upon her flesh. "I am Teufel, as I told your husband.

But I have other names. Lucifer is one of them. Perhaps I will use that one. Much less harsh-sounding than Teufel, don't you think?"

She took in a gasping breath. "You are mad!" Surely that must be it. He must have escaped from Bedlam. Anger cleared away her fear, and she thrust his hand away from her. But his hand closed on her wrist like a vise, and pain coursed through her arm.

"Oh, please!" he said plaintively. "Clairmond thought the same thing. How unoriginal. I am not mad at all. Shall I prove it to you?" He waved at the mist, and it swirled and came apart. A hole, black as a starless night, appeared, and then flames flickered in it. There she could see two figures entwined, a quilt twisted about their bodies. It was herself and Richard in the cottage. How could Teufel show her this?

Teufel sighed sentimentally. "How . . . romantic, yes? And such unrestrained . . . passion. My, my, my."

She looked at the young man again, at his unearthly, beautiful face, and his ancient pitiless eyes. The mist curled around him in a caress, and she realized she could see him clearly, as if in daylight. Yet, she knew it was night, and there was no light that could glow from an indefinable source as it did here. The mist closed in around her, chill and oppressive. Eveline drew in a large breath, trying to feed her lungs with air.

"Who . . . are you?" she whispered again.

Teufel smiled gently at her. "I told you. My name is Lucifer."

Eveline shook her head in denial. "No," she said. "No."

He pulled her closer so that the buttons of his jacket pressed against her. He looked at her consideringly. "Yes," he said. "Oh, yes. You really should consider becoming a courtesan. Think of the respect you would receive, the adulation! You would command the attention of every male eye; you would be irresistible. Riches—no, you have that already, eh?" He flicked her chin with his finger. "Ah, definitely hold the salons. You are a fairly clever woman, are you not? You could invite the most famous minds to your house and have them converse, admire your intellect, and write sonnets to your most delectable lips." He smiled again and bent toward her, and Eveline's mind filled with horror at the idea that he was going to kiss her. But Lucifer stopped, his expression arrested, and straightened himself. He looked past her as if in expectation, then raised his eyebrows.

"Ah, yes," he said, and the mist slowly parted. Eveline could see night again, though the glow that seemed to come from Lucifer still remained. He held her arm less tightly now, but firmly nevertheless. "Ah, yes. It seems we have more players now in this game."

The music and the noise from the ballroom came hard and sharp to Eveline's ears once again after the muffling fog. The last of the mist curled away, and the hedges and walls came into sharp focus.

"Eveline!" came Richard's voice. Eveline swirled around and breathed a sigh of relief.

"Richard, here!" she called. She half expected Lucifer to keep her from crying out, but he only stood still, as if he were waiting.

The viscount appeared at last from around a wall of shrubbery. He caught sight of her, and he smiled, relieved. Then he saw her companion, and his expression shifted to that of alarm, then anger. He strode toward them.

"Your business is with me, Teufel, not my wife." Richard pulled Eveline away and held her tightly to him. "Leave her be." He bent his head to her. "Go, Evie, now. I will deal with him."

Eveline raised her eyes to his and grasped the lapels of his coat. "No, Richard. You will *not* deal with him. Not again."

Richard looked at her, his eyes despairing. "So, you know."

"Yes."

He closed his eyes briefly as if in pain. "I see," he whispered. "I see." He let out a long breath. "Go, Eveline."

"No. I will not leave you here with him."

This time it was Richard who grasped her arm tightly.

He shoved her toward the noise of the ballroom. "You *will* go, Eveline. It is too late for me, for I've sold my soul to the devil and there's no retrieving it."

Anguish, cold and sharp, clutched her heart in a way that the deadening mist had failed to do. She gazed into his eyes and saw they had grown more shadowed and cold than ever, his expression chill and remote. Her own Richard, the laughing one who loved her, was dying, slowly being replaced by this cold and dreadful creature. He had to come back to her, he had to! Eveline let out a wild sob and grasped the sleeve of his coat. "No. Listen, only listen to me, Richard! Come back with me! There must be another way," she cried desperately.

Lucifer smiled and shook his head. "He is mine, Lady Clairmond. Most certainly, he is mine. He will come to me—not to you. I need only crook my finger"—he curved his finger—"and he will do as I say."

Richard stared down at her, his eyes old and tired. He pulled Eveline's fingers from his coat sleeve. "I must, Eveline. You can see that, can't you?"

"No, I cannot! What has he done for you that you owe him anything?"

"He offered to restore the estates and ensure Marianne would live a good life."

"I have not seen any evidence of it!" Eveline retorted. "It seems to me that if anything has happened on the estate, it was through your own efforts!"

"My efforts were nothing, Eveline; not enough to keep my tenants from starving. You must see that." His voice, remote and icy, chilled her, and his face seemed almost as inhumanly cold as Lucifer's. Richard shook his head and took a step toward Lucifer.

"Richard! Oh, God. Don't go! Please don't go!" Eveline ran and seized his arm again, but he shook her off and she stumbled to the ground.

"Lady Clairmond!" A hand grasped her arm, helping her up again, and she looked up into the face of the Earl of

Wyvern. "Are you hurt?" Before she could reply, she was thrust aside.

"You!"

Clairmond's voice came hot and angry, and when Eveline looked at his face, the stonelike expression had transformed into one of fury. But she was glad, for his face seemed human again, and he had taken a step away from Lucifer.

"Wyvern, you must stop him!" she cried. "He is going with this . . . demon, this Teufel, who is trying to hurt us!" Neither Wyvern nor her husband paid her any heed, for Richard had seized the earl by the neckcloth. Wyvern, his face startled, then angry, pried the viscount's fingers from his neck, then punched him in the stomach. Richard reeled backward, staring furiously at the earl.

"You bastard! It wasn't enough that you wanted to buy my sister from me, you had to bring my wife here, too! I could kill you for that!" His breath came swift and heavily, his eyes narrow with rage.

"Stubble it, Clairmond! I did nothing of the sort." Wyvern's hands tightened into fists, however, as if ready for the next attack.

"Don't lie! I know you're in league with Teufel; why else come to me about Marianne right after I met with him? And why else bring my wife here, where he could get to her?"

"You are mad. I did nothing of the sort. Your wife would have come here alone to save you if I had not agreed to accompany her. And I damned well never met this Teufel before, and so I tell you!"

A soft laugh came from behind Eveline, and she turned to see Lucifer gazing at Wyvern and Clairmond with an odd, avid expression. "You know, you humans do have a talent for conflict. It is one of the most delightful things about you, and immensely entertaining." He sat upon a bench and leaned his chin upon the end of his walking stick. "But we lack some equipment here. . . . Oh, yes," he said brightly. "Swords. I do like swords. So very refined and elegant, don't you think, Lady Clairmond? And your husband can be quite the fire-eater; how diverting!" He nodded his head toward the two men.

Richard felt something solid in the palm of his hand and raised it. It was a rapier. He glanced at Wyvern; the earl was also looking at a sword in his hand, and he was clearly bewildered. The earlier deadening chill had risen from Richard's mind, but it had been exchanged for a red haze of anger at finding Eveline with Wyvern; clearly the man was in league with Teufel, and clearly he had brought Eveline to destroy her. He could not allow it! His heart twisted with agony at the thought of her brought to degradation in the coming years, and it fed the rage within him—rage at his father, at himself, at the powerlessness he felt before the poverty facing his tenants, and his hopelessness he felt before Teufel. He looked at Wyvern and found a focus for his rage.

Richard lunged. Wyvern had only time enough to raise his rapier to deflect the viscount's sword and jump back. He lunged again, and this time the earl parried, and parried again when the next thrust came at him.

"Damn it, Clairmond, are you mad?" He moved aside, Richard's sword just missing his chest by inches.

A breathless chuckle came from Richard's throat. "Perhaps. But at least I'll keep Marianne from your filthy hands before I'm locked up."

"Think, you idiot! Would I have asked to marry your sister if I didn't mean honestly by her?"

Uncertainty flickered within Richard's mind, and he faltered for a moment. Quickly, Wyvern pressed his advantage and tried to disarm him. He was not quick enough. Richard was used to battle where the earl was not, and the viscount's fury-fed energy returned in full force at this attempt at diversion.

Horror filled Eveline's mind and heart as she watched the two men battle. "Stop! Stop this!" she cried. "There is no need to fight, for God's sake!" The men paid her no heed, caught up in the thrust and parry, deflection and lunge. She looked about her for help, for she feared she'd cause an injury to one or the other if she intervened physically, but it seemed their group was wholly ignored. People passed the small clearing they were in, and it seemed they were oblivious of the duel going on before them. Eveline gazed at Lucifer's beautiful, avid face. He was the cause of it all, she knew. He must stop them.

She moved to him and touched his sleeve with a trembling hand. "Stop them, Lucifer. I beg of you, stop them."

He looked at her, eyebrows raised. "What? Do you not like the little play before us?"

The oppressiveness of his presence overcame her again, and she almost sobbed with despair. Swallowing her tears, she lifted her chin firmly. "This is not a play, but real life. Either one of them could die. Is there no pity in you? Stop them, please!"

Lucifer eyed her coldly. "I have no pity; haven't you heard?"

"A bargain then!" she cried desperately.

He smiled. "Ah! A bargain!"

Hope rose in her heart, and then, suddenly, she was wary. Lucifer's face was interested now, turned away from the combatants before him. Her every instinct was on the alert, her mind sharp and calculating. She realized what had come over her and almost laughed hysterically. Each time she had gone into negotiations with her father's solicitors, or with rival businesses, she had learned. Each time she faced an investment in a calculated risk, she had learned. It was not long before she had cultivated a frame of mind that clicked into place as soon as she stepped into a house of business.

And here it was again, appearing at the very mention of the word "bargain." This time, however, it was bargaining on a scale she had never approached before: for the soul of her husband and her own happiness. It frightened her, but she knew this was her only chance. Lucifer had no pity, he had said so himself; but he was open to bargains.

"Yes, a bargain," she said. Eveline sat down on the bench next to Lucifer and made herself relax. "But you must tell me the usual terms of your agreements first." She forced her gaze away from the two fighting men, to Lucifer instead.

"Oh, my, very much the merchant's daughter, are you not?" Lucifer laughed. "Very well, then. I usually grant a favor—and very generous I am, too—in exchange for a few tasks and one's soul. The favor and the tasks are negotiable."

"The terms are too vague," Eveline returned, frowning. "I need guarantees." She had to have time to find loopholes; there was always one, she remembered from the stories her nurse had told her when she was a little girl. Indeed, the tales were fresh in her mind, for she had heard them only a little more than a month ago. She hoped those stories were true.

Irritation passed across Lucifer's face. "I guarantee all my bargains. I always come through with my agreements."

"How do I know that? You have given me no paper you will sign; there is no proof I can hold in front of you if you renege."

Almost it seemed that Lucifer would snap at her, for anger flared in his black eyes. "Let us talk terms first, and I will give you your paper."

"Very well." Eveline took in a breath and let it out slowly. "Can I assume your bargains would be according to human laws? That all contracts are binding on both sides, just as they would be, say, in England?" She wanted to look at her husband and Wyvern, but did not. All her concentration must be on her negotiations.

"Of course. You humans are incapable of understanding more than what your own minds have put together." Lucifer sneered. "Get on with it. Your husband tires."

Eveline ignored the insult and the threat. "Very good. This is what I want, then: I wish for you to relinquish my husband's soul, contingent on the validity of his contract with you. I will do what tasks you put before me, and I must have my favors first before I do my tasks—if and only if this is how you phrased your contract with Clairmond." She clenched her hands, and then flattened them on her lap. It would be worth it, she told herself. Never could she live with the thought that the Richard she knew would die and become the cold and remote creature that had faced her earlier. She focused her whole mind and heart on that thought.

"Done!" Lucifer laughed triumphantly, and waved a hand. A paper appeared upon her lap, already signed with his name. He gave her a quill dipped in ink, she read the paper carefully, and then signed her name.

The fire in Richard's mind slowly faded, and fatigue overcame him. He looked at his opponent, at Wyvern's angry face, and the rage within him flared low. He fought on, but he knew he could not last. Suddenly, the earl's words came back to him, and the last of his fury died out.

"Anthony!" Marianne's voice screamed from behind him, and he saw Wyvern's attention waver just as he thrust forward. The earl's eyes widened, and he dropped his rapier and grasped his left shoulder with a gasp. He fell to his knees then sat, leaning against a bench.

A hurtling form thrust Richard away and fell next to Wyvern. Marianne's confused and agonized eyes met her brother's and she shook her head. "Why?" she whispered.

"I . . . I thought I was protecting you." He shook his head. "I was wrong." They heard running footsteps, and Sir John Grey appeared as well, looking anxious, obviousy trying his best to keep to his role of Marianne's escort. A sound behind Richard made him turn around, and he saw Eveline sitting next to Teufel with a paper in her hand. He strode toward her and tore the paper from her grasp.

"What is this?"

Eveline looked at him, smiling, with tears in her eyes. "You are now released from your agreement, my love. I have signed a contract, trading my soul for your own."

"No!" Grief shot through him, as sure and sharp as a sword thrust. "No! Not you. Oh, God, not you, Eveline!" He grasped her shoulders and shook her. "Do you know what you've done?"

She smiled up at him. "Oh, yes, I do. Most certainly, I do. You will see, my dear one."

Teufel grinned and held out his hand to her. "Come, my lady. You are mine now."

Eveline looked at the outstretched hand, and then at Teufel. A small smile crossed her face. "My husband's contract first. I must have it in my hand, and then I will come with you."

The smile on Teufel's face grew strained. "Regardless of whether you come with me now or not, at some time, I will come for you."

"True. However, the condition of *our* contract was that my husband's contract must be valid. How can I be sure of its validity if I do not see it for myself?"

"Eveline, this will not work," Richard said. "I made a verbal agreement with Teufel."

She smiled at him, then turned and raised her brows at Teufel. "A verbal contract? How is this?"

"A verbal contract is still binding, oh merchant's daughter!" Teufel laughed.

"And the witnesses?"

Richard looked at her, an odd expression on his face. "There were none," he said.

"No witnesses?" Eveline shook her head mockingly. "Then how do I know if this supposed contract existed at all?"

"Your husband admits it."

She turned to Richard. "Then tell me the terms of the contract, please."

Richard did not know what she was trying to do; going over the agreement with Teufel was useless. Had he not done so over and over in his mind already?

"Tell me, Richard!" There was an urgency to her voice. Hope flared within him. Perhaps, perhaps she knew something he did not.

"I was to seduce and abandon you, and then I would receive enough wealth to redeem my estates and save my sister from poverty."

"What is this, Mr. Teufel?" Eveline's voice was mocking now. "It seems this is different from what you agreed upon in my contract. Here you say I will get my wish first, and then I must do my task, but in your contract with Lord Clairmond, it is quite the opposite!"

"He does not remember it accurately. It was as yours," Teufel said, but his smile was uneasy.

Richard opened his mouth to protest, but Eveline's hand closed on his arm tightly.

Eveline smiled in mock sympathy. "In which case, Mr. Teufel, both contracts are null and void." She turned to Richard and took his hand, pressing it to her cheek. Her eyes were full of love and joy, and hope rose in his heart.

"You are lying!" Fury burned in Teufel's voice, and Richard took a step toward him, moving protectively in front of Eveline. But his wife moved out from behind him and shook her head mockingly.

"Oh, no, Lucifer! It is you who are lying, and have lied. You are the father of lies, are you not? Never did you come through with your promises to Richard; there was no money that came to him before he seduced me. And what you say does not agree with what you wrote in your letter—which I read, I should mention."

"You cannot deny he prospered afterward!" Lucifer cried.

"According to you, that was not in the contract. As for his prosperity, it was all through his own efforts, I assure you! Where were your favors when he dug ditches side by side with his tenants? What aid did you provide him when he spent his days poring over the estate records? *I* do not recall anything magically appearing in our midst that helped him drain swamps or irrigate cornfields." Her gaze was severe. *"None of it was in the contract."*

Richard looked at Eveline and shook his head. "Eveline, this will not work. I agreed to the bargain, and I did indeed seduce you."

She let out an exasperated sigh and put her arms around his neck and kissed him. "You silly man! You never seduced me. I loved you and came to you willingly. How is that a seduction? It was never against my will."

Reluctantly, he pushed her away from him. "But your inheritance! What of that?" He glanced at Lucifer, who watched them carefully.

Eveline rolled her eyes. "Oh, for heaven's sake! I would have inherited the money regardless of whom I married! It was there before you ever made your bargain with Lucifer! And as for your benefiting from it, when did that occur? I seem to remember you rejected it as soon as I mentioned it." She grasped the lapels of his coat and shook him a little. "Do you not see? It has all been a lie; Lucifer had manipulated all your perceptions to such a point that you believed all he said—even that poor Wyvern here was some vile seducer, when anyone could see that he is top over tails in love with Marianne." She turned to Lucifer. "No matter which way the contract was, you have no case, and both our contracts are invalid. Indeed, you cannot even show me a signed one for Richard, nor have you even delivered on this nonexistent contract. The burden of proof is on you, Lucifer, as the contract holder. Where is your proof?"

"You think you are so very clever, do you not, Lady Clairmond?" Lucifer sneered. "However—"

"Enough, Lucifer!"

They all turned, and there was Lescaux, looking impeccably neat and very grave indeed. He bent over Wyvern, examined his wound, and shook his head. "Such mischief you cause, my brother! Eh, *bien!* A clean wound, at least." Light seemed to flow from his fingers as he passed his hand over the earl's bloodied chest, and Wyvern breathed deeply.

The earl opened his eyes. "Marianne?"

"Anthony!" Marianne cried, kissing him fiercely.

Lucifer turned angrily upon Lescaux. "You said you would not interfere! You said—"

"And so I have not! Did I move them here and there, as you certainly did? I did not!" The valet pressed his lips together, then smiled. "I will not argue with you, Lucifer! Admit it. You have lost."

"Clairmond did as I told him, if you'll remember!"

Lescaux shook his head. "No, he did not. Did I not say that love would overcome all? And so it did. Milord le Capitaine"—and here he grinned at Richard—"loved his lady, and though you fooled him into thinking he had done her harm, he could not abandon her, but married her instead. And did he ask anything for himself?"

Richard looked back and forth between Lucifer and his valet, confused. What did his servant have to do with the devil? Eveline moved from his side and faced Lucifer.

"No, he did not," she said. "He bargained for the lives of his tenants and that of his sister. He did not ask anything for himself." She held out her hand to Richard, and when he grasped it, she smiled lovingly at him. "I always knew you were a good man, my love. Even when you thought you had lost your soul, you did it out of care for those who depended on you. How could that ever be evil?"

An upsurge of emotion made him swallow, and he shook his head. "I don't know," he said.

"*I* know," she said, "and I will never let you forget it."

Richard laughed shakily. "I am sure you will not." He drew her to him and kissed her softly, then with more fervor. His heart felt light, as if a stone once lodged in it had been pulled away. There was no doubt he had made mistakes, but he had not made one when he married Eveline. She had saved him, saved him from the darkness of his soul, and he would love her forever.

"Lucifer," came Lescaux's voice again, "admit it. I have won."

Richard looked up from Eveline, then gazed, astonished, at his valet. Lescaux had changed, though he was still neat and precise as ever. A brilliant light seemed to come from him, and his eyes twinkled when he glanced at his master.

"Who are you?" Richard whispered.

The valet chuckled. "Why, I am Lescaux, your guardian angel. Did you not say so yourself?" The valet's coat and trousers faded into gleaming robes, and a shimmering flicker shone at his shoulders. He turned to Lucifer. "Come now, my brother, answer me."

Lucifer stared at him, his hands balled into fists. "Very well, Ariel. You have won."

"And . . . ?" the angel prompted.

"It will end at Waterloo. 1815. And you will get the rest of your reforms through."

"Thank you." Ariel turned to the group and smiled at their amazed faces. "You may go now. Lucifer will bother you no longer."

Richard took Eveline's hand and with one long backward look signaled his friends to leave. As one they moved from the Dark Walk; Wyvern, a stunned expression on his face, Marianne looking anxiously at him, and Sir John shaking his head and muttering under his breath.

Ariel raised his hand to them in blessing and turned back to Lucifer.

"You will never win, you know," he said.

Lucifer looked at him, sneering. "Persistence is a virtue, and I have an abundance of it."

Shaking his head, Ariel smiled. "You have more than that positive attribute, if you would but exercise it. That is all it takes, after all."

The Fallen One rolled his eyes. "Oh, please! I have heard the lectures before. You have won, and that is the end of it. I am sure you have your duties to perform—as have I."

"Very well, then." Ariel stepped away, and his light faded slowly. "I look forward to our next encounter, dear brother."

Lucifer said nothing and watched the angel fade into the night. He lifted his eyes to the stars; then he, too, disappeared into the darkness.